Paul Lynton

Paul Lynton was born in New Zealand and lives with his wife in London. His interest in creative writing began as an antidote to a career in retail advertising and marketing. INNOCENCE is his first novel.

SCEPTRE

INNOCENCE

PAUL LYNTON

SCEPTRE

Copyright © 1996 by Paul Lynton

First published in 1996 by Hodder and Stoughton
First published in paperback in 1997 by Hodder & Stoughton
A division of Hodder Headline PLC
A Sceptre Paperback

The right of Paul Lynton to be identified as the Author of the Work has been asserted by him in accordance with the Copyright, Designs and Patents Act 1988.

10 9 8 7 6 5 4 3 2 1

All rights reserved. No part of this publication may be reproduced, stored in a retrieval system or transmitted in any form or by any means without the prior written permission of the publisher, nor be otherwise circulated in any form of binding or cover other than that in which it is published and without a similar condition being imposed on the subsequent purchaser.

All characters in this publication are fictitious and any resemblance to real persons, living or dead, is purely coincidental.

British Library Cataloguing in Publication Data

Lynton, Paul
Innocence
1. English fiction – 20th century
823.9'14 [F]
I. Title

ISBN 0 340 67466 0

Typeset by Palimpsest Book Production Limited,
Polmont, Stirlingshire
Printed and bound in Great Britain by
Caledonian International Book Manufacturing Ltd, Glasgow

Hodder and Stoughton
A division of Hodder Headline PLC
338 Euston Road
London NW1 3BH

Innocence is a work of fiction. It is a figment of the imagination, and contrary to popular wisdom regarding first novels, it is not an autobiography masquerading as fiction.

It is dedicated – with much love – to my wife Jan, without whom it would not have been possible.

I would like to thank Harvey Unna, Giles Gordon and Roland Philipps for the help and encouragement they gave to me when I was struggling with *Innocence*.

Paul Lynton, May 1996

We were as twinn'd lambs that did frisk i' the sun,
And bleat the one at the other: what we chang'd
Was innocence for innocence; we knew not
The doctrine of ill-doing, no, nor dream'd
That any did.

William Shakespeare, *The Winter's Tale*

Part One

Elme 1671

1

Mother and Father and I sleep in the same bed. He sleeps in the middle, she sleeps against the wall, and I sleep facing the fire. Most nights we snuggle into each other and share the warmth and the calm, and the soft snoring that is like sandpaper. It smooths away the rough edges of the day. But some nights, and last night was one of them, he climbs on her, and grunts and snorts like a wild boar digging for roots.

I lie still and keep silent and watch the flames die in the fireplace.

On the beam above the fire Father has carved the date AD 1658. It was the year Mother came to live in The Fens, and it was the year my brother was born.

I close my eyes and shut out the past, the past that took my brother from me, and I hear the bedboards squeak, and heave and shudder. After a while the noises begin to change. They become more regular, like the beat of a drum. The bedcovers rise and fall, and the wind blows around me, and in my mind I am walking along the edge of the great drain towards one of the new windpumps. It looks like a small windmill. It is painted black, and its sails are white, and they form a cross in the sky. The sails are catching the wind. They are beginning to turn, and in the bank below them the wheel is beginning to turn, beginning to lift the water out of the ditches that drain the marshlands.

The wind is blowing in my face. It is growing stronger and stronger, and it is making the sails turn faster and faster. The waterwheel is spinning round and round, and the water is spurting into the drain. It is spurting hard and fast like water from a hand-pump. It is white with froth and bright with sunshine.

After a while the froth vanishes, and the water becomes clean and pure, and it sparkles with life.

Then I hear a gurgle, and a sucking-slurp, and I know that the water is pumped and the ditch is dry.

Then the wind dies away and the bedcovers lie still. The white cross hangs in the sky again, and the windpump is wrapped in silence.

Father rolls into the middle of the bed and lies on his back, and his panting softens to sighing, softens to sleep.

Mother sniffles, groans, tosses and turns, and somewhere in the night that follows I hear her voice come over the black mountains that are my Father. 'Go to sleep, Martyn,' she whispers to me, 'there's a good boy, go to sleep.'

My dog sleeps with me, sleeps with us. I call him Dog, in my mind. Father says his name is Patrick. He says he hates the Irish, and he hates my dog. And he hates me when I forget that Patrick is Patrick, and I call him Dog. He clouts me round the ear and tells me that the Irish are an abomination in the eyes of the Lord. I look at Dog with his black coat and his black eyes and his slobbering pink tongue, and there is no hate in him, and I wonder why my Father would want to call him Patrick.

Dog farts in his sleep. He fills the bed with the smell of rotten eggs, and I push him onto the floor, and he scratches at the dirt and stretches out in front of the fire. But he sneaks back into bed again when he's cold and I'm fast asleep. He never hears the sound of the windpump, he never has to cover his ears and pretend that nothing is happening; and he doesn't even know that I cuddle him and tell him not to be afraid.

This morning, before the first rays of the sun began to creep through the cracks in the wall above our bed, Dog licked my face and nipped my ear and nudged me with a nose that was wet and black and sloppy with love. I slipped out of bed and we went outside, to a world that the dawn had painted grey, and we peed on the grass together. We ran and played and bounced around, and we put away the ghosts of the night. Then the colours of the day – the greens, the yellows, the reds and the blues – they flowed into the sky, the grass, the trees and the flowers. And they flowed into the things he calls my work.

He came outside, and saw me, and grunted. He sniffed the air, licked his finger and held it up to test the wind. Then he grunted again, and picked up his sack and his scythe, and strode off down the path.

I let the geese out of their cages, and looked under the hedge to see if the hens had laid any more eggs. The nests were empty. I told the hens to start laying, and I told them what she'd been saying about the axe. They looked at me with disbelieving eyes, and then they turned away and scratched and pecked at the dirt and cackled to themselves.

I walked down to the stream, filled two pails with water, and carried them back to the wooden trough that sits beside the pigsty. Dog put his nose into the trough, and lapped at the water. The pigs grunted and pushed him away, and he barked at them. I smiled. It is a game they play every morning and he always loses, and I gave him a pat and he licked my hand.

Then I went inside and shut the door.

Mother moved along the stool she had placed in front of the fire. I sat beside her. She sighed, and took my hand, and enclosed it in hers. 'Martyn,' she said, 'dear Martyn, you must try to do better. For your own sake, you must try to do better, and if you can't try for your own sake, then you must try for my sake.'

I looked at the floor. The dirt was hard and flat and strewn with the dry meadow grass we call litter. I stirred the litter with my toes and it rustled and scratched the air; and then I said: 'It's not up to me.'

'Yes it is,' she said.

'No it's not!' The words rang in my ears. I hadn't meant them to sound so loud, it was just that I was sick of having to do things for her sake. They weren't for her sake, they were for his sake. That's what she meant, and she knew it and I knew it, and it annoyed me.

I waited for her to say something, but she sat and stared into the fire. The silence unnerved me. It made me feel that I had to say something, I had to explain. I took a breath and let it out. 'The eels go into the trap, or they don't go into the trap. It's not up to me, it's up to them, and that's all there is to it.'

'No, Martyn,' she said, shaking her head from side to side. 'I don't agree with you. There's more to it than that. There's you, with your soft heart and your funny ideas.'

She pulled my hand up and twisted it, and she forced me to look straight into her eyes. They were brown and black and full of sparks. They looked like chestnuts that had been left in the fire too long. I wanted to pluck them out of the ashes before they burst into flames, and I tried to reach for them; but she must have felt me moving because she took a tighter grip, and she said: 'You let them go. Don't you?'

'No!' I yelled at her. 'No I don't!'

I jumped to my feet and yanked my hand free.

She reached over and picked up the empty bucket. She stood up, and thrust it into my face. It was warm – it had been left too close to the fire – and it stank of fish.

'Take it,' she said, 'and make sure you catch some today.'

I grabbed the bucket, and I ran out of the house and down the path. Dog barked. He came bounding after me, and he barked some more and ran in front of me. 'Get away from my bloody feet,' I yelled at him. I tried to boot him, but he was too fast for me and he ran on ahead.

Silly old cow, I thought, what does she know? She knows nothing, that's what she knows, bloody nothing. And I yelled: 'Shit! Shit! And shit again!' at the top of my voice.

Then I started to slow down, and some of the heat began to go out of my face, and after a while I was walking, and whistling, and swinging the bucket round and round. Then it came to me. It was sudden and shocking, like being hit from behind. She was afraid of him. That's what it was.

I sat on the bank of the stream turning my new-found fact round and round in my mind. It kept bringing me back to one question: why was she afraid of him? I turned it round and round some more. It was like a wild strawberry, firm and red and ripe. But the more I turned it the softer it became. Then the skin broke, and it bled, and I took a bite. It was soft and full of pulp, and there was nothing to it, and it made me feel confused.

I put my hand up to my eyes, and cut out the glare of the sun, and watched the waters. They were rising, inch by inch. And all the old dangers were returning, like unwanted visitors.

Yesterday I found a sheep.

It had left its tread in the soft earth of the water meadow, and it had walked over the flats and broken the thin crust of sun-baked dirt, and then it had wandered into the bog. The mud had sucked at it, and held it firm, and it had drowned in the rising water. It was fat and bloated, and the maggots were wriggling in its nose and its eyes; and it was filling the air with a heavy stench. The wool was long and black and laced with mud, and as it dried in the hot sun it was twisting into curls.

I slipped my knife into the belly and slit it open. I thought I'd take some of the meat home, but it oozed a green slime and it slid to bits as soon as I touched it. I had to step away and take a couple of deep breaths, and swallow hard.

I pulled off the fleece and washed the wool and tied it into a roll. And I thought: in the evening, when I've nothing to do, I'll scrape and salt the skin and tack it to the wall inside the shelter. At the back of our cottage the thatch runs from the roof to the ground, and it makes a shelter that looks like a long thin triangle. Inside this shelter the turf is stacked from end to end, and it touches the beams. I was beginning to think I might have to move some of the turf, when I saw that the leg that was deepest in the mud was still firm and pink.

I cut off the leg and threw a bit of meat to Dog. He sniffed it and left it lying on the mud. I shrugged and picked it up and shoved it in my pocket, and we walked back to the river.

I cut the leg into chunks and tied them into my eel traps. Then we walked over to the pond by the south stream. The reeds stood tall, taller than me by five or six inches, and from time to time a slight breeze was stirring the stems and the leaves and the plumes of seed, and they were filling the air with a soft swishing sound. In the wintertime, when the water is slushed with ice, and the leaves have curled and died and their sound has become harsh like the sound of grating, I have to sit in the punt and cut the reeds. I have to cut them long, six inches below the surface of the water, and it freezes my fingers and the cold creeps through my hands and up my arms.

I would like to cut and bundle them in the early autumn, while the weather is still warm, but that would make for a poor thatch, and I must wait, I must wait till the chill is in the water.

I sat down and looked at the water.

It lay around the reeds. It lay quiet and still, and it looked like a mirror. It was reflecting the blue of the sky, and the green of the reeds and the pink of the plumes.

As I watched, the dragonflies hovered and darted, and the sunlight passed right through them, and it made them look like diamonds, like the dew-drop diamonds that sparkle in the dawn.

In the mirror, when I half-closed my eyes, I could see the faintest of images, and they too were sparkling with diamonds. And amongst the diamonds, shimmering as if they had a life of their own, came specks of red and gold, and beads of turquoise. For a moment or two I did not know what to think – what to believe – and then I began to understand that the dragonflies were showing me the life that was inside them: they were showing me their souls.

I kept very still, and shut my mouth and tried not to breathe. But then a cloud came over the sun – for a moment or two – and the dragonflies took fright and flew away, and the images were gone.

I pulled down the top of my breeches, freed my cock, and pissed in the water and shattered the mirror. I gave it a shake, and looked down. The mirror was restored. And there it was: long and white with a droopy hood and a few black hairs. I couldn't take my eyes off it. Never before had I seen my cock in a mirror. I left it hanging out, spread my legs, and made it swing from side to side, and bounce up and down.

Then it went hard, harder than it had ever gone before, and it started to ooze a sort of oil that was clear and slippery. I rubbed it round my knob, and it shone like a small red plum with a polished skin. I squeezed it a few times, and then my brain and my body exploded. I gasped and cried out, and I let go of my cock, but it had a life of its own, and it pumped white froth into the air. It made me sweat and pant, and it made my mouth go dry.

I didn't know what I'd done to myself. I thought I was going to die, and that was why I'd been allowed to see the souls of the dragonflies.

When the pumping stopped, and I could feel that I was still alive, I looked down. Blobs of white floated like snowflakes on the mirror-water. I wet my lips and swallowed, and wiped the sweat out of my eyes. I couldn't make any sense of it, and I stood, looking down at the snowflakes. Soon hundreds of tiny fingerlings were darting everywhere, breaking the mirror, and feeding on the snowflakes. Then the snowflakes were gone, and if it hadn't been for the warm feeling that lingered deep inside my belly, I could have shut my eyes and pretended that it was all a dream, and nothing had happened.

I lay on the bank and stared at the sky, and an hour later or maybe it was two hours later – I can't be sure because I think I went to sleep – I stood up and pissed into the water.

Then I found I was feeding the snowflakes to the fingerlings again, and they were snapping at the surface of the water and they were hungry for more, and so was I.

But that was yesterday.

Today the waters are pushing and shoving and swirling, and they are not interested in sitting still and making pretty pictures. They were fed with the rains that fell in the night, and they are carrying the dust of yesterday. They are carrying it down to the sea. It is an offering. It will be left in the salt marshes, with all the other offerings from other years, and it will help to calm the pounding of the waves.

I wished there was something that would calm my cock. It was behaving like the water. It was pushing and shoving inside my breeches, and I thought about the eels and how long and slippery they were, and then I was holding it, and thinking about pulling in the eel traps. And somehow these thoughts became my hands, became all I cared about, and my snowflakes were falling onto the water. The water stirred them round and round, frothed them into strands of white foam, and the strands became brown, like the water, and then they were gone, carried away, like the fingerlings of yesterday.

Then I remembered that the rising waters could also carry away the eels. I sat and looked at the ropes that stretched into the water, and I remembered the times I'd pulled them in and found the traps empty; found the meat was still in the trap, and the water had leeched all the blood out of it, and made it white and stringy.

Then I began to think what he would say, what he would do, if I came home with another empty bucket.

2

The eels I catch breed in the swamps, in the wetlands that lie beyond the reach of the seas that wash around the coast of East Anglia. We don't think of the wetlands as swamps, we think of them as The Fens. In the winter they are cold and full of gloom, and the branches of the leafless trees form cages in the sky.

As a child I used to feel that the cages were closing in on me and I was to be their prisoner. I'd jump the flooded drains with my fenpole, and I'd find an open space, and I'd look up at the sun and warm myself. Then I'd climb a willow or an elder tree and try to see the hills. But there are no hills. The horizon is flat in every direction, and all I ever saw were the tops of other trees; and the wet bogs; and the water that drowns the paths of summer; and the beds of reeds that stretch for miles and miles and close off The Fens and make them into a secret place.

My Father says The Fens are like a huge basin. It has filled with water, and when the tide goes out some of the water can pour over the lip of the basin. But when the tide comes back in again the water is trapped, and the basin never empties, and The Fens stay wet.

At night the air is filled with a dampness that is cold and clammy.

Men live and breed and die in this dampness. My Father is one of these men, and so was his father before him. He knows the things we have to hide from strangers, and he can grow corn on the land that comes out of the swamp in the springtime. And he can find the places where the fish are hiding, and lure the wildfowl out of the air. And he knows the plants and the berries and the seeds that are safe to eat.

These are his secrets and he is teaching them to me.

To him, this is an obligation, a trust laid on him by his father, and he tells me that my success will be his success. It is a heavy burden for both of us, but it is heavier for him than it is for me, because I think of the hills beyond the horizon and I dream of leaving The Fens. I dream of going south to a place where the land is firm and the air is warm, and my feet and my clothes will be dry instead of being wet all the time. But I can't tell him that. He is a man of The Fens, he has water in his blood, and he believes that a man should live and die in the place of his birth.

He has a special word for the things that he is teaching me. It is watercraft, and when he says it, he lowers his voice. He makes the word sound like a prayer, and once I bowed my head and closed my eyes for a moment or two, and when I looked up, I looked into his face. He was smiling. And that is the only time I can ever remember him smiling at me.

I too have a special word for the things he is teaching me. Frogcraft, I call it, but not to his face. That would earn me a kick in the arse, and each time he remembered my word, he'd give me another kick. Then he'd say what he always says when he kicks me in the arse: 'That's to teach you a bit of respect.'

He'd like to teach the strangers, the outsiders who live beyond the hills and talk about draining The Fens and making them into fields, he'd like to teach them a bit of respect. They think we are frogs and they call us yellow-bellies and they say we have web-feet. I haven't got a yellow belly, I've had a look. It's white and covered with tiny hairs. And I haven't got webfeet. I've spread my toes and held them up in the air and wiggled them, and there's nothing there, apart from the dirt that keeps my feet warm, and there's no harm in that. But I have to say that when I'm in the water, I can swim like a frog, and on hot days I like to lie in the water with my legs and arms outstretched, and my nose just above the surface, and watch the day drift away. At night I like to hear the frogs croak. It means the ponds and the ditches are safe, and when they are safe, we are safe.

The thought of being safe made me feel warm inside and sleepy. I took a deep breath and yawned, and I looked down at the river. My legs were wide apart, and my right foot was sinking into the soft mud that sloped from the edge of the grass to the edge of the water. I lifted my foot and wedged it into one of the branches of the willow tree. The branch stuck out over the water. It was long and thin, and as it took my weight it bent, and the leaves almost touched the surface of the water.

I picked up the rope I'd tied around the tree yesterday, and I tried to drag the eel trap out of the water but it didn't want to come. I jerked the rope and flexed my knees, and took a firmer grip, and pulled as hard as I could.

The branch moved up and down and smacked the water. It sounded as if the water were being punished, and I knew if I were being hit that hard it would hurt like hell and I'd be jumping up and down. But the water moved on, without a murmur, and I wished I could be that brave. I looked at the water, it was still rising. In its own quiet way it was staging a rebellion, and a beating from me was not going to make the slightest bit of difference.

Tonight, under the cloak of darkness, the water will flow over the marsh meadows. It will flow without a sound, and it will fill the drains and the ditches and the swamp holes. The small streams will overflow and the bogs will flood and all will be joined in a seamless sheet of brown water. And once again a long mound of solid silt will rise from the waters and be as God and nature intended it to be. It will be an island. On this island, that they say looks like the black hump of a whale surfacing for air, the village of Elme grew. It was here that I was born, eleven winters ago.

Mother counts the passage of time by the winters, and it's a habit I've picked up from her. She finds the winters long and cold. Too many wet days and too many black nights, that's what she says.

February and March bring out her worst fears. By then our store of food is almost gone, and there's nothing to be gathered outside, and the iron pot hangs in the fireplace. Its mouth is open wide. She says it's mocking her and asking for something to eat.

The wheat for the spring planting sits on the high shelf. It was poured into earthen crocks and sealed with beeswax. It is dry and warm and free from the black mould that can turn it into slime. It sits on the shelf like an evil temptation. In my mind I see the wheat ground between stones, turned into flour and baked into bread. It is brown and the crust is hard. I can see the crust softened with gravy, and it wipes my plate clean.

But my March-eyes see an empty plate, and the wheat waits for spring, and I must live with the temptation.

Poor Mother: her childblains itch and hurt, and despite the goose-grease she rubs into her hands at the end of every day, her fingers crack open and her blood runs thin in the cracks. Rheumatism puffs up her ankles, sends fingers of fire into the joints of her feet where bone grinds on bone. It wakens her from her sleep, cramps the muscles in her legs and shapes them into spears of iron. The spears jab her, force loud gasps and cries of pain from her lips and tears from her eyes. Hidden in the blackness of the night she crawls out of our bed and drags herself over to the fire. She rests her leg on the iron spit, and to my sleep-filled eyes it looks like the leg of a sheep that has been smeared with fat and salt and made ready to roast.

Eel skin garters cure rheumatism, that's what she tells me. I don't know how the skins of eels plaited together and worn next to the skin can suck out the hot pain, can calm and cure. She says it can. But I don't see any calming, or any curing.

To survive, to live through another winter, is a great triumph for Mother. When she counts her winters, she is counting her triumphs. But when I look at her stooped shoulders, and the bent head that is always searching the ground, and the hands that are quivering like a bird that is about to have its neck wrung, I know that she has paid a terrible price for each year, for each victory. It's a price that fills me with dread. It sucks the warmth out of me and makes me shiver. Then I remind myself that she is an old lady. She has thirty-one victories to her name, and her own mother was dead at twenty-seven.

Mother smiles when she talks about my birth. It's the only time when the burden of the years, the victories, slips from her shoulders and she straightens up. A girlishness, almost a skittishness comes upon her, and she is like a young filly that is being led to the stallion for the first time.

'They celebrated the year of your birth,' she says. 'They rang the bells in Elme and Ely and Norwich. And there was feasting and bonfires. In London they fired rockets, and they filled the nightsky with stars. The stars were red and yellow and green, and they say they were a wonder to behold, and those who saw them will never forget them.'

I respond with a big beaming smile, and a wide-eyed look. I've heard this story a hundred times before. It has become a game and we have both learnt how to play it. So I ask: 'Why would they want to celebrate my birth?'

She always laughs out loud and says: 'Not your birthday, silly, the year of your birth. It was 1660, the year of the Restoration. The year the King came back. That's what they were celebrating.'

And the game calls for me to nod, and to be wise as the revelation dawns on me, and I have to say: 'Now I understand.'

I understand more than Mother thinks. I know Charles II is our King and we have to do what he says. And I know his father was King Charles before him and his head was chopped off, because he wouldn't do what Oliver Cromwell and the Parliament said he had to do. Mother goes to church each year on 30 January, the day of his death. We have a special service for him and she used to make me go with her. I'd stand beside her, thinking hard about him, and I'd see his white face, and his long brown hair, and his pointed beard, and his thin neck stretching over the block. I'd hear him say his final prayer and I'd hear him say, 'Amen.' Then I'd see the axe swing high, the sharp edge was glinting in the cold light of winter, and then it came down with a mighty thump. His head fell off, and rolled in the straw, like a ball with chattering teeth. And blood, gallons of thick red blood, spurted out of his neck, just like a rooster with its head chopped off. He didn't run around like a rooster does, no, he just sagged, and lay there, fingers twitching. When they turned him over, laid his body out flat, I saw the front of his breeches were wet and they smelt, and I knew the great man had pissed himself.

It was the best service of the whole year.

I don't go now, now that I'm a man. I'm off doing other things, better things, like catching eels. I would never say that to Mother, she would sniffle and cry. She says King Charles is a martyr, a saint who died for his God and his Church.

Father says he was a fool and got what he deserved. She tells him that he can't say such things any more, and he tells her he'll say what the fuck he likes. She goes red in the face and her eyes fill with tears and she blows her nose. When he's gone she says that he is wrong and she is right, and if I don't remember that, it will be me that is the fool.

I'm not a fool, I thought, and I shook my head and I looked at the rope that was in my hands. It wasn't moving, and nor was the branch that was supporting my foot. I pulled on the rope. I could feel the eel trap stirring as it came off the bottom and out of the mud. The trap was woven from willow. It was long and thin with a fat middle and a mouth at one end, and it looked like a slug. I gave it a hard yank, and the mouth shot up and out of the water. It felt as if I'd hooked a large fish and it was fighting for its life. It started to twist and jump, and then it slumped, and all the weight slid into its tail. I pulled it to the side of the bank, and poked my fingers into the weave and heaved it up the mud and onto the grass. I sat to catch my breath. The eels twisted and turned and seethed, and knitted themselves into a ball. Some were opening their mouths and snapping, and I wondered what they were trying to say.

Each of the eels was a strand of life, about twelve inches long, and each was as black as the sin that the Reverend Mister Salthouse likes to preach about on Sunday. Each of them was doomed because they came to eat the meat of the sheep, and no one was willing to die for them and take away their sin and give them the gift of life eternal.

I looked at them and I said: 'I'm sorry,' and I thought how he would be pleased to see them.

Then I opened the trap and lifted it up and the eels slid out. For the briefest of moments they were free, and then they fell into the bucket, and they made a loud plopping sound. But one eel, more alert, more alive, or maybe more blessed with luck, bounced out of the bucket onto the grass. It pulled itself into the shape of the letter S, and it slithered towards the water. I grabbed it and held it between my thumb and my finger, just below its mouth. I looked into its round eyes and saw nothing, nothing but blackness. Its mouth opened and shut and I saw the white rasps that were its teeth. Then it twirled and curled up on itself and covered my hand with slime. Without thinking I threw it up in the air and it fell into the river. It made a splash, a small splash, and then it was gone.

I picked up the bucket and started to walk back to the village. I could hear myself whistling, and I was thinking: one has got away, one has escaped from the trap and found freedom. Then I stopped and the whistling died. I felt strange and I found myself thinking about the snowflakes. I felt hot in my breeches, and I wanted to put my hand on my cock, and my face was going hot. I put down the bucket and I stood on the path with my hands outstretched, like Jesus on the cross, and I yelled: 'Dear God! What the hell are you doing to me?' The wind carried away my words, and after a minute or two it carried away the heat that was in my face and in my breeches, and I lowered my arms.

I thought about what I'd said, and I swallowed hard. I knew that I should never have spoken to God like that, and I wondered what He was going to do to me. I felt sick in my stomach and I could taste it in my mouth, and I kicked at the dirt. I was glad He was not my real father, and I was glad that it would be a long time before I met Him face to face and had to explain my rudeness.

My thoughts wandered along on their own for a while, and I found I was thinking about the eel. Why had I let it go? Why had I been so kind to it? There was no sense in it. Most days I'd pick up an eel and proclaim it King Charles and chop off its head with one swipe of my knife. And that was that.

I looked up at the sky, and I wondered what was happening to me. I felt uncertain, and there was no help in the sky. I lifted up the bucket and looked into it, and there was no help in it. I felt a blackness rising within me. It was like the stench that comes from a shit-hole on a hot day, and I wanted to back away from it and breathe the air that is fresh and clean.

I put down the bucket, put down what seemed to me to be the source of my despair, and I put my foot near the rim, and looked away, and I gave it a gentle push. The bucket fell over and the eels slipped and slid, and broke away from the knotted mass, and with wild S-shaped thrusts they made for the water. The dry dust powdered them, and black became brown, and sin was taken away. They wriggled down the mud bank and into the water. The water washed them cleaned, baptised them, and restored their sin.

I shook my head and sighed, and I remembered what Mother had said about my funny ideas. I took a deep breath and the air was fresh and clean. I looked into the empty bucket, and I knew that no one was going to save me from my sin.

3

I opened the door and walked into our cottage.

Mother looked at me and the empty bucket, and she shook her head. 'Martyn,' she said, and I could hear the sadness in her voice, 'what is to become of you?'

'There weren't any,' I said.

She sighed. 'Martyn. You are telling me lies.'

'Mother. There weren't any. Honest. Cross my heart, and hope to die.'

'I'm not a fool,' she said. 'I've lived here for thirteen years, and I know. I know in here,' and she tapped the side of her head with her finger. 'I know that you can always catch a few eels. I used to do it when you were young. So don't you go telling me any more lies.'

I stepped back from her. 'The waters are rising. You didn't know that. And the eels have swum away. That's why the traps are empty.'

'Liar!' she screamed at me. 'Liar!' Her face puffed up and it went bright red, like the wattle on a fowl; and her bosom heaved up and down. She shook her fist in my face. 'Martyn Fenton, you will rot in hell!'

In my mind I could see the flames of hell. They burnt the air I was trying to breathe, and I felt as if I were choking, choking to death. I started to sweat, and tremble. I couldn't think, and I blurted out: 'They got away.'

'Got away?' she repeated. 'Got away?'

'Yes. They got away.'

She turned and picked up the poker, and bent to prod the fire, and after what seemed like an age, she said: 'You can tell your father. I'm not going to.'

I went outside and walked up and down, and kicked at the grass, and drew circles and squares in the dust with my big toe. I closed my eyes and wished that everything would come to a sudden stop, and nothing else would ever happen. But when I opened my eyes, everything was still moving, still inching towards the time when he would come home.

I looked at the door, counted all the bits of wood that had been shaped and nailed to form it, and then I looked at the window. It's a hole with a wooden frame. It's a bit deeper than it is wide, and Mother often talks about filling it with glass. Once I saw her touching the windows in our church and running her fingertips over the lead frames. When she saw I was watching, she smiled and said: 'One day. Maybe one day.'

I smiled back at her.

There are no smiles today, and the black shutters on either side of the window made it look like a black eye. I remembered Mother's eyes and the times he slapped her face, and then I shut the shutters. I pushed the locking-bar through the brackets and pulled it down tight, and made sure it wouldn't rattle if a wind came up in the night.

She says we have to close the shutters in the afternoon and keep out the night airs that rise from the wetlands as soon as the shadows deepen, and the sun begins to die. The night airs carry the ague, the malaria fever that makes us sweat and shake. I've seen it make Father sleep and sleep, and when he wakes his strength is gone, and he can't even lift a spoon to feed himself.

Mother sewed strips of leather together and made a curtain. It rolls up on a stick and fits into the slots above the window. She says we have to keep out the draughts, and every night she insists on tying the curtain around the window. She checks that it is tight and firm, and she taps it with her fingers, and listens for the drumming sound that tells her she will be safe in the night. She says this is woman's work but I think she doesn't trust me to do it right.

Far in the distance a squat brown shape is rising and falling. Its head is swaying from side. It looks like a bull that is snatching at the grass as it plods along. It has come from Coldham Manor; it has come over Fryday Bridge and past the open fen fields with their stubble of corn; and past the two trees that are heavy with fat-bottomed pears; and past the long trench where we stood in the water and cut the turves of black peat and stacked them into piles.

The summer sun dried the peat, and it made the turves shrink and crumble and curl at the edges, and it made them look like a row of tree stumps, the sort of stumps that rise out of the soft bog from time to time. The stumps are harder than iron when they are wet, and they can break the blade of a plough. Father calls them bog oaks and he says they have been hidden in the earth since the time of creation.

The squat brown shape vanishes from sight. In my mind I follow it, step by step, along the path that leads to the river with the eel traps, and through the reeds with their plumes of dapple pink. I know that in a minute or two it will be in front of our cottage and it will walk on the grass that the geese crop.

The geese are like sentries. They hiss and honk and peck at strangers. I looked at them and said: 'You know him and I know him, and we've nothing to fear.'

As he stepped onto the grass I looked up, and tried to pretend that I was pleased to see him. 'You're home early,' I called out; and I ran forward to meet him.

But he didn't look up, and he left me standing in the middle of the grass, and I watched him walk towards the geese. 'Get out of my way,' he said to them, and he swung his scythe to the ground and pushed them away.

He stooped and went inside. I stared at the wall we had whitewashed at the start of summer. For a few weeks it had sparkled in the sunshine like a slice of snow. But now the moss and the mould had grown again, and the snow had melted and the sparkle had died, and our cottage looked as though it had come out of the ground, like a mushroom, a mushroom with a cap of thatch that the years had greyed and scabbed with moss.

'What's to eat?' he bellowed, and I knew I had to go inside.

Mother fluttered towards him. 'Bread and cheese. And some of the broth from last night. I've cut up the last of the duck and put it in the broth, so it'll be better than last—'

'And what about the—'

'The apricots? I managed to buy four of them. And they're ripe, and they're the ones you like.'

'The eels, woman. What about the eels?'

'We're not having eels tonight,' she said, rushing her words together. 'We're having pickles instead.'

She was trying to protect me, I could feel it. I wanted to reach out, to take her hand in mine. I wanted to say thank you and—

He grabbed me by the neck and hoisted me off the floor. 'Did you empty the traps?'

'Yes,' I said. 'Yes, I did.'

'Then where are the eels?'

'They got away.'

'Got away?' His voice rose and curled like a wave that is about to crash.

I wriggled and tried to break free. He shook me the way a dog shakes a rat when he's got it by the neck, and death is a second or two away. Mother started to cry. He looked at her and she went quiet. He looked at me. His face was hard and pale, like the rind on a new cheese, and he said: 'Tell me how they got away.'

'I tripped. And the bucket fell into the water. And by the time I pulled it out of the water, they were gone.'

He let me go, and I dropped. The floor jarred my feet and my ankles. The jarring ran up my spine and snapped my teeth. It made my head ache and my eyes water. I staggered back and leant against the wall, with my mouth opening and shutting, like a fish that is about to die.

'Broth,' he said. 'Broth. And a bit of bread. And a bit of cheese. And a few old pickles. That's not enough for a man to work on.'

He ran his hands up and down the handle of his scythe. He'd oiled the wood, and it shone. The curves were soft and rounded, like the curves of the girls who have to stack the corn he cuts. I've seen him watching them as they bend down, and I've seen his face take on a faraway look; and that same look was coming onto his face as he stroked the curves of the scythe. He saw me watching him, and some of the colour came back into his cheesy face, and he said: 'It's hot out there. And the dust and the bits of straw get up your nose and in your mouth and you can't breathe, and you can't spit. It's hard work, much harder than you think, and it goes on and on, like this!' He swung the scythe in fast low sweeps, cutting corn that only he could see. And as he cut he moved forward and the long blade swished across the floor. His back was bent and his head was down, and he didn't seem to know that we were there in the room with him.

I pressed against the wall. Mother opened her mouth but I couldn't hear the words she was trying to say. She pointed at the table. Her hand was shaking.

'The leg!' I screamed. 'Look out for the leg!'

He stopped, and straightened up, and looked at me.

'I'm sorry,' I said, and I could hear my heart thumping, 'I thought you were going to cut the leg. I thought. I thought you were going to nick the blade.'

'I'm not blind! I can see it. I watch what I'm doing, which is more than we can say about you and that bucket of eels, isn't it? And I never put any nicks in my blade. Never.'

He swung the blade up and held it in front of my eyes. 'See!'

I ran my eyes along the sharp edge. It gleamed from end to end, and it looked as though it had just been whetted and rubbed with the stone. 'Yes,' I said, 'it's perfect.'

The slightest of smiles came and went on his face; and then he hooked the handle of the scythe onto the three pegs that jut from above the door and the window. The pegs are shaped and curve upwards and come to a point like the horns of a cow. In my dreams I've seen the cow with the three horns. It's a fearsome creature, like the dragons of old, and Father can't get near it. I have to milk it, and sometimes it turns into a bull, and I still have to milk it, and it hasn't got an udder and milking it doesn't make any sense. Mother says it's just a silly dream, and it has no meaning, and I'm not to worry about it. But it's not her dream, and she doesn't know how real it is, and I do worry about it, and it's not the sort of thing I can talk to him about.

The blade of the scythe hangs to the right of the window. It hangs like a curved sword, and I dream of the day when I can take up that sword, and slay the cow that is a bull. I dream of being a soldier, and I see myself with a sword of my own. It's a straight sword, a thin sword, and I am fighting for the King. We are carrying bunches of flowers. It is spring and the petals are falling and blowing about in the wind; the bells are ringing and we have won a great victory. The land is dry and the land is mine; and The Fens and the waters that keep them wet belong to the past, to the past that I have left behind.

I looked at the end of the blade. Father had honed it into a sharp point and it fitted into a hole in the wall. The hole is shaped like a snowdrop. The point has scratched it out, bit by bit, as the years of summer scything have come and gone. If it wasn't for this flower, this flower that is whitewashed in the spring, there would be little to show for all the work that he has done.

Sometimes Father puts the scythe up the wrong way and the blade hangs to the left of the door, and the point sticks out into the room.

Mother looks at it, and she sucks in her lips, and she waits a few minutes, gives him time to forget the day, and then she says, in a quiet voice: 'I don't want to cut myself on that.' And she'll wave her hand in the direction of the door.

Sometimes he grunts and leaves it that way – just to annoy her, I think – and sometimes he gets up and takes it down and turns it round, and scratches another bit out of the snowdrop.

Those are the better nights, the nights when he is in a good mood, and because he is in a good mood, she is in a good mood. But tonight won't be a good night, despite the fact that the blade is pointing towards the wall.

Hunger makes him twirl his wooden plate round and round. He shows off its emptiness and he makes sure that Mother knows that he is annoyed.

One night last winter he was sitting at the table, and there wasn't much to eat. He was becoming more and more annoyed, and I was wishing we had two rooms, or a loft to which I could retreat, when he jumped to his feet and thumped the table with the flat of his hand. He screamed at her. I can't remember the exact words, but I can remember the sound of them. They sounded like the scream of a wild animal. They made me tremble and they made my mouth go dry.

Then he grabbed his knife, swung it high in the air, and brought it straight down. He stabbed the table. He let out a yell, and shook his hand as if to shake the pain out of it. The knife quivered for a second or two, then it went still. He stood and looked at it. I could hear him breathing. He was making a rasping sound. Then he told her to pull the benches together and make our bed; and he lay down, and she covered him with quilts.

The knife scarred the table, and time has not healed it, and I've often thought, if the table had been a living thing it would have died that night.

Tonight he ate, and said nothing, nothing at all. He drank his mead, and belched, and then he went to bed. I put away his mug, and Mother put away his knife and plate.

We sat close together by the fire, both pretending to warm ourselves, but in truth we were waiting for him to go to sleep.

4

In the autumn, the green leaves of summer turned yellow and orange and brown; the rosehips fattened and became bright red, and like pimples they spotted the face of the land. The balance of light shifted: the days grew shorter and the nights grew longer. Then the first frost sucked the warmth out of our cottage and out of our lives; and at the start of December, sheets of ice spread like a shroud over the fen water. The Isle of Elme became a white whale, locked in a solid sea of white.

The white glittered in the pale sunshine, and it hid the dirt of life. And everywhere we looked there was a sort of purity, a sort of innocence. In my mind I used to think that this could have been the Garden of Eden, and I'd think of Adam and Eve walking around in the snow with no clothes on. I'd see that they were shivering and that their feet had gone blue, and the cold had shrivelled his cock, and it was smaller than mine; and I'd think about snakes, and apples, and temptation, and God throwing the two of them out of the garden. And I'd think of Eve, and that secret place between her legs, and I'd think of her covering herself, and my cock would go hard, and I'd wonder if that was a sin.

We walked to church on the morning of the second Sunday in January, and our footprints marked the snow that had fallen in the night. The inside of the church was cold, much colder than the outside. Our breath formed a mist in the air. It fogged the windows, and the walls took on a wet sheen and they looked like the inside of an oyster shell.

Father and Mother stood side by side, and I stood in front of her. I could feel her rubbing her hands together, and then she came a bit closer and she put them on my shoulders. After a while she ran them down my arms, and she slipped them into my pockets, and she whispered in my ear: 'That's a lot warmer.'

The words of the Reverend Mister Salthouse painted pictures in my mind. In the pictures the three wise men followed the star. It took them to Bethlehem, and the baby Jesus; and they offered him gifts of gold and frankincense and myrrh. Mister Salthouse said that we could offer these same gifts to God, and ours would be the gold of sexual innocence, the frankincense of true love, and the sweet myrrh that rises from a soul when lust has been defeated.

I looked at my feet and wriggled my toes, and in my mind I began to yawn. And then he roared: 'The path to hell is paved with immorality, and carnal knowledge, and perversions too terrible to mention in the house of God.'

No one coughed or mumbled or shuffled their feet or made the slightest sound, and I wriggled my toes some more.

Mother's hands moved deeper into my pockets and I put my hands over hers, and I wished that she could be as warm as me.

I twisted my head and looked up at Father. His mouth was shut and his eyes were fixed on Mister Salthouse.

He was leaning over the edge of his pulpit looking down at us. His mouth was shut, and his hands were on his hips. His surplice floated around him. He looked like a white butterfly and I wondered if we looked like cabbages to him. The thought made me snigger. Father poked me in the ribs. I gulped and swallowed and looked at the floor, and Mother pulled her hands out of my pockets.

I tried to think what all the long words might mean. I'd never met them before, and I couldn't make much sense of them. My eyes ran around the edges of the puddles of slush that were starting to form on the stone floor, and they climbed the wall and walked out onto the beams. I looked at the heads and the wings of the angels who hang there in frozen flight, and I wondered if they ever feel the cold.

At home that afternoon Mother was in a sour mood. She was itchy and irritable. There was no reason for it, that I could see. It was just her time for being itchy and irritable, and I kept out of her way, and so did Dog. I don't know how he can tell when she's in a sour mood, but he can, and he knows before I know. It's strange, and I know some people say he's just a dumb animal, but he's not as dumb as they think he is.

The four of us went to bed as soon as it was dark. Father lay in the middle as usual, and Dog was keeping my feet warm. I was tired and I was thinking about the angels in the church and the fact that they haven't got any bodies, and they couldn't commit what Mister Salthouse called the sins of the flesh. I was drifting, and half-asleep, and the night was folding around me like a soft blanket, when I heard her say: 'No!' Her voice was far away, and then it came a little closer. 'No. Not tonight.'

'Yes,' he said, and his voice was closer, and louder.

I felt him moving. He pulled the bedcovers, and the cold air rushed in, and I opened my eyes. The flames were flickering in the fire, like the will-o'-the-wisp that flickers across the bogs when the smell of marsh gas is in the air.

'I'm bleeding,' she said, 'bleeding.'

'Doesn't matter,' he said.

Mother was hurt. She was bleeding. I hadn't seen her fall, or trip, or cut herself, so how could she be bleeding? I turned it round in my mind but it didn't make any sense. I tried to pull the bedcovers back but they wouldn't move, and I was starting to shiver. And then they were fighting.

She was hitting him, and kicking, and I saw her hand go up in the air, and her fingers were curled, like cat claws, and she cried at him: 'No-o-o-o! My belly hurts. And I've got the cramps.'

'Christ, woman. Be still!' He smacked her. It was a loud slapping smack, and it was full of hurt and full of sting.

She flopped back into the pillows, sobbing and snuffling, and she kept saying: 'No. No. No.' Each 'No' was becoming weaker and weaker. Then she was silent, and she lay still. I knew that he would move onto her, and the pump would grind into life, and the sound of his pumping would fill the room.

My mind cried out to help her, to pull him away, to make him stop.

I grabbed at him. And somehow I had him by the cock. It was big, and hard, and throbbing, and I was shaking, and I could feel a sort of madness burning within me. I moved my hand up and down, and then his oil was on my fingers and I rubbed it round and round. Then he cried out, and his cock spat hot snowflakes onto my hand, and onto his belly, and onto the bedcovers, and the smell of it, the smell of him, was all around me. Dog sat up and whimpered and jumped off the bed, and lay with his nose to the fire looking at the will-o'-the-wisp.

I ran the tips of my fingers up and down his cock, soothing the thick muscle, and calming the knotted veins. It became softer and some of the heat started to go out of it. I pulled down his shirt, and it soaked up the snowflakes.

Then there was silence, and deep inside I was shaking, and I felt frightened.

Hours passed. Hours and hours. I listened to Dog snoring, and to Father snoring, and I tossed backwards and forwards, and I couldn't get comfortable. I heard Mother whisper: 'Go to sleep, Martyn. There's a good boy, go to sleep.' But the words had lost their soothing power and I couldn't go to sleep.

In the morning he left without a word, and without looking me in the eye. She wrapped her arms around me, and she cried – and I cried – and she said: 'I'm sorry. I'm so sorry, but I don't have the strength to fight him any more,' and I hushed her words, and held her tight and tried to kiss her tears away.

In the dark of the months that lay ahead, Mother slept undisturbed, and I lost all sense of shame, and each night, without any prompting from him, I ran my hand up his leg and under his shirt and took hold of his cock. If the day had been hard, full of splitting wood, or punting or netting, he would lie on his back and stare at the beams, and I would roll the end of his cock between my fingers and I'd play with his balls, and he would sigh and go to sleep. But if the snow or the rain or the driving sleet had kept him inside, he was full of energy, and restless, and his cock would grow in my hands and he would need me.

In my mind I was like a small boy leading a great ox: I'd tied a rope through the brass ring that hung from its nose and it would go where I wanted it to go, and it would do what I wanted it to do. I felt safe and I wasn't afraid of it.

Then came July, and the ox gored me, and our lives were never the same again.

It began as an ordinary day with a long twilight, and when it was dark the warmth stayed in the air. Dog was asleep on the floor, twitching and snoring and making slobbering noises, and the three of us were lying in bed. I was holding his cock and feeling full of sleep, and tired from walking to Outwell and back to carry the first of the fenberries to Granny Wilkes. I thought he was tired after hours of scything, and I thought he'd drop off to sleep at any moment, but he put his hand over mine and moved it up and down and stirred his cock into life.

'Turn over,' he grunted at me. He lifted my shirt and spread my legs and shoved his finger up my arsehole, and moved it round and round, and in and out. It bloody hurt. I squirmed around and bucked up and down, and then he was on me. His weight pressed me into the bed. I thought he was going to crush me, and I couldn't breathe and I could feel him pushing his cock into me. It went in and in and in, and it felt as if he'd shoved a stick up my arse. Then he was ramming it in and out, and I could hear the pump, and it was sucking and slurping and echoing, and he slipped one hand under my belly and in behind my balls and he lifted me up and his cock slid in some more and he ground himself against my arse, and I thought I was going to split in half. Then I felt him explode within me. It was hot, searing hot. And I was sweating, and my legs were trembling.

When he pulled it out, the shit dribbled down my leg, and the smell of it was in our bed.

I lay on my belly. My tears wet the pillow, and I shoved some of it into my mouth and bit it. Every time I tried to make the slightest move the pain roared through me, and in my head I could hear myself screaming.

In the early morning, before he was awake, I walked down to the stream. I was bent over, like an old lady. It felt as though my arse were on fire. I sat in the stream till the fire went out. And then I thought it would be all right but it wasn't, and I had to eat my breakfast standing up.

In the evening, just before he was due to come home, Mother began to cry, and she took me into her arms and ran her hands through my hair. Then she handed me her pot of goose-grease and she said: 'Rub a little of this onto him and put a bit on yourself, where it hurts.'

I looked at her and I could feel my jaw sagging, and the trembling came back into my legs.

'You'll find it helps,' she said. And then she sat on her stool – hunched and aged – and looked into the fire, and she started to cry again.

5

Winter came early – within a few days of the Harvest Festival – and it was cold and bitter. It kept my Father inside, and it kept him idle, and he did to me what he wanted to do; and I have shut it out of my mind and will speak of it no more.

The spring thaw brought the spring floods, and they filled the basin that is The Fens to overflowing, and the bitterness of winter stayed with us till late April. May was soft and warm, and in June and July and August the heat haze blurred the flat line between the earth and the sky and it made them into one; and it blurred the lines between the months and it made them into one long hot summer. And for a while I thought it would last for ever. But then autumn returned and it put a chill in the air, and I realised that two years had passed since I first began to release the eels.

Sometimes I let all the eels go, and sometimes I kept a few and they calmed his suspicions. And sometimes I called them 'Father' and chopped off their heads and threw them back into the river.

The river had been quiet for a long time, but last night it was starting to stir, starting to rise again, and this morning the waters were heavy with silt and they'd lost their sparkle.

I picked up the rope and began to pull in the first trap. It felt light and it sprang from the water and slid up the bank. It was empty. And so were all the other traps.

I felt uneasy, and my stomach gurgled.

Last night, and the night before, Mother served a stew thickened with marrowbones, and it left me feeling hungry. Father twirled his plate around a couple of times, and we both knew that he was missing his eels. I saw her mouthing words at me, and in my mind she was saying: you make sure you get some eels tomorrow.

And now it was tomorrow and there were no eels.

Father came home looking tired. He was carrying his hat and his sack in one hand and his scythe in the other. He was stooped, more stooped than normal, and he complained about not being able to stand up straight. He said his fingers were going numb, and there were bands of pain in both of his arms.

The salt marks on his shirt, the tidelines of perspiration, glistened in the firelight, and his speech was strange and rambling as it is when the fever is upon him. 'Fourteen hours,' he was saying, 'fourteen hours I been in that field, and it's your fault. No one can cut as much as I can. And I know it's your fault. It's hot in that field. And I helped with the stacking. You let them go. That's what you do, I know you do.'

'No, Father,' I said, keeping my voice soft and pretending to a calm I didn't feel. 'There was a lot of mud in the water last night and I put some more bait in the traps so the eels would see it, but it didn't make any difference.'

'Hmm,' he said, picking up my soft tones. 'Hmm. When I was a boy the eels could see the bait. And I never had any trouble catching them. Never. Never ever.'

He sat back in his seat, and fixed his eye on me. 'I think you're telling lies. Or you've gone soft in the head, and you let them go.'

Then he lifted his arm and pointed his finger at me. 'You have to kill to eat! Animals is animals! We kill them, and we eat them! That's what we do!'

His words were screaming in my ears. I gulped and swallowed. For one mad moment I wondered if an eel was an animal. Then the thought vanished, and my mouth went dry. 'The traps were empty. The eels must've swum away. Or maybe the current's too strong for them and—'

'I don't believe you! I don't believe a single word you say!'

He jumped up and ran at me, and his open hand came hurling through the air. It slapped my face.

I reeled backwards. The room went black and stars exploded in my head. I fell into the fire. It was hot. I screamed, and scrambled out and leapt to my feet. Ash covered my hand. It was burning, burning hot, and the room was swaying, and in my head I was seeing red, bright red, and I yelled at him: 'I didn't let them go! I told you that! There weren't any. Not today! There were some yesterday. And I let them go. But not today. It was yesterday . . .'

The words died on my lips. The room swayed some more, and my stomach heaved, and I felt as if I were going to be sick at any moment.

Mother put her hands to her mouth, and she seemed to shrivel and become part of the wall.

He stared at me. His face was getting redder and redder.

'What did you say?'

His voice felt cold. It sent shivers running through me.

I kept my eyes on his hands, and inch by inch I backed away from him.

The fire sparked and flared. In the silence it sounded like a roaring inferno, and I felt as if I had arrived at the gates of hell. And I knew that the man who guarded the gates had asked me a question, and I knew that I had to answer it, but the question kept breaking into little bits, and the bits didn't make any sense. I felt helpless, and I didn't know what to say.

He looked down at his feet, and then he turned and he started to talk to the fire. 'I worked,' he said, 'I worked all day yesterday and it was stinking hot, and I was tired, and hungry, and what did I get? More of that bloody stuff she has in the pot all the time. That's what. And what do I get tonight? A fish, and more of the bloody same.' He shook his head from side to side. 'That's not a proper meal. Not for a man who likes his eels.'

He lifted his foot, eyed the pot as if it were a ball, and then he booted it. It swung in and slewed to the side and hit the bricks. The stew, thick and full of jelly, flew out of the pot. For a moment it hung in the air like a brown puffball, then it exploded, and flung bits of stew at his foot and his leg and the crutch of his breeches. The bits stuck to him like hot glue.

'Ahhhh!' he screamed.

He staggered backwards, trying to kick off his shoe and undo his breeches at the same time.

He crashed against the wall. His head whipped back and hit

the shelf. The plates rattled, and two of them slid to the floor and broke.

His jaw sagged and a wailing roar came out of his mouth. It was the roar of an animal, an animal in pain.

He rubbed the back of his head and then he stared at his hand. It was covered in blood. He closed his fingers, and forced the blood to run between them.

'This is your fault!' he screamed. 'You did this!'

My throat went tight, and my mouth tasted of copper.

He rushed to the door, grabbed his scythe in both hands, and swung it to the ground. He turned round, and for a second I caught the terrible madness that was in his eyes. Then he seemed to be measuring the distance between us, measuring the corn that was still to be cut. He grunted, and his arms began to move, and the blade began to swish across the floor.

Mother screamed: 'Stop it! For God's sake. Stop it!'

His head stayed down. And his mouth stayed shut.

I edged away towards the fire, but he followed me, step by step. And then with a slow deliberate swing, he scythed at my legs.

I jumped. The blade swished under me.

He looked up, and shook his head, and roared.

He swung the blade again.

I jumped again. And grabbed at the beam. The blade swished under my feet. My hands slipped, and I dropped to the floor. Sweat was pouring from my face, and running down my back and under my arms.

He scowled and stepped back. He swung the blade into the air. It howled through the long beams, and it came straight down, at my head.

I screamed. And tried to leap away.

The blade tore past my ear and down my arm. The point hit the hearthstone. A clanging ringing sound filled the whole room, and it echoed in my head.

In the silence that came when the echo died, I turned and looked down, and my hands started to shake.

The blade was broken. It had snapped in half and the sharp end had fallen into the fire. The point, made thin by years of gentle honing, took on a faint glow, a sort of delicate blush. As I watched, the blush deepened and became red and angry, like a boil, and for some reason the pain of that boil was in my arm. I rubbed at it, and my hand was covered in blood.

I looked at my hand for a moment or two. It didn't make any sense. Then I saw that my sleeve was cut from the shoulder to the cuff, and blood was oozing from the cut. I tried to hold the cut, tried to stop the bleeding, but the blood ran between my fingers as it had run between his fingers. It made me shudder and my stomach heaved.

Mother began to cry, began to wail and howl as she did when my brother drowned and we brought him home and laid him on the table. She held his head in her arms and the water ran out of his mouth, and she mourned for him for three days and three nights. Then he was laid in the ground, and she never spoke of him again.

I knew that she was mourning for me, and the chill of death was upon me, and in her mind I would be buried and gone for ever. The vomit rose in my throat and it flowed from my mouth in the same way that the water had flowed from my brother's mouth.

I turned to Father. He was swaying from side to side, like a man who has drunk too much, and he was talking to his scythe. I could hear the word 'sorry'. He was saying it over and over again. Sometimes it was loud and sometimes it was soft and mumbling. His hands were moving up and down the wooden handle, as if to sooth away the hurt, and the tears were running from his eyes. He picked up the scythe, held it in both arms like a new-born baby, then he shuffled over to the door, and with a tenderness he'd never shown to me, or to her, he placed it on the pegs.

The broken end of the blade rested against the wall. The end was bright and clean, and it shone like polished silver. It picked up the light of the fire and it laid a thin flickering line on the wall, about eighteen inches above the snowdrop, and it told me what I had known in my heart from the moment I saw the broken blade: he would never reap again, and he would blame it on me.

He took his chair from under the table. He sat down and stared into the fire. His head began to sink forward, and his back rounded, and I thought he was going to sleep, but his eyes were open, and they were fixed on the blade.

No one touched the fire. We let the peat burn away and we

let the blade sink into the red-brown ash. When it was gone, Mother dabbed at her eyes, and she said to me, in the softest of whispers: 'You have destroyed him, and he will destroy you.'

I gulped and swallowed, and I wanted to say something but there was nothing that I could say. And there was nothing that I could do.

Our eyes met. Her eyes were the eyes of a stranger, and I looked away, as strangers do.

Then I heard her say: 'You must go.'

6

I shut the door, shut out the light and the warmth of the only place I have ever called home, and as I walked into the night, the geese hissed and honked for a moment or two; then they seemed to recognise me, and they settled down and the night became still and quiet. I wandered about in an aimless way, and the black of the night seeped into my mind and filled it with gloom. I couldn't think what I should be doing or where I should be going. Then I felt afraid and I started to run. My arm throbbed and my hand hurt, and I stumbled and fell. I could smell the earth, the earth in which my brother lay. It was cold and wet and it stank of death. And I started to shiver.

Later, I found myself standing beside the stream, and I can remember putting my hand in it, and wishing the pain would go away. And I can remember bending down to drink some water, and the taste of sick came flooding back into my mouth. I tried to spit it out but it was right inside my head, and it was sour like bile.

Then I was in the village, opening the door to the church and climbing the stone steps in the tower, and sitting on the wooden floor with my back to the wall. The stones felt hard and they kept digging into my back, and I kept thinking about the morning, thinking about Father, thinking that he could take his scythe to the smithy. I've seen old Blackie shoe horses and make hooks and chains for the fire, and I've seen him toast his bread on the forge; but try as I would, I could not remember seeing him repair a blade.

I sighed to myself and stretched out on the floor and the blood rushed to my head. I'd forgotten that our soft soil had tilted the tower and sloped the floor, and I sat up and turned around and lay the other way.

In the darkness high above me, the wind was stirring the bells and creaking the beams and feeding the draught. The draught was running down the wall and across the floor and it was feeling my hands and my face, and it was sneaking inside my coat and through my shirt and under my arms. It was carrying the chill of the night, and I could feel it right inside me, and it was making me shiver.

I crawled into the corner and curled up in a tight ball, just like Dog used to do when he was a little puppy, and Mother said he had to sleep on the floor.

I woke numb. My hand ached and my arm throbbed. My legs had stiffened and locked against my belly, and they hurt as I tried to stand up. My face felt cold, cold as the ice that creeps across the face of the pond. My teeth were chattering, and they weren't making any sense, and nor were the thoughts that were in my head.

Outside the birds were beginning to sing, beginning to form the choir that would greet the dawn; and in the big brick house just across the road, they were starting to stir, starting to stretch and yawn and scratch themselves and think about the day that lay ahead. With a sudden shock I realised I didn't want them to think about me. I slipped down the steps and out of the church and into the shadows. I crept through the village and down our lane and I hid behind the hawthorn hedge.

Every few minutes I pulled the branches aside and peered through the mesh of thorn and leaf, and I waited. I waited for him to go out. I waited all day but he didn't go out.

In the evening, when our cottage had merged into the dark of the night, and the door and the window were shut tight, I walked back to the church and climbed the tower.

In the rafters above me the bats stirred and stretched their wings, and the smell of their droppings filled the air. I could taste the smell, at the back of my mouth and in my throat. It was sour and full of vinegar like the bile of yesterday. I swallowed hard, and I felt hungry, more hungry than I'd ever felt before. I thought of fish baked in clay and served with watercress and stewed apples. It made my belly go flat and hard, and it twisted my insides round and round.

I sat in the corner and leant forward and hugged my knees. I rubbed my belly and tried to ease the pain, and I wished I'd never thought of food. I shut my eyes and tried to go to sleep.

Sleep came and went and came again, and somewhere in this drifting dreaming time, I had an idea. I took off my shirt and flung it high into the air. Like a net, it wrapped itself around two of the bats. I grabbed their legs and banged their heads against the wall and broke their necks. In the corner I built a fire and I roasted them. They smelt like a duck, a fat succulent duck, and the flesh fell away from the bone. It was dark and tender and full of juice, and as I opened my mouth to take my first bite, I woke up.

For a moment or two I could still see the meat in my fingers, and I could still smell the smell, and my mouth was moist and my insides didn't hurt any more. But then the meat and the smell were gone, and I felt as if I had been cheated, and I could taste the disappointment that was welling up in me. I jumped to my feet and screamed. My scream echoed inside the bells, and I shook my fist at them, and my insides began to twist again. I slid down the wall, and sat in my corner.

I couldn't go back to sleep. The cold kept me awake, kept me thinking. Why did it have to be his scythe? Why did it have to be the one thing he valued most? And how often had he said to me: 'That's my scythe. I own it, and no one can take it away from me. I saved the money for that scythe. It took me three years, it did. But I did it, with the sweat of my brow, and these hands.' And then he would stretch out his hands and turn them over so that I could see the scars, and the scabs that felt like cow horn. 'There's always work for a man with a scythe at harvest-time. And those who own their own scythe, they get the most work. And they earn the most. And they don't go hungry. And nor do their women. And nor do their children. So just you remember that.'

It was the longest speech he ever made, and he made it over and over again. I knew it by heart, and I used to say the words with him, under my breath. In my mind the words were soft and sleepy, like some of Mister Salthouse's prayers, and they didn't mean much, till one day he looked me up and down and said:

'Won't be long now till you're big enough to use a proper scythe. And you'll have to earn the money to buy one. And that'll make a man of you. By Jesus it will.' I looked at him, and I knew I didn't want to be like him. And it hurt to nod my head, and pretend to an eagerness that I could never feel in my heart.

Next morning, still cold and hungry, I went back and waited again behind the hawthorn hedge. In the late afternoon I watched him go. He plodded along the path, more bent, more ox-like than usual. His head had flopped and he looked lifeless. Dog ran beside him, barking and sniffing and shoving his nose under the clumps of bog-weed, and he was full of life. The contrast between them was there for all to see and it hurt. I felt sorry for him and I wanted to help him, but deep inside I knew that he wouldn't want me to help, and he wouldn't want me to be sorry for him. I looked down at my feet, and my eyes filled with tears, and when I looked up he was gone.

I ran inside calling: 'Mother! Mother! Where are you?'

She opened her arms, and we hugged each other, and sniffled. I took her hands and for a moment her forehead rested against mine and our noses touched. Then I stepped back, and felt ill. Her whole face had puffed up and her eyes were black and blue and yellow and green. She looked like a pumpkin that had gone rotten. I remembered the pumpkin I'd found in the meadow beyond Fryday Bridge. I was going to kick it, then I changed my mind and I tossed it high in the air. As it fell I ran towards it and gave it a punch, a hard vicious punch. It exploded into a thousand bits. The bits splattered my hand and my face and my shirt, and they stank, like the slime that edges the ponds in summertime.

I looked at my hand and I thought of that punch, and I thought of him, and his hands, and I said to her: 'Why does he do it?'

She shrugged and looked away.

I went to touch her face, to sooth the pain away, but she held up her hands and formed a grille in front of her face, and she said: 'It's all right. It will heal. It always does, so don't worry about me. Worry about him. He's the one that's sick. He won't talk to me. And he won't eat anything. He just stares at the fire. I've tried to make him go to bed but he won't. He just sits in that chair of his and he mutters to himself. Sometimes I think he's talking to you, and sometimes I think he's talking to his mother. But she's been dead for ten years, and I don't know what to make of it.'

Her words weighed me down, and for several minutes neither of us said anything.

Then I heard her mutter: 'You have destroyed him and he'll never forgive you, and no words of mine will ever make him change his mind.' Then she straightened up, as she always does when it is time for her to tell me what to do. 'He'll be back soon,' she said, 'and he mustn't find you here. You must go. It's not safe for you here,' and she sighed and shook her head. 'I've been thinking about what you should do. And I want you to go to my sister, to your Aunt Mary, in Ely. She'll know what to do. And I want you to do what she says. Do you hear me?'

I nodded, and she flung her arms around me and pulled me into her bosom. She was crying and mumbling words that had no meaning. Then she seemed to find her composure and I felt her fingers in my hair, felt them running down my neck and down my spine. She made me feel warm and safe; and my fingers moved up to her shoulders and down her back, kneading the muscles that were hard and tight.

Then she whispered in my ear: 'You must forget about our bed and the things that happened there. If you tell the truth they will not understand, and they will not accept what has happened, and they will not accept you. So you must pretend that you do not know about these things, and you must lock them away in your mind and never speak of them again.'

We looked into each other's eyes and the tears streamed down our faces, and I nodded to her, and she kissed me on both cheeks. Then she locked me into her arms and we swayed to and fro, half-asleep and half-awake, and an eerie calm filled my head. And all the gloom, all the blackness that was in my soul, flowed from me to her, and she made me feel clean again.

She took my face into her hands in the same way that Mister Salthouse takes the communion cup, and she said: 'I give you back your innocence. It is a precious gift, as precious as the body and the blood of our Lord. There was no sin in Him and there is no sin in you.'

She hugged me again and said: 'And now you must go,' and

she touched my hair with her fingertips and brushed it away from my eyes, and her tears wet my coat.

I stepped back from her and took both her hands into mine. 'Tell me,' I said, 'what was it like in the year of my birth?'

'Oh,' she said, and I could hear her voice beginning to brighten a little: 'Oh. They celebrated the year of your birth. They rang the bells in Elme and Ely and Norwich. And there was feasting and bonfires. And in London they fired rockets, and they filled the nightsky with stars. The stars were red and yellow and green, and they say they were a wonder to behold, and those who saw them will never forget them.'

The tears were rolling down my face. 'Why would they want to celebrate my birth?' I asked.

'Not your birthday, silly, the year of your birth. It was 1660, the year of the Restoration. The year the King came back. That's what they were celebrating.'

'I will be like the King,' I said. 'I will come back.' I kissed her on both cheeks, and I ran outside. I didn't look back. I ran and I ran and I ran.

7

I ran down the path and along the lane and onto the road. I ran without thinking, splashing through the puddles and leaping over the ruts and running around the cows and the geese and the boys who were driving them back to the village.

In my mind I was like the eels that slid out of my bucket: I was escaping, I was finding my freedom.

The swamp and the reeds and the ditches that follow the road blurred into each other. Half a mile became a mile, became a mile and a half, became two miles, and then I was running through a line of trees and past the church and the graveyard and into Wisbech.

The shadows felt cool and the cobbles felt hard and they grabbed at my feet, and like a brake on the front wheel of a coach they slowed me down, and I started to walk. My heart was thumping. I could hear myself puffing and panting. I leant against the wall of a house and took a couple of deep breaths.

To my left, looming over the roofs and the chimneys, was the Castle of Wisbech. Its walls were smooth and made of stone. They were catching the last of the sun and they had taken on a pink glow. It was soft and delicate like the pink that comes to the dog rose when the petals are falling and the blooms are dying.

It wasn't a real castle. It was a house that was built when Mother was a little girl. She says she can remember the real castle, and she went inside once, just before they pulled it down, and she saw the dungeons and the shackles.

She climbed the tower and she could see all the way to Elme. And when she looked in the opposite direction she saw a haze on the sea, and she couldn't tell where the salt sea met the salt marsh. She said that this place of meeting was a mysterious place, a place where the spirit of the Lord still moved across the water, a place where the waves divided and the land grew, as it did in the days of creation.

And she would tell me that the land was pushing Wisbech further and further away from the sea, and she could foresee the day when the river would silt up and the port would be no more. And I would smile at her and think she had strange notions in that head of hers.

I heard a window open, and I felt a sudden rush of hot air, and it brought to me the smells of cooking. They filled my head and they made my mouth water. I stepped away from the wall, almost into the middle of the street, and I turned and looked up. A fat face filled the window. It was glossed with sweat and speckled with warts and black moles, and it looked like a suet pudding.

It was a face that came to me in my dreams. And every time it came, it came with a piece of cake or a slice of pie.

'Mother Jackson,' I called out, and I waved to her.

She leant out the window and peered down at me.

'It's Martyn,' I said, 'Martyn Fenton.'

'What you want?'

'I'm hungry. And I'm on my way to London. And could I have something to eat?'

'And where are the eggs?'

'I don't have any eggs. Not today I don't,' and I opened my hands and stretched out my arms to show that I wasn't carrying anything. 'The ducks aren't laying, and nor are the hens, and it's too late for the quails, but I'll bring you some as soon as I can.'

She sold her baking from a stall at the Saturday market and I had been bringing eggs to her for as long as I could remember. She always patted me on the head and gave me something to eat. I was her friend, and she was my friend. I smiled at her but she shook her head. 'You won't be bringing me any more eggs. Not from London you won't. So you won't be getting anything from me. Not unless you've got some money and you can pay for it. Have you got any money?'

I shook my head, and she shrugged.

'But I will be back,' I said, 'and I can bring you some eggs then, and I won't forget.'

She made me feel like one of the beggars who sit with the whores on the quay where the ships tie up. They sit with their hands outstretched, and they used to follow me with their eyes, and I'd look away and pretend they didn't exist.

Then she was telling me to go away, and I remembered the man who inspects the goods and collects the taxes when the ships are being unloaded. I remembered him telling the beggars to go away in the same tone of voice that she had used to me, and I had watched them go, watched them shuffle away. She shut the window, and I yelled: 'I'm not going to bring you any more bloody eggs. So don't you go looking for me in the spring because I won't be here.'

Her window stayed shut, and I sniffed and wiped my nose on my sleeve. Then I shuffled away.

I was somewhere near the quay, and the twilight had given way to night, when it occurred to me that I mightn't be in Wisbech in the spring. I might be in some other place. I felt afraid and I burst into tears. Then I saw a couple of men looking at me in a strange way, and I rushed into a doorway and wiped at my eyes.

Another man came from the shadows and put his arm around me. He was wearing a hat and riding boots and a long cloak, and he smelt of scent, and I knew that he was a gentleman, and a gentleman could be trusted. That's what my Mother said, and I felt myself relax. His draped one side of his cloak over me and then the other, so that only my head was showing. It felt warm and safe. He took my hand and pressed a coin into it. The coin was also warm, as if he'd had it in his hand for ages, and I thought of Mother Jackson and her pies and how warming they were. I wanted to run all the way back to her and push the coin into her hand, and then his hand was running down my belly and into my breeches and he was playing with my cock and rolling my balls between his fingers.

For a moment I was like a man with the palsy: I couldn't move. Then I felt an anger, a wild mad anger rising in me, and I yelled: 'No!' and I wrenched myself away from him. He flung his arm around my neck and hooked me under the chin, and pulled me back to him.

'I thought you Dutch boys liked this sort of thing,' he whispered. He lifted my head with his arm, and it felt as if he were going to choke me. I struggled, and he punched me high in the back. The pain shot through me and thumped into my head, and I felt myself sag, and I grabbed at his arm.

'That's better,' he said. And he pulled my breeches down and his fingers were in my arse and they were hurting me. I jigged around and tried to shake him off, and he jerked my head up again. I gasped for breath and sagged again, and I could feel myself trembling.

He put his mouth to my ear. His breath was hot and it smelt of peppermint. 'You do it on the boats, don't you? I know. I know your sort. You do it in the dark, don't you? And you think nobody knows. Well, I know. And God knows. And he's sent me to punish you. And that's what I'm going to do.'

There was something in his voice, something evil, something that made me fear him, and I tried to pull away. He held me tight, and I felt helpless, as helpless I had been with my Father, and in my despair I cried out. But it did not come out like a cry, it came out like a moan, a soft submissive moan.

'So you do like it,' he said. 'I knew you would. You're all the same. Now bend over.' He pushed my head down, and I could feel him fumbling with his breeches. Then he was rubbing his cock against my arse and I was struggling, trying to break free. He leant down and bit my ear and pulled my head up against his, and he said: 'I do like it when they put up a bit of a fight.' He twisted me to the side and slapped my arse with the flat of his hand. It was sudden, and hard, and it stung, and I felt the tears in my eyes. He slapped me again and again. Then he ground himself against me and he shuddered and cried out. His seed ran down my arse and down my legs and the smell of it came up through my clothes. It was ripe, and rancid, like the smell that lingers on the billy goat.

'Christ,' he said, 'that was just what I needed,' and he took my hand and pushed another coin into it. He pulled me into his cloak and wrapped both his arms around me, and held me tight. I could feel him breathing and I could hear his heart thumping.

'We can do it again,' he said, 'and this time I'll get inside you, and you'll jump up and down, and then you'll know what it's like to have a real man. By Jesus, you will.'

His voice had changed. It had lost the huskiness that was there earlier on, and the tones were more mellow, more familiar, more like the voice of a preacher.

It was a voice I knew, a voice I had often heard. I felt myself go rigid and I sucked in my breath so fast it made a whistling sound.

'Let me go,' I said. 'I want to go.'

'You speak English?' I could hear the surprise in his voice. 'I used to ask if they could speak English but none of them ever could, and it didn't matter. They all knew what I wanted and I knew what they wanted, and we never had any difficulty.' He paused and ran his hand through my hair and he bent down and bit me on the neck. 'So, where did you learn to speak English?'

'In Elme.'

I felt him shudder, and his grip softened a little. 'Elme, you say?' and the huskiness was back in his voice. 'Is that in the Netherlands?'

'No,' I said, 'it's about two miles from here.'

He let go of me, and backed away into the frame of the door.

I put my hands on his cloak and I pulled him back towards to me. 'What would they say in Elme,' I asked in a voice that was no more than a whisper, 'if they could see you now, Mister Salthouse?'

He let out a screeching sound, like a gull in distress. Then he reached out for my face, and he held it, and he peered at it for a long time, and then he said: 'Fenton. Martyn Fenton.'

His hands dropped from my face to my shoulders – and I could feel them trembling – and I pushed them away.

He pulled up his breeches, and for a while he just stood in the doorway with his hat hiding his face and his cloak hiding his body. Then he said: 'This. This will be our secret. And I will be able to help you . . .' and his voice drifted away.

He dug into his pocket, and grabbed at my hand and pushed some more coins into it.

The coins felt sweaty, and they slid about in my fingers, and they unleashed in me a sudden burst of anger. Without thinking, I swung my arm high above my shoulder, and I threw the coins at the cobbles. They filled the air with the sounds of spinning and ringing; and in the distance one or two heads turned towards us, and then they turned away.

'I don't want your money!' I yelled at him. 'I'm not a whore, and I'm not for sale like the women over there. And I wasn't down here looking for a sailor. I was walking along. That's all I was doing.'

He shrugged – as if it didn't matter – and I wished that I could make him pay for what he'd done to me. And then he put his hands to his face, and I remembered doing the same thing when I was young and I wanted to hide from my Mother. I thought of her and the innocence she had returned to me. And I felt bitter. And I did not know how this man could preach the gospel of love and forgiveness.

I could not forgive him, and the anger that was within me exploded, and I clenched my fist, and I eyed the black shape that was his head, and I punched it. His head hit the door. His knees sagged and he slid to the ground. He moaned and rolled forward, and lay in a heap.

His head was about a foot from my foot. Without thinking, I stepped back and swung my foot, and my toe touched his head. I smiled to myself and I swung my foot again, and in my mind I heard his skull crunch and crack. It sounded like a spoon hitting the shell of an egg. It made me feel sick in my stomach and sick in my head, and I wanted to stop my foot. But it had become a savage dog. It was off the leash and it had scented blood. It tore at him and struck the side of his head and it crunched the bones at the top of his neck.

He made a soft moaning cry, and I could hear the pain that was within him. His feet were twitching and drumming at the ground, as if they knew they should be carrying him away from me. Then his feet went still, and he lay without making a sound or any sort of movement. He sent a chill, a feeling of horror, a feeling of panic, running through my body. It set my heart beating in my ears, and it made my hands tremble and go numb, as if they had been bitten by frost, and I thought: I've killed him.

I fell to my knees, and I tried to pick him up but he flopped in my arms. I remembered the picture of Mary with the dead Christ in her arms; and in the blackness that was in my heart I felt some of the sorrow, some of the agony that she must have felt that day; and I was crying, and I could remember she was crying. She had seen them kill her son, and I had killed the man who taught me to read and write; the man who used to pat me on the head and call me son, and I could not think what evil, what madness, what perverse trick of the devil, had made me want to kill him.

I stood up with him still in my arms as if I were offering a sacrifice. I closed my eyes and I bowed my head and I tried to say I was sorry, but the words would not come from my mouth, and I stood there swaying backwards and forwards.

A minute swayed away, and then another, and another. He was growing heavier and heavier, and my arms were starting to ache. I could feel that I was losing my grip on him, and I tried to lift him to get a better grip. But his legs slid away from me, and his feet hit the ground with a thump. I felt the thump. I felt him shudder. Then he coughed in my face and groaned in my ear.

He had come back from the dead. It was the only thought that was in my mind. It made my skin tingle and it sent a feeling of relief screaming through my body, and for a moment I felt quite light-headed. Then this feeling gave way to one of happiness and I sensed that his return from the dead was more real, more worthy of celebration, than anything he had ever preached about on the day our Lord came back from the dead. I know this is a mad thought, a thought that would have me thrown out of the church if it were known. But it was what I was thinking and it made me hug him and it sent me dancing around him till he started to wobble, and I had to grab him and hold him, and stop him falling to the ground.

'Mister Salthouse,' I said, when my high spirits were no more and I could see him again with sober eyes, 'it's time for you to go home.' I straightened his cloak and picked up his hat and stuck it on his head.

He mumbled something but I could not catch it, and then he staggered away.

I looked down at the cobbles, and I thought of the coins, and

I told myself not to be a fool, and I crawled about like one of those black beetles that come out at night, and I found a farthing, and then I found another one. Then I bumped into a woman. She was crawling about on all fours, feeling the cobbles. Then I bumped into another and another and another. They giggled, and one of them said I could have her if I found a coin, and I said, 'No thank you,' and they laughed.

Then one of them ran her hand over my back and down my arse.

I pushed her away and felt my face go hot and my cock go hard, and I said: 'No, that's not what I want.' My throat felt dry; and my voice sounded high, as high as it used to be in the days when I sang in the choir, and I knew that it had betrayed me.

I jumped up and ran away, and their laughter came running after me.

8

I sat down in the Market Place, on the marker stone by the corner where the street leads down to the bridge, and I caught my breath.

A soft light came from some of the houses. It was not enough to disturb the darkness in the middle of the market or to show where the roofs touched the night sky, but it was enough to put a flat outline on some of the doors and I could see that no one was hiding in the ones behind me.

The market was quiet. The noises of the day had departed, and so had the man who swept up the dung; but some of the smells – the smells that taste of cabbage and onion and apples – they were lingering in the air.

In my mind the whores were still laughing and I was thinking of all the things I could have said to them if my wits had been a little sharper and my voice had been a little deeper.

I remembered Mother Jackson, and I wondered why I had told her I was going to London. If Mother had overheard what I had said, she would have told me I was showing off, or talking nonsense, and she would have told me to put such thoughts out of my mind. She would have reminded me that I was a Fenton, a man of The Fens, and that was where I belonged; and London was not for the likes of me.

I wondered what Aunt Mary would say. In size and shape and face she was just like Mother, but in her head, her thoughts walked in a strange land. She was full of surprises and I could never guess what she was going to say. She was older than Mother, by ten years or more, and she was older than Father, and she said she could remember the summer Mother was born, and the winter Father was born. Sometimes she would talk of those times and sometimes she would push aside my questions and shake her head and say: 'Some things are best forgotten.'

I ran my fingers down the marker. The years had weathered the stone and rounded the edges of the letters and they were not as deep as they used to be. My fingers found an E, and an L, and an M, and another E. I traced the outline of the arrow that pointed to Elme, and below it my fingers found the letters K I N G S and the letters L Y N N. For a moment I felt as if my fingers had touched the red-hot prongs of a toasting fork. The letters seared my fingers and they seared my mind, and they sent a shock running through my body.

I had come the wrong way.

I jumped to my feet and swore. And I cursed the madness, the blind panic, that had sent me running towards Wisbech instead of Ely. I should have gone to Fryday Bridge and over Coldham Fens, and here I was, miles away, in the opposite direction. I sat down again on the marker and the point jabbed into my arse. It hurt, like Mister Salthouse's fingers, and I burst into tears.

By the time I was back in Elme and walking along the bank of the drain they say the Romans dug, the moon was starting to rise and the puddles had taken on a bright sheen, and I could see where I was putting my feet. I was beginning to feel a bit better, but by the time I was past Coldham Manor and over Waldersey Bank and onto Northwold Green, the clouds had covered the moon and the blackness had swallowed my feet and I was feeling lost and lonely.

Then the dogs of March found me. They came bounding up to me, barking and sniffing. I patted one of them, and he followed me through the village. I gave him a hug and I talked to him, and in my mind he was Dog; he was my friend with the pointed nose. I said goodbye to him and he licked my hand and I told him to look after Mother. I told him he could have my place in bed. I told him he could lie beside her and keep her warm. Then he seemed to know that it was time to go and he gave me another lick and he bounded away. I could hear him barking, and I yelled: 'And when I get back you're going to have to lie by my feet again. You hear that? By my feet.'

Just beyond Doddington, where the path softens and the men

have built a gate to keep the cattle on the high ground, I found a plum tree. Or maybe I should say it found me because the branches hit my face, and as I reached up to push them away some of the plums fell on me. They were small and very ripe; more stone than flesh and not worth the trouble is what Mother would have said of them; but to me, with my dry mouth and my dry throat, they tasted like honey and they eased the ache in my belly. I put a few of them in my pocket, thinking I'd eat them at Vermuyden's Drain, but as I walked that last couple of miles the skins burst. The flesh came away from the stones, and the juice wet my breeches and the wet rubbed at the top of my leg. I reached into my pocket and brought out a handful of mush that smelt of eels and fish and salted mud. I threw it away and walked on, and the ache came back into my belly.

The air grew cold and a few spots of rain fell on my face, and on the wind I could hear the sounds of the drain. They were faint and far away but as I drew closer they gathered strength and I could hear the sounds I used to hear in our bed. They were the sounds he made when he forced himself upon her. They were the sounds that haunted my dreams. I swallowed hard and told myself I was not in bed. I was on The Fens, and the sounds were the sounds of the windpumps. The sails made a swishing sound, and the wheels made a grinding sound, and the water made a sucking, sloshing sound. It was this last sound, of water moving from a low drain to a high drain, that raised the fear in my mind, the fear of what he was going to do to her in that bed of ours. My mind went black, as black as the bank that lay in front of me. I felt myself tremble, and I was afraid for her.

If it had been daylight this fear might not have troubled me, because I could have seen the bank, and seen the bend from which the bank ran straight and true for miles and miles in both directions. And I could have seen the windpumps perched in twos and threes along the side of the bank, like black crows seeking company. And I could have seen that the waterwheels were turning, passing the water up the side of the bank. And if I could have taken wing and soared into the sky, I could have seen the water bubble away from the wheels and into the tunnels and come frothing out the other side to run down the bank and join the waters that were moving towards the sea. But it was dark, and my eyes were tired and I could not see; and I could not push the fear out of my mind.

Pools of water lie at the base of the bank. They have turned the soft peat into bog, and the reeds and the rushes that should have been cut and cleared have spread from the bog to the drains that suck the water out of The Fens. When the wind dies and the wheels stand idle, the water rises and flows from the ditches and covers the paths, and the bog grows by a few more feet.

The firm tread of my feet gave way to the soft squelching of mud. Then there was a splashing sound, and I was wading through water that was up to my knees, and the reeds and the rushes were cutting my hands and scratching my face. I pushed them away from my face for thirty feet or more; and then my hands were on the bank and I was clambering up the side of it.

I stood on the rim, and the wind came gusting across the blackness where the water ran. It threw handfuls of rain in my face. It stung, like hail, and I turned and scurried along the rim till one of the windpumps reared up beside me. I slid down the bank and crawled under the windpump and leant against the piles. I was out of the rain, and out of the wind. I shut my eyes and let myself drift off to sleep.

Somewhere, in this time of drifting and dreaming, I heard the voice of my Father. It came up through the clay and the peat and the piles, and it spoke of the past, and I heard it say: 'They dug the drain about ten years before you were born. They were always short of men. No one from round here would work for them, so they used to bring them up from the south. I remember some of them were sailors, and they spoke Dutch, and they looked different when they arrived. But after a couple of days in the drain, the mud made them all look the same.' I heard myself asking why would sailors want to come and dig? And he said: 'They were prisoners. There was a battle and their ship sank, and they were captured. They were made to dig and a lot of them died.' And he laughed. 'We didn't want them and we didn't want their drain and we didn't shed any tears when we heard that another one had been sucked into the mud, or drowned, or found dead in his bed with the fever on his brow.' He laughed again, and I felt myself tremble, and he put his hand on my shoulder.

'Take away the water,' he said, 'and you take away the eels and the fish and the wildfowl. Then they take away the corn that grows where the eels used to swim. And they sell it, to pay for the drains. And there's nothing for you and nothing for me. And we will starve; and then it will be time for you and me to lie down in our bed and die.'

Then Mother came towards me saying: 'He used to go out into the night, him and the other men. They were young then, and their backs were straight, and there was fire in their bellies. And they'd take the punt, and be gone. In the morning he would put his finger up to his lips, and the questions would die in my mind. And in the afternoon we would hear that a windpump had burnt down, or a lock-gate had been smashed or a bank had been breached and the waters were back in The Fens where they belong.'

She said they called themselves the tigers, the tigers of The Fen. I asked what a tiger looked like and she said it looked like a ginger cat, bigger than a man. And I saw this cat that was a tiger; I saw it coming through the reeds. The reeds were golden brown, and smelt of summer, and the wind was making them tremble, and the tiger was no more than a shadow, a shadow moving in the shadows. It was stalking a bull, a bull with the face of my Father. I wanted to scream, to warn the bull; and I wanted the tiger to kill the bull, to kill my fear of what that bull could do to my Mother.

The tiger stopped. And crouched. And sprang. It filled the air with claws and a roar that set my heart pounding. I jumped to my feet, and started to run; and I hit my head.

I hit my head on a beam or the underside of the floorboards. It sat me down with a thump and a jolt. For a moment I was stunned and screaming in my mind, and my hands were shaking. Then I realised where I was, and I crawled out from under the windpump and rubbed my head.

The wind had blown the rain away and the air smelt clean and cold. The cold seeped into my arm. I tried to stretch it but my elbow had locked and it was stiff and sore and wouldn't move. I touched the upper muscle, the muscle that the blade had cut, and I felt as if I were stirring the embers of a fire and it was flaring into life. Then the pain was roaring through my shoulder and up my neck; and my feet were like a pair of bellows. With every step I took they blew more air onto the fire, and I felt hot and cold and hot again. And the sweat was pouring down my face.

I looked at the water. It was forty feet wide and running high, and the dawn was making it browner and browner with every passing minute. I knew that I couldn't swim it, not today I couldn't, and not tomorrow; and I couldn't walk to the end and back up the other side. I looked at a boat – it was tied to a stake and it belonged to the ferryman – and I put my hand in my pocket and I felt my two farthings.

'Are you waiting to cross?' The voice came from behind me. It was deep and full of sleep, and as I turned I looked into the yawning mouth of a man who was no taller than me. His legs were thin, like those of a heron; but his arms were like those of a bear, short and thick and covered in hair.

'Yes,' I said. 'Could you row me over to the other side?'

'You got any money?'

I shook my head.

He shrugged, and walked to the edge of the bank, and peed into the water. He turned and flicked the drops off the end of his cock, and he looked at me for a second or two, and then he pulled up the front of his breeches. 'I could use a boy like you,' he said.

I could understand his words, the meaning was plain. But his words were like the skin of an onion, peel them away and there was another skin and another meaning. I clenched my teeth and I backed away, and I saw in his face the face of Mister Salthouse.

He came towards me. 'I'm too old to do all the rowing. And my hands hurt in the morning.' He held them out. His fingers had curled and grown fat at the joints. 'It's all right up here in the daytime; there's always someone wanting to cross over. It's the nights. I don't like the nights, when I'm here on my own, and I can't sleep, and there's no one to talk to. Oswald and me, we used to talk and talk, till he went soft in the head and couldn't remember his own name. Then he died; and I've still got his things up there.' He pointed to a tiny black hut. It jutted out from the side of the windpump and ran down the bank for a few feet. Smoke was coming out of the chimney and it was drifting up through the sails. He smiled a toothless smile, and he put his hand on my shoulder. 'You could have his things. You're about his size, and they're too small for me. And you could sleep in my bed and . . .'

For a second I couldn't believe that it was happening again. Then a wild blinding rage exploded in my head and I brought my hand up, and knocked his arm away. It flew up in the air and he staggered backwards on his heron legs, and for a moment I thought he was going to fall over, but then he swayed and recovered his balance.

I could see the anger on his face. And I could feel a searing pain in my arm. I put my hand in my pocket and pulled out a farthing. 'I can pay,' I said, 'and I want to go to the other side. And I want to go now.'

The coin was like a magic talisman. At the sight of it he became the servant and I became the master, and the anger drained out of his face. He went up to his hut and came back with the oars; and after he'd taken me to the other side and had my farthing in his pocket, and was back in his boat in the middle of the drain, he yelled out: 'You would never have made a good ferryman! Liars are no good for nothing. And that's what you are. A liar.'

His words echoed in my head as I walked through the village of Chartres; and they were still echoing when I left the Black Fens of Mepall and climbed up the bank and stood on the edge of the Old Bedford River. This time I didn't think of saving my money. I gave my farthing to the ferryman and he rowed me to the other side. We walked through the washes and he asked me if I was all right. I said I was seeing double, and he thought I meant the two rivers – they run side by side – and he laughed, and I didn't try to explain. Then he rowed me over the New Bedford River – some call it the Hundred Foot Drain – and he insisted on helping me up the steps. He left me sitting in the sun on the top of the bank. In July, when I last sat in this spot, both the rivers were low and the corn was growing in the washes. The ears were heavy with seed and they bent and swayed and rippled in the breeze and Father had said he was coming back to cut them in a week or two. And now they were cut, and gone, and the rivers were running high. They had flooded the washes once or twice and the stubble was brown, like the spikes of a hedgehog; and it was starting to rot, starting to put a stench in the air.

I walked from Mepall to Wicham and on to Wichford, and in the early afternoon when the heat or the wind or the haze in my head had blurred them all into one, I came to the lower slopes of Ely Field. There was no stench here. The stubble had been burnt, and the ash had blackened the earth. The wind was lifting the ash and it was fluttering in the air, like black butterflies. I tried to catch some of them, to see if they still had the spots of fire burning on their wings.

I knocked on Aunt Mary's door, and there was no reply. I was confused. She takes in travellers and I expected her to be at home waiting for someone to come knocking. I sat down on the step and looked at the ash the butterflies had left on my hand. It was black like the disappointment that was rising in my mind. Then I shut my eyes, and the black became blacker, and my head became heavy. I rested it against the door. It felt soft, like a pillow, and the pain flowed out of my arm; and I went to sleep.

The pain came back to me in my sleep. I couldn't open my eyes but I knew it was there. Then I felt some hands and some arms and I was being lifted up, and a voice came into the blackness. 'Did he do this?'

I heard myself saying, 'Yes,' and she said: 'I thought so.'

Then I was sitting at a table, dipping bread into soup, and the blue lines that ran around the top of the bowl were moving up and down. I laid my head on the table, and shut my eyes, and I could still see those lines. They made me feel as if I were going to be sick at any moment, and I lay without moving, and without making a sound, and I thought I was going to die.

From behind me I could hear her voice, and the voice of another woman. Their words were coming and going like the dry rustle that comes and goes when the wind stirs the leaves of autumn. '. . . this one's got the same black hair . . . and the same green eyes . . . and he looks just like Patrick O'Sullivan . . . no . . . old man Fenton . . . he wanted a wife . . . and he wanted a son . . . and she had one . . .'

When I woke it was dark. I could feel the bedclothes, and I thought I was back in Elme in my own bed. I rolled over expecting to see the fireplace, but I saw instead a window. It was full of glass and each pane was a different size and a different shade of green. The moonlight was coming through the panes. It was filling the room with a glow, a soft moss-green glow, and I remembered: I was in Ely. After a while I sat up and the pain came back to my head and arm.

Then I heard her coming up the stairs.

'Ah,' she said, 'you're awake.'

'Have I been asleep all day?'

She smiled and nodded. 'And all of yesterday.'

'*All* of yesterday?'

'It's how you get better.'

I shook my head. 'I can remember coming up Ely Field. It feels like it was just a few minutes ago, and the stubble was burnt,' and something was fluttering in my mind. It was black, and I couldn't put a name to it. And I had a feeling, a strange feeling, that I had caught something, or heard something, something that had been hidden from me; and now it was hidden again, and I didn't know what it could be.

She put her candle on the table, and took off my coat and shirt and laid bare the cut on my arm. The cut ran from my shoulder to my elbow. It was red and swollen and it hadn't knitted together and it was weeping blood and pus. It smelt like rotten meat and it made my stomach heave. She washed it with hot water and the pain brought tears to my eyes. I wanted to cry out, and I put my finger in my mouth and I bit on it, and I prayed for the pain to go away.

She tied the cut together with eight pieces of string and they made the top of my arm look like a roll of pork. Then she took a piece of stale bread that was covered in green mould, and she crumbled it and laid the crumbs along the cut. Then she wrapped a cloth around my arm and tied it with some more string.

'Father would have heated up his knife and seared it,' I said, 'and then he would have rubbed in goose-grease, and that would have taken away the pain.'

She smiled with her eyes and said, 'Hmm,' and then she brought me a mug of her poppy tea. She called it an infusion. I didn't know what the word meant and I was too tired to ask. It was dark brown, and hot, and I held it between my hands and sipped it; and when it was gone it left a bitter taste in my mouth.

She blew out the candle.

I snuggled down into the bed and I lay there quiet and still. The golden colour of ripe corn filled my mind and I could see the white petals of the opium poppy. They were waving above the corn like little white flags. And I could see the women. They were bending over, and cutting the green seed heads and collecting the milk that flowed from the cuts; and they were picking the ripe seed heads and dropping them into baskets. And I was thinking how strange it was that a mixture of milk and seed and hot water could dull my pain, and make me float above the fields of corn.

Then I was in the fields, walking with the women and scything the poppies – not the tall opium poppies, but the small red poppies that blood the corn – and I found my Father and my Mother. They were lying on the ground, side by side, looking up at the sky. The years had slipped away from their faces, and they were young again. I closed their eyes and filled their arms with poppies and I closed my own eyes, and said a prayer for them; and when I opened my eyes they were gone. The earth where they had lain was raw and mounded, as it is on a new grave; and their red poppies were beginning to wilt, beginning to die.

Part Two

Ely

9

After three days the pain in my arm softened to a dull ache. The swelling went down and a pale pink replaced the angry red. Then the pink faded to a white, a washed white that lapped along the edge of the blood-brown scab. Sleep narrowed my eyes and filled them with prickles, and it made the scab look like a long fat caterpillar. I kept wondering when the caterpillar was going to crawl down my arm and go away and turn into a butterfly, a black butterfly that would be lost in the blackness that bound the days and the nights into one.

I can hear myself asking Aunt Mary about the caterpillar, and her voice is telling me to go back to sleep.

On the morning of the fourth day, or it might have been the fifth day, Aunt Mary pulled across the curtains and filled the room with sunshine. She helped me out of bed and I walked up and down. The room smelt stale. I opened the window, and when I turned round I saw she was watching me. I stretched out my arm and wiggled my fingers. The pain was gone and I felt myself smile. She caught my smile and it softened her face, and I thought how pretty she must have been when she was young. She saw that I was looking at her. She blushed, and her fingers fluttered from her face to her side. Her fingers were white with a touch of pink and they looked like apple blossom fluttering in the wind, and I felt the stirrings of spring within my loins. I looked away, and she said she'd be back in a moment.

She came back with a coat.

'Try this on,' she said. 'It belongs to your uncle. He used to wear it a lot, till he put on all that weight, and I couldn't let out the seams any more.'

'But won't he mind?'

She shook her head. 'These days he's never here long enough to mind about anything,' and then she did up the coat buttons and straightened the collar. Her fingers ran down my back. They pulled the coat into shape and smoothed away the ruffles.

'It will fit,' she said, 'if I put the seams back to where they used to be.' She tapped me on the shoulder. 'Now turn around and let me have a proper look.'

She looked at me for several seconds without saying anything. Then she walked right round me and inspected me with a quizzical eye. She reminded me of the farmer who has to look at his young bulls at the end of autumn and choose which will be slaughtered and salted, and which will spend the winter in the barn and be allowed to breed in the new year.

'Green suits you,' she said. 'It goes well with your black hair and your pale skin.'

I smiled and looked away and hoped she would say no more, but she touched my chin, and our eyes met, and she said: 'You're a good-looking young man.'

I was taken aback. No one had ever told me I was good-looking. I didn't know what to say. I shuffled my feet and then I giggled. It was a nervous giggle, and for some reason it made me tremble, and I felt my cock go hard.

'Give it me,' she said.

For one mad moment I thought she meant my cock, and it went harder. Then her fingers were on the buttons, undoing them from the top, and she said: 'I'll shorten the sleeves.' Then she was undoing the buttons over my cock. My face went hot, and I looked down. The front of my shirt was sticking straight out. She undid the rest of the buttons and slipped off the coat and let it drop to the floor. Then she bent and lifted the bottom of my shirt and I raised my arms, as if to surrender, and she pulled the shirt up and over my head, and left me standing in front of her stark naked. I tried to cover myself, but she took my hands and kissed them, and said: 'Don't be afraid. This will help you to get better.'

She pulled the curtains across, and in the gloom she took off her dress and hitched up her underskirts. She led me to the bed and I lay on my back. Her fingers ran up the inside of my leg and they felt me, and she murmured, more to herself than to me: 'You're going to be bigger than him. Much bigger. And your eyes are a nicer green.'

When I woke she was gone, and the curtains were pulled, and once again the room was full of sunshine. I put on my shirt and breeches and looked out the window. Some of the houses were thatched and some were tiled. The tiles were orange and red, and a dull brown with tinges of red, like eyes in need of sleep. Then I remembered: my uncle's eyes were brown with tinges of red, and my Father's eyes were green. I felt as if I had walked into a bog, and the slime was about my feet and the mud was like quicksand. It was sucking me into a past that I did not want to know about.

In a daze I opened the door and went to go downstairs. A voice came from below. 'Do you know where the boy is?'

It was the voice of my Father. I felt it box my ears and punch me on the nose; and I stood with my hand on the door, unable to go forward, and unable to go back.

'No,' she said. 'I've not seen him, not since he was last here with you, when the corn was cut.'

She came to the bottom of the stairs and looked up. She saw me, and she smiled. Her smile unlocked the muscles in my legs and I crept back into the room, and shut the door. And I knew that I was not to be slaughtered and salted by him. I was to be kept till another time.

The days settled down into a pattern. I rose late and she made my breakfast. Then I walked around Ely, soaking up the sun and trying, as my uncle put it to get my strength back. In the afternoon I took her arm and we walked to the cathedral to hear Evensong; and in the evening, if he returned to the house, she served a plate of cold meat with bread and boiled cabbage. I went to bed when it was time to light the candles; and later, when he was gone, she would come to me in the night, and she would run her hands over my naked body. I would feel myself stirring and she would nibble at my ear and whisper: 'Shall we see if your strength has come back?'

Towards the end of the month my strength had come back, and Simon was asking when I was going back to Elme. He was her only child, and he was three years older than me. And like the boy in the rhyme who meets a pieman going to the fair, he was a simple soul. When I was little he used to follow me round and do what I told him to do. But now he had grown tall, and his arms and his legs and his chest had swelled, and the hairs on his face had started to curl and go black, and he walked with a strange slouch. He said that I was a boy and he was a man. I asked him if he'd ever had a fuck. His cheeks blushed red, cherry red, and he bit his lips and shook his head; and I told him he was still a boy. He wanted to know what it was like. I smiled, and I told him he should ask his mother.

His jaw sagged, and he said: 'I can't ask her things like that.' Then he thumped me on the arm, and mumbled something about me needing to have a little more respect for his mother.

10

Aunt Mary and I walked along Saint Mary's Street, and past the house of Oliver Cromwell, and headed towards the cathedral. I told her it was time for me to go, and she told me about the days when he was the Lord Protector. I told her we were not supposed to talk about him and the things that were done in his name. She said he meant well, and to begin with he did look after The Fens and the rights of those who grazed their cattle on them in the summertime.

Then tears came into her eyes. I don't know if the tears were for him, or for me, and I tried to pretend they were not there.

I asked about my Father, and had he said anything about Mother? She shook her head, and I remembered the fear that was on Mother's face on the day we said goodbye.

I thought of my own fear, the fear that his voice had caused to well up in me again, and the tears came into my eyes. I blew my nose and looked away.

I told Aunt Mary about Mister Salthouse, and the things he'd done to me, and the things I'd done to him.

She put her arm around my shoulder and held me close, and as we walked across the cathedral green she said: 'You must be careful of men like him. We see them standing in the pulpit week after week, and we grow used to them telling us what is right and what is wrong. And we assume that they will always tell the truth. But we forget that they can sin like other men; and when they do they have more to lose, and they hide behind a thicket of lies.'

I thought about what she said, and then I told her about my idea.

She stopped walking. Our faces came together. 'If you asked him to help your mother, and he said no, and you said anything against him, they would not believe you. They would believe him. And he could have you put in the stocks; and if you persisted with what he would call your lies, he could have you hanged. And don't think he will help you in private. He won't. I know such men. They forget the promises they make. And if they do remember them they don't honour them, because someone could ask questions which might uncover their sin.'

She relaxed her grip and we began to walk again. 'So it's best you forget all about him and the things he did to you.'

We stepped into the cathedral. It was dark and damp, like a winter's afternoon; and the smell of mud and rotting leaves rose from the flagstones. The mud had come in on the wheels of the haycarts – they were dragged in through the ruins of the left wing – and it made the stones feel slippery.

The cold frosted my breath and the draught brought a chill to my ears and my hands. I turned up the collar of my coat, and did up the buttons, and slipped my hands into my pockets.

The draught was coming from the aisle to the right where the dark was made darker by the boards and the canvas screens that covered the windows. Some of the boards had fallen away from the top of one of the windows, and the lead that used to hold the tiny pieces of coloured glass had sagged, like a cobweb battered by the wind and the rain, and it was starting to break away from the frame.

'We don't have the money to repair them,' she said. 'And the roof leaks, and that wall over there is starting to tilt. Can you see it?'

I shook my head.

'It's easier to see in the morning when the cathedral is full of light.'

Then she told me that Cromwell was to blame. He had shut the cathedral, and apart from the Lady Chapel, which had become the Church of the Holy Trinity, it stood silent and empty for more than ten years, and that was when the rot had set in.

I said we didn't need a cathedral as big as this. And she said it had a spirit and she could feel it. I told her that all I could feel was the cold, and she sighed, and said that I sounded like my Father.

She covered her head with her shawl and the shadows chipped away her eyes and her nose and her mouth. And like the statues in Holy Trinity that have had their eyes and noses and mouths chipped away, her face became a bowl of stone. It was emptied of all the love and the tenderness that she used to have for me, and I saw in her a hardness I had never seen before.

I began to feel uncertain, almost apprehensive, and I found that I was walking behind her. The distance between us was growing bigger and bigger with every step she took. And when she went through the stone screen and into the great octagon, and left me alone in the nave, I knew what a thousand words could never make any clearer: the closeness that we had shared in the night had come to an end.

She was standing by the stalls. I came and stood behind her – it seemed to be my proper place; and we waited, with eight or nine others, for the boys from the school. They came gliding out of the shadows and they filed into the stalls.

My eyes ran along the faces of the boys and they came to the clergy. Among them, close to the Table of the Lord, was the face of Mister Salthouse. His head was bowed and his lips were moving, and he was clasping a prayer book to his chest.

I tapped her on the arm and whispered: 'That's him.'

She stared at him for a long time, and then she half turned and said: 'You remember what I said.'

The cantor led the boys into the first of the psalms of Evensong. His voice was like him, old and thin; and I remembered him coming to Elme. He was looking for boys to join the choir school. He told me to call him Mister Hamilton, and I had to sing for him. He said I had perfect pitch, and I was like a young horse. I needed a set of reins and I needed breaking in. This amused him, and he laughed a lot, and so did Mister Salthouse.

They sent for Father. They told him I had the voice and the learning, and he said to them: 'He don't need no learning for what he has to do. And if he wants to sing he can sing to the birds. And maybe he'll be better at catching them than he is at catching eels.'

That night Mother said to me: 'I told you so;' and like so many of the things that happened between him and her and me, we never spoke of it again.

I turned away from these memories, and the sound of the singing filled my mind. It was high and pure, and in my head I sang with the boys. My voice had not aged or cracked. It was as pure as theirs, and I opened my mouth and began to sing.

Aunt Mary twisted round and hissed at me, and pointed to the floor beside her. I closed my mouth and shuffled forward.

At the start of the third psalm Mister Salthouse shut his eyes and so did Aunt Mary. I looked from one to the other. The hard lines in their faces were softening and they appeared to be going to sleep. I knew in my heart I could not soften, and I could not go to sleep. Aunt Mary was wrong. Mother needed help, and that help had to come from Mister Salthouse. There was no one else.

Mister Salthouse said the prayers. His voice had lost its usual strength. It was soft and full of mumbles and his words drifted through the arches. I hoped that God could hear what he was saying because I could not and I don't think Aunt Mary could: she was looking up and her eyes were wandering from pillar to pillar. She still looked half-asleep, and as she lowered her head she whispered: 'When you came to me you said I was to tell you what to do. You said that was what your Mother wanted. I have given it a lot of thought, and I have kept it in my prayers; and there is only one thing that you can do.'

I felt the temperature drop. It turned the cathedral into an ice cave, and it chilled my bones and froze my mind. I turned and looked at her. 'You must go back to your father. You must make your peace with him, and as the years go by – and you grow bigger and stronger, and old age creeps up on him – you will be able to look after her, and she will be safe.'

'No,' I said, 'I can't go back to him. Not after what he did to me.'

'Yes you can. If you tell him you're sorry. And make it sound as if it was all your fault.'

'My fault?'

'Yes. Your fault. You should have kept your hands to yourself. And you're sorry you didn't. And from now on you'll sleep on the floor, in front of the fire, with that dog of yours.' She paused and sucked at her lips. 'And there's something else.'

'Something else?'

'You must tell him you're going to earn the money to buy a new scythe. It will be a gift from you to him. And you must tell yourself that when he's dead the scythe will be yours. It's not much of a thought, I know that, but it might—'

I clenched my teeth and shook my head, and I stormed away from her. I would not do it! I would not do it! The words went screaming round my head like angry bees. They stung me into madness. I jumped up and down and my arms flew out. I punched the air, and I yelled: 'I won't do it!'

My words echoed in the stones, high above me; and they were chased by laughter, a soft muffled laughter that added to my madness.

I spun around. The boys from the school were walking towards me in a line, two abreast, with the small ones at the front and the tall ones at the rear. Their faces formed a wave, a wave that was grinning and smirking; and on the crest, bubbling along like froth, came the faces of the clergy. And behind them, bobbing up and down in the undertow, came the face of the Beadle.

Mister Salthouse caught my eye, and he held my gaze. I could see that he was interested in me and I smiled and fingered my lips, and tried to make him understand that I wanted to talk to him.

After a second or so, his jaw sagged and a look of horror swept over his face, and he stumbled. The Beadle banged into him and dropped his staff and tripped. And they both fell to the floor.

I rushed over and helped Mister Salthouse to his feet, and I said: 'I have to talk to you.'

'Get away from me!' he yelled. 'Get away,' and he tried to push me away.

I grabbed at his robe, and I pulled his ear to my mouth. 'He beats my Mother, that's what he does. And I can't stop him.'

Then their hands were pushing me away, and the Beadle was raising his staff in the air, and I was yelling: 'I want you to help her! That's all I want you to do!'

The staff hit me across the back and the arm, the arm that was healing; and the pain sent me reeling away.

I leant against one of the pillars. I felt my legs sag and I slid towards the floor.

When I looked up, the Beadle and Mister Hamilton were

holding onto Mister Salthouse. He was swaying from side to side. I heard him say: 'That's the one I was telling you about.'

The Beadle turned towards me. He stood with his legs apart and his head to the side, the way some dogs do when they are about to attack; then he was running at me. He had the staff in both hands and I could see the knob. It was wooden, and carved, and spiked with silver; and it was going to hit my head.

I jumped to my feet and I ran at him. He roared with rage. The knob screamed past my ear. I felt the swish of the air and I laughed.

Aunt Mary yelled: 'Have you gone mad?'

I shook my head, and yelled: 'No!'

I ran through the stone screen and into the nave, and on towards the main doors. I could hear the Beadle coming after me. His clogs were clattering on the stones, and he was puffing and panting, and calling to me to stop.

I laughed some more, and the madness drove me on. I pushed on the door to the left. It wouldn't move. It was locked, and I couldn't see how to open it. I tried the other door, and it was locked. I thumped it with the flat of my hand, and I spun around. He was coming at me, and this time he was holding the staff like a spear, and he was aiming it straight at my heart.

My eyes locked onto the end. It was silver and pointed, and it killed all thought of fleeing.

I dropped to the ground. The staff flew over my head. It hit the door with a thump, and it filled the air with a twanging humming sound. The Beadle swore. He ran past me, grabbed at the staff, and tried to pull it out of the wood. It wouldn't budge, and he swore again.

I slipped away to the side, to the wing where the haycarts are stored, and my fingers guided me along the wall, and into a corner, and they found a door. I lifted the latch and gave the door a push. It opened with a rush and the iron hinges banged against the stone wall. The sound was explosive, like the firing of a musket. It made my heart race, and it sent me shooting up the steps.

They took me round and round, and along an open gallery and then up, and round and round some more. They sent my head into a spin, and they slowed my feet, and they made me stop and gasp for breath. I trudged up and up, and I came to another door. I leant on it, and listened for the Beadle.

I could hear the wind. It was whistling through the slats that covered the open windows. And I could hear the birds. They were coming to roost in the tower, flapping and twittering, and pecking at the slats.

I could not hear his voice. And I could not hear him huffing or puffing. I put my ear to the stones, thinking they might be alive with the clatter of his clogs, but they were dead; and all I could hear was the thump of my heart.

After a while a sense of calm began to return to me. I lifted the bar from the door, and climbed the ladder, and walked around the thin spire that rises from the top of the tower.

Below me the town stretched away from the cathedral. It looked like the back leg of a dog. The houses that formed the toes led my eyes down to the water, and along the River Ouse and into The Fens. The mist was rising. It was joining the water to the reeds, and the reeds to the trees, and the trees to the sky; and it was taking on the colours of the sky: pinks and purples in the west; blues and blacks in the east.

The top of the spire of Saint Mary's church was catching the last of the sun. It was glowing, like pink and grey marble, and it was pointing the way to heaven. It was a signpost in the sky, and it made me wish that there was some sort of signpost that I could follow.

I watched Aunt Mary walk home. Her shawl was still over her head and it made her look like a little black doll. She had been a signpost to me for as long as I could remember; and I started to think of all the times she had set my feet on the right path, and it hurt to know that this time she was wrong.

'I'm sorry,' I said to her, 'but I'm not going back to Elme.'

The wind picked up my words and it carried them away. I tried to tell myself it carried them to her, but she kept on walking, and she didn't look back.

11

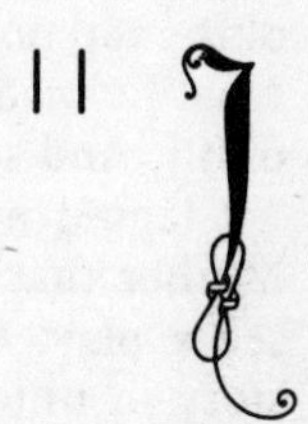

I sat at the top of the cathedral tower, looking towards the glass lantern that covered the octagon, and I listened to the birds. They were singing in harmony, like a well-trained choir. But as more and more of them arrived, and the ledges filled up, a strident note came into their singing, and it began to sound as if they were bickering. I remembered Mister Hamilton telling us, on the day he came to Elme, that choirboys should not fight amongst themselves because it would come out in their singing. At the time I thought him a silly old fool, but here was living proof, and for some reason it offended me.

I jumped to my feet and clapped my hands and shouted. The birds took fright. They flew into the night sky; they circled around the tower and the spire, and they filled my ears with squawks and screeches.

As they began to return to their places on the ledges, their anger cooled, and they began to bicker again. This time the bickering was louder, more intense, and more annoying; and I was about to jump up and send them flying around again when I found myself wondering why Mister Salthouse had been talking to Mister Hamilton about me. Was he still annoyed with me, and was this his way of showing it? Or had he been preparing their minds, filling them with lies that would take on the colour of truth if I ever said anything against him?

I looked up to the heavens, from where they say all our help is supposed to come, and I said: 'Mister Salthouse used to say that we should tell You all our problems.' I paused and sucked at my lips, and then I said, in a voice that was much quieter than before: 'I remember when choir practice was finished, and we were getting ready to go home, and his fingers were starting to fidget, he would ask one of us to stay behind. To try some more of the top notes was the way he used to put it. But we all knew what he meant, knew what he wanted to do with those fingers of his. And so did You. And You never helped us. Did You?'

I lapsed into silence, and I remembered the night I'd told Mother that I thought God was like a man who had paid to see a play: He was sitting and watching and waiting for the story to unfold. And if He didn't like what He saw He would punish the actors. She told me I must never say such things, and I must never think such things, and if such things came into my mind I must think about other things. So I thought about the Beadle and my need to escape, and I watched the moon rise and grow fatter, and I said: 'Could You please help me to get out of here?'

He didn't reply.

I suppose I should be used to His silences by now but in truth I'm not, and sometimes they upset me, and without thinking, I yelled: 'Father was right. God helps those who help themselves, and that's the truth of it.'

The words rang in my ears and they filled me with a sense of shock. Never had I admitted that my Father might be right about anything. It was one of the cornerstones of my life: he was never right and I was never wrong. And here I was shouting out the opposite.

Some of the birds took to the air. They had heard my confession and it had scared them, and it set them chattering. And I knew that by tomorrow afternoon they would have spread it, like common gossip, from one end of The Fens to the other.

Cold and confused and bereft of any sign of help, I left the top of the tower and shut the door behind me.

I felt my way down the steps. There was no handrail, and in the darkness my mind played tricks on me, and I kept thinking I was about to lose my balance. It was a long way from my head to my feet, and I could feel my confidence seeping away. I lifted up the back of my coat and sat down, and I eased myself from one step to another. The steps were like some of the psalms, they went on and on and on, and I began to think I would never get to the end. Then I crawled along the gallery, and I became aware that I was seeing the outline of the steps. They were spread in front of me, like the ribs of a fan. I stood up and crept down.

I put my head round the corner of the door and I froze. The Beadle was sitting at a table, about ten feet from the door. His staff was lying on the table, and he had both hands on it. His hat was lying beside the candle. The flame was level with his eyes, and it was enclosed in a glass bowl. It would last through the night, and the draughts would not be able to blow it out.

I retreated back up the steps and walked along the end gallery till I came to a door. It was locked. I turned around and walked back and sat down at the top of the steps. I felt a sickness rising in my gut. I would never be able to sneak past him, and in the morning he would have me. I sat with my head in my hands, looking at my feet, and wriggling my toes and wishing they would warm up. I started to wonder why he hadn't seen me. Could he be asleep? The thought was like one of the great alleluias of Easter. It rang through my mind; it filled me with joy; and it restored my faith. I crept back down the steps and stuck my head out. Nothing had changed. I put out my hand and wiggled it around. He didn't move. Then I saw that his eyes were shut. I sat down again and took off my shoes, and I eased myself out of the door.

A low growl came rolling across the stone floor. It sent a shudder through me, and it sent me back to the door and up the steps.

A dog came padding out of the shadows. He sniffed at the haycarts and lay down beside the table with his nose pointing towards the door. He was the size of a sheep. His coat was shaggy and in need of cutting. The spikes on his collar made me gulp and swallow, and they made my hands tremble.

I waited for him to go to sleep. But he was restless, and he kept getting up and padding around the table.

An hour passed, or maybe two, and I was beginning to despair, as they say men do in the hours before their execution, when I thought I saw something. I rubbed my eyes and peered into the darkness but whatever it was, if it was anything, it was gone.

I waited some more. And I wished I was home in bed.

Then I saw it again. A sort of twitching in the shadows. I eased myself back down to the edge of the door, and the twitching became a hand. The dog sat up and turned towards the hand. The hand rolled something towards the dog. He sniffed it, and ate it. And he padded over to the hand. The hand was putting food on the floor.

I didn't know if this was the work of God, or the work of man, but I took my chance and I eased myself out of the door and along the wall. The hand saw me. It pointed to my right and I slid further along the wall, past an old chapel and a couple of haycarts and round a pillar and into the nave.

Simon came out of the darkness. He put his fingers to his lips. He grinned at me, took my hand and whispered in my ear: 'She said to come and get you.'

We crept up the nave and into the octagon and through the dark places beyond it till we came to a door. He gave it a push and we walked out into the night, and I heaved a sigh a relief.

'How did you know where to find me?'

He gave a soft chuckle. 'It was easy. I saw the birds fly out of the tower.'

Half an hour later I lay in my blankets in front of the fire in the downstairs room. Aunt Mary had moved me out of the upstairs room. She said a traveller was coming and she had cleaned the room, and she didn't want to clean it a second time. She looked away when she said these words, and I knew she was easing herself out of my bed, and I knew she didn't want to talk about it. I thanked her for sending Simon, and she said I could sleep with him in front of fire. Then she said the strangest of things: 'He's not simple. People say he is, but he's not.'

I bit my tongue, and in my head I sighed, and I pitied her as I would pity any mother who cannot face the truth about the child she bore, and I said: 'He knew where to find me.'

'And so he should. He played in the cathedral for five years when he was little. He knows all the secret places. And he knows how to get in and out without a key, and he's too quick for the Beadle.'

Then she laughed. 'Oh dear,' she said, 'I shouldn't laugh, but I did enjoy seeing that pompous man fall flat on his arse.'

I felt my jaw drop, not at her laughter, but at her use of the word 'arse'.

'Don't be a prude,' she said, and she put her hands on my

shoulders. I could feel her trembling; and she said in a soft voice: 'I didn't know you felt so strongly about your mother, and what your father has done to her. It would be nice to help her. I'm the first to acknowledge that. And it would be nice to think that Mister Salthouse was the man to do it. But the truth is your father despises men like him, and he would never do what he said, and to suggest it would lead to a lot of trouble. You must remember that when they were married she gave him her body, and she promised to obey him; and in the eyes of the law it's right for a man to punish his wife if she won't obey.'

I shook my head and shrugged off her hands, and I looked away.

'It's hard, I know,' she said, 'and I've been thinking about Elme and what I said, and maybe we should talk about London.' She put her hands back on my shoulders. 'I'm too tired to talk now, but tomorrow, when Simon's gone to work, we could talk then.'

I couldn't wait for tomorrow. It was a hundred years away. So I talked to Simon. I talked and talked and talked. The words bubbled out of me and I forgot that he was a simpleton. I told him about Mister Salthouse and the night at Wisbech. I heard him suck in his breath, and he sat up and looked at the fire. And I told him his mother was wrong: Mister Salthouse had to help my Mother, there was no one else. Then my words failed, and I sat up, and we both stared into the flames.

I didn't know what to do.

Then Simon began to speak. He took my breath away and he sent my head into a whirl. His plan was bold and mad and full of cunning, and I could not believe that such a scheme had come from him.

'You're not simple at all,' I said. 'You're just as smart as all the rest of us.' The words were still fresh in my mouth when I began to think that he might be smarter than me, smarter than all the rest of us. It was like a kick in the belly. It hurt. It hurt like hell, and I said: 'So why do they call you Simple Simon?'

He picked up a pine cone and tossed it into the fire. We watched it flare, watched the red petals bloom and fall away, then he said: 'I was simple when I was small and I couldn't hear.'

'Couldn't hear? You've got ears just like me, so why couldn't you hear?'

'They were blocked up. She said they were full of grease, and it had set and gone hard like beeswax. She poured some oil into them, warm oil, and it melted the wax and I could hear.'

I stared at him. I couldn't accept what I was hearing; what I had seen with my own eyes for so many years. 'So why,' I asked with some hesitation, 'have you pretended to be simple?'

'People expect me to be simple. So I am. And they tell me all sorts of things,' and he burst out laughing. I realised he was laughing at me, who had told him all sorts of things.

When my embarrassment faded away, we talked some more, and then some more; and somewhere in that night my idiot cousin became my friend. And we agreed that Simon's plan was the right plan and Mister Salthouse was the man to help my Mother.

12

It was dark. I heard Simon sit up and yawn. The blanket was still over his head. His hands felt for his clothes and they pulled them under the blanket.

I rolled over and blew at the ashes in the hearth, and a flurry of sparks filled the air.

His hands and his elbows and his knees were flying at the blanket. They were struggling to get free, and they made the blanket look like a net that had fallen over a flock of birds.

I yawned and asked him how he knew when it was time to get up.

'I always wake up at the same time,' he said, and he stood up and slipped his feet into his shoes.

When he pulled the bolts and opened the door, the wind blew at the ashes, and raised another flurry of sparks.

'I've done it every day for six years,' he said. 'So I suppose it's a habit or maybe I've got an hourglass in here,' and he tapped his head, 'and a little man, and he keeps turning it round and round, and when it's time to wake up he shouts in my ear.' He laughed; and I said I'd see him in the afternoon. He shut the door and the sparks died, and the room was dark again.

The cold was coming up from the stones beneath me. It was making me shiver, and I couldn't get back to sleep. I rolled onto his blanket and pulled it around my legs and I began to think about his work in the kitchens at the choir school. His words of the night came back to me: 'I have to let myself in at five in the morning,' he said, 'and I have to stoke the fire, and draw the water and put it on to heat. Then I have to knead the dough, and measure out the barley, and chop the vegetables, and pluck the doves, and take the bones out of the red meat. And then it's time to eat.'

'Do you eat with the boys?'

He laughed. 'No. They eat in the refectory with the Master and old Mister Hamilton. I eat in the kitchen with the cook and the porter and the doorman from the gatehouse.' Then he said they were always complaining, complaining that four of them were not enough to look after all of the school, and there should be five or six of them.

'And should there be five or six?' I asked.

He shook his head: 'They don't work in the afternoon. They pretend they do but they don't. They leave me to do the sweeping and to scour the pots and pans with sand, and they go up to the loft or down to the barn and they play cards; and sometimes they take some wine and sometimes they take a sleep. If the Master comes looking for one of them, I have to say: "I know where he is and I'll fetch him for you." And I have to be out of the kitchen and across the yard before he can say another word.'

I laughed. 'So that's what friends are for.'

'They're not my friends,' he said. 'The boys are my friends.'

He told me that the young ones, the ones who were seven or eight and were still missing their mothers, they knew he wasn't simple. To them he was a friend and a brother, and they could trust him. But by the time they were ten or eleven they were seeing him through the eyes of the Master and he had become a servant who was a simpleton. Then they made fun of him and their words were layered with scorn, and they began to pity those who still called him their friend.

'It used to hurt,' he said with a shrug. 'And it still does if I'm being honest, so I play a game. When a new boy arrives I tell myself he's going to be different, and he is, for a year or two. Then he becomes like all the rest. And when his voice breaks and it's time for him to go, I tell myself that I was his friend when he needed a friend. And I know that his pride will not let him come and say goodbye to me, so I say it for him.'

Inside I felt cold and full of gloom. To me Simon was like a mud-crab. He had found a shell, and he had crawled into it, and now he was carrying it around. He was thinking it would protect him but he was wrong. His shell had none of the strength of a periwinkle. His shell was a shell of wax, a shell that deafness had made; and every time somebody stamped on him, it crumpled and broke, and he was hurt some more.

I stood up and shrugged off my blanket. And I wondered if it would be possible to prise him out of his shell and out of that school, and talk him into making a new beginning. And I wondered if we would be able to rely on the young boys who were his friends. Without them, without their help, we could not help my Mother.

13

In the afternoon I waited for Simon in the Market Place. When I arrived the sun was shining and the wind felt warm. When he arrived, an hour or so later, the clouds had covered the sky and the wind had picked up a chill; and I was feeling tired and bored. 'I was going to come over to the school and knock on the door and ask for you,' I said.

'That would have been stupid,' he said. 'They would have sent someone to find me, and they would have asked what I was doing up in the room where the boys sleep.'

'It was just a thought.'

'I'm not allowed up there and God knows what I would have said.' He threw his hands up in the air, and shook his head at me. 'Did I tell you they found the old porter up there? One afternoon, last year, towards the end of winter when it was dark, and the boys were going to bed early; and they made him leave next day.' He shook his head again, and turned away from me, and he sank into a glum silence.

He made me feel sorry for something I hadn't done. I was going to say so, but I could see that it would provoke another outburst, so I bit my tongue and shoved my hands in my pockets and waited. I thought of all the times I'd been caught in a storm and had to run and shelter under a tree. And I thought of the question that had been jumping in and out of my mind all day. I was tempted to ask it, but I bided my time, and when at last he turned around, the clouds were clearing from his face and there was a hint of sunshine in his eyes.

In my mind I stepped out from under the tree, and I asked: 'How did you get on with the boys?'

'It was more difficult than I thought,' he said. 'The best I could do was five.' I could hear the thunder rumbling in his words. It was closer than it should have been. I kept my mouth shut and waited for the thunder to die away. 'And they're very young,' he said, 'but then we knew they would be, didn't we?' I nodded. 'You'll know Patterson and Elliot. They're from Elme.' I nodded again. 'And you might know Clarkby, he's from March.' I knew of the family. There was a boy my age, and an older girl, but I didn't know of a younger brother. I shook my head. 'And there's the Russell twins. They're from Wisbech, and I think Mister Salthouse might know them.'

'He might,' I said. 'He goes over there often enough. But it will be dark, and if they say they're from Elme, and they give another name, they should be all right.'

'I haven't told them about that yet.'

'But I thought we agreed?'

'I know. But it didn't feel right, and they might have said no, so I decided to tell them tonight.'

'Tonight?' I felt a sudden sense of panic. 'We said we were going to do it tomorrow night.'

'It has to be tonight. Mister Salthouse has Matins in the morning and then he's going back to Elme. It was in the notices. They ring a bell, and we all have to go in and listen to them every morning, just before the second grace, so don't go thinking I've got it wrong.'

The thunder was back in his words. I looked away and thought about his plan. In the night we had agreed to ask seven boys to help; and we'd said if two of them changed their minds and wouldn't come with us, we would still have five, and that would be enough. But now we were starting with five and if we ended up with three, the balance would swing in his favour. And once the surprise had worn off he might think he could deal with them, and us, and we wouldn't be a threat to him. And our plan would fail.

'Is something wrong?' Simon asked.

'No,' I said. 'We can manage with five, but you'll have to make sure they all come. And if one won't come, you'll have to find another one right away or we'll have to forget all about it.'

'They say they'll come and I'm sure they will. But you know

what boys are like. They change their minds, or they think they're sick and they won't get out of bed. And I'm not going to argue with them, not in the middle of the night with old Mister Hamilton trying to sleep in the room next door. He leaves his door open. Did I tell you that?'

I shook my head.

'The boys say he gets up in the night and he walks about, and they can hear him pissing in his pot.' Then his voice went quiet, almost apologetic. 'And by the way, I had to tell Patterson he could have a lantern. He's scared of the dark and he won't come without one. I know you said we wouldn't need one. And I know there's less chance of us being seen if we go without one. And I told him this, and I told him I walk to school every morning and it's dark most of the time, and I know my way and I'd make sure he was safe. But he didn't want to be convinced, and I knew we needed him, so I said I'd get him one.'

It was the same careful sort of reasoning that my Father used, when he was in a mood to explain things to me. And long ago, with the help of his hands, I had come to understand that some things are meant to be, and this was one of them. 'Is there a lantern in the kitchen?'

'There is,' he said, 'but we can't take it. The cook's put in a new candle. It's marked with rings and he'd know if we used it. He'd say the boys had been in the kitchen, stealing food, and the truth would come out, like it did last time. So we'll have to find another one.'

I thought for a moment. 'What about the one your Mother uses?'

He shook his head. 'She likes to have it in her room at night. And anyway, some of the glass is missing and the wind would blow it out.'

I looked up at the sky. The clouds were thickening and becoming dark and heavy with rain. I thought of the boys creeping down the alleyway behind the cathedral and going through the gates and across the garden and into the privy cloister. I thought of them getting wet. The rain would muffle the sound of their feet and in the night they would be safe from prying eyes. But in the morning their clothes would be wet and they would betray them; and they, in their turn, would betray us.

I felt uneasy. We hadn't thought that it might rain. In our minds the night was fine and clear and lit by moonlight. We had talked about flitting from shadow to shadow like moths, and we saw ourselves standing on the path below Mister Salthouse's window. Simon had said it would be open and in my mind it was. But in my heart I was not so sure. I remembered the care my Mother took to shut her window every night and I could not imagine how a man like Mister Salthouse could sleep by an open window. It was the act of a fool, a mad man, and I began to think that the rain would bring him to his senses, and I could see him shutting the window – and that would kill our plan.

Then I remembered that Simon had also said that the gravel on the path was old and bound with dirt and it wouldn't squeak when we trod on it. But tonight that path might be wet with water, and if the window were open, our feet might carry the dirt up the wall and over the window ledge and into his room. And when we were gone the dirt would be like streaks of cow dung, it would mark the passage of a herd of small boys, and it would be there for all to see.

I sighed to myself and I shut my eyes for a moment. Then I looked at Simon. He was staring at me.

The lantern came back into my mind. 'We're going to have to borrow one,' I said. 'If you could think of someone who knows your Mother, I could go and ask. I could say it's for her. But I fear they'll look at me and see a stranger, and they'll think of their lantern, and what it cost, and they'll say no.'

He frowned and nodded.

'So I think we ought to go together and I can do the asking, or you can, if that's what you prefer. Or you can go on your own. I don't mind.'

'What I prefer won't make the slightest bit of difference,' he said. 'They won't lend me a lantern.'

There was no need to ask why. The reason was plain, and I hadn't given it a thought. In their minds he was a simpleton – and simpletons, as my Mother was fond of saying, can be humoured but they cannot be trusted.

Simon was not to be humoured. I could see that. I kept my words flat and serious. 'We can go together,' I said, 'and you can tell them my name and I can do the asking. You could say that

I'm staying at your house. And they'll know that I'm a friend, and not a stranger, and I think they'll trust me.'

'You can think what you like,' he said, 'but they won't lend you a lantern, not as long as you're standing next to me they won't.'

'But they know Aunt Mary, and they trust her. So why won't they trust you?'

He met my eyes, then he looked away. 'I started a fire once, when I was about eleven. I didn't mean to. I was in a barn with the straw pulled around me, trying to keep warm, and the candle was in the lantern and it was about to go out, and I went to—'

I held up my hands.

He bit his lips and mumbled: 'I'm sorry, there's nothing I can do about it.'

'Nothing? Oh yes there is,' I said in a loud voice. 'You can go back to Patterson, and you can tell him you can't get a lantern. Then you can see a couple of the older boys and you can get them to come. That's what you can do.'

He shook his head and swore at me, and he said it was me that was the stupid one, and not him; and couldn't I remember anything?

We glared at each other for a moment or two. I could feel the anger burning in me. It was hot and destructive, like the straw that had burnt in that barn of his, and it set fire to my words, and as I opened my mouth to say: 'Of course I can bloody remember what you said,' he began to tell me again about the younger boys and the older boys and the way his friendship changed as they changed.

His words poured over me like buckets of water, and they put out the fire. I was left feeling foolish and sorry for myself. And I thought of how he must have felt when he looked at the barn that burnt, and I felt sorry for him. I flung my arms around him and I gave him a hug.

He blushed and pushed me away. It was a gentle push. There was no anger in it, and I could feel the imprint of his body on mine. It was like a warm glow and I thought how well we fitted together. The thought embarrassed me and it brought confusion to my mind, and I heard myself say we should think again about the lantern, and he said that was a good idea.

We talked some more about the boys and what we expected them to do. Then he wanted to talk about himself and I mentioned the word shell, and the word wax, and then the two were linked together. And a silence, a heavy thoughtful silence, settled upon us.

A minute passed, and then another, and then he said he had tried to crawl out of this thing I called his shell, but he had failed. He had failed because they knew he was stupid, and they expected him to be stupid, and when he did something that was sane and sensible, they said it was amazing what some idiots could do. Then the men would laugh and pat him on the head, and the boys would giggle and pull faces and roll their eyes.

I could feel the sadness that was within him. It swirled from him to me like a thick fog, and I remembered my thoughts from the morning, and I said in a quiet voice: 'I think I know what you should do.'

He came closer. Our noses were about two inches apart.

'And what would that be?'

I looked him in the eye, and I took a deep breath. 'You should make a new beginning. You should forget about all this,' and I waved my hand towards the school, 'and you should leave Ely and go to another town where they don't know you. And you should stop playing the fool.' The colour drained out of his face. It became white and wrinkled like that of a man who has drowned; and I could see the face of my brother in him. I swallowed hard, and backed away and said: 'I'm sorry. I didn't mean to shock you.'

He mumbled something. I caught the word 'not', and I said: 'Sometimes there are things that have to be said.'

'And you think you're the one to say them?'

'I'm your cousin.'

'You're more than that.'

'All right. I'm your friend, and friends should be able to say what they think, and still be friends.'

'You don't know, do you?'

I looked at him and I knew that if I said 'No', he would lead me down another path, and we would not talk about the things

I wanted to talk about. I shook my head, and I said: 'Could we talk about it later on?'

He shrugged and looked away.

I wet my lips and took a deep breath. 'You have to change. You have to stand up straight,' and I pulled my shoulders back as if to add emphasis to my words. 'And you have to walk like I walk,' and I walked a few feet to show him that I wasn't ambling along and I wasn't bouncing up and down and I wasn't dragging my arms like a great ape. 'And when you talk, keep your tongue in your mouth and stop grunting. You're not a pig, you're a man, and a man says yes and no. He doesn't grunt.'

He was nodding, not to me but to himself.

I felt encouraged, and I said, 'And one last thing. If you behave yourself and don't do anything stupid, the people in your new town will accept you for what you are, and they will treat you like any other man.'

He shook his head. 'Not with a name like Simon they won't. And I don't know if I can stop. It's so easy for me. I can do all those things without thinking. And I'd only have to forget once. That's all it would take, once, and someone would call me Simple Simon, and that would be the end of it.'

You're trying to fob me off, I thought, and as I opened my mouth to say so, the tears welled up in his eyes and they told me that I was wrong. I shut my mouth, and walked up and down. Then an idea began to quicken in my mind. 'Do you have another name? A middle name?'

'No,' he said. 'I don't.'

My idea was dead before I could put it into words. I walked up and down some more, and I looked around the Market Place, and I looked at the well and the bucket that was sitting beside it, and I thought some more.

'If you could choose another name, what would you choose?'

He frowned and shut his eyes. Then a smile came over his face and he said: 'William.'

I started to laugh. In the games we played when we were young, I was Hereward the Wake and he was King William. The Normans were his soldiers and they were chasing me, and I was hiding in The Fens, and they couldn't catch me.

Hereward was our greatest hero. We spoke of him in whispers, and we remembered how he fought to keep The Fens in the hands of those who were born in The Fens. And we prayed that we might have the courage to be like him.

Simon had always wanted to be Hereward, but I would never agree. It was selfish of me, I suppose, but that was how I was, and I saw that this might be the time to make amends. I touched him on the shoulder. 'You can be Hereward,' I said.

'No,' he said. 'I don't want to be Hereward. I want to be William.'

I looked at him in silence. He wasn't making sense and for a second or two I thought he had become a simpleton again. But his eyes were glowing, and his face was alive, and he was standing up straight, and there was nothing stupid about him. I shook my head, and I asked him why.

'Because he won and Hereward lost. You always used to forget that. You pretended that he escaped and he was still alive and fighting in The Fens, and I let you. But in my mind, I knew he was betrayed and put to death on the Isle of Ely. And I knew that I was William . . . the Conqueror.'

I stared at him, and he smiled, and I smiled and shrugged. I let him think that he had won what he had lost so long ago, and I told myself that no words of his could steal my memories. They are stored away in my mind like treasure in a chest, and there they shall remain.

I looked down at the cobbles that circle the well. They were wet and green with slime, and they shone like the eyes of the black cat that came to live with us when I was young. We called him Alfred, and when he grew into a large tom, we called him Alfred the Great.

I remember the day we gave Alfred his name. My brother said we had to do it the proper way, and he made me fetch a pail of water. The cat hated the water. He hissed and scratched, and he made my hand bleed and I had to let him go, and he ran up the quince tree. And when I sucked my fingers they tasted of salt.

I put Alfred out of my mind, and I looked into the bucket. It was half empty, and the surface of the water was dark, almost black, like the wood of the bucket.

I looked at Simon and said, 'Are you sure that William is the right name for you?'

He stood for a moment and pursed his lips; then he grinned and nodded.

'You wouldn't like to be Charles, or James, or Henry?'

He shook his head.

'Or Richard?'

He shook his head again.

'And you're not going to change your mind?'

He laughed. 'No.'

'Then you shall be called William,' I said, and I rolled the word around in my mouth. I wondered if it would sit upon his shoulders and be right for him as some names are for some people. Then I saw his nose, the nose that some call a Norman nose, and I smiled.

He smiled back. It wasn't an ordinary smile. It was like a spring. It bubbled up from deep within him and it was full of excitement.

I sensed that this was a special time for him, and I said: 'We have to do this properly.'

He laughed. 'What do you mean, properly?'

'Well, you can't become William just because I say so, or you say so, can you? It has to be done by Him up there.' And I pointed up to the sky.

He looked up, and I picked up the bucket. He looked at me and he looked at the bucket, and his smile died.

He made a sudden grab for the bucket. I stepped to the side and swung the bucket and heaved the water at him. It hit him in the face and it wet his hair and it fell from his shoulders like a waterfall.

His jaw sagged, and a wild look came onto his face. I backed away and yelled: 'I baptise you, in the name of the Father, the Son, and the Holy Ghost.'

He clenched his fist and swung his arm. I tried to duck but his fist was in my face. Then he started to laugh, and I laughed, and he rubbed his knuckles across my nose. Then he flung his arms around me and he hugged me, and he danced me round and round. We slid on the slime and fell onto the cobbles, and we rolled about and we laughed some more.

Then he sat up and said: 'You forgot to say "Amen".'

I nodded, and he became solemn and serious, and he made

me feel solemn and serious. I bowed my head, and I was silent for a moment, then I said: 'Amen.'

'Amen.'

I stood up and stretched out my hand. 'William,' I said, 'may I call you William?'

He nodded and smiled, and took my hand.

Then I saw that my hand was scratched and it was bleeding. And I remembered Alfred and the taste of salt, and I prayed that this baptism would not leave a bitter taste in my mouth.

14

Simon and I walked from the Market Place to the cathedral, and then on towards the church of Saint Mary. His hair was still wet and so was the front of his shirt. He turned to me and said: 'You won't say anything about this, will you?'

'No,' I said, and I gave him a gentle punch on the arm. 'It will be a secret between you and me. And when you're gone from here, I won't tell anyone that Simple Simon is dead and buried, and William the Conqueror is riding round The Fens again.'

He laughed.

I had never heard him laugh at a joke about himself before. It was a good sign, and it encouraged me to ask: 'Have you thought any more about leaving Ely?'

'No, I've been thinking about tonight and the lantern. And how are we going to know when it's time to wake up?'

'We won't go to sleep. We'll just pretend to go to sleep and when she's in bed we can get up and slip away.'

'And what if we do go to sleep?'

I didn't have an answer to that. We fell silent, and we walked some more. Then he stopped and grabbed me by the arm and said: 'I'm sorry. I forgot to ask. What did she say this morning?'

'About going to London?'

'Yes.'

'She said she was going to think about it.'

He stared at me. 'She said she was going to think about it?'

'Yes, that's what she said.'

He shook his head. 'That's her way of saying no.'

'Don't be silly. She said I needed some money and she was

going to see a man she knew. And if he couldn't help she knew another one who might. And next week she would talk to me about it, and she was sure she could help me.'

He laughed again. 'So you've agreed to stay another week?'

'Yes, but it's just till—'

'You hear from her. Yes, I know that. And next week there'll be something else, and she'll want you stay for another week. And then there'll be something else again, and you'll stay for another week. And it will go on and on, and you'll keep hoping. Then autumn will be over, and the snow will be here. And she'll put her hands on her hips like this,' and he put his hands on his hips and stood with one foot forward as she so often did, 'and she'll say: "It's too cold. And the Thames will soon be freezing over, and there'll be slush in the streets. And you'll have nowhere to live and nowhere to sleep; and how am I going to tell your mother that you went to London in the middle of winter without a penny in your pocket?"'

He had slipped into Aunt Mary's voice, and if I had shut my eyes I could have sworn she was standing in front of me. Then he slipped back into his own voice: 'And you won't be going to London, you'll be staying right here in Ely. You mark my words.'

I laughed. It was a nervous little laugh. 'You're wrong,' I said. 'Quite wrong. I heard what she said. And I heard the way she said it. And I could tell she meant it. She wasn't lying.'

'I didn't say she was lying. I just said that this was her way of saying no.'

I didn't believe him. I couldn't believe him. She had come to my bed, and I knew her well. I knew her better than he did.

He had known her longer than I had, and he'd seen her more often, but I had heard her words. I had seen the look on her face, and I trusted her. And besides, she was right. There was no denying that. I would need some money when I arrived in London, and I could wait for a week.

15

Simon and I lay in front of the fire. We lay together with both blankets wrapped around us, and every few minutes we were giving each other a shake, or a dig in the ribs, or a tickle, and counting from one to ten. When we first lay down we didn't need to do anything to stay awake. We were annoyed, and impatient, and neither of us thought we would go to sleep; but now my eyes were growing heavy, and I was wondering if we had waited the hour we thought we had to wait.

The log at the back of the fire was burning in the middle where it touched the ashes, and a hole was forming. The hole was curved and it made the log look like a bridge. In my mind I was crossing the bridge, and looking down into a river of fire, when I felt a sudden gust of wind. It stirred the flames and they rose and wrapped themselves around me. I opened my mouth to scream but the flames filled it with fire, and I could not scream. I tried to run but I slipped and I fell on my back, and the flames bound me to the bridge. I fought to free my hands and I grabbed at the air, and I sat up with a jolt.

The jolt snapped my teeth and rolled my head, and I bit the side of my tongue. For a moment I didn't know where I was. Then I saw the fire, and the log, and the hole that had grown some more.

I shook Simon. 'Come on,' I said, 'you weren't supposed to go to sleep. It's time to get up.'

He began to count, 'One, two, three, four . . .'

I shook him again. 'Get up.'

I crawled out of the blankets and stood up.

He sat up and reached for his clothes, and he pulled the

blankets over his head. I could hear him talking, but his words were muffled. I leant down and lifted the blankets.

'. . . and I'm still annoyed,' he said. 'And don't do that. I'm cold,' and he pulled the blankets out of my hand.

I grunted and took my breeches off the peg. They felt warm and dry. The mud on my shoes had cracked. I banged them together and it flaked off. The mud was no more than three or four hours old. It had come from the ruts, near the corner, at the top of his lane. We were running. He'd said he could beat me, and I'd said he couldn't, and we came hurling round the corner like a couple of dogs that have sniffed a bitch in heat. Then he flung out his arms, and skidded to a sudden stop. I crashed into him and we fell in a heap.

'Shit!' he said. 'Look at that.'

I looked at the mud on my breeches and my coat, and I held out my hands. They were thick with it, and it did look like shit.

'Not that!' he said. 'That!' And he pointed to a brown horse with white hocks. It was saddled and tethered to the rail by Aunt Mary's front door. 'You know what that means, don't you?'

'Yes,' I said, trying to ignore the sick feeling that was rising in my belly, 'yes I do.'

We helped each other up, and I forgot about the race, and we walked towards the house.

The last time I stayed with Aunt Mary she had a guest sleeping in the upstairs room, and in the evening he sat at the table by the fire, and wrote a letter. It was hours before he went to bed, and it was hours before she would let us snuggle up to the fire and go to sleep. If the same thing happened again tonight, it would be hours before we'd be able to slip away, and by then the night airs might be cold and noxious, and the boys might be afraid to go outside. I could see our plan beginning to fail before it had even begun.

In my mind I wanted to take Aunt Mary's hand. I wanted to sit her down and tell her what we were doing, tell her we were doing it for her sister, and she should be helping us, and not making it more difficult. But I knew that I couldn't do what I wanted to do, and it annoyed me.

I kicked the air, and then I kicked her door, at the bottom

where the stepping stone is worn and the draught comes in. The door rattled and stayed shut.

Simon shook his head, and waved me away from the door. He leapt in the air. His leg flew up and his foot hit the door just above the bolt. The door rattled and swung open.

She was standing in the front room with her hands on her hips, about a foot away from the door. 'How many times have I told you not to do that?' she screamed at him.

We backed away, and she rushed out and stood on the step. She scowled at him, and she scowled at me and she made me feel very small. Then she said: 'We have a visitor from London. His name is Mister Woodgate, and he says he's looking to buy some things up here. And if he finds what he wants he might be back to buy some more. So I've told him he can have the room at a special price. And I want you two to be on your best behaviour. And I want you to be polite to him. And I want you to help him.' She sucked in a breath and it made her bosom heave. 'Do you understand?' I nodded and so did Simon. 'And you can begin,' and she pointed to me, 'by walking his horse down to the stables at Ely Field. He's been to see them and he's paid his money, so they're expecting him. And you,' and she pointed to Simon, 'can go over to Mother Malloney's. She's been baking this afternoon. And she knows I want a couple of loaves of her raisin bread.'

She turned her back on us and lifted her skirts and stepped inside. Simon pulled a face at her, and I shook my head from side to side, and the flints in the wall to the right of her doorstep came into focus. They were blue and silver and grey with a blush of white, and the mortar that held them firm was black with mould. In my mind the flints were precious stones. They were set in silver – like a brooch – and time had tarnished it. I wanted to polish the silver and I wanted this brooch to be a gift, a gift that would—

'Don't you shake your head at me!' she screamed. Her face was screwed up, and her eyes were blazing. 'And when you get back you wash the mud off your breeches.'

She banged the door shut. The bang was louder than the noise our kicks had made. It startled the horse. He tried to rear up but the reins were short and they held him firm. I rushed to him and patted him on the nose and the neck. He became calm, and in my hands I could feel the quivering that had been in him.

I undid the reins and gave him another pat, and as I waited for him to get used to me, Simon shrugged and slouched away with his arms dangling at his side. And once again I saw in him the shape of the great ape, and it roused in me feelings of sorrow, and feelings of anger.

On my face and my hands I could feel spots of rain. The warmth of summer had gone out of them and they sent a shiver running through me. I gave the reins a gentle pull. 'Come on,' I said. 'She didn't mean to scare you. She's upset. She thinks I should stay here in Ely and she thinks I should stay out of her bed. But I want to go and I want to stay, and I want to be in her bed; and it's all mixed up in my head. And every time we see each other she tells me what I have to do, and we argue, and I hate the sight of her. But in the night I can smell her, and I can taste her, and I can feel her body against mine, and it hurts, right here,' and I pointed to my belly.

We turned out of the lane and onto the road that would take us to Ely Field. The horse had relaxed, the reins were slack in my hand, and we were walking along side by side with our heads close together like two old friends.

I told him about the first day she came to my room. And I told him about my uncle and the nights when he didn't come home. Then I told him about Simon, who was William, and leaving Ely; and I was struck by a thought. It was hard and brutal, and it stopped me dead.

The horse kept walking. He pulled me forward. I stumbled and the reins bit into my hand. He stopped and turned his head. His eyes were like hers had been, big and round and full of scorn.

'He's not going to leave,' I said. 'He's going to say he will, and he's going to think he will, but when it comes to picking up his things and saying goodbye, he won't be able to do it.'

I thought of all the reasons he would give for staying, and in them I could hear the echo of Aunt Mary telling me why I should go back to Elme. To me her reasons were like dust – they would blow away in the wind. But to him they were safe and solid like rocks, and he would use them to build a shelter. Then I knew in my head what I think

I always knew in my heart: he would have to be forced to leave.

By the time I was back at the house, pulling the bolt and easing the door open with my toe, I knew that nothing physical would force him to leave. He was too big and too strong for that. It would have to be a thing of the mind, or the spirit, and it would have to make him want to leave. And in the years to come, it would have to make him want to stay away.

I was trying to think what this thing might be, when I saw Mister Woodgate. He was sitting at the table chewing mutton bones, and Simon was pouring him a tankard of black beer. He was bald and dressed in brown, and his book was leaning against the candlestick. The light was good for reading, but it filled his face with shadows and it made him look old and gaunt.

He reminded me of a monk, and I thought of the picture that used to hang in our school room. It showed the monks leaving the old abbey that stood on the edge of the marshes at Ramsey. Some of the monks were looking back – through the gatehouse to the church that was now locked and barred – and some were looking at the ground, and some were looking bewildered like little children who have lost their way and are about to burst into tears.

The monks had been ordered to go. And they had been told that they were now like other men, and they could take a wife, and have a child, and come to know the true meaning of the word Father. But most of them were not like other men. They had slept alone for far too long. Their cocks had shrivelled and their juices had dried. And the cold had seeped into their hearts and they could not love a woman.

In some strange way that drew the past into the present and made it live again, Mister Woodgate appeared to be at one with them. He appeared to be their brother.

He looked up and asked me if they'd fed his horse. I said they had. And did they rub it down? I said they were doing that when I left. He grunted and broke off a piece of bread and dropped it into the gravy on his plate. Then I remembered Aunt Mary saying I had to be polite to him, and I said: 'Were you able to buy what you came to buy?'

He shook his head. 'No,' he said. 'I saw some. And I like what

I saw. And I think I'll go back tomorrow and tell them I could buy a lot over the next few months. And then I might get the sort of price I'm looking for.'

I nodded in that slow way that is supposed to acknowledge wisdom, and I said: 'May I ask what you want to buy?'

He laughed. 'You may ask but I shan't be telling you. It would break what I call the second law of commerce, and I wouldn't want to do that.'

I looked at Simon, and he looked at me and shrugged. Mister Woodgate chuckled to himself and then he said: 'The second law says: never tell anyone what you intend to buy. If you do tell someone they might buy it before you, and so you miss out; or, they might tell the person who is selling, and that person might put the price up, and then you'll have to pay more than you want to pay.'

'But you don't have to buy,' said Simon. 'You could say "No thank you." And the man would be caught by his own greed.'

'That's true, but I'm a merchant, and a merchant lives by buying and selling. And if I don't buy, I don't have anything to sell. So I keep my mouth shut, and that is a vulgar definition of the second law.'

Simon laughed and I smiled, and we were silent for a moment or two, and then Simon said: 'And what would the first law be?'

He smiled. 'I wondered when you were going to ask that.' He looked at me. 'Do you know what it is?' I shook my head. 'It's very simple. You buy things at a low price and you sell them at a high price. And sometimes that means carting them to another town, and sometimes it means storing them in a warehouse for a few months. And that's what I do. And that's how I make money.'

'I thought money was made in a mint,' said Aunt Mary, who came flustering into the room with both arms wrapped around a large cheese that she had anchored under her bosom.

Simon and I looked at Mister Woodgate, and the three of us burst out laughing. Her face flushed and she slid the cheese onto a wooden platter, and then she looked at Simon and me, and said: 'Aren't you supposed to be doing something about that?' and she pointed to the dirt that had dried on our coats.

Our laughter died away. Mister Woodgate looked down at his book, and we slunk outside.

I washed the dirt off my coat and breeches, and wrung them out, and hung them on the pegs by the fire. By the time I was finished Simon had wrapped himself in his blanket. I did the same and I sat beside him. We toasted bread and spread it with bacon fat and honey. The wax from the honeycomb stuck in my teeth. I picked at my teeth, and flicked the wax into the fire. It melted and flared and then it was gone without a trace. I remembered the beetles that used to drop out of our thatch when the night was dark and still. I used to catch them, and then I'd let them go on the wood that was burning in the fire. They would run up and down, and then they would curl up and die and burst into flames. Sometimes the flames were yellow and sometimes they were orange and sometimes they were tinged with blue and green, but they all had one thing in common: they left black marks that looked like moles.

I yawned and blinked at Mister Woodgate's candle, and then I leant against Simon, and asked – in a loud whisper – if he thought we could have another piece of cheese.

Aunt Mary glared at me, and I shut my eyes. In my mind I could still see the flame of his candle. It was about five inches above the top of his book.

When the candle was four inches high, I heard him shuffle, and his stool scraped on the stones. He asked for some more black beer, and then he said to her: 'You can go to bed. There is no need to wait up for me,' and he smiled. 'The boys can keep me company.' But she said it was only polite. He might be needing something and she liked to look after her guests.

Simon swore in my ear and said we had to do something. I drew four lines in the ash at the front of the hearthstone and put a cross in the middle of them. He said that wasn't what he meant, and he put in a nought, and I put in another cross. I won that game, and the next five, and Simon won the next seven, and the candle was now about three inches above his book.

Mister Woodgate stood up and said he was going to read in bed, and he asked if he could have another candle. She unlocked the big chest to the right of the fire and replaced the candle. As he went to go up the stairs, he hesitated, and she asked if there was anything else. 'I was wondering,' he said, sucking his lips in, 'if the young man there,' and he nodded at Simon, 'could come up and read to me? My eyes are sore and it would be good to give them a rest.'

'I'm sorry,' she said, 'but he can't read.'

'And what about him?'

She smiled at me. 'He's very good. He used to read to his uncle and his voice is easy to listen to.'

He was looking at her, and he couldn't see my face.

I shook my head, and my hands pretended to shoo him up the stairs on his own.

She ignored me. 'I'm sure he'd like to.'

He turned to me and smiled. He said that was very kind and he'd have to think of some way to show his appreciation.

I reached for my breeches. They were still wet.

'No need for those,' she said, 'just keep wrapped up in that blanket and you'll be nice and warm.'

Mister Woodgate shut the bedroom door, put the candle on the table, and handed me his book. It was called: *A History of the Martyrs of the Early English Church*. It was printed in Southwark in 1664 and written by the Reverend Dr James Fisher, Precentor of the Cathedral Church of Saint Paul.

He asked me if I had read it. I shook my head, and he told me to turn to page 149, and find the paragraph that began with the words: 'They tied ropes to his wrists and his ankles, and they passed them through the rings on the floor and the roof.'

I found the place, pulled the blanket around me, and went to sit on the chair. But he said I should stand, it would help my breathing and my reading.

I moved closer to the candle, and then I began to read. '"And they pulled him into the air and stretched his arms and his legs into the shape of the letter X. Then they tied the ropes to the hooks on the wall."'

He told me I was reading too fast, and he was right. I'd been thinking of Mister Salthouse and wanting to get out of the room as soon as I could.

I slowed down, and my words formed a knife, and it cut off the man's leather breeches, and it cut into his hip and his leg, and he began to scream. The blood dribbled down his leg and it dripped from his toes. In my mind I could see the puddles forming on the stone floor. They made me feel uneasy, and they dried my throat, and I could not read any more.

He waited a few seconds, and then he handed me his mug of beer. I took a sip and he told me that the story always brought a lump to his throat and he knew how I felt.

I nodded and took a breath and tried to concentrate on the words. '"They cut off his shirt, and the cross and the beads that hung around his neck. Then they carried a brazier down the steps and into the cellar. They placed it on the floor between his legs, and they blew on the ashes."'

The book was fat and heavy. The pages didn't want to stay open, and as I tried to take a better grip on them, the blanket began to slip off my shoulders. He came and stood behind me and put the blanket back on my shoulders.

'She was right,' he said. 'You do read well,' and I thought he would sit on the bed or the chair, but he stayed behind me and rested his hands on my hips.

I tried to ignore him and I went on with my reading. '"Then one of the men asked him if he wanted his clothes back, and he said: 'If the Son of God wants me to be naked I shall be naked.' The men laughed, and the one with the face that had been painted blue, tossed the man's breeches onto the brazier."'

His hands ran down the outside of the blanket and they gripped my ankles and eased my legs apart.

I shivered and swallowed hard. I wanted to scream. But I thought of Aunt Mary and the shame it would bring to her, and I could not do it. I wanted to run but his hands were like the ropes: they were binding me to the floor and I could not move.

I read some more and I could hear my words. They were tumbling over each other and they weren't making any sense. He told me to go back to the start of the paragraph. And this time I was to read with more care.

'"Speckles of black began to appear on his breeches. They grew into black spots and began to smoke, and then they burst into flame. The man twisted and turned and tried to swing away from the flames, but the flames fed on the leather and they grew bigger and they reached for his legs."'

I could feel his hands reaching for my legs, and in my mind I twisted and turned and tried not to think about what he was doing. And I thought about the man in the flames and I wondered what he had done, and my eyes went back to the page.

'"And then the flames reached into the place between his legs, and he began to scream."'

His hands reached into the place between my legs and they set me on fire. My hands began to shake and they made the words on the page shake. He told me to keep on reading but the flames were roaring out of control – like bracken in a forest fire – and I couldn't read and I couldn't move, and nothing was making any sense any more, and the book slid out of my hand. And he knelt in front of me.

Later, when the flames had died away and I was beginning to feel the cold, I wrapped the blanket around myself again, and he stood up. Then he took my hand and said his would seldom do what mine would do, and I must stay, and he would do it again.

I said she wouldn't go to bed till she had seen me tucked up in front of the fire. And he said I could come back later on, but I thought of Mister Salthouse and Simon, and what we had to do, and I said I couldn't do it.

He took a silver threepence from his pocket and placed it on the table and said: 'If you come back you can have that.'

I thought of London and I was tempted, as that man on the ropes must have been tempted, but I shook my head. He shrugged and said, if you change your mind it will still be there waiting for you. I said I wouldn't, and he said: 'We'll see.'

16

Simon pulled the cord over his neck and slipped the key into the lock on the school door. The key was cast from iron, and it had stained the front of his shirt. Aunt Mary said the stain was rust and it was caused by sweat, and he shouldn't wear the key all the time.

He said they trusted him and he had to wear the key, and he wasn't going to take it off.

At home, or around Ely, he wore the key inside his shirt, and he pretended that it was a secret and he had to hide it. But I knew that when he was at the school he wore the key on the outside of his shirt, and it looked like a badge of office, or a symbol of authority, and I wondered if he were trying to impress the boys.

He turned the key, and we slipped inside. It was dark, much darker than it was outside. I stretched out my hand and tiptoed after him. When he stopped I came up behind him, and he whispered: 'There's someone in the kitchen.'

I looked around the corner. A few yards away a door was ajar, spilling light into the passageway.

I froze, and my heart began to pound.

'Stay here,' he said. He crouched down, and crept along the passageway on all fours, and he lay on the floor and looked into the kitchen. He crept back. 'It's the cook and the porter. They're sitting at the table. They've carved a ham and opened a crock of pickles. And they're drinking beer.'

'It won't matter,' I whispered. 'We can sneak past the kitchen, and on the way back, we can warn the boys to be quiet.'

He shook his head. 'The lantern is in the kitchen. And we have to get it.'

I cursed the boy who had to have the lantern, and then I began to feel that something was wrong. 'But didn't you tell me we couldn't take it because it had a new candle and he'd know if we used it?'

He reached into his pocket and held up a candle. It was the one that Mister Woodgate thought too small to take to bed. 'Oh my God,' I whispered, 'I never thought of that.'

He smiled and beckoned me to follow him.

We crept past the kitchen door and down the passageway and through the end door that led to the refectory. We eased the door into the lock, and I said: 'We could go up and get the boys, and hope that the two of them have gone by the time we get back.'

'We could. But what do we do if they're still there, and young Patterson starts to cry, and says he wants his lantern and we have to take him back upstairs, and we can't get anybody to replace him?'

There was no need to answer his question. We both knew that it would spell the end of our plan and the end of any hope I had of helping Mother.

I slid down the wall and sat on the floor.

I tried to think, but nothing that made any sense came into my head. I began to despair, to think of silly things, and I said: 'I suppose we could pull our shirts over our heads and go into the passageway and moan and groan and pretend to be ghosts, and hope they'd run away.'

He snorted. 'They were both in the Queen's Regiment of Foot, and they've seen too much and they've drunk too much. And they won't be frightened by the likes of you and me.'

We sat in silence for a while, and then he said: 'They're not supposed to be in the kitchen. The Master changed the rules after the boys were caught stealing food, and no one's allowed in there now after dark.'

'But that wouldn't include the cook?'

'Yes it does.'

'But that's stupid. The cook works in the kitchen and he buys the food and he looks after it.'

'And he steals it.'

'What?'

'He steals it. That's what he's doing right now.'

'He's eating it. He's not stealing it.'

'Eating is stealing. That's what the Master said. And we all know if a boy is caught stealing, he'll be birched in front of the whole school, and then he'll be expelled; and if a man is caught, he'll be dismissed. And if someone enquires about his character, they'll be told that the man is a thief, and is not to be trusted.'

His words filled my soul with sadness. They were so cold and unforgiving, and for a moment I thought the Master had spoken them himself. I could sense the fear that was aroused in his presence. Then I began to wonder if this fear could be used by us, and I turned to Simon. 'What would the cook do if the Master came down the passageway right now and pushed open the kitchen door?'

Simon started to giggle. 'He'd shit himself.'

I laughed. Simon hissed at me and jabbed his finger in the direction of the kitchen. I gulped and said I was forgetting. Then I asked: 'If the cook thought the Master was coming down the passage in a minute or two, what would he do then?'

'He's not a fool. He'd put the food away and slip out the side door, and he wouldn't make any noise. Then he'd go to his room and get into bed. And if anybody went up and asked him, he'd say he'd been in bed for an hour or two, and he'd want to know why we were disturbing him. And he'd complain like bloody hell, and you wouldn't do it a second time.'

I knew a man just like that, and I nodded to myself, and I said: 'This afternoon, you were mimicking your Mother's voice. Do you think you could mimic the Master's voice?'

'Oh,' he said, 'I don't know. It's deep and it rumbles like a belly full of wind,' and then he giggled as if he couldn't contain himself, 'and the boys say I sound just like him.'

I smiled, and I told him what I thought we should do. He refused to do it. He told me there was no point in my saying he could do it. He couldn't, and that was that. I told him we should think of it as a play and we should do what actors do. We should walk up and down and say our lines, and act our parts. He told me I was being stupid, and I asked him if he had a better idea. He said he didn't, and I said it's either this or we go home. And he said he'd do it, just once, and I'd see what a silly idea it was.

We tried it. His heart was not in it, and it did sound silly. I said we should try again; there was no harm in that was there? He said I suppose not. And we tried it again, and again, and he said it might work. I said we should try once more, and we did. Then he was grabbing my arm and saying: 'Come on. It's easy. There's nothing to it.'

I took a deep breath, opened the refectory door, banged it against the wall, and clattered along the passageway. I tried to make my voice sound old and thin, like that of Mister Hamilton, and I called out: 'Master! Do you want to look in the kitchen?'

'In a minute! Will you come back to the refectory? I want you to have a look at this serving hatch. I think it should be bigger.'

I clattered back along the passageway and slammed the door shut.

Simon grabbed me. 'How was I?'

'I would never have known it was you,' I whispered.

We stood and waited. I thought I heard a door open and shut. Then we crept up the stairs and along the top passage, and past Mister Hamilton's room, and into the long room where the boys slept.

A boy was sitting on the end of his bed. 'We thought you were never coming,' he said in a loud voice.

Simon wrapped his arms around him and gave him a hug, and he said we had to speak in whispers.

'No we don't,' the boy said. 'I told Robert you'd give him a farthing if he slept the night with old Mister Hamilton. He says we're nice and warm, and he makes us promise not to tell the Master, and he never wakes up when we sleep with him.'

I patted him on the head, and Simon said Robert could have a farthing, and he'd make sure it was bright and shiny. Then he lifted him up and said: 'Come on. It's time to get dressed.'

'I am dressed,' he said. 'We all got dressed hours ago. We were wide awake and we practised the psalm, and then it got cold and they went back to bed. And now they've gone to sleep and there's just me.'

Simon took his hand. 'Can you wake them up?'

'Of course I can,' he said. 'But I don't want to wake up Richard Constable. He wants to come with us and I said he couldn't. And then he got dressed and he said he's going to ask you. But if he's not awake he can't ask, can he?'

They walked away from me, and I did not catch what Simon said.

Then I felt a tugging at the leg of my breeches. I knelt down. A small boy was looking at me. 'What's your name?' I asked.

'Mark,' he said, in the softest of whispers. 'Mark Patterson.'

Then I recognised him from Elme, and I smiled and said: 'We've got a lantern for you. It's in the kitchen, and in a minute or two we can go down and get it.'

'I don't want a lantern. Richard said only babies need a lantern. So I don't want one.'

'Oh,' I said, and I could hear in my voice a tone that my Mother used to call exasperation. 'I don't know if Richard's right or wrong. But we do need a lantern, and if I carried it, would you like to walk beside me?'

He took my hand.

When Richard and the others were ready, we crept down to the empty kitchen, and blew on the embers. We lit the candle, and walked out into the night.

The wind had cleared the rain. The air smelt cold and clean. I took a deep breath. It made me feel cold inside and I shivered.

'Are you nervous?' Mark asked.

'A wee bit.'

'I'm nervous.'

'You'll be all right,' I said. I gave his hand a squeeze, and he gave my hand a squeeze.

In silence, we walked through the yard where the dead lie beneath their crosses of wood, and through the shadows at the back of the cathedral, and along the alleyway, and across the garden, and into the privy cloister.

Simon came up to me. 'You see,' he said. 'He does leave his window open at night.'

It was most unnatural, and despite our need for that window to be open, I still found it hard to believe that a man like Mister Salthouse could be so foolish. 'Hmm,' I said, 'the man in the next room has more sense.'

Simon chuckled. 'Your old friend lives in there – the Beadle.'

I swallowed hard. In my mind I saw the spikes on his staff,

and the spikes on the collar he fastened around the neck of his dog. 'Does he sleep with that dog of his?'

'Yes. You can hear it barking in there sometimes.'

'Then we're going to have to be a lot quieter than we thought,' I said. 'That dog is very restless. It keeps getting up and prowling around and I wouldn't want to disturb it.'

'And nor would I. And this time I didn't put any meat in my pocket. So, if he opens his window and lets it jump out – as he does every morning as soon as its light – we wouldn't be able to keep it quiet.'

It was a grim prospect and there was nothing I could do about it, and I tried to put it out of my mind.

I crouched down and spread out my arms, like a Mother hen spreading her wings, and I gathered the boys around me. And Mark whispered in my ear, 'I like dogs.'

'You wouldn't like this one. He's got big teeth and he bites. So we have to be very quiet when we go inside.'

'Can we go in now?'

'In a minute or two. Simon's gone to get the stool. And when he comes back he'll climb in first, and then he'll help you in, and we'll all sit together on the floor.'

I told them that we wanted Mister Salthouse to think that he knew all of us, and that meant we would have to tell him that we all came from Elme or March.

'But I come from Wisbech,' said Richard.

'And so do we,' said one of the Russell twins.

'I know,' I said. 'But in the dark he won't be able to recognise you, and if you tell him your name is David Brown, he'll think you're David Brown. So, can anyone tell me the names of three boys who come from Elme or March?'

'I come from Elme.'

'And what's your name?'

'John Elliot. And I don't know anyone called David Brown.'

The name Elliot reminded me of Luke Elliot. He came to school for a few months in the winter of '67 when the snow was deep and the ice wouldn't melt, and he sat next to me. He was slow to speak and slow to think, and we used to laugh at him.

In John I could see the face of Luke. 'Are you Luke's brother?' I asked.

He nodded his head, and I told him we used to be friends. I asked if he would be my friend and he said he would. Then I said: 'I don't know anybody by the name of David Brown either, I was just using it as an example.'

He bit his lips and then he seemed to understand, and I said: 'Do you know the names of any other boys who *do* come from Elme or March?'

'Of course I do,' he said. 'And I don't want to be Peter Monkton. I don't like him.'

'You can keep your own name,' I said. 'It's just the boys from Wisbech who have to pretend to be someone else.'

'Oh,' he said. And before he had time to think or to open his mouth again, James, the boy who had been sitting on the bed, was telling me the names of two more boys and whispering in my ear that John was very slow.

When Simon came back with the stool, he placed it under the window. I asked if the three boys from Wisbech could tell him them their new names. He crouched down with me and put his hand to his ear and he listened to them. He said they sounded very good, and he was proud of them. Then he slipped the latch on the window, and climbed inside.

As I handed the lantern up to him, the light brought the thorns of the climbing rose into sharp relief. The thorns were curved and barbed, like fish hooks. I broke off the ones that I could see, but some that I couldn't see pricked at my hands. I swore to myself and Simon hissed at me to be quiet. I said I was being quiet and I tapped Mark on the shoulder. He climbed onto the stool, and Simon reached down and gripped him under the arms. I took him by the ankles. We counted one, two, three, and we lifted him up in the air, and over the bricks of the window ledge, and into the room. It was easier than we imagined and apart from a soft snuffling sound that could have come from a hedgehog looking for snails, the night still lay about us, quiet and undisturbed.

17

When I eased myself off the windowsill and into Mister Salthouse's room, the boys were sitting on the floor, with their shoulders touching and their legs crossed. Simon had placed the lantern on the table. It was casting a dim light, and it was painting their faces with browns and blacks. It was making them look nervous and wide-eyed.

The boys reminded me of baby owls and the way they huddle together when their Mother is off the nest. I thought of my own Mother and what they were doing for her, and my heart went out to them. I wanted to protect them, and to keep them safe; and as I sat down my eyes filled with tears.

I blinked my eyes and wiped away the tears. As I became used to the dark, my eyes found a chair and a chest and another table. They could not find a bed or a shape on the floor, and I began to realise that the room was empty.

We were going to fail. That was the first thought that came into my mind. It dried my mouth, and it reached into my guts and tied them into knots. I slumped forward and I hissed at Simon: 'He's not here.'

Simon pointed to the far wall. 'He sleeps in the alcove behind those curtains.'

I sat up and some of the knots in my gut unravelled. Then I understood why he could sleep with his window open: the curtains were protecting him from the fevers that ride on the night air.

Simon stood up and pulled the curtains along the rail. The bed filled the whole of the alcove. Mister Salthouse was lying just above my eye level. His head was under the blankets and his body was forming a chain of hills, soft rounded hills, like those that have been ploughed for hundreds of years.

Simon sat down, close to the bed, and nodded at James.

James lifted his head, closed his eyes, and sang: '"The Lord is my shepherd, I shall not want."'

His pitch was perfect. The other boys picked it up, and together they sang: '"He maketh me to lie down in green pastures: he leadeth me beside the still waters."'

The rise and the fall of the plainchant filled the room with sound. It came and it went. It was eerie. It made me tremble; it made Mister Salthouse stir; and it brought Simon to his knees.

Simon patted the air and calmed the singing. It became soft and mellow, and the words of the psalmist led me along the paths of righteousness and through the valley of the shadow of death, and I came to the table that the Lord has prepared for me 'in the presence of mine enemies'.

'Enemies' is a harsh and unforgiving word. It raised in my mind the sounds of battle and the clash of will that goes before the clash of swords. It sat me up, straight and hard. And it sat up Mister Salthouse.

His mouth opened and his eyes flared. He pulled at the blanket and tried to cover himself.

Simon said: 'We are your friends. We have come to ask your help. We are not going to harm you. And we are not going to steal anything.'

The boys strained to hear Simon and their singing began to falter.

Simon turned towards them. He lifted his hands, and he lifted the sound of their singing, and the final words, 'I will dwell in the house of the Lord for ever', appeared to flow from his fingers like a benediction.

These words restored my soul and untied the last of the knots that were in my gut, and with a calmness that I had not felt for some days, I fixed my eyes on the skull that was the face of Mister Salthouse; and I waited for Simon to speak.

'We are here, Mister Salthouse, to ask for your help. And if you can help us, we will thank you; and if you cannot, we will ask you to pray for us; and then we will leave.' Simon looked down for a moment and lowered his voice, and in that slow precise manner that some teachers use when the lesson is hard or their pupils are being thick in the head, he said: 'No one saw us come, and no one will see us go, and no one knows that we are here. So there is no need for you to worry about what others may think or say.'

Mister Salthouse slid his feet from under the blanket, and placed them on the floor. For a moment I thought he was going to stand, but he stayed sitting on the edge of the bed. His head was twisting from side to side and nodding up and down, as if he were counting, or checking to see that we had all arrived.

I looked down at the floor. His feet were white, and bare, and the bones were raised, and the flesh hung between them like the webbing on the feet of a dead frog.

We waited in silence, and I counted his toes and the bones in his feet, and then he cleared his throat. 'What do you want?'

In my head I breathed a sigh of relief. Yesterday we had decided that we would have to wait for him to speak. It would give him time to wake up, Simon had said, and time to think, and time to unchain the secret fears that live in the mind of every man.

'We need your help. But first we would like to tell you who we are. We know your name and we think you should know ours. I am Simon and I work in the kitchens, and you may have seen me serving in the refectory last Sunday.'

'Are you Simple Simon?'

'I am Simon. They call me simple, but that is not my name. And I am not a simpleton.'

There was a second or two of silence, and then I said: 'And I am Martyn Fenton, and I used to sing in the choir in the parish church at Elme. And sometimes I went with you to the church at Emneth.'

He stared at me for a long time. Then his head sagged, and I tapped James on the shoulder.

'My name is James Clarkby,' he said, 'and I come from March, and I live at the choir school, and I sing in the cathedral.'

I smiled to myself. It was more than we had asked him to say but it didn't matter. He said it well, and I thought it would help the others, and it did. Each of them gave their name, or their supposed name, in a voice that was crisp and clear and free from any hesitation that might have raised a doubt in Mister Salthouse's mind.

Simon looked at me. I gave him the briefest of nods, and he said: 'A week ago the Master announced that the Bishop of Ely is to be our Canonical Visitor. He is to inspect King's School, and that of course includes the choir school, and he is to see that everything is as it should be. He is to talk to each boy, and they may, if they wish, go to Prior Crauden's Chapel and speak to him in private.'

He shrugged. 'Such visits are common. They are provided for in the charters that govern most of our schools, and I don't see what this one has to do with me.'

'The boys from Elme want to talk to the Bishop about the man who was their choirmaster. And the boys from March remember that the same man came to take their choir when their Minister was ill. They say that things were done to them that should not have been done. I do not believe that a man in holy orders would do such things, but I am told by Martyn Fenton that such things have been done for many years. And I have to tell you that, after much hesitation, I have agreed to go with the boys. They will see the Bishop, and I will help each of them to tell his story.'

Mister Salthouse pulled his feet up from the floor and wrapped his arms around his legs. He laid his head on his knees, and he rocked back and forth. He looked like a demented bird that was about to fall off its perch.

Mark took my hand, and I whispered: 'He'll be all right. He's thinking about what Simon said.'

Mister Salthouse lifted his head and Simon said: 'If one of the boys went to the Bishop, he would not be believed; and it might be so for two or three. But for six, or seven if Martyn came with us, he would have to accept that we were telling the truth.'

Mister Salthouse laid his head back on his knees. He didn't rock back and forth; he just sat there.

'Before going to see the Bishop,' I said, 'we wanted to ask your advice, because there may be other things that could be done, other things that—'

'Yes,' he said, letting his feet slip back to the floor, 'there are other things that could be done, other things that might help a man who has strayed from the path of righteousness.'

I bowed to him in a humble submissive way, and I said: 'It's late and the boys should be in bed, and some things are best kept from the ears of the young. I suggest that Simon takes the boys back to the school, and you and I can talk about this man, and what should be done.'

When Simon and the boys were gone, I said: 'I want to say I'm sorry for what happened in the cathedral. I did not intend it to happen, and I am sorry that it did, and you have my word that it will not happen again.'

He nodded.

It was a strange reversal. I, who thought I held all the power, was sitting on the floor like a supplicant; and he, from whom I thought all the power had drained away, was sitting on the edge of the bed. I felt as if I were looking up at a man on a throne. I stood up and pulled over the chair, and sat in front of him. I looked at him for about a minute, and then I said: 'I would like to tell you what I think you should do.'

He listened to my words and to my reasons, and his fingers drummed the bed. Then they fell silent and he asked: 'And why should your father do what I say?'

'You could always make him pay the tithes. He would curse and swear when he heard you were coming. And he'd say he wasn't going to pay. Then you'd come and he'd pay, and when you were gone, he'd curse and swear some more, and say that was going to be the last time. And I thought if you could make him pay the tithes you could make him do other things.'

He shook his head. 'It's not the same.'

I kept my lips shut tight, and I waited.

He stood up, and I stood up, and he said: 'I don't have any choice, do I?'

I felt a great sense of relief. It made my head feel light enough to float away. I flung my arms around him and gave him a hug. Then I let him go, and he pulled me into his arms, and he held me. I felt sorry for him. But then his hips began to grind and his breathing became heavy. I tried to pull away but his grip grew stronger. I tried to push him away but he was too big for me, and I yelled: 'You're bloody mad!'

'Just this once,' he said, breathing into my ear, 'and I'll do anything you want.'

'You've already agreed,' I yelled. And I butted him with my head.

He staggered backwards, knocked the chair over, and fell against the wall.

A dog barked, and a man's voice floated in through the open window: 'I don't know what's going on in there. First I hears singing and now there's voices.' He thumped on the wall. 'Is you all right in there?'

Mister Salthouse walked to the window and rubbed his head. 'I was having a nightmare. I'm sorry. It made me feel sick and I knocked over the chair.'

'That's what comes of leaving your window open.'

Mister Salthouse turned towards me.

'That was your fault,' I said.

He shrugged. 'I wanted you. And you were here. And I couldn't help myself.'

I shook my head, and then the voice of the Beadle floated in through the window again. 'Go on,' he said, in a gentle affectionate way, 'get on out there. And don't you come back barking and wanting to come in, because I'm not going downstairs to open the door for you.'

He banged his window shut, and I looked into the garden. The dog was sniffing along the path, and it was wearing its collar.

'Jesus,' I said. 'What am I going to do about him?'

Mister Salthouse came and stood beside me, and he sighed. Then he opened his chest and brought out a pestle and mortar. 'I'll grind you up some pepper,' he said, 'and when he gets close, throw it in his eyes and on his nose, and he won't give you any trouble.'

'But pepper is like gold,' I said. 'It's worth a fortune.'

'Hmm,' he said, 'and so is my reputation.'

18

Simon and I sat in our blankets and watched the fire. We were wide awake and bubbling with excitement and not in the least interested in going to sleep. We talked about the cook, and Mister Salthouse, and the Beadle and that bloody great dog of his. We relived each threat, each moment of danger, and somehow – as we talked – they seemed to grow, and swell, and throb with a life of their own.

I said this to Simon and he laughed. Then he stared at me for several seconds, and he picked up the poker and said, in a voice that was not much more than a whisper: 'You were upstairs for a long time before we went out, and I heard some funny noises.' He thrust the poker in and out of the ashes, 'and it crossed my mind that this is what you might be doing.'

On a normal night, I would have denied everything and lied till I could lie no more. But it was not a normal night, and what we had done had bound us together. I felt close to him, and I told him about reading the book and Mister Woodgate running his hands up my legs, and then kneeling in front of me. And I told him about his head coming up under the blanket and forming a belly. And I told him about my cock being sucked into that mouth, that belly; and I was afraid that it was going to be bitten off.

Simon's face flushed and his mouth trembled. Then he wanted me to go upstairs and wake up Mister Woodgate, and let him do it again.

I shook my head, and told him I didn't want him to do it to me again, and he said: 'He can do it to me.'

I shrugged and said: 'If you go upstairs he will.'

It was a stupid remark, and I should never have said it, and I knew it the moment the words were out of my mouth.

He stood up and paced around the room, and flapped his arms as if he needed to cool off, and then he said: 'I've never done it before. And I don't know if I could.'

In my head I sighed, and then I said: 'It's easy. You take off your breeches, and you go up there, and give him a shake, and he'll do the rest.'

'You think so?'

'Yes I do.'

He paced some more, and took off his breeches – with a slowness that was hard to bear – and he hung them on the peg. Then he came and sat by the fire. 'I'm not sure.'

'Well, you're always talking about it. And you mightn't get another chance like this.'

He stared into the fire. I lay down and slipped a cushion under my head, and a few minutes passed. I closed my eyes, and I heard him say: 'I think I will.'

The stairs creaked, and I remembered that they had creaked when I had gone up to read to Mister Woodgate. Then I saw myself in the room. I saw the table and the threepence. I sat up with a start. I hissed at Simon, and he came back down the stairs. The front of his shirt was sticking straight out, like the top of a tent. I told him about the threepence, and I said: 'I want it.'

I shut my eyes and I thought I'd wait for him, and we could talk about that mouth and those teeth. Then I remembered I hadn't told him about those teeth and what they could do, and I laughed in my head, and I felt my cock. It was all there, it hadn't been bitten off, and I sighed.

Then I was dreaming about dogs with no teeth and no bark, and I heard Aunt Mary's voice. 'Get up,' she was saying. 'Come on, get up. You've slept in.'

I rolled over and forced my eyes to open. She was shaking Simon.

He sat up and swore, and she told him to watch his mouth. Then she lifted the latch on the door and went outside.

He threw off his blanket and reached for the leg of his breeches, and he flicked them off the peg.

I waited for a moment, then I said: 'I thought you always woke up on time.'

He told me to shut up. I laughed and yawned at the same time, and it made me choke. I sat up, and coughed and spluttered, and I couldn't catch my breath. He thumped me on the back, and then, with his hands resting on my back, he said: 'We did it three times.'

'Three times!'

He shrugged. 'The first time was so quick it hardly counted. And the second wasn't much better. And then we waited a while, and he did it again, and he said I was better than you.'

'And you believed him?'

'He said I was a man and you were a boy, and there's a big difference.'

In my head I didn't want that man, and I didn't want his mouth, and I didn't want his hands on me. So I shouldn't have been annoyed, but I was. I felt as if my body were betraying me, and I rounded on him. 'Did you get the threepence? Or did he get you so bloody excited you forgot all about it?'

He lifted up his cushion and uncovered the threepence.

I turned it round in my fingers and I was sorry for the words that had come from my mouth. 'Half of this is yours.'

'I don't want it.'

'Why not? You earned it.'

'I'm not a whore.'

'What do you mean, a whore?'

'Whores are paid to do what we did. And I'm not one of them, and I don't want the money.'

'You're being stupid. Women are whores, and men are men. If men were whores there'd be a word for it, and there isn't. So men can't be whores. And that means that half the money is yours.'

'You were always clever with words,' he said in a cold slow voice, 'but you're not clever enough to know that a bull existed before we called it a bull. And there's lots of other things that exist right now, and they still have to have a name, and being a man who is a whore is one of them.'

He put on his hat and pulled it down around his ears as if to shut out any arguments that I might be about to offer, and then he stalked out the door. I picked up the blankets and the cushions, and lifted the seat on the settle, and dropped them into the chest.

I looked at the threepence and I thought about his words. Then I saw the black cross that we had made in the ash when we played our last game of noughts and crosses. I placed the threepence in the centre of the cross. Somebody had polished the threepence, and the image of King Charles, with his circlet of laurel leaves, could have been the image of a saint. I laughed at him on his cross of ebony, and I gave him a mock bow. Then I remembered what they say about him and his whores, and I envied him. And I remembered the whores on the quay in Wisbech, and I told myself that I'm not like them. Then Aunt Mary came puffing into the room, and she dropped a bundle of wood beside the fire.

'Good God,' she said, 'where did that come from?' She picked up the threepence, and held it out to me, as if it were an offering.

'It's for you,' I said with a shrug. 'It's from Mister Woodgate.'

'But he's already paid.'

'It's for the extra candle. He asked if he could have the small one, so I gave it to him.'

She nodded. 'I was wondering where it was.' She blew on the ashes and covered them with dry leaves and twigs, and then she said: 'I must thank him for it.'

I swallowed hard and said: 'It was meant to be a surprise. I was supposed to give it to you after he'd gone, and I don't think he'd like you to spoil his surprise.'

She arranged the wood on the fire in a crisscross pattern. Then she held out her hand and I helped her to her feet.

She sighed and looked at me. 'Sometimes, Martyn, I don't know if you're telling the truth or telling lies.'

'I always tell the truth.'

'Always?'

I nodded.

'Last night you read to the man upstairs. Did anything else happen?'

'No.'

'The walls are thin upstairs and the sounds go through

them. You know my room is next to his, and I heard what happened.'

I bit my lip and looked into the fireplace. I watched the flames dance from leaf to leaf, and I felt sick in my belly.

'I heard you and Simon go out, and I got up and I sat in the window, and I waited for you to come back. Then I heard you go to his room again. And to say that nothing happened is a lie.'

I looked at her and I thought how we had been in the days that followed my sickness, and the will to lie, the will to hide the truth, slid away from me. 'And you want to know what we did?'

She nodded, and I sat down at the table. I had to tell her what had happened. It was part of our plan. I had been dreading it and I wished I didn't have to do it, but we needed her help, and she had to know what we wanted her to know.

I spoke of the boys, and the school, and Mister Salthouse, and what he had done to them. I told her that he was going to see my Father, and after that my Father wouldn't hit my Mother any more; and in the night he wouldn't force her to do what she did not want to do.

She shook her head. 'I told you before: a man like Mister Salthouse will never get a man like your father to do what he doesn't want to do. I know your father. I know him better than you think. I've seen what he's like when he's in a temper, and God help Mister Salthouse if he comes between your father and your mother. That's all I can say.'

'I don't care what happens to Mister Salthouse,' I said, 'and I don't care how he does it. I just want him to do it. And I told him he has to do it by next Tuesday.'

'Tuesday? Why Tuesday?'

'Because that's her birthday. And ever since I can remember you've been coming to see her on her birthday. I told Mister Salthouse that he has to tell her that he's talked to Father. And I've told him that you will see her on Tuesday, and on Tuesday night, when you come back, we will know if we have to see the Bishop.'

She stared at me for a long time, and then she shook her head. 'And you really would take those boys to see the Bishop?'

'Yes, I would.'

'God help us,' she said, and she pushed her stool away from the table and stood up. 'You sound just like Patrick O'Sullivan.'

'Who?' I said.

She stared at me and her cheeks flushed. She swayed a little, and she reached for the table and steadied herself. Then she said in a voice that was almost too quiet to hear: 'I'd forgotten all about him. He lived here in the days before your father was born. And he had a lovely Irish accent. Such a soft lilt. And such a lovely smile.' Then she smiled. Not at me, but at some distant thing – some distant memory – and then she said: 'I don't think I can go to Elme this year. The cart only goes as far as Wisbech and my legs are sore and swollen, and I don't think I could walk that last couple of miles. And I'm having trouble with my breath, and those stairs,' and she waved her hand towards them, 'they seem to be getting steeper every day.'

'But she's your sister,' I said, 'and I thought you'd want to help her.'

'I do,' she said, 'and it hurts right here,' and she touched her bosom, 'but I can't interfere.'

'But it's not interfering. It's helping.'

'She would see it as interfering and so would he.' She closed her eyes and sighed. 'They used to like me helping when they were first married, but then Simon was born, and things changed, and she said I had to stay away. And I did, for about five years. Then she relented a little, when you were about two years old, and she let me come over for her birthday. That was the very first time I ever saw you and that poor little brother of yours.'

She went silent, as if the past were too much for her, and then she said: 'I would like to go on Tuesday. There are some things I want to say to her, things that should not be left for another year. And I've been thinking if I bandaged my legs, I might be able to manage it. But I can't make any promises. We shall have to wait and see how I feel on the morning. And if I am all right, and I do go, I can tell you one thing right now: I will not be asking about your father and Mister Salthouse. That would be interfering between him and her. And I will not do it!'

I had never heard her speak like this before. It unnerved me, and I sucked at my lip and looked down at the stone floor. When

I looked up she was staring at me. I broke away from her stare and looked back at the floor. 'If she said she had a message for me, would that be all right?'

'Hmm,' she said, 'that would be all right. That would not be interfering, that would be helping.'

'And would you be prepared to ask if she wanted to give me a message?'

She thought about that for a while, and she gave me a gentle nod.

I reached out and took her hands. 'I know you didn't want me to talk to Mister Salthouse and I'm sorry I had to go behind your back to do it, but I have to help her. I have to do what I have to do. I can't explain why. It's right inside me, here,' and I laid my hand on my heart, 'and I have to do it.'

She looked at me with watery eyes, and she lifted my hands up and she turned them over. She looked at the scratches, and then she kissed them. 'They smell of pepper,' she said, 'and dogs, and roses. And they smell of men. And I worry what men like him up there,' and she rolled her eyes towards the ceiling, 'are going to do to you.'

19

Next day, long after Simon had gone to the choir school, and my uncle had said he would not be back for a couple of days and had gone to the house that we were not supposed to talk about, Aunt Mary filled two wooden mugs with hot mead, and we sat down at the table.

'While that cools,' she said, stirring in a spoon of honey, 'I want to talk to you about Mister Bradbury, the master mason.'

The honey left a twirl of white bubbles on the top of the ale. I blew on them and sent them scudding into the rim of the tankard. It was made of pewter, dull and grey, like the rain that comes with the dawn.

I thought of Mister Bradbury, and the rain that had eaten into the brick and the stone and the mortar in the church tower at Emneth. He and his brother had been repairing the tower about a year ago, and one of the capping stones on the south side gave way and fell to the ground, and his brother fell with it. When they buried him, Mister Bradbury carved his brother's name on that stone and they set it on his grave.

In my mind, I went again to see the stone. I walked through the marshlands and along the paths of summer that cut the distance from Elme to Emneth to less than a mile and a half. The stone was still covered in lichens of grey and green and yellow, and each letter was brown and bevelled and smooth to touch.

Mother said it was not a fit and proper thing for a man like him to have a stone like that, and she thought it should be put back where it belonged.

Aunt Mary sipped at her ale, and then she said: 'You heard what happened to his brother?'

I nodded, and I wondered what they would do with the stone when the time came for someone else to lie in that grave.

'It was sad,' she said. 'He was going to be married. And that other brother died when he was fourteen. And now there's only young Bradbury, and he's just turned seven, and his Father doesn't want him to start on the stone for another year. So he needs some help for a year, and maybe another year after that.'

I could see what she had in mind and I didn't like it. I said: 'But he knew this when his brother died. He could have hired someone a year ago.'

'He did. But the boy didn't last. And nor did the one after that.'

'And nor would this one.'

She gave me a pinched smile. 'But you might have something they didn't have.'

I shook my head. 'A mason needs a strong back, and a brick – or should that be a stone – between his ears. And I don't think I have either of them.'

She took my hands. 'Don't frown,' she said. 'It's what's in these hands of yours that's important. You have to feel the stone, to feel what's inside it; and you have to cut it and shape it and let it be what it wants to be.'

I laughed and pulled my hands away. 'Look at them,' I said. 'They're cut and cracked,' and I sniffed them, 'and they still smell of eels. And when the water's cold they shrivel and go white, and I can't feel a thing.'

She took my hands again and held them against the lacing that kept the top of her dress smooth and flat. 'You have feeling,' she said. 'You have it in every single finger.'

I felt my face go hot, and I pulled my hands away.

'He's expecting you,' she said, 'this afternoon. He says you can live with him and his wife, and you can be his apprentice. He won't pay you anything, but he will teach you what he knows. And when it's time for you to go he'll give you a letter for a friend of his. This friend is a mason, and he lives in London, and you'll be able to finish your apprenticeship with him.

'He says there's a lot of work in London for masons since the fire and the new laws about building in stone. So you'd never go hungry. And who knows? If you became a master mason and other masons worked for you, you could become a rich man.'

The idea of being rich drove all other thoughts out of my mind, and, that afternoon, like thistledown on the wind, I floated down the High Street and along the side of the River Ouse. At the quay they were unloading stone. It was brown, like the water in the river, and it was heavy. It had splayed the wheels on the cart. The wheels had slid into the gaps that had opened up between the planks and they had locked the cart to the quay. The men from the boat were pushing and heaving but they couldn't get it to move. They waved at me to come and help, and I lent them a hand, and so did a couple of others, and we eased one wheel out and then the other.

We pushed the cart up the slope, and past the sign that read:

ROBERT BRADBURY
MASTER MASON
and purveyor of memorial tablets
for the embellishment of churches
and places of burial.

Mister Bradbury came running out of his house and pointing to the side of the yard. We turned towards the fence and the piles of rock that were covered with straw, and we brought the cart to a halt. I stood up straight and wiped my brow. He gave me a puzzled look.

'Are you Martyn Fenton?' I nodded. 'You've made a good start,' he said and he smiled, 'and I like that.' Then he thumped me on the back and said I could help with the rest of the stone, and in the late afternoon we could have something to eat, and we'd have a lot to talk about.

When I sat down at his table, my arms and my back and my neck were aching so much it hurt to pick up the spoon and lift the food to my mouth.

'I like you, lad,' he said. 'I like you a lot, and I think you could do well.'

I smiled and nodded, and the spoon grew heavy, and I felt some more of my strength dribble away. He touched his wife on the arm. 'Don't have much to say, does he?'

She grinned at me. 'Give him time,' she said.

We ate in silence for a few minutes and the food warmed my belly; and I began to wonder how I could tell him about my desire to walk the streets of London, and see what there was to see.

'When did you first hear about me?' he asked.

'Oh,' I said, 'it must have been when your brother fell from the tower at Emneth, and I went to see the gravestone, and I looked to see if it still had any blood on it.'

He roared with laughter. 'Poor old Cuthbert. I shouldn't laugh. But everyone seems to know about that stone, and since he died business has never been better.' He paused and put his hands to his lips and formed a steeple, as some people do when they're praying, and he said: 'I think of that stone as an advertisement. She says I'm wrong to think that way and maybe I am, but it does have the name Bradbury on it, and that's my name, and you know what?'

I shook my head.

'If we stopped using the same graves over and over again, a mason could make a lot of money out of headstones. I think most people would like to know that once they're dead and buried they'll be staying put . . .'

'And resting in peace.'

'Hmm,' he said, 'and we could carve on the stone: "AT REST". And the more letters we carved, the more we could charge.'

'I don't think it right to make money out of the dead,' she said, 'and I think we should be talking about the living, and what we would expect from Martyn.'

He pushed his plate into the centre of the table. He looked at her, and he looked at me and said: 'Yes, you're right. And it's getting late, and he should be going home soon.'

He settled back in his chair and he asked me to tell him all about myself. I think he expected to hear about eels and wildfowl and the school at Elme; but I knew that I had to get to the point, and the point was that I wanted to go London. And I didn't want to be a mason.

I don't think I explained myself very well because he made me say it all over again.

Then he said: 'I think this is just a whim or a passing fancy. And in a month or two, when you've settled down and you're getting to know the stone, I think you'll be glad that you came to live with us.'

I looked at the table and I bit my lip, and I shook my head.

'I don't understand you,' he said. 'You don't know anyone in London and you don't have anywhere to live. You don't have a craft and you don't belong to a guild. And you haven't got any money. And on top of all that you don't know why you want to go.' He shook his head and turned to his wife. 'She didn't tell us about this,' and there was a touch of bitterness in his voice. Then he turned back to me. 'Has anyone told you there are hundreds of boys in London, and they're all looking for work, and there isn't any, and they end up begging and sleeping in doorways? And that's what would happen to you.'

His wife reached over and put her hand under my chin, and lifted my head, and said: 'And you still want to go, don't you?'

I nodded.

'And you're not prepared to wait for a year or two?' he asked.

My stomach was churning around. I looked for a long time at the ruffle of green, bilious green, that ran around the edge of my plate. Then I said: 'I feel, I feel if I don't do it now, I might never do it.'

'And if you go, and nobody wants you to row on the Thames or serve in a tavern, and you're tired, and hungry, and miserable, what are you going to do then?' she asked.

I looked at the table for a long time. 'Come back to Ely, I suppose.'

She turned to Mister Bradbury. 'I was speaking to Father this morning. He's going to run them through the tar on Saturday and Sunday and he says he'll be ready to leave on Monday morning. I was thinking, if Martyn could go with him, he could be back in a month and—'

'What about John?'

'He's going but you know what he's like. And he's not getting any better.'

'Hmm,' he said, 'and what about old Frogmore and that son of his?'

'He says it's too late in the season, and they have too much to do.'

He laughed. 'I don't know about too much to do. But it is too late. He's right about that.'

'I know, and I've told him. But he says he'll get a good price, and that's all that matters.'

'So he could afford to pay Martyn a shilling?'

'He could afford more than that.'

'A shilling would be quite enough.'

He stared at her till she lowered her eyes, and then he said: 'I don't like it. I'd much prefer him to start right away. But I know your father does need someone, and I know you're worried about him. I suppose you could see him in the morning, and if he liked the idea, I could go over in the afternoon, and we could talk about the money.'

For a few moments they both appeared to be lost in their own thoughts, and then Mistress Bradbury reached out and put her hand over mine. 'Let me tell you,' she said, 'about my father – Mister Edwards – and what he would want you to do.'

20

I left Mister Bradbury's house and walked down to the quay. Darkness had settled on the day, and I could just see the men from the boat. They were sitting on the barrels that were waiting to be loaded onto the boat. I wanted to join them, but at the same time I wanted to be alone. I wanted to think about Mistress Bradbury and the words she had said to me.

I stayed in the shadows, and I sat on a pile of bricks, and I leant against the beams of wood that brace the back wall of the old fishmonger's house. And I let her words take me to London.

I saw the bridge that crosses the River Thames. It was covered with houses and tiny shops, and they were all engraved in black and white as they are in the book that was kept in our school room. The tops of the houses leant in towards each other and they trapped the smoke. The smoke smelt of coal, and the cobbles smelt of horse dung, and I could hear people walking and talking. They were coming towards me and their steps and their voices were growing louder. I began to catch a word or two. Then I realised I was hearing the voice of Mistress Bradbury, and she was saying: 'And I think you should have offered him more than a shilling.'

Between them the Bradburys were carrying a large box or hamper. She was on the right side, closest to me, and he was on the far side, and it wasn't till they were almost beside me that I heard him say: 'And I don't think he's ever had a penny in his pocket in his whole life. It wouldn't matter if we gave him one shilling or two shillings, he'd still spend the lot. So I say we give him a shilling and the sooner he spends it the sooner he comes back to us, and I think . . .'

One of the men ran over to Mistress Bradbury and took her side of the box, and the rest of their words were lost to me. I slipped away into the night and I remembered her saying she was making a duck stew for the men. I'd asked her what the smell was, and she said it was rosemary and thyme, and I could smell it again in my head, and I began to think I'd like to live in that house of hers.

Aunt Mary was waiting for me when I walked in the door. She listened to what I had to say and she told me I was a disappointment to her. I said nothing was settled and she said she thought it was.

Then she asked Simon to help her up the stairs, and she went to bed.

Simon came and sat beside me. 'I've been thinking,' he said. 'If you leave on Monday morning, and she comes back from Elme on Tuesday night, and says Mister Salthouse didn't see your Father, what am I going to do?'

'You'll have to come and get me.'

'And how far away would you be by then?'

'It's hard to know. Eight miles.'

He nodded. 'That's about what I thought. And it means if she gets back by five o'clock, or six at the latest, I might still be able to find you before it gets too dark.'

'Hmm,' I said, and I thought about the second part of our plan. I remembered saying to Simon we'd have to give Mister Salthouse as much time as possible. Simon had wanted to give him a day, or two days at the most, and he wanted me to go back to Elme to see my Mother. But I had remembered about Aunt Mary and her birthday visit. And I thought that her presence, and her knowledge of Mister Salthouse's secret sin, would add to the fear that was in his mind. And it would prove to him that we were serious, and he would not be tempted to push us out of his mind and pretend that we did not exist. And we had agreed that if we had to see the Bishop, we would see him on Wednesday morning.

'Is the Bishop still going back to London on Wednesday afternoon?' I asked.

He nodded. 'The Communion Service is set for half-past ten. Then the Bishop is going to dine with the Master and Mister

Hamilton. And they say the carriage has to be ready for two o'clock.'

'And he's not coming back for a year?'

'That's what they say.'

I thought for a moment. 'So if the worst came to the worst, we'd have to walk back through the night. And first thing on Wednesday morning before anybody could stop us, we'd have to take the boys out of the school and go to the chapel. And we'd have to wait for the Bishop to see us.'

'And we couldn't take the boys from Wisbech.'

'No,' I said, 'we couldn't take them.'

It was the flaw in our plan. We had talked about it on the night Simon first suggested the plan. Then, it had seemed a long way away and we did not think we would have to knock on the Bishop's door. But now it was beginning to look as though we might have to, and I wondered if the Bishop would believe the story of three little boys, and an older one if they would let me in to see him.

A blackness came into my soul, and I said: 'Maybe your mother's right. Maybe the Bishop would say it's a lie and the boys would be sent home in disgrace; and I would be accused of corrupting children, and it would be me that would be punished, and not Mister Salthouse.'

Simon was silent for a long time, then he said: 'And what about me and the work I do in the kitchen? Have you thought about that?'

I nodded. 'They would throw you out.'

He was silent for several seconds, then he said: 'I think they'd want me to leave Ely. And my Mother wouldn't want a scandal so I'd have to go. I know you'd say that was a good thing, but I don't know. And anyway . . . we don't have to decide till Tuesday night. And who knows? Maybe on Tuesday night there'll be nothing to decide.'

I nodded, and picked up my cushion and hugged it, and for a while I was lost in my own thoughts, and then I heard him say: 'I've been thinking. If she's not well on Tuesday, I could go to Elme instead of going to the kitchens. And she could tell the cook I had the flux and—'

I shook my head. 'To my Mother you're a simpleton, and she

would never talk to you about my Father or Mister Salthouse. If you told her what you know about him and her, she would think I had betrayed her trust, and she would shut her lips and send you away. And she would never forgive me.'

He stretched out on the floor and pulled the blanket over his head, and he didn't reply.

Part Three

Gander

21

On the Monday, as the first rays of the sun were beginning to break into the dawn, we turned our backs on Ely and set out on the road that would take us to London.

The road was wide and rutted, and because the September rains had failed to arrive, it was still layered with the dust of summer. As we walked, our flock of geese stirred the air, and the dust began to rise. It was like a cloud of brown fog. It powdered my coat and matted my hair, and it put the taste of mud in my throat. I spat and blew my nose, and tried to wipe my eyes.

Mister Edwards laughed and for a moment he looked younger, and I could see Mistress Bradbury in his eyes and his smile. Then he waved his stick in the air and called out: 'I didn't tell you about this, did I?'

I shook my head, and the thought of walking in the dust for two weeks annoyed me. I booted one of the smooth egg-shaped pebbles that lay loose on the road. It rose in a high arc, then it dropped straight down like a mortar bomb. The geese at the front of the flock exploded with fright. They hissed and honked and flapped their wings, and they fluffed up the feathers on their necks, and their eyes were bright with anger.

Mister Edwards yelled: 'What the bloody hell do you think you're doing? That's how you bruise the meat. And that's how you make them scatter. And I'm not running after them. I'm too old for that. So don't you do that any more! You hear me?'

I looked at him and I nodded in a sheepish way, and I took a tighter grip on my stick. The shaft was stripped of bark, and the top was curved like a shepherd's crook with a broken neck. He said it had been to London and back twice this year, and I was to look after it, and to rub it with grease at night. If I lost it, or broke it, or allowed it to crack, he'd have to pay the willow weaver to steam and bend another one, and that would cost me tuppence.

For the next mile or so, I watched my feet, and I watched the geese, and I hooked a couple of them out of a deep ditch. I made sure I did as he asked: I hooked them at the base of the neck, and I grabbed them by the tail and I lifted them up; and I kept away from their beaks.

He gave me a curt nod when I had the second one out of the ditch. I felt myself relax a little, and I eyed the second thing he hadn't told me about. It was goose poo. It was unrolling in front of my feet like a wet carpet, and it was making a soft farting squelch as I walked through it.

The goose poo seemed to excite John. He came towards me dancing on the tips of his toes, like a bear at a market-fair. He was twirling his stick through his fingers. His stick was not like ours. It was short, and fat at one end like a cudgel. I spoke to him but his eyes were far away and he kept his lips shut, and he danced along in front of me. As the road dipped and took a slight twist to the left, his feet slipped and he fell in the poo. He sat, and drummed his feet up and down, and he laughed and giggled, and he stretched out his hands and looked at his fingers. They were like lumps of poo: white and grey and black, with a dribble of green. He sniffed them, and I felt sorry for him. And I felt sorry for Mister Edwards. He had warned me that his son was not like other men. He said his ways were simple and his wits were dim, and he was like a child: eager to please and eager to help, but after a few minutes he'd lose interest, and he'd forget what he was supposed to be doing, and he'd go and do something else.

'And you mustn't make the mistake,' he said, 'of thinking you can trust him. He doesn't understand about such things, and no amount of telling will make him understand.'

I felt sorry for him, and John, and I prodded a goose that wanted to sit down in the shade, and I walked on and on.

In the late afternoon, when all the warmth had gone out of the day, we came to a small village. The houses and the high wicker fences crowded the road, and they made it appear dark and narrow, like a tunnel. Mister Edwards walked down this road to the middle of the village, then he turned and waited for us to drive the geese towards him.

I could hear doors and windows being opened, and by the time I was level with the first of the houses, we were being watched by twenty or thirty people. The faces of the children were wide with smiles and cheeky grins; but the faces of their parents were cold and glum, and their eyes were narrowed by greed.

'If a door shuts,' Mister Edwards had said to me when we were about half a mile from the village, 'it means we've lost a goose. So you watch those doors and you watch those hands, and put a couple of stones in your pocket. I've seen them toss a dog into the flock, and I've seen them take a goose when they think they've got me chasing that dog. So you be ready with those stones. And remember: it's not the dog you have to hit, the geese'll take care of him for you, it's the man.'

When the first of the geese waddled up to Mister Edwards, he stretched out his arms and his stick. He made them wait till the others had closed up all the gaps and then he began to walk backwards.

I looked at John. He had both hands on his cudgel. He was carrying it in front of him, on an angle, like a fighting stick; and his head was jerking from side to side.

The children lost their smiles and turned away from him; and the men and the women appeared to shrink a little; and again he reminded me of a bear, a large lumbering beer, and I sensed what the villagers were sensing: this man was dangerous and not to be baited.

Somehow our four hundred geese also sensed the danger and they stopped being noisy and nosy, and in a solemn silence that would have honoured a corpse on the way to its grave, we passed through the village.

There was a certain degree of irony in this silence because the geese were on their way to the axe and the roasting spit, and they were as good as dead.

On the other side of the village Mister Edwards whistled at John, and he stabbed the air with his finger. John hung his head and grunted, and swung his arms around, and then he led us down a long lane. 'Two months ago we spent the night in one of the fields by the road,' Mister Edwards said. 'They'd just cut the corn, and there was enough for the geese to eat. But now,' and he shook his head, 'they've burnt the stubble, and there's nothing here for us.'

Twenty minutes later we turned to the right, and we drove the geese along the stones and the mounds of sand and the banks of crumbling dirt that marked the path of a stream that had run out of water, and we came to a small pond. It was shaded by willows, and yellow leaves had matted the surface of the water. I took off my shoes and sat with my feet in the water.

I pushed away the geese that wanted to drink on top of my feet, and I thought of Mister Salthouse, and Mother, and Simon; and I wondered how Simon would find me, if he had to find me, if our search for grass and water took us far away from the main road.

This thought was still in my mind two or three hours later, when the flock had settled down for the night and our bellies were full and the fire was burning low.

John had not said a word all night, and when I asked him about tomorrow and the number of villages we would have to pass through, Mister Edwards said: 'He won't be answering you. He used to talk when he was young. But he doesn't any more. I don't know why, and he won't tell me, and there's nothing I can do about it.' He yawned and closed his eyes, and soon his head began to nod, and he fell asleep with his chin resting on his chest.

I drew circles in the dust with the end of my stick and after a while the circles became letters, and I wrote my name. I tapped John on the arm, and I told him that was my name; and I wrote JOHN in the dust and I told him that was his name. He smiled the blue-mouth smile of a baby that's full of wind. I wanted to thump him on the back and burp the word out of him; but that would have been the act of a fool, or a madman, and I cast around for another word to write.

Three halfpennies weighed down the corner of my pocket.

Aunt Mary had given them to me when she was crying, and I was about to leave. She said: 'I think you earned them in your own way. And I think a man should have some money in his pocket, so I want you to have them.'

The word 'earned' stiffened my spine and my neck, and I

looked her in the eye, and I said I didn't want the money. But she said I was to take it, and she forced it into my hand, and she closed my fingers and she held them tight.

I came to love the hard feel of my money – and the look of it.

I pulled it out of my pocket and I said: 'Money.' I wrote the word in the dust, and I pointed to it and I pointed to my three halfpennies, and I looked at John. His eyes were fixed on the money, and the smile had gone from his face. And I knew that I had been a fool.

The cold woke me next morning, or maybe it was the hardness of the ground. I sat up and watched the dark of the night begin to slip away. I felt uneasy, not just in my stomach but all over, and I wondered if Aunt Mary would be well enough to walk from Wisbech to Elme. I tried to imagine her getting up, brushing her hair, and putting on her shoes, and walking through the dark and getting into the cart that would take her to Wisbech. But my mind was like a wall without pictures: there was nothing to see. And I looked at the geese.

They were lifting their necks and eyeing the world, and standing up and stretching their legs, and showing off their black boots.

The boots were a perfect fit, more perfect than a cobbler could cobble; and they walked my mind back to Saturday and the trough of tar. The tar smelt hot. It was full of sawdust, and we forced the geese to walk through it, and a pit of sand. They honked and hissed and bit at us, and they flapped their wings and filled the air with feathers; and at the end of the day, they were tarred, and we were tarred and feathered. Mister Edwards said I'd make a lovely goose. I laughed, and he squeezed my leg, and I pulled away.

I ate my bread and cheese and cold sausage, and I filled my flask with water, and we herded the geese back to the London road. A slight breeze was coming from behind us and for most of the morning it carried the dust over the heads of the geese and away to the right, and it made for easy walking.

Late in the morning we moved off the road and into the shade of an old oak tree. John stretched out and closed his eyes. Mister Edwards began to talk about the geese, and how the tar protected the webbing on their feet; and I began to think about Aunt Mary arriving in Elme. I could hear her voice and I could hear the voice of my Mother, and in my mind I was hearing what I wanted to hear. It lulled me into a state of contentment, and the afternoon and the walking that was becoming more like ambling, passed away in a soft blur.

But in the early evening, soon after we had settled on a water meadow about half a mile from the main road, my mind began to strip away the blur in much the same way that the geese were stripping away the soft blur of autumn grass, and like them I was being left with the dirt of summer. It was rock-hard and parched of life, and it spoke of crops that fail. As the minutes passed, I became more and more certain that it was an omen, and Mister Salthouse had failed us, and Simon was on his way.

This omen – this warning of evil to come – stood me up and sent me pacing around the fire.

Mister Edwards stopped picking his teeth and flicked the straw into the fire. 'What the hell's the matter with you?'

I shrugged. 'I don't know. I'm not feeling well. And I was thinking I might go for a walk.'

'A walk?'

'To the top of the road and back.'

'You're bloody mad,' he said. 'You should lie down and go to sleep.'

'I can't,' I said, and I picked up my blanket and wrapped it around my shoulders like a shawl. I walked back to the top of the road, and I sat on the corner, and I waited.

As the clouds crossed the moon, they filled the road with shapes that moved, and in them I kept seeing the shape of Simon. Twice I stood up and moved towards him, and the cold or the shock of seeing him was making me tremble, and then he wasn't there, and I sat down again.

Later, when the clouds had covered the sky and darkened the night and taken away any feeling that I might have had for the passage of time, I began to think of Elme and Coldham Manor House and the clock that stood in the great hall. In my mind I saw the hands move around the dial and I saw the weights unwind. When I was sure we were approaching five o'clock and the greying of the sky, I stood up and walked around. But the sky stayed dark, and I could not see the slightest glimmer of grey, and

I gave up watching the clock. I sat down in the same spot, like a bird returning to its nest in the grass, and when next I opened my eyes I could see to the end of the road. The wind had died away, and the road was empty, and not even the dust was stirring. I waited for what I thought were thirty minutes, then I walked back to Mister Edwards and the geese.

For the next two or three hours I was haunted by the thought that Simon had walked past me in the dark, and I half expected to see him coming towards me. I peered at every stranger like a man who has lost his mind, and thinks he is seeing everyone and everything for the very first time.

Now and again I turned and walked backwards for a few yards in case Simon was still coming after me. I caught Mister Edwards watching me out of the corner of his eye. I gave him a shrug and he shook his head, and I booted a stone, when I thought he wasn't looking, and he yelled at me. And I settled into a sullen silence.

At midday, when it was no longer possible for me to return to Ely by two o'clock, even if I ran every inch of the way, my spirits began to lighten, and I dared to tell myself that Mister Salthouse had talked to my Father, and from now on everything was going to be all right. In my mind I saw my Mother as she used to be so long ago. Her eyes sparkled, and her skin was clear and all the bruises had gone, and she walked with a spring in her step. I was following her, and the same spring was in my step, and we were singing.

Mister Edwards laughed at me, and he said: 'You're a funny lad.'

'She's going to be all right,' I said.

He nodded and turned away, and I didn't care a bit. I went on singing at the top of my voice.

22

Four days later, when the spires of Cambridge were far behind us, and the fields had taken on the purple blush of the autumn crocus, I said to Mister Edwards it was just like spring, and just as beautiful. He wrinkled his nose, and said I wouldn't think like that after I'd spent a day on my knees picking the bright orange bits out of the middle of each flower. He called them styles, and when they were dried on a charcoal fire and ground into a powder, the tiniest pinch would be worth twenty of them. And he waved his hand at the geese.

'They call it saffron,' he said, 'and they use it to dye cloth and cake. And over there,' and again he waved his hand, and this time it was towards the houses that clustered on a ridge about a mile away, 'that's Saffron Walden, and it's best we stay out of there. They don't like my geese. They say they eat the crocuses. And last year they closed the road, and that cost me ten shillings, and a goose for the man on the gate.'

The thought of somebody getting the better of Mister Edwards brought a smile to my lips, and I turned away so that he couldn't see my face.

'We'll take the next lane on the right,' he said, 'and we can spend the night on the bank beside the River Cam. The geese'll like that. And then we'll go over to Littlebury and down towards Bishop's Stortford.'

In the evening, long after the fire had died down, and long after I'd written a few words in the dust and helped John to copy them, it began to rain. At first the drops were light, and they washed my face and that felt good. But then they grew heavier, and they brought a wind with them, and they made me shiver. I pushed my way into the middle of the hedgerow and tried to keep dry.

The geese were stirring and making cackling sounds. I wondered what were they talking about. Was it the rain? Or how far they'd walked today? Or the state of their boots? Or did they gossip about us and what we did? And I wondered what they'd make of John, who never had anything to say to them, and then I heard him roar. There was a madness in it, and a feeling of pain, and for a moment it was like waking from a nightmare. I didn't know where I was, and I was so wet I thought I'd been swimming in the river. I tried to stand up but branches hit my head, and thorns grabbed at me and forced me to crawl out of the hedgerow on my hands and my knees.

John was running. His club was up in the air.

Mister Edwards was running after him. 'Where is he?' he was screaming. 'Where is he?'

I wiped the rain out of my eyes and I grabbed my stick.

The geese hissed and honked and milled around, and they blocked my way.

Mister Edwards yelled: 'Come on, Martyn!'

I tried to push the geese away, but they hissed some more and bit at me. And they flapped their wings.

I ran to the left and then to the right, and I jumped over a couple that wouldn't get out of the way, and Mister Edwards yelled: 'There he is!'

John roared, and ran towards the river bank. I ran past Mister Edwards. He was puffing and panting and waving his stick in the air.

I saw a shape, a black shape. It was running and jumping, like a deer in flight. And just as I thought we would never catch it, it seemed to trip and stumble, and it became a jumble of legs and arms and it fell to the ground.

John laughed. He swung his club over his shoulder, and he ran at the shape.

It screamed.

The sound was the scream of an animal – an animal that knew it was about to be killed.

It reached into my soul, and it tore at my guts, and in a flash I knew that I had heard that scream before. I had heard it when I was young and the fear was coated with laughter, and we called it a game.

I didn't think. I didn't scream. I ran straight at John. I swung my stick and hit him on the back of the head. The stick broke and the hook shot into the air. John staggered, and slipped, and dropped his club. His knees buckled, and he curled into a ball, and rolled down the bank.

I heard the splash of water.

And half-drowned by the noise of the rain, I heard a soft whimpering.

I reached down and lifted up the shape. It wrapped its arms around me, and it said: 'He was going to kill me.'

I swallowed hard and I held him tight. And when the trembling that was in him, and in me, began to die away, I said: 'What in the name of God are you doing here, in the middle of the night?'

I felt him shrug.

'I had nowhere else to go and I thought, I thought you and I . . .'

'What?'

He took my hands. Then he jumped up and screamed, and pushed me away.

Mister Edwards was standing about three feet from me. He had stabbed him in the back with his stick. And as he swung his arm and prepared to stab him again, he yelled: 'And who the bloody hell are you?'

'It's Simon,' I said, and I grabbed at his stick.

'My name is William,' Simon said, and there was in his voice a nervous dignity that I had never heard before, 'and we are brothers.'

'Brothers? We're not brothers. We're cousins. That's what we are.'

'I don't care what you are,' Mister Edwards said. 'I don't want you here. So you get going. And you get going right now!'

Simon backed away from him and he lifted his arm and he pointed. And in spite of the rain and the dark, I could see that his hand was shaking. I turned around.

John was standing on the edge of the bank.

The sight of him dried my mouth. I looked at my headless stick and it made me feel sick in my gut.

John peered to the left and then to the right, and he patted the back of his head with long soothing strokes. Then he crouched down, and with his fingers sweeping the ground he began to waddle towards us. After a few seconds he stopped, and chuckled, and stood up. He spun the club through his fingers, and he held it up to his face and he said: 'I dropped you, didn't I? And I told you I'd always come back for you. And you didn't believe me. And I have. So don't you go complaining any more.' He kissed the club and swung it over his shoulder, and walked back towards the geese.

'Oh,' said Mister Edwards, his voice quivering with excitement, 'he can talk. He can talk!' He grabbed me and shook me. But I could not feel what he was feeling, and he ran after him.

I turned to Simon.

He put his arms around my neck, and he said: 'She's dead.'

The warmth drained out of my body. I went cold, as cold as I have ever been. My fingers dug into his arm. I pulled him closer. 'Dead?' I said. 'My Mother is dead?'

He shook his head and his voice became a whisper. 'No, not your mother. My Mother.'

'Aunt Mary?'

'Yes.'

I sighed, and closed my eyes and I felt relieved. It was wrong of me, I know, but the sigh slipped out of my mouth without my thinking. I could not take it back, and it made me feel ashamed of myself. Then I felt empty, and sad, and sorry for him. I rested my forehead against his, and I thought of her and all she had done for me, and I cried; and the rain washed away my tears.

Hours and hours later, or maybe it was minutes later – I don't know how much time passed away – we crawled under a tree, and sat side by side with our backs against the trunk. I reached for his hand. 'How did it happen?'

For a long time he said nothing and then he sniffed and sighed to himself, and said: 'It was Tuesday. The day she went to Elme. I came home at about five o'clock and she was sitting at the table. I said, "You're back early," and then I went upstairs. When I came down she was still sitting in the same position. I said: "Can I take off your shoes?" She used to like me doing that, it saved her having to bend down, but she didn't say anything.'

I gave his hand a gentle squeeze, and he turned towards me.

'Then I saw her face. Her eyes were open and that wet sparkle, it was gone. Her mouth was wide open, and I thought of all the times she'd told me to shut my mouth when I was eating. And I knew she was dead. I sat and looked at her for ages and ages, and then I touched her hand. It was cold and her fingers were starting to stiffen. I held them and I rubbed them, and I warmed them, and I said, "They won't hurt you any more." Then I carried her upstairs and I laid her on the bed, and I took off her shoes, and I lit the candle. It was a wax candle, one of the ones she saves for special occasions. I told her this was a special occasion, and she was not to worry about the cost.

'Then I went to the other house, the house I'm not supposed to talk about, and I told my Father that she was dead.

'"Dead?" he said to me. "How can she be dead?"

'"I don't know," I said, and four little faces crept up behind him and they looked at me. I tried to smile at them but it came out stiff and twisted, and I burst into tears.

'We buried her next day, in the evening when the ground was cold and the grave was full of shadows. When I came home he told me the other house was too small. And he said: "I think you should live with your father, your real father. He's never done anything for you and that's what she wanted. But now, things have changed. And I want you to go, in the morning, before I get back."

'I didn't know what to say. I went upstairs and I lay on her bed, and I wrapped her blanket around me, and I could smell her smell. I knew I didn't want to live with the man who is my father, and your father, and I remembered what you said about leaving Ely, and calling myself William. And I thought of London, and you, and how they say brothers should help one another. And that's why I'm here.'

I sat hunched and quiet. I should have known. It was obvious. It was like a thread. It sewed together all the little things she'd said to me and it gave to them a meaning and a logic that they had not had before. Then I felt disappointed that he, and she, had kept their secret from me, and I said: 'Why didn't you tell me?'

'I tried to. That afternoon in the Market Place. But you didn't want to listen, and I told myself there'd be another time. But somehow, it never seemed to arrive.'

I nodded, and for a while I listened to the steady drip-drip-drip of the water as it passed from one leaf to another, and then I said: 'My Mother. Do you know what she said to your mother?'

He shook his head. 'I thought there might have been a note, or a sign, but there was nothing. And she didn't come to the funeral, and nor did he, and I knew you didn't want me to go to Elme and . . .'

I sank into a pit of blackness. It was cold and it froze my mind, and I saw the stone walls that our plan had built around my Mother. I saw the Angel of Death, and I heard him sound his trumpet. I saw the walls come tumbling down, as they had at Jericho. And I knew that my Father had rolled her onto her belly, and he had done to her what he had done to me; and our plan had failed.

In the dawn, when the rain stopped, Simon said I knew no such thing. I said I did, and I tapped my gut, and I said I can feel it here, and I think I should go back to Elme right now. He said it would do no good. If Mister Salthouse had tried and failed, or not tried at all, it was too late to do anything about it. The opportunity had passed.

I wanted to know why he hadn't come to me on the night she died, and I said I could have gone to Elme and we would have known. He shrugged and said he hadn't thought of it, and in truth he didn't know what he'd thought about that night.

Then I asked him about last night, and creeping up on us.

'I thought I could do it,' he said, 'without making any noise.'

I shook my head at him. 'John thought you were going to steal a goose.'

'I never thought about that. I thought about you, and what you would say, and what I would say, and . . .'

I looked down at the black earth and the pink worms that the water had brought to the surface, and I felt cold and wet and miserable.

In the distance Mister Edwards was heaping up the fire. The wood was wet, and the wind was catching the smoke and blowing it towards us. It smelt of goose-grease and it made me hungry, and I stood up. Mister Edwards saw me, and he beckoned. Then Simon said: 'Don't forget,' and he stood up, and Mister Edwards beckoned again; and I said: 'And make sure you say you're sorry.'

Simon bit his lips, and looked at the ground.

'This is William,' I said to Mister Edwards. 'He's my brother. And I was hoping he could come to London with us.'

'I'm sorry about last night,' Simon said. And I looked at him and wondered if I would ever be able to think of him as William.

Mister Edwards nodded, in a slow thoughtful way. 'I like a young man with manners,' he said, 'and I'm glad you came.'

He looked at me and smiled, and his face softened. 'John hasn't said anything for ten years and I thought he'd never speak again. It was a great thrill for me to hear his voice, and it took me back to the time when he was young and his mother was still alive.' He sniffled and tears began to run down his face. 'I'm sorry,' he said, 'I didn't think it would affect me like this,' and he looked away and wiped his eyes.

When he looked back, the tears and the smile were gone, and his face had hardened. He turned to Simon. 'I couldn't pay you anything. You'd have to understand that.'

Simon nodded.

Then Mister Edwards seemed to notice that we were both wet through. 'You'd better take off your clothes,' he said, 'and dry them by the fire.'

I looked at Simon and he looked at me, then he shrugged as if he didn't care. And I thought if he didn't care I didn't care.

We stripped off our clothes and hung them on sticks about a foot or so away from the flames. It didn't seem right but as soon as my clothes were off I started to warm up, and the heat from the fire felt good on my skin.

Then I noticed that Mister Edwards was staring at us.

'You do look like brothers,' he said, 'with your green eyes and your black hair. He's bigger than you,' and he nodded at me, 'in all sorts of ways,' and he laughed. It was a sniggering laugh – the sort of laugh men make when they tell jokes that are coarse or crude – and it made me feel ashamed of myself, and I covered my cock with my hands, and he laughed some more.

I felt my face go red and my cock go hard, and it burst out of my hands. I looked at Simon. His cock was hanging limp and his hands were on his hips. I wasn't sure what to do, so I put my hands on my hips, and I felt a fool – I felt embarrassed – and I wished I had another hand to cover myself.

Then I felt that other hand. I felt it running up the back of my leg. I felt it making for my arse. I jumped and yelled. And I ran round the fire and through the smoke and grabbed my stick and whirled around.

John was standing where I had stood. His eyes were flaring and his neck was stretched and his back was arched, and he looked like a cat that was about to pounce.

Simon turned towards him, and for one dreadful moment I thought he was going to strike him, but then he stepped to the side and grabbed his breeches. They were steaming and it looked as though they were too hot to put on, and he held them up in front of himself, like a shield. Through the smoke and the steam he took on the shape of an ancient warrior – and he reminded me of the man on the brazier, the man who died in Mister Woodgate's book – and then I caught a whiff of goose-grease, burning grease. I thought of the man with the blue face, the man who could torture and kill, and in his face I saw the face of John, and I knew that we were helpless, as helpless as the man on the ropes had been. And I began to tremble.

Then John did a strange thing. He seemed to lose sight of us and he pulled at the front of his shirt, and eased his belt and slipped his hand inside his breeches, and moved it up and down. He began to rock backwards and forwards, as if his feet were glued to the ground, and a dreamy faraway look came into his eyes, and he made a soft moaning sound that rose and fell like the strumming of a harp.

Mister Edwards shook his head, and pulled his face into a tight smile. 'He won't hurt you,' he called out, 'not when he's doing that he won't. And lucky for you he doesn't seem to remember much about last night, and that lump on the back of his head.' His eyes shifted from Simon to me, and they settled on my stick, my stick with the broken hook, and the smile slipped from his face. 'Is that your stick? Is that the one I gave to you?'

I nodded, and my heart thumped and my cock shrivelled, and I felt sick in my belly.

He scowled, and a blue flush came into his lips and it spread towards his nose and his chin, and he said: 'That will cost you tuppence.'

23

During the next six days the sun lost all its heat, and the wind blew the first of the autumn leaves along the road and gathered them into clumps. The rain came and went in the night and it made the leaves slippery, and it left us feeling cold and wet, but never once did we take off our clothes and try to dry them in front of the fire.

I took to keeping an eye on John. When he walked behind me he made me feel uneasy, and without thinking I fell into the habit of walking away from the flock, and dawdling along till he was back in front of me again. I don't know if John noticed, but Mister Edwards did, and several times he scowled and beckoned me back.

Mister Edwards and Simon, who was becoming used to being called William, were walking side by side with their heads close together. I had come to resent their friendship which left me on my own for most of the time, and as the sound of bells came floating across the fields, I longed to see the last of Mister Edwards and John and the geese that went with them.

It was early in the morning and the sun was still low in the sky, and I was surprised when Simon – William – stopped and waited for me. Some of the resentment drained out of me, and I said it must be Sunday, and I meant that it was a special day, a special time for friendship. But he shrugged and said: 'What does it matter? One day is just like another.'

I remembered all those early Sunday mornings when I stood in the choir – and believed that it did matter – and I thought of all the sermons I had heard on friendship and forgiveness, and then we turned a corner and a narrow lane opened up in front of us. The stone walls on either side had been raised and filled with earth and topped with hawthorn.

The roots of the hawthorn had loosened the grey stones and some of them were lying in the lane; and high above them, the branches had knitted a canopy of green. It shut out the sun and filled the lane with shadows, and it chilled the damp that still lingered in my coat.

'I've not seen anything like this before,' I called out to Mister Edwards.

'You see a lot of them in Cornwall,' he said, 'where the stone lies on the ground. It's an easy way to clear the fields, and it makes a good windbreak.'

I'd heard of Cornwall, but I couldn't remember where it was. 'How do you get to Cornwall?' I called out.

William – Simon – was moving towards the front of the flock. He stopped and whirled around and yelled: 'You walk. That's how you get there.'

Mister Edwards burst out laughing, and the two of them exchanged a knowing look, and then he said: 'It's in the south. The south-west. And that's as far as a man can walk, if he's of a mind to walk.'

I nodded to myself, and I looked at my wet shoes and I didn't want to walk another step.

I tried to remember what the map of England looked like, and I was sure there was some place called The Lizard, and it was in Cornwall. But I couldn't remember – the map was buried deep in the sleep of lessons past – and then we were out of the lane, out of the shadows, and into the sunshine.

I turned to check that none of the geese had strayed, and at the far end of the lane, where the trees formed an arch of light, a man on a horse rode into the arch and blacked out most of the light.

He wore a long riding cloak and a chimney-pot hat. The hat blurred into his face, and his face blurred into his cloak, and his cloak blurred into his horse; and the shadows coloured them black. The horse slowed to a walk, and its front legs nobbled the rest of the light, and it picked its way over the rocks.

Then I noticed its back legs. Both of the hocks were white, with a touch of light that was coming right through the hair.

The light gave the hocks an eerie look – a look of premonition – and I shook my head and thought: It can't be. His horse was brown.

I heard Mister Edwards yell at me, but I did not turn around.

I stood and stared, and I saw that black horse become a brown horse, and I saw that black face become a white face, and I knew that face, and it made me shiver. I wanted to turn away, I wanted to run, I wanted to forget that face and that night of shame, that night of weakness, but my feet were cast in lead. They weighed me down, like sinkers on a fishing net, and I shuffled back a foot or so, and that was all I could do.

'Get out of my road,' Mister Woodgate yelled.

I rocked on my feet, and he leant towards me and slashed the air with his riding crop.

I felt the air and I felt his anger. I shuffled back a little more, and he yelled: 'Next time you move a lot faster. Or you'll feel some of this,' and he flicked the crop over my head.

Then he seemed to hesitate – as he had hesitated on the staircase in Aunt Mary's house – and he pulled on the reins, and his horse stopped. Its head was about a foot from me. I reached out to pat it on the nose but it shied away.

'You look familiar,' he said. 'Do I know you from somewhere?'

'From Ely,' I said.

He stared at me. 'Ely? I don't remember you in Ely,' and then frowned. 'Were you on the quay when I bought the smoked eels?'

I shook my head, and then his face burst into a smile. 'Then it must have been when I looked at the salted eels, and the new way of packing them into barrels.'

'No,' I said, shaking my head. 'I read to you in the evening, before you went to sleep.'

The colour leached out of his cheeks, and he nodded his head. 'Yes,' he said, 'now I remember you. And your friend.' His eyes drifted from me to the front of the flock, and he stared at William for several seconds. 'Is that him?'

I nodded.

'I thought so. You don't forget someone like that.'

I didn't know what to make of that, and I looked down and I didn't say anything.

Then he said: 'I was in Ely last week. I went to your house and a man told me the woman was dead. I said I was very sorry, and he said he wasn't. For a moment I was lost for words, and then I said I didn't know her very well, but she did look after me, and she did cook my supper, and I was hoping to rent the room again. He shook his head and said he didn't want me in his house. He said he didn't want anyone in the house who used to be a friend of hers. Then he slammed the door in my face. It made a dreadful rattling sound, and for a moment I thought it was going to come off its hinges.'

He shook his head and he laughed to himself. 'I didn't laugh at the time. I was bloody wild. "Steaming mad" is the phrase my old Mother would have used.' He paused for a moment. 'Did I tell you I was still sitting on my horse?'

I shook my head.

'Well I was. I kicked the door with the flat of my foot – just above the lock – and the bolt broke. It broke clean in half, and the door swung open and it slammed against the wall. It made a hell of a bang, like a musket going off inside a house, and it brought him running out, and he stood on that doorstep of his and he swayed backwards and forwards and he shook his fist at me, and he swore.' He laughed. 'I used to think the fishwives down at Billingsgate could swear. But they've got nothing on him. Nothing at all. I told him he's got the foulest mouth I ever heard. And I told him it served him right, and it would teach him a lesson, and maybe next time he'd know how to mind his manners.'

I shook my head. 'He's usually such a quiet man.'

He frowned, and a puzzled look came onto his face. 'Is he your father?'

'No. He's my uncle. My uncle by marriage.'

'And what about him?' and he nodded towards William. 'Would he be his father?'

'Yes,' and then I paused as the truth flooded back into my mind, and I looked into his eyes and said: 'Yes and no.'

'Yes and no?'

I shrugged. 'It's a long story.'

He laughed. 'And I don't have time for a long story. Not today I don't,' and he gave me a smile, and a nod of his head, and then he rode off. He raised his hat to Mister Edwards as he passed him by, and then he was gone without a word to William.

About fifteen minutes later he came back, and he rode up to Mister Edwards and said: 'Do you think I could buy two of your geese? And maybe your man,' and he gestured to John, 'could break their necks and tie them together. And then I could hang them over the horse's neck.'

Mister Edwards' face bloomed like a wreath of flowers opening in the sunshine, and he hurried over to John.

Mister Woodgate dismounted and walked his horse over to me. He leant towards me, in what some would call a confidential manner, and said: 'I would like to hear that story. And I thought if you could bring your friend, we might have a mutton pie, and maybe a glass or two of sack. Have you ever tasted sack?' I shook my head. 'It's a wine. It's very sweet and it comes from Spain. And you'll like it.'

I could remember Mother saying strong drink befuddled the mind and made a man forget his morals, and I said: 'I'm not sure.'

'Come and try it,' he said. 'And if you don't like it you can drink beer. And if you don't like that you can drink water. But I wouldn't recommend that,' and he laughed. 'So what do you say?'

I smiled – it would have been crass to do anything else – and he said: 'You won't have any trouble finding me. I'm at the north end of Bishopsgate, in the old part of the city, the part that didn't burn. If you start at London Bridge, you go straight up Fish Street Hill and into Gracechurch Street and that runs into Bishopsgate. I'm on the left – as you come up from the bridge – right next to The Three Crowns. It's a small tavern, and they have a sign near the door, and you can't miss it. I eat there most afternoons at one o'clock, and again in the evening at six o'clock. So if I'm not in my rooms I'll be in the tavern. And if you forget all those names just remember it's the main road up from the bridge, and the tavern is called The Three Crowns.'

I nodded and patted his horse on the nose, and this time it seemed to recognise me, and he said: 'I've been thinking. If you and your friend were of a mind to accept my hospitality, and maybe stay the night, I might be able to find some work for you.

It would be hard work – and your arms would ache, and so would your back – but it would put some money in your pocket, and I think you'd like that.'

He smiled, and this time his smile was limp, as limp as the necks of the dead geese that John was carrying towards us.

Part Four

London

24

In the evening, as I lay in my bed of straw against the wall of a thatched barn near Shoreditch, the lights of London cast a soft glow into the sky. The glow was orange with a flicker of red and yellow, and it made me think of the number of times I had lain in our bed at home and looked into the dying embers, and seen things that were not there.

I blinked my eyes and blinked away the embers of the past, and I watched the wind play with the smoke from the chimneys, and I counted the towers and the steeples. It was a rough count, a count that was blurred by the mile or more that still lay between us and the selling of the geese.

When the smoke cleared, the stars brightened and the steeples became black spears with pointed ends, and I saw them stab the glow.

Then the glow began to die, and I heard the bells. I counted the strokes, all twelve of them. I heard them ring again in my mind and this time the clapper was muffled, and the sound was heavy and more measured, like the sound of a mourning bell.

In the hours that followed, when sleep would not come and the bells continued to toll the passing of the night, the night became a watch – a death watch – and I remembered my Father's father, the man they used to call 'old man Fenton'. We sat with him on his last night, and I yawned the hours away, and I remember him saying to my Father: 'You must be true to Patrick – true to him who gave you life.' And my Father said: 'You are my Father, and I will be true to you.' But the old man shook his head, and said: 'He was your father,' and my Mother took his hand and said: 'Patrick O'Sullivan's gone,

gone back to Ireland – and popery – and he doesn't matter any more.' Then the old man died, and the voices slipped away with him.

Some of the straw wriggled into my hair and it itched my scalp. I scratched at it, and I lifted my head. The lights had gone out and the glow was dead, and the geese had snuggled into me. They raised their heads, and I told them to go to sleep.

The embers came into my mind again. I saw burning feathers, and I knew that the death watch was not for my Father's father, and it was not for the lights of London, it was for the geese who would die tomorrow. I reached out and patted them. They pushed my hand away, and they made a soft hissing sound, and I said: 'I know you think you can look after yourselves, and you can, but this time,' and I hesitated, 'this time is different.' The tears welled up in my eyes, and I could not tell them about tomorrow.

Then I realised it was tomorrow. It was the day to say goodbye. It was the day that would see the end of them, and the end of us.

My mind sank into blackness, and the blackness sank into a pit, a restless pit, and the dross of sleep came and went and came again.

In the dawn I felt the chill coming up through the straw. I opened my eyes and beyond the dark grey of the thatch, the grey of the sky was blurring into the grey of the mist. The wind had dropped, and in the distance the chimneys were smoking again, and the smoke was feeding the mist.

I ate my bread and cheese, and the pickled herrings I'd saved from the night before, and in less than an hour the mist became a fog, a thick fog. It took my mind back to the Lea Valley, and Waltham Abbey, and the last time we were caught in a fog. That was also early in the morning, but it was colder then, much colder, and the frost had crisped the grass and the geese wouldn't eat it. We walked for about half a mile in a muted silence. It was strange, almost unnerving. My ears were used to the sounds of honking and hissing, and the flapping of wings. And they were used to the sounds of grazing, to the sounds of grass being snatched and twisted and torn away from its roots. These sounds made a melody, and it played in my head as I walked along, and I did not notice it.

But I noticed the silence. It was right inside my head, and it was seeping into every part of my body.

Then the geese began to stir, began to waddle a little faster, and I heard a faint sound. The sound began to gurgle and run. Then a bridge came out of the fog and the road softened, and the reeds grew higher and the road trickled into the marsh. And so did the geese. And they made their sounds, and the melody played in my head again.

Mister Edwards screamed at me, and he screamed at the geese, and for a moment the melody faltered. Then it came back again and I sighed, and tied my shoes around my neck, and my bare feet squelched the soft mud, and I peered into the fog.

After a while we found an old man with a squint in his eye and he grinned at us, and said we were the second lot this week. Then he waved his hand at his punt and his hunting horn, and he said: 'Everything has a price.'

Mister Edwards shook his head and he would not pay the price. The man said it could be the price of luck, and Mister Edwards said luck could be good or bad. The man shrugged and grinned again, and he slid the punt into the water and handed the pole to William.

We rounded up the geese, and herded them onto the road and out of the marsh. Then it was time to pay the price.

We counted the geese, and then we counted them again.

Nine were missing. And they were to be the price of the punt and the hunting horn.

Mister Edwards swore and slapped his leg with the flat of his hand, and he turned to me and shook his fist, and he yelled: 'This is your fault! You were at the front. You should have stopped them. That's what you should have done.' Then he glared at William and John, and he turned his back on me and he said: 'Come on, you two.'

They followed him back to the marsh, and an hour later when the sun was trying to burn a yellow hole into the fog, they came back with four geese.

It made for a sour day and a sour night.

And now, it would make for another sour day. I cursed the fog, the fog that London bred, and I buttoned up my coat. Then I heard the barn door open and Mister Edwards came out.

'Christ!' he said. 'Look at that.'

I looked, but apart from the geese who were fluffing up their feathers and trying to fluff away the fog, there was nothing to see.

The geese looked back at me. Their eyes wore a wet sheen and they looked like black beads. I remembered that black was the colour of death, the colour of mourning, and the thoughts of the night came back to me and a feeling of doom, of gloom, settled in my mind.

Mister Edwards leant over the hurdles – they were penning the geese to the side of the barn – and he coughed and spat and cleared his nose. Then he blinked at me and said: 'What's wrong with you?'

I shrugged. 'It's our last day. And I guess it's their last day,' and I nodded at the geese.

'I've been thinking,' he said, and he paused, 'a fog like this. It's no good. It brings out the rogues with the fast hands and the long cloaks. And the trouble is we can't keep an eye on everyone. Not with a flock this size, we can't,' and he paused again. 'You remember that man with the punt?' I nodded. 'I think he might have done me a favour. Brought me a bit of luck you could say,' and he grinned. 'Do you remember what he said?' I shook my head.

'He said we were the second lot this week. And that means they came through here three or four days ago, and they would have gone into the city through Bishopsgate, and gone to the market in Leadenhall. It's no secret. It's the quickest way, if you're coming in from Ely or Norwich. So, if we waited another day, and split the flock, we might get a better price, and we might be able to keep an eye on those bloody rogues. And I might be able to get each lot into the cages at the market, and that would be even better,' and he smiled. 'So I think we'll go on to Spitalfields and down to White Chapel. And we can spend the night there, and in the morning we can go in through Aldgate.'

I felt some of the gloom lift from my mind, and I prodded one of the geese and said: 'And that gives you another day,' and instead of smiling, or whatever it is a goose does to show it's pleased, it tried to bite me. Mister Edwards laughed, and I said: 'That's gratitude for you,' and he said: 'There's no such thing in nature. And there's no such thing in that city there. And you'd do well to remember that.'

Then he looked around. John was crouched down, prodding the fire.

'Where's William?'

'He's still asleep,' I said.

'Well, give him a shake. He doesn't need that much sleep,' and he yawned. 'Do you know,' and he lowered his voice, 'there's something about that boy. Something that isn't right. I know it. I know it in here,' and he tapped his head with his finger, 'and I can't think what it is.'

In the late afternoon, in an apple orchard to the left of White Chapel Street, William and John and I pushed wicker hurdles into the soft ground. We tied them together, and we tied them to the trees, and after an hour we had the orchard divided into three pens.

Mister Edwards leant on the hurdles and tested the fence. It swayed a little, and he grunted, and then he grabbed a goose by the feet. 'Fat ones like this, they go in this pen,' and he dropped it over the fence. 'And skinny ones, and ones that don't look too good,' and he grabbed one that had worn away the tar on its feet and torn its webbing and gone lame, 'they go in this other pen. And all the rest stay in here,' and he waved his hand at the largest pen.

I pulled a face – I was sick of working and the cold was making my nose run – and Mister Edwards shook his head at me, and turned to William and said: 'There could be tuppence in this for you, if you make a good job of the sorting. And in the morning we can herd the fat ones into Leadenhall. It's a good market, and we should get a good price,' and he nodded to himself. 'It's where all the big houses do their shopping, and they're the ones with money. And next morning John and I can herd the skinny ones into Billingsgate. It's a fish market but it does sell a lot of other things. And the funny thing is, they know the price of fish down there, but they don't always know the price of a goose. And I've heard you can sometimes get a good price for a bad bird,' and he burst out laughing.

'And what about all the rest?' I asked.

'I'll feed them here for a couple of days, and they might fatten up a bit, and then I'll take them into Leadenhall in two or three lots, and that'll keep the price up.' And he smiled at me. 'And that's how you make money.'

It was a phrase I had heard before. I tried to think who said it, but it slipped my mind. I picked up a goose, a large fat goose, and sent it flapping over the fence.

25 

Mister Edwards prodded me with his foot and I opened my eyes. It was still dark. The sky was clear, the air smelt damp, and the fog had lifted. He said it was time to go, and if we were lucky we'd be through the gate and into the market before the roads became too crowded.

We herded the fat geese through the hurdles and out of the apple orchard, and past the tavern of The Old Cider Master and onto White Chapel Street. Within a few minutes the trees took on the shape of houses, and they crowded the street. They made it feel narrow, narrower than I think it was, and they made the dark feel darker. High above us, the roofs cut into the sky like the teeth of a saw, and they began to saw away the darkness and expose the grey of the dawn.

The road was black with a dusting of grey that looked like ash from a wood fire, and it was soft, like the earth of autumn, and it deadened the sound of our passing.

At Aldgate, eighteen carts had lined up in front of us, and they were blocking the road. Most were two-wheelers with one horse, but one was the size of a hay cart with eight wheels and six horses. It was loaded with stone. The stone was cut and dressed and laid out on a bed of straw. It looked like the surrounds for a door with corners of trailing ivy.

Mister Edwards stepped over the chains and walked along the footpath to the gate. It was closed, and he shook his fist at the gatekeeper, and then three or four other men gathered around and they blocked my view.

I shut my eyes and I began to think about Mister Bradbury and what he said about work always being available for a stone mason in London. And I remembered him talking about the things that were inside the stone and how a mason could bring them out; and in my mind I touched the ivy, and it began to grow, began to cling to me and I was locked in its grip. I grabbed a chisel and hit it with a mallet. It shattered with a sudden bang – and a clattering of hooves – and it opened my eyes, and the carts in front of me began to move.

The carts were loaded with bricks. Some of the bricks looked black, as if they had been through a fire; some looked purple; and some looked like dry mud with speckles of red. They were piled high and they weighed on the wheels, and the wheels ground their hoops of iron onto the cobbled stone, and they filled the air with a screeching. It sounded like chalk scratching on slate, and it made my ears ring and my skin itch.

I blocked my ears with both hands, and they calmed the ringing but not the itching – that stayed with me like the hot itch that comes from the leaves of the stinging nettle.

Then Mister Edwards came running back to us. 'Have you ever heard such nonsense?' he yelled. 'They've been complaining about the noise in there,' and he gestured towards the city, 'and now they're shutting the gate, and keeping it shut, till half an hour after dawn.'

He waved his arms and clapped his hands and yelled at the geese. Two or three of them took fright and they flapped and honked and hissed and ran towards a horse. It shied and the cart slewed and the wheels slithered and sparked and the driver swore and yanked on the reins. The horse stopped and the cart bounced. A cloud of grey dust rose in the air and covered the geese. 'Christ Almighty!' Mister Edwards yelled. 'That's lime. And who's going to buy a goose covered with lime?' And he shook his fist at the driver.

The driver leant over the side of the cart, clenched his fist and yelled: 'Get out of my road, you bloody old fool! And if you do that again I'll drive over the geese and then you'll really have something to complain about.'

Mister Edward's eyes bulged and his face reddened, and he turned to us. 'What are you staring at?' he yelled. 'Come on! Get them moving!'

We followed the lime cart through the gate and into the city.

The street was wide and cobbled and it rumbled with noise. It was lined with houses, old wooden houses like those in Norwich, and I felt a sudden sense of disappointment, and my jaw sagged.

'What's the matter with you?' Mister Edwards yelled.

'I thought all the houses were going to be new.'

'The fire didn't get this far. You'll see a lot of new ones in Leadenhall.'

I nodded and looked up. The chimneys were clumped together and all of them were smoking. Some of the smoke was drifting away, and some of it appeared to be too heavy, and it was streaming down the tiles and over the gutters, and it was filling the street with a white haze.

I took a breath, and it made me cough and splutter. I spat and tried to clear my throat but the taste of sulphur stayed in my mouth and burnt my throat.

I have never liked the smell of burning coal. To me it is a foreign smell that dries the air and lingers in the thatch. I like the smell of peat. It smells of the earth and the bogs that used to be, and late at night when the air is still, it smells of dreams, and it smells of home.

I sniffed and sniffed again. I could smell lime and horse dung, and in the smoke I could smell burning bacon, but there wasn't a whiff of peat – or the things my Father used to do to me – and I looked at William, and he grinned. And I grinned back.

Then I started to cough again and I spat and wiped my mouth on the sleeve of my coat. It tasted of pig shit, and I remembered the farmer in Shoreditch saying his pigs slept on my side of the barn because it was out of the prevailing wind. I spat again, and this time I did not wipe my mouth on my sleeve.

At the market in Leadenhall the cages stood empty.

Mister Edwards allowed himself a slight smile, and some of the anger seeped out of his face.

The geese were quiet, almost too quiet, and as they waddled up the ramps and into the cages I wondered if the smoke had affected them in some way.

They poked their heads through the wooden bars and they looked at me with trusting eyes. They made me feel like a false friend, like a man who could betray the ones he loved.

It hurt. It hurt right inside my gut.

'I know what it's like,' Mister Edwards said. And he put his arm around my shoulder and walked me to the side of the market.

Here the hens and the roosters scratched at the dirt that lay on the cobbles, and pecked at the ropes that bound their legs to the hitching posts. When they saw us they stopped and lifted their heads and tilted them to the side, and they looked as though they were reading the sign that said: 'LIVE POULTRY.'

I turned away from them and the sign that would not be true tomorrow, and I watched the ducks huddle together and sink to the ground.

Mister Edwards reached into his pocket and he said: 'This'll cheer you up.'

He counted eight pennies into my right hand and four halfpennies into my left hand, and he closed my fingers around them. 'Put some in your shoes,' he whispered in my ear, 'and some in each pocket. And should you get drunk,' and his laugh echoed in my head and became mixed up with the sounds of crowing and cackling, 'and someone goes through your pockets, you might still have a couple of pennies when you wake up in the morning.'

I sat down, and leant against the tiers of cages that held the quails and the thrushes and the other small birds, and I undid my shoes.

He gave William his tuppence, and he said to him: 'Have you ever earned any money before?'

William nodded. 'I used to work in the kitchens, in the choir school at Ely.'

'Ahh,' he said, 'then you'll have some money of your own?'

William shook his head. 'I don't have any money. I used to give it all to my Mother. My Father said we deserved each other, and he wouldn't pay for anything.'

Mister Edwards gave him a strange look, and then he appeared to become uncertain about something. He took a step backwards and eyed William up and down. 'I knew there was something about you – something that wasn't quite right – and I was saying that only yesterday, wasn't I?' And he looked at me, and I nodded, and then he looked back to William. 'You're Simon, aren't you? Simple Simon. I remember when you used to come with your father to buy my suckling pigs and you were this high,' and he patted the air about eighteen inches above the ground. 'And I remember when he sent you to work in the kitchens.'

The colour dribbled out of William's face, and his shoulders slumped.

'You never looked like him,' he said. 'You looked like her. And my wife used to say you looked a bit like that young fellow from Elme. He used to come around with his eels and his wildfowl, and he'd knock on the door, and his words would flow like honey. My wife could never resist buying something from him. She said he had the gift of the gab. And he made her smile a lot.' He paused and smiled to himself, and for a moment he was lost in the past. Then he said: 'He had a way with women, he did; and there was a lot of talk about him and your mother, in the days when she was Mary Mourant. Then he married her sister. She was much younger, and more pretty, and they went to live in The Fens. And I can't think of his name.'

He frowned. 'It was something simple, something obvious.' He looked at me and he looked at William, and then he smiled. 'Fenton. That's what it was, Fenton. I knew it was something obvious.' He looked at me again and the smile slid off his face. 'That's your name, isn't it?'

'Yes.'

'And your mother . . . oh dear, oh dear . . . your mother was the sister.' He burst out laughing, and his eyes began to water. 'You are brothers,' he said, dabbing at his eyes, 'you really are.'

I nodded and then William nodded, and we both looked at the ground.

'Dear God,' he said, 'and I thought – well, it doesn't matter what I thought,' and he shrugged and laughed some more. 'I wish my wife was still alive. She would have enjoyed this.'

I shut my mouth and tied my shoes. And I wished I could tie his mouth, and keep it tied when he went back to Ely. Aunt Mary would be mortified if she knew what he knew. And so would my Mother. In my mind I saw Aunt Mary's grave. I saw the mound of raw earth and I said to her: Nothing can touch you now. And the earth smiled that smile of hers. I felt sorry for my Mother, for she would hear. And she would have to bear the shame that would keep my Father mute and full of anger.

I pushed my fingers into the corners of my eyes and stopped the tears that were welling up. Then I sniffed and cleared my nose, and stood up and tried to walk. The pennies felt like pebbles with lumps and hard edges. They hurt my feet and they made me limp.

He pulled his lips into a thin smile. 'You'll get used to them,' he called to me, and then he turned to William. 'The geese trust you, and you work well with them. And next year if you'd like to come with me, I could pay you a shilling, and a halfpenny for every night we spend on the road.'

William's face broke into a smile, a forgiving smile, and he pulled back his shoulders.

I looked at Mister Edwards. His face had softened a little, and I thought: I have to ask. And I said: 'He's worked very hard, and we were wondering if you could pay him a little more,' and my voice sagged, 'maybe threepence?'

Mister Edwards stared at me and he shook his head. 'You've got enough. And if he needs any more you can give him some of yours.' Then he turned away and called to John.

John hadn't spoken a word since the night I hit him on the head. He looked at me, and I saw in him the same anger that had been in Mister Edwards when the lime dusted the geese and greyed the road. He grunted, and it made my gut rumble, and I was glad I wouldn't be coming back to help again next year.

Mister Edwards walked back to the geese, and John helped him to climb onto a barrel, and he waved to us. Then his words came pattering over the noise of the market: 'Get your Norfolk goose here. Fat and plump he is and very tender. And he's a good walker,' and the crowd laughed. 'And he's a good eater. And the price is a bargain. A real bargain. And I don't have to tell you there won't be any more. Not this year there won't.'

John lifted a goose above the crowd. His left hand was holding the two legs, and his right hand was sliding up and down the neck, and he was pretending to pull off the head. Then I realised that that wasn't what he was pretending to do, and I felt a sense of disgust, a sense of shame; and my mind filled with snowflakes; and the crowd laughed again.

I booted a stone, but it wasn't a stone. It was a rounded lump on the corner of one of the cobbles. It stubbed my toe and I swore.

William giggled, and that made me mad, and I yelled: 'I tried! And that's more than you did.'

He turned to me and for a second I caught his eye. It was like looking into a pond that was still and cold and about to freeze over. I felt the chill that was in him, and I was ashamed of myself, and I said: 'You can have half of mine.'

He shook his head. 'I don't want it.'

I took a couple of steps. My toe hurt some more, and it made me hobble. 'Of course you do,' I said. 'It's what we agreed. So stop your bloody arguing,' and I rubbed at my toe. 'And anyway, I don't see why I should have to look after the lot.'

We pushed our way through the crowds and past the stalls with the bunches of dry herbs. The herbs scented the air and they filled my mouth with the taste of sage and rosemary and thyme; and I could smell stuffing-bread and roast fowl and giblet sauce and they made me feel hungry, starving hungry. I grabbed William by the arm and yelled in his ear: 'Come on! Let's get something to eat. And then we can look at London.'

His face broke into a smile, and he punched me on the arm and laughed and yelled: 'Who wants to look at London?'

I punched him back and I laughed with him. And all the fears that were bottled up inside me fizzed away, and left behind a calm, a flat calm, and I said: 'This is like those games we used to play.'

'Games?'

'When we were little boys.'

'And I was William.'

'And I was Hereward.'

'And you were hard to wake.'

'Wake?'

'Hereward the Wake. It was supposed to be a joke.'

I laughed and played with the words in my head, but I couldn't see the joke and I didn't know why I was laughing. He seemed to sense this, and he smiled and said: 'You used to get tired out, and want to sit down and go to sleep. And I had to carry you home. And I used to say you should be called Hereward the

Asleep. And you'd screw up your eyes tight and say: I'm not asleep. I'm Hereward the Wake. And then you'd go to sleep.'

I smiled at him and the past that was not the past I remembered, and then he said: 'If anybody asks me my name I'm going to tell them it's Fenton, William Fenton.'

I stopped and stared at him, and for a moment I wondered what my Father would say, and then I knew that it did not matter. And I laughed, and said: 'If you take my name you have to take my money,' and I held out my hand, and he smiled and nodded, and we shook on it.

26

We sat on the stone steps to the left of London Bridge and ate a smoked mackerel with two rolls of bread and a handful of dried plums. The tide was high and about to turn, and the water lay still at our feet. I knelt on the steps and cupped my hands and leant down to drink, and a fat turd floated by. It was cast in a spiral and it turned my stomach. I let the water trickle through my fingers, and I stood up and looked at William and said: 'I don't think I will.'

He shrugged and said: 'I told you we should have bought some milk. She had the cow tied up, and it would have been warm and straight from the udder. And you can't get it any fresher than that, can you?'

'No,' I said in a quiet voice, 'you can't. But that's not what we agreed, is it?'

He shrugged, and I could hear his voice in my head telling me that we would have to make our money last. We would have to drink water from the public conduit, and sleep outside, and buy nothing but food till one of us earned some more money.

'But I like milk,' he said. 'And my Mother used to say I should drink a lot of it because it was good for me.'

I started to laugh. 'Was this when you were a little baby, or a big baby?'

He began to grin, and then he laughed and gave me a shove on the arm. 'Did you ever think you'd really be here, in London, looking at London Bridge?'

My eye drifted along the stone arches of the first section of the bridge, and then along the next section with its stone piers and boats of stone encased in wooden buffers, and over six blocks of houses, and I began to grin. I couldn't help it. It was deep inside me and it came bubbling to the surface like a natural spring; and I said: 'Sometimes I did, and sometimes I didn't. But all the time I kept hoping and praying,' and I sat back and listened to the carts rumbling down Fish Street Hill, and I watched the drivers pay the early morning toll.

On the other side of the river, in Southwark, the houses looked old and they leant against each other. Their steep roofs were clad with tiles that might have been an earthen orange when they were new, but now they were mottled with ash, lichen and the grime of old age, and it looked as though nature were trying to reclaim them. The walls bulged with cross beams and uprights – painted black to match the windowframes – and the plaster between them was a dull white with a tinge of grey or brown. Not a single house was painted bright red. It was strange.

Mister Salthouse had been so precise in his sermons. These were the famous houses of Southwark: 'The scarlet houses of the scarlet women.' There was supposed to be a woman leaning out of every window, but I couldn't see a single one, and I felt disappointed.

I began to wonder if I had heard him right. Or had his words confused me, as they so often did when I was young? I began to think it might have something to do with the red light he said each woman hangs by her door at night. The red of the light would reflect on the white of the plaster and the white of her face. It would make her house into a scarlet house and it would make her into a scarlet woman. And like Eve in the days of the Garden of Eden, she would lead a man into temptation, and he would fall from grace; and later he would have to confess to what the prayerbook calls: 'Those things which we ought not to have done.'

For a moment I shut my eyes and shut out these sins of the night, and then I looked at the sky. It was a soft grey with a hint of brightness, and some of this brightness was beginning to wash the brown and the grey out of the plaster. It was restoring the white, and it was exposing my thoughts to the light of the day, and it was making a nonsense of them.

Then I knew in my head what I had known in my heart for a long time but never dared to put into words before: when the blood is pounding in a man's cock, it is pounding in his head, and that is what puts the red – the scarlet – before his eyes. It is not the fault of a woman. It is his own fault, and no prayer or penance will ever make the slightest difference. It is, as they say, in the blood.

Then Mister Salthouse came back into my mind, and I remembered the perversions of his thought, the private perversions when he and I were alone together and he said: 'A man can lead a man into sin, and he has no need of Eve, no need of the scarlet woman. The serpent is in his breeches, and it will rise again and again, and that is the resurrection of the flesh.'

And I remembered Mister Woodgate, and his book, and the martyr who died for the man who died on the cross. His book was printed in Southwark, in the land of the scarlet women, the women who are the whores of the night. The women, whom my sane mind was telling me would now be asleep, with the windows closed.

Then my mind drifted down the river.

Two small boats were edging into a quay on our side of the Thames, about a hundred yards away. As they touched the quay, they furled their sails and slung ropes around the bollards; and within a couple of minutes a sting of men were clambering on board and hoisting baskets onto their heads. The baskets looked like wicker hats, with a glint of silver in the crown.

As the men began to cross the quay, the seagulls found the baskets. They circled and screeched and swooped on the fish, and the glint of silver rose high in the air.

Then the sounds of shouting reached us, and William laughed, and nodded at the quay. 'That must be Billingsgate.'

'Or it could be the next one along, the U-shaped one that looks like a harbour.'

'There's a lot of room in there and they could tie up ten or twelve boats.' He yawned. 'Do you want to walk along and have a look?'

I shook my head. 'I can smell it from here, and that's enough for me,' and I closed my nose with my thumb and forefinger and pretended to lift it off my face. Then I saw some moss. It was growing in the shade beside the steps. It was bright green and a bit damp, and I pulled it free and squeezed it hard and said: 'If we put some of this in our shoes, it would take the hard edge off the pennies, and we wouldn't limp so much.'

A few minutes later, at the stalls near the bridge, he said: 'You're right. It is better. But it's a bit wet, and I don't like wet feet.' He paused for a moment. 'If we could buy one of those papers over there,' and he pointed to a paper stall, 'and stuff it in our shoes, we could have dry feet.'

I laughed. 'If you were a real Fenton, a real man of The Fens, you'd be used to wet feet, and you wouldn't complain.'

He gave me a hard stare. 'I seem to remember someone I know who used moan about wet feet all the time, and wasn't that one of the reasons he wanted to come to London?' And he gave me a shove.

I shoved him back, and then I started to laugh, and I looked at the paper stall and the old man who was sitting in a chair with his head against the wall. His eyes were closed and his mouth was open and his teeth looked like the black stumps I used to use to tie up my eel traps. And I said: 'How much is a paper?'

He shrugged and we tiptoed into the stall, and the man stayed asleep. The *London Gazette* sold for fourpence, and I said that was a lot for a sheet of paper that was printed on both sides and folded in half.

'This is cheaper,' William whispered, and he handed me a copy of the *London Reporter*. It was one sheet, smaller than the *Gazette* and unfolded. I said we'd need two of them, and as I stooped to place it back on the rack, I saw it was talking about houses. 'Listen to this,' I whispered. 'A census was taken a month ago and London still has 1,000 building plots available, and 3,500 new houses are still unoccupied, and the Lord Mayor of London has been asked to—'

He tapped me on the arm. 'Look at this.'

It was the *Ely Examiner*.

'Good God,' I whispered, 'I haven't seen one of them for ages.'

'And who'd want to read one here, in London?'

I shook my head, and slipped my paper back in the rack.

'There's a report here from the Mayor. He says they are going to repair some more of the causeway between Ely and Stuntney. And it's going to cost another sixty pounds. And here's something about digging some more drains by Wicken Fen; and he says the High Street should be cobbled.' He laughed to himself. 'He says that every winter, when the mud gets churned up. And in the summertime he complains about all the dust. But he never does anything about it.' He turned the paper over, and he was silent for a moment. Then he said: 'Here's something about the Bishop. Listen to this: "His Lordship the Bishop of Ely is now resident at Ely Place, Holborn, London, and persons wishing to petition His Lordship should write to him at this address."'

'Hmm,' I said, and I remembered the part the Bishop had played in our plan. He had played it in the mind of Mister Salthouse and he had played it without knowing that he was playing it. It was a mystical part, a magical part; and like a play, it was an act of the imagination. Then I remembered the last act: the act that never was. I wondered if I would have had the courage to knock on his door.

Then I remembered my Father and his empty pockets. And I remembered the tithes he paid through the hours of work he said were a waste of time and a waste of sweat. He paid them at the end of summer when the harvest was in. For him it was not a time of festival, it was a time of giving and a time of taking.

He gave and the Church took.

'And that's the way it's been,' he said to me, 'since that woman Etheldreda founded the abbey. And now they call it a cathedral and we have a Dean, a Chapter and a Bishop, but it hasn't made any difference. They want their money, and they want it every year. And don't go confusing what it says in the scriptures about rendering unto Caesar the things that are Caesar's, and unto God the things that are God's. Here in Elme, the Bishop of Ely is the Lord of the Manor. He is Caesar, and he wants the things of Caesar, and as for God . . . well . . . I suppose he renders unto Him the things that are His. But he doesn't do it here. He does it in London, and you and I pay for him to do it.'

This tithe of bitterness ran from generation to generation, like a river of brine. It had soured my Father, and his Father, and his Father's Father before him. And in time it would sour me. And it would sour the children who would be born of my body. It was a reason for leaving Elme. It was more powerful than anything to do with wet feet, or dry feet, or the seed that had flowed in our bed of pain. This was to do with the future. With the generations to come. With the flowing of sweet water. And it would not be taxed or tithed or rendered unto Caesar It would be a thing of the spirit. A thing of God. And for the first time I felt at ease with myself. I felt I knew why I had left Elme. And I turned to William and said: 'Is there anything else?'

'No. I don't think so. There's a list of clerical appointments,' and he ran his finger down the list, and then he stopped. 'Good Lord,' he said, in a voice that sounded more like a prayer than an exclamation. 'There's one here for Elme.'

I laughed, and leant over his shoulder. 'Is it still there? Or has it just vanished in some mysterious way?'

He smiled and pointed to a column in the left-hand corner.

I read to myself: 'The Reverend Mister Joseph Cotter has been appointed to the Parish of Elme with Emneth.' Then I said: 'I've never heard of him,' and I stole a glance at the man in the chair. He was still sound asleep.

I put fingers to my lips and William looked at the man and nodded, and I gestured for him to put the paper back in the rack. But he held it as if his hand and the paper had frozen solid, and he said: 'Christ Almighty! Listen to this: "The Reverend Mister Lawrence Salthouse, Master of Arts (Cambridge) and Bachelor of Theology (Oxford) of the Parish of Elme with Emneth is appointed Secretary to His Lordship the Bishop of Ely." And that means,' and his voice dropped to a whisper, 'he's living here in London, in Ely Place.'

I felt sick in my belly, and I swallowed hard. 'What does a secretary do?'

'Write letters. I think.'

I nodded and I thought of Mother. I saw her face. I saw the bruises and the swelling, and the pumpkin colour that came to her skin, and I said: 'I'd like to know what happened.'

He nodded, in a solemn way. 'Maybe you could write him a letter.'

I shook my head. 'I couldn't write what I want to say to him, and if I did, it would be a betrayal.'

'Betrayal?'

'Of her, and the things I promised to keep secret.'

He nodded. 'Then we should go and see him.'

'They wouldn't open the door to us. Not looking like this they wouldn't,' and I stretched out my arms. The dust and the dirt had browned my green coat, and it had greyed my black breeches. I sniffed, and I could smell myself and the pigs from the barn. And I could smell William. 'You bloody stink,' I said, and I laughed. He gave me a shove, a hard shove and I toppled against the stand, and I laughed again.

'We could go and sit by his door and wait,' he said. 'And when he came out he'd have to . . .'

'Are you going to buy that? Or are you just going to put your grubby fingers all over it?'

The man's voice screamed in my ear and it confused me, and I handed him the paper. He stretched out his hand and said: 'That'll be one penny.'

'I was just looking,' I said. 'I don't want to buy it.'

'And how am I to sell a paper that's already been read?'

I shook my head. His face was long and thin and his mouth was wide and it bowed like that of a snake and I felt it was about to swallow me. 'You've read the words,' he said. 'They've gone from the paper into your head,' and he tapped my head with his finger. 'You've sucked the meaning out of them. And now they're not worth as much to me as they were a few minutes ago,' and he grabbed my arm. 'So I want a halfpenny.'

I shook my head. 'A halfpenny? I don't have a halfpenny.'

'What?' and his teeth wobbled, and I remembered how the eels could pull out the stumps when they wobbled, and he said: 'You come to my stall. You read my papers. And you can't pay!'

I shook my head.

'Then I will have to think of some other way for you to pay, won't I?'

William came and stood beside me, and I could taste the mackerel. It was swimming up my throat and into my mouth.

'Let him go,' he said, and he raised his fist. 'Let him go.'

'You get out of my shop!' the man screamed at him. 'And don't come back.'

William shook his head. 'We arrived together and we're going to leave together. And you say you want a halfpenny before we can leave?'

'Yes, I do!'

'Right,' he said. 'I have a halfpenny here in my shoe, and it's all yours,' and he stamped on the man's foot.

The man screamed. His face flushed. And he hopped up and down.

William grabbed me by the coat and we ran up Fish Street Hill.

We slithered to a halt by a square on the right, and leant against a hoarding. It was made of wood and plaster and canvas and it covered half the footpath. We looked back towards the bridge and the stalls, and the man who was standing in the middle of the road shaking his fist at us, and William said: 'That was a pity.'

'Pity?'

'Hmm. He had a sign asking for "good reliable boys" to deliver papers every Tuesday and Thursday. And we could have done that. And we could have made some money.'

I shrugged. I would never have trusted a man like him, and I walked around the hoarding. It was the size of a house, a square house, and I could see what looked like an enormous chimney beginning to poke above the awning. A large sign was fixed to the hoarding. It bore the arms of the King, the same arms that hang in the Parish Church in Elme, and it read:

By ACT of PARLIAMENT,
this monument is being erected
to commemorate
THE GREAT FIRE OF LONDON
which began here on
September the Second 1666

And underneath, in black tar, someone had written:

THE PAPISTS DID IT AND
THEY SHOULD BE MADE TO PAY FOR IT!

William stood with me in silence for several seconds, then he said: 'You'd never know, would you, looking at it today?'

I shook my head. It was not the London that was pictured in my school book. That London was gone. This was the new London. The London of wide streets and flat-faced houses and paving stones. And cobbles. Never had I seen so many cobbles.

'There's enough here,' and I pointed to the cobbles around the monument and in the street beside it, 'to do all of the High Street in Ely. And maybe the Market Square.'

He nodded. 'It's so big you don't get a sense of proportion,' and he strode across the road and back again. 'It has to be fifty feet across. And it might even be a bit more.'

We wandered around for an hour or more in a dreamlike daze, and when we were somewhere near Leadenhall, I thought I caught sight of a black figure, a figure that was following us. And I said: 'I think I've seen John. In truth I think I've seen him half a dozen times.'

William laughed. 'You're so used to keeping an eye open for him, so used to making sure he's not behind you, that I think you're still doing it, like a habit. Like talking to yourself, when you think no one's around.'

I laughed and I felt my face flush, and I shrugged.

'I'll have a look for you,' he said, and he turned round and put his hands on his hips. He peered along the street and shaded his eyes with his right hand, and he shook his head. 'There's no one there,' and then he laughed. 'Apart from this lot who look as though they would like to shove us off the path.'

I nodded and hoped he was right, and about half an hour later a little boy came towards me. He was leading a goose. Someone had tied a red rope around its neck and under its wings and between its legs, and it looked like a harness. It had a white face and there wasn't a trace of lime in its feathers or tar on its feet.

I stopped and smiled, and said to the boy: 'He walked all the way from Norfolk and we walked with him.'

'He did nothing of the sort!'

I took a step backwards, and a brown cloak was flapping around in front of my eyes, and a woman said: 'His goose came from a farm in Bromley. It's a pet. A family pet. And we've had him for two years,' and she grasped the rope and steered the goose and the boy round me. I turned and watched her. To my surprise the boy turned and smiled, and I winked at him. I watched him for a moment or two longer, and as I lifted my eyes and went to turn, I saw that shape again. I grabbed at William, and I said: 'He is there. I just saw him again.'

He shook his head, and began to run. He dodged through the

crowds and past the woman with the boy and the goose, and past the spot where the shape had been, and then he walked back. He walked at a slow rate, and he let the crowds bump him along.

Then he looked me in the eye and shook his head again. And he touched my head, just above my right ear, and said: 'It's all in here,' and he ruffled my hair, and then he smiled.

We ambled on for a mile or more, and then he said: 'I want to talk about earning some money,' and I nodded. And he went on: 'I've been thinking of Mister Edwards, and what he said about the big houses in Covent Garden. And I think the kitchens would be like the ones at the choir school, and if I knocked on the back door, I could tell them what I've done, and maybe I could do some work for them.'

'And that would get you in out of the cold, and maybe they'd give you a bed for the night. And maybe they'd want me to give you a hand.'

'Are you any good at cleaning fatty dishes?'

I pretended to scrub and rinse a dish and hold it up to the light to see that it was clean, and he laughed, and we crossed the street in Cheapside and drifted along some more.

A small church caught my eye. It stood near the corner of Foster Lane. It was dedicated to Saint Vedast, and it looked brand-new. The stones on the side wall were rough-cut and thick with mortar. But the stones on the front, on the side that would always be seen from the lane, were smooth and the joins were straight and hard to see. The windows were large and rounded at the top and they filled the inside of the church with light. It reminded me of a small hall, or an assembly room.

I turned to William. 'The first churches must have been like this.' Then I thought of Ely Cathedral and the remnants of popery that still chain it to the past, and I said: 'The man who designed this has gone right back to the beginning, and it's pure and simple, like the gospels.'

He curled his lip and said: 'It's just a church. It's just a building with four walls and a roof, and one day they'll spend some more money, and then it will have a tower and a spire like that,' and he pointed to a drawing hanging on the wall.

The spire was topped with a ball and a weathervane that looked like a bird squashed flat and frozen in flight.

'And as far as I'm concerned,' he said, 'the money could be better spent on other things.'

I shrugged, and I tried to shrug away the sourness that was in him when it came to matters of the spirit. It was a sourness that reminded me of my Father, and in many ways it could have been him speaking. I suppose I shouldn't have been surprised. They are father and son, and it is natural that they should be alike in some ways. But I had closed my mind to the sameness that was within them, and I had accepted that Simon was Simon, and William was William, and that was that. But now it was plain before my eyes and I didn't like it. And it was nothing to do with Simon or William, it was to do with my Father, and it raised in me a feeling of sourness too, a feeling that made me the kin of both of them.

In silence I walked out of the church and down the steps and into the lane, and I ran my fingers over the stone at the front of the church. It looked white with a softening of grey, and I traced the faint outlines of the shells that were caught in it, and I knew that I too was caught, and I said: 'I have to go to Ely Place.'

27

The ruins of old Saint Paul's stood gaunt against the sky. The great fire had consumed the roof and the innards, and now the pillars that used to hold up the tower were to be pulled down.

The men had built a wooden scaffolding to the height of seven or eight storeys, and from there they were climbing up ladders and ropes, and picking away at the stones with axes, chisels and hammers. Some of the stones were still blackened from the fire; and the weeds that had flowered in the summer were now hanging in clumps, and they looked like pale gingery beards. Through my half-closed eyes the beards belonged to black faces, gargoyle faces with water-spout mouths drawn into tight smiles. The smiles were smug or complacent, and they gave me the impression that they knew something the men did not know.

For a long time nothing seemed to happen, and the crowd muttered and mumbled, and grew impatient. Then some rock broke free and fell on the scaffolding, and it swayed, and a woman clapped and the man behind me cheered in my ear. I turned round and grinned at him, and he said: 'At this rate I'll have to live to be a hundred to see the new Saint Paul's.'

I laughed and said: 'What's the new cathedral going to look like?'

He shrugged. 'I don't know. I hear they can't make up their minds.'

Then William tapped me on the shoulder. 'Come on,' he said, 'we could be here all day and still see nothing come down,' and he pushed me through the crowd.

I half turned and looked back at the men, and I knew what

the gargoyles knew: they weren't going to budge. And I said: 'They need a battering ram.'

'Or a few barrels of gunpowder.'

'You'd blow out all those windows,' and I pointed to the new houses.

He shrugged, and we drifted along Cheapside, and past the shops with their rolls of cloth, and their shelves of blue and white plates, and he said: 'We could be going the wrong way. I think we should ask someone.'

I shook my head. 'We're sure to see a sign,' and we wandered along Cornhill and into Gracechurch Street. Then something began to feel familiar and I said: 'This looks like the road to the bridge.'

Willian looked up and down the road, and he nodded, and then I saw a sign. The end was arrowed, and it read: 'BISHOPSGATE'.

'Let's go as far as that,' I said, 'and if we don't see a sign to Holborn we can ask someone.'

We walked in silence for a few minutes, and then the names began to ring in my head: Fish Hill Street, Gracechurch Street and Bishopsgate. I stopped and looked around.

'What's the matter?'

'I think Mister Woodgate lives around here somewhere. On the left going up from the bridge, that's what he said. And right next to a tavern.' I ran my eye along the street, but I couldn't see any hanging signs, and I remembered reading they had been taken down because of the fire risk.

'Does it have a name?'

'Hmm,' I said, 'but I can't remember what it was.'

'Can't remember?'

'I didn't take much notice. I didn't intend to go looking for him.'

'Why not?'

'Why not?' and I paused to think. 'Because I don't want him to do that to me again.'

'I thought you said you liked it.'

'I did.'

'And what's wrong with doing it again?'

'It's wrong.'

'Wrong?'

'It's not what God intended. When he created Adam and Eve.'

He stopped and we stood about four inches apart, almost nose to nose, ignoring the people pushing around us. 'I don't give a fuck about Adam and Eve. And if Mister Woodgate wants to suck my cock, he can. And I don't think there's anything wrong with it.'

I broke his gaze and stalked ahead, and then I stopped and turned. 'Yes there is,' I said, and I could feel the heat in my face. 'A cock is for pissing. And a cock is for fucking. That's what a cock is for.'

Then I saw a woman looking at me. Her mouth was wide open and the colour was seeping out of her face. I covered my mouth with my hands, and I shook my head like a dog shaking off water, but I couldn't shake off her stare, and she made me feel like a fool, and I turned away from her.

'So when you play with yourself,' he said, 'at night, when you don't think I can see you, that's not fucking, is it? So it's wrong. And you shouldn't do it.' And then he laughed. 'But it's all right for me to do it because I don't think it's wrong.'

I felt the anger boiling up inside me. 'A sin is a sin,' I said. It was the same cold logic that Mister Salthouse employed in his sermons. And there was no love in it. And it drove me on to say: 'And no amount of thinking, or wishing, or denying what is obvious to every man will make right into wrong, or wrong into right.'

'I don't think it's a sin. And I don't think it's a matter of right or wrong. And if he wants to do it again, as far as I'm concerned he bloody well can. And the sooner the better.' And he gave me a hard look. 'And I'll tell you something else. You've been to church too much. And you've listened to too much rubbish. That's the trouble with being a choirboy. It fucks your mind.'

The shock of his words and the madness of his logic exploded in my head, and without thinking I hurled across the road and stormed up the footpath – on my own.

I stood at Bishopsgate and watched the carts trundle along the road that had brought us to London. I remembered Mister Edwards saying the Romans had built the road, and in my mind

I saw our geese again – they were still alert and bright-eyed – and they calmed me.

And I remembered Mister Edwards thinking there was something wrong with William – something he didn't understand – and I began to have the same feeling. It was something obvious. Something I had been told. But I couldn't think what it was. And it began to niggle at me, the way a boil does when it's still growing and it's red and there's no sign of puss or whiteheads that can be squeezed.

Then William came and stood beside me and said: 'I found the tavern. It's called The Three Crowns. I remembered you saying the name as soon as I saw it. And I've found his place. He has a sign painted on his windows. And I'll tell you something that will surprise you: he has a couple of sons.'

I followed him down Bishopsgate and our friendship began to mend. To me our friendship was like a sheet of ice. It had broken and we had drawn apart. But now as we walked in silence the break closed and joined and healed, as it does with ice. But it left a line, a weakness that had not been there before.

He stopped and pointed to a small door. It was down an alley that was no more than three or four feet wide, and hanging above it, half-hidden in the shadows, was a wooden sign with three crowns.

The building at the front of the tavern ran to twenty paces and it rose to four storeys. The frontage was glassed above waist height, and the door in the left-hand corner was open and latched to the wall inside the shop. It was a shop in the sense that it had a table and three chairs, and a low bench and two men standing behind a counter. But there was nothing on display. There was nothing for sale. And there were no signs, or prices or invitations to buy.

The writing on the window was hard to read. It had been lettered onto the small panes of glass, and these had buckled in their lead mountings, and as the light caught the various angles it made the black lettering vanish. I stepped back to the edge of the footpath and stood by the bollards that keep the carriages off the path and I read:

A. & J. WOODGATE & SONS
Merchants & Purveyors of Imported Goods
Contractors to the Navy Office
& Suppliers to the Gentry
Established: AD 1635
Offices in London & Plymouth

'It must have been established by his father,' I said. 'And he'll be the A. in the sign, and our Mister Woodgate will be the J., and I suppose the man behind the counter, the young one with the cropped hair, he'll be one of the sons.'

'And what about the old one?'

'I don't know. He's too old to be his son and too young to be his father. He could be a clerk.'

'What do they do?'

'They keep the books.'

'I could keep the books.'

'It doesn't mean to look after the books. It means you write down everything that's bought and sold. And you record the prices. And then you add up all the figures and you know how much money you've made.'

He gave me a slow gentle nod, and I could see the words sinking deep into his head, and then he smiled and stood on the stone step and peered into the shop. I took his arm and pulled him away. 'You know what they say about temptation,' I said.

He shrugged, and let me lead him away. In my head we crossed the ice that was our friendship, and it held.

I called out to a man who was ambling along: 'How do you get to Holborn?' He pointed towards Cheapside, and I said: 'Thank you,' and he gave me a smile, a lopsided smile that sucked me into a mouth with no teeth.

In Cheapside another man sent us on towards Newgate.

On the other side of the gate, beyond the rules and regulations that order life within the city, a pedlar stood in the sunshine. She was displaying her tray of wares. It hung from a ribbon around her neck. It was bright with colour and some of the tiny things that looked like thimbles, were picking up the sun and they filled my eyes with glitter. 'Could you tell me the way to Holborn?' I said to her.

'Holborn. Whereabouts in Holborn?'

'Ely Place'

'My,' she said, 'that is a grand address. And would I be right in thinking you might be from Ely? And you might be going to see the Bishop?'

I smiled and nodded, and I warmed to her.

'And might I also be right in thinking this is your first visit to London?'

'Yes.'

'And you, sir,' and she smiled at William, 'is this also your first time in London?'

'Yes.'

'In that case,' and she lowered her voice, 'I think I should let you into a secret.' We both stepped a little closer. 'There is an old custom, you might call it a tradition, that a man on his first visit to London, to the greatest city in the whole world, buys a gift, a little gift to take home to his mother.'

'My Mother's dead,' William said, and his face drooped and his eyes clouded.

'Oh,' she said, 'I'm so sorry. And you so young,' and she shook her head and patted him on the arm. Then she looked at me. 'And your mother? Is she still alive and well?'

'Yes,' I said, and in my mind I could see her as clear as clear. She was smiling at me. And I wanted a gift, I wanted something to give to her.

'Then you'll be wanting something for her. Something not too dear. But something nice. Something she can't get in Ely. A little mirror,' and she held it up to my face. 'Or a hairbrush,' and she pretended to brush her own hair. 'Or a pair of scissors,' and she snipped the air.

The scissors were about six inches long. They were pointed, and they were just what my Mother would like. In my head I could hear her voice, I could hear her saying: 'If they were pointed,' and she was fingering her old scissors, the small ones with the blunt end, 'if they were pointed I could cut the threads so much closer, and all this darning,' and she waved her hand at the socks and the shirts and the breeches that needed mending, 'it would look like new. And no one would know that it was darned.' And then she smiled at me and her face drifted back into the past.

'How much are they?'

She took a red ribbon and she held it towards me and cut off about half-an-inch. 'See how they cut. Clean and quick. And no tearing or pulling. You don't get that with a cheap pair of scissors. These are quality scissors. These are scissors for a lady,' and she leant towards me. 'And these are only threepence.'

'Threepence!' William said with a shriek. 'We could eat for two days for threepence.'

'Hmm,' I said, 'but they're just what she wants, and I'd like—'

'Then buy them when it's time to go home. That's the sensible thing to do.'

The lady nodded and said: 'He's right. That is the sensible thing to do,' and William smiled at her. 'But let me tell you something. In this city there are hundreds of things to tempt a young man. Things he'll never see in Ely. And I've seen the young men. I've seen them in their hundreds. They give in to temptation and they spend their money, and when it comes time to go home they haven't got any money. And they can't buy their mothers a present. And they go home contrite and shame-faced, and they don't have a gift for their mother. And I wouldn't care to be in their shoes. Not if I loved my mother I wouldn't.' And then she smiled. 'And the sensible man is the man who buys his present when he first comes to London, because that's when he's got some money in his pocket. And I'll tell you what,' and she came so close I could smell the garlic on her breath, 'I'll let you have them for tuppence. Now, I can't say fairer than that. Can I?'

I dug in my pocket and pulled out a halfpenny and a farthing.

I turned to William. 'Have you got any money in your pocket?'

A look of disgust came over his face and he pulled out a penny and a halfpenny, and she took the money from us.

'I'll show you something,' she said, 'and it'll only cost you that extra farthing.' She cut off a length of green ribbon and tied one end to the scissors and the other end to a loop on my breeches. 'This is a secret. A secret weapon. You slip them in your pocket with the point down, and if anyone attacks you, you pull them out and stab him like this,' and she stabbed the air. 'And because they're tied on, you won't lose them.'

William began to giggle and shake his head.

She turned to me. 'Your friend doesn't believe me, does he?'

I shrugged, and fingered the scissors in my pocket. The point felt sharp, as sharp as the point used to be on my Father's scythe.

Then she smiled at William, and flicked a pair of scissors out of her pocket and stuck the point to his throat. The smile died on his face and the red drained out of his cheeks.

She slipped the scissors and the ribbon that tied them to her coat, back into her pocket, and she turned to me. 'You have to learn how to do it. Practice. That's what it takes. And look the person in the eye when you do it. It gives them a terrible fright, and it loosens their bowels. As I'm sure your friend will tell you.'

William ground his teeth and grabbed me by the sleeve. 'Come on,' he said, 'before you buy anything else we don't need.'

She gave me a nod. 'Ely Place. You were asking about Ely Place. Some call it Ely Palace. You keep going straight up there, for about half a mile, and it's on the right.'

28

Ely Place clustered around two chapels, and at first glance it looked like a small village. Some of the buildings were of wood, and some were of stone with slate roofs and battlements, and a feeling of decay – of neglect – seemed to have settled upon them. Even the coat of arms, which was carved in stone and set above the door, had suffered the weathering of the years; and now the heraldic quarterings, the symbols of pride, the symbols of possession, were nothing more than vague shapes.

For a while I stood and watched the smoke drift among the brick chimneys, and I remembered my Father saying: 'We paid for Ely Place, we did, and by rights it should belong to us and not the Bishop and not the King who took it off him.' When I was little, I couldn't make much sense of this. But as the years passed, and the repetition of these words became part of the annual ritual that accompanied the paying of the tithes, I came to know that 'we' did not mean my Father and me. It meant all the generations of our family who had lived and died in Elme, and paid their tithes to the Bishop of Ely.

The King in my Father's story was Henry VIII. The name of the Bishop has slipped my mind, but I do remember that when the King was intent on reforming the Church and breaking the power of Rome, he bent to the will of the King.

Today our Bishop still bends to the will of the King, but he has managed to slip back into Ely Place. It is not the place it used to be, for his rights are much reduced, and now our tithes can only lay claim to a few rooms and a private chapel, and that, in the words of my Father, is like robbing the dead. It is a grave crime, a grave injustice.

He could not recognise the humour that lay buried within his words, and I had to keep a sober face, and after a moment or two I was able to say: 'But it led to the Church being reformed, and now the purity of the past has been returned to us, and popery is banned and we can read the Word of God for ourselves, in English. And we don't have foreign priests telling us what to do, and what to think.'

'Hmm,' he said. 'It is a freedom of sorts. A freedom to think, and you'll always have it, up here,' and he tapped his head. 'But what you won't have, and what you're not going to get back, are the tithes we paid. They're gone. They're the price we had to pay for King Henry and his greed, and just remember that freedom is a strange thing: it does not always allow you to say what you think in public, and it does not allow you to break the law. And all things considered,' and he paused, 'I would prefer to have the tithes, or the things they could have bought for us.'

I let these memories drift back into the past where they belonged and I watched a carriage come into Ely Place. It was painted black, and drawn by two black horses. The driver had perched himself at the front, on the edge of the roof, and he had wrapped himself in a black cloak and a black hat. His face was white and his flesh was stretched, and if I had wanted to paint a picture and call it *The Visitation of Death*, I could not have found a more perfect model.

Six men with brown leather coats, cream breeches, black shoes and iron helmets, marched behind the carriage. Each of them carried a pike on his right shoulder. The pikes were about twelve feet long, and topped with a long spike and a metal barb, and they reminded me of the gaffs fishermen use when they want to land a big fish.

I began to wonder what sort of a big fish could afford a carriage like this. I thought of the grouper, the big black grouper. We learnt about it when we learnt about the colonies and the plantations, and the strange things people have to eat in the Americas. The crudeness of the name – when shortened to groper – had amused me, and it stuck in my mind, as crudeness does, and now it brought a smile to my lips.

Then the driver spread his arms and pulled on the reins, and the carriage came to a halt beside a small door. The door opened and Mister Salthouse came out.

My smile slipped away, and my mouth gaped.

I suppose I should have been prepared for him, but in truth I wasn't, and as I stood and stared, he opened the carriage door and another man – an older man with robes of black and white and red – walked out of the house and stepped into the carriage.

Mister Salthouse followed him into the carriage, and shut the door and pulled down the blinds.

The men shouldered their pikes and paired off again, and as the carriage began to roll, they picked up the pace of the horses and they began to trot.

In less than a minute they were gone, and the whole thing took on an eerie feeling. It was as if we had somehow been in the face of death, or the face of the bringer of death, and I could make no sense of it.

I turned to William. 'Did you see him?'

He nodded. 'He's more confident. He's put away the past, and I suspect he thinks it doesn't matter any more.'

I looked at him and bit my lips. 'It doesn't,' I said. 'Not now it doesn't,' and I thought how well the word groper would have fitted Mister Salthouse in the days gone by. I walked over to the door and looked at the plaque.

THE BISHOP OF ELY
Petitioners, and persons having business with His Lordship,
will be received in the first instance
by His Lordship's secretary.
From 10 o'clock to 12 noon
except on Sundays and Holy Days of Obligation.

I turned away from the plaque and whatever a Holy Day of Obligation might be, and as we walked back to Newgate, William said: 'We have to look for some work. And it's no good putting it off. So I think we should go to Covent Garden, right now. And I suggest I ask the way, and then we won't waste any more money.'

I pulled a face to myself and fingered the scissors. They still felt sharp, and they reassured me, and I did not think I had wasted my money.

Then the pedlar spied us, and she waved and smiled. We waved and smiled, and William took a firm grip on my elbow, and we crossed to the other side of road.

Covent Garden, or Convent Garden as I heard some people pronounce it, was not a garden. It was a square of pink houses. The houses on the east side and the north side enclosed a long walkway that was arched and filled with shadows. Each house looked like its neighbour and each lay to the sun. To me they had lain there too long, for the sun had burnt them, and much of the pink was red, and it hurt my eyes. In a strange way these houses were just like the ones Mister Salthouse used to describe in such loving detail when he preached against the pleasures of the flesh.

In the middle of the west side, pushed high by its neighbours, stood the church of Saint Paul. It did not look like a church. It looked like a Roman temple, like a place where false gods might be worshipped in the privacy of the past. It made me think of Rome and Spain and Queen Mary – Bloody Mary – and I saw the stake and the fire, and the chopping block that waited for the men who could not renounce the faith they had reformed.

I could not have died for my faith. I do not have that measure of courage that some would call a measure of madness.

I let my mind slip back from the past and I looked away from the Church that asks so much of us, and my eyes wandered along the stone wall that enclosed the south side of the square.

A square white stone was set in the middle of the wall, at eyelevel. It was inscribed with black letters, and I thought they were painted on, but as I came closer I could see that the letters had been cut into the stone and then filled with paint. They said:

THIS WALL
BORDERS THE PROPERTY OF
THE EARL OF BEDFORD

Behind the wall lay the Earl's house. In front of the wall, and spilling into the central part of the square that was fenced and closed to horses, lay the dregs of the morning market.

It appeared to be a market for fruit and vegetables, and the cabbages and the winter greens were being shouted down to half price. I looked at some late plums. They were polished purple, and I fingered one, and William moved me on before I could say a word.

To the side a man was fitting wicker baskets into one another and stringing them onto a waterseller's yoke. Next to him another man was folding up an awning, and another was emptying the ashes out of a roasting tray and tying up his sack of chestnuts.

I remember once when I was young, thinking about my Mother's eyes, thinking how they looked like burnt chestnuts: hot with sparks and hot with anger. I could still see that anger, and I could still hear it in her voice. And the water that drained from The Fens and made them into fields had never been able to put out that anger. From the past two names came into my mind, two names that always sparked her anger. The first was Vermuyden: the Dutchman, the digger of ditches, the man who dyked her precious water and sent it to the sea. The other was a man of money, a man of shadows, a man who was never given the title of 'Mister'. His name was Bedford.

I began to feel cold, to feel the chill of a winter that was still to come. I turned and walked back to the stone in the middle of the wall, and I read the name again: Bedford.

I felt her anger. I felt her hate. And I felt the despair that this man had brought to The Fens. In my mind I saw him drain more of the wetlands. I saw the water flow into the two great rivers that bear his name. And I saw the fish and the eels that were left behind on the drying mud. I saw them wriggle and seethe and gasp for water, and die in their thousands. For a week or two they would feed our hungry mouths, and when they were gone they would breed no more. And the wildfowl would look for the water that was not there, and they would fly on to feed and breed in other places. And our mouths, our empty mouths, would open and shut and feel the pangs of hunger.

Many of the men who used to walk the waters must now walk the land. And food that was once free must now be earned. And so they plough the land and sow the seed and cut the corn, and it does not profit them. It profits the men in London: the men with money. To them it was an adventure: an act of creation. To us it was a death: an execution. And it ended the life that had been ours since the beginning of time.

The hate and the anger that was bred in those days when the drainage began live on in my Mother. They live on in my Father. And they live on in me.

I looked at the stone: at black Bedford. And I spat on it. I spat on him, and his money. It was Fen money. And it built his wall, his house, his square, and God knows: it might have built his church too.

I turned my back on the stone and the past that was locked in hate and anger, and I looked at William.

He was watching three girls. They had been walking around the square selling flowers from the baskets they carried over their arms. Now they were clumped together with their heads touching, like dead sunflowers at the end of summer.

I tapped him on the shoulder and said: 'We can't put it off any longer,' and he gave me a curt nod.

One of the girls straightened up and looked towards us, and she said something to the other two and they began to giggle.

William giggled – and I wondered if the air were infectious – and then he said: 'I like the look of the one with the dark hair,' and he grabbed my arm. We followed them along the walkway and into James Street, and he kept whispering in my ear, kept telling me what he'd like to say to her – do to her – and I began to laugh. Then an old man with a cart full of flowers pulled up and they clambered on, and the girl with the dark hair hung her arm over the side and wiggled her fingers at us.

William looked at me and grinned, and I laughed at him, and I pointed to the lane that led to the back of the houses. It was not like other lanes in the city. It was wide and cobbled, and edged with high stone walls and wooden gates.

We opened the first gate. The garden was large. The grass had been scythed and the paths had been filled with cockleshells. To the left the stable doors were open and to the right a flight of steps took my eye up to the back door. It looked safe – almost welcoming – and we stepped onto the path and crunched the cockles. Within a second, a large dog was barking and hurling towards us. We scrambled back to the lane and slammed the gate.

The next house had a dog on a chain that ran along the path, and we looked at each other and shut the gate. At the next house the gates were locked; and they couldn't hear us knocking.

At the fourth house we walked up the path and under the trees – the leaves had fallen and a boy was raking them into a pile – and William knocked on the door. A man in a red livery opened the door, looked us both up and down, and pointed to the gate. Then he shut the door without saying a word.

At the fifth house the man yawned and said: 'Yes?'

'We're looking for work,' William said.

The man shook his head, and yawned again and shut the door.

The next house was locked up, and at the one after that William said: 'I used to work in the kitchens at the choir school and I was wondering if I could come and work for you. I can bake bread and carve meat and scour pans and . . .'

The man smiled. It was a tired smile, and he looked as though the years had worn him out. 'You're not from here, are you?'

William shook his head.

'In this house they like the servants to speak the way they speak. And they like them to be clean and tidy, and it's much the same for all the rest around here,' and he waved his hand towards the other houses. 'And if I were you I wouldn't go knocking on any more doors till I'd had a bath, and a haircut, and changed my clothes,' and he smiled. 'I can smell you from here.'

In silence we walked back to the city, and in through Bishopsgate, and William said: 'I wasn't expecting it to be as hard as this.'

I don't know what I was expecting. My eyes had been so set on getting to London, I hadn't thought, or looked, beyond that moment. I felt the coins in my shoe, and I said: 'We still have our money, and tomorrow we can go to Westminster and see if they want us to row. They say there are hundreds of boats down there, and we might have some luck.'

He gave me a nod and turned away, and I could sense his disappointment. I ambled towards a sign. It was tall and thin and nailed to a wall inside a porch, and the shadows made it hard to read. After a few moments I could make out the words:

Chapel of
The Ancient and Honourable
Guild of
WARRENMASTERS

I called to him: 'What on earth is a warrenmaster?'

He came and looked over my shoulder. 'They breed rabbits in warrens. So I suppose he's a rabbit farmer.'

It sounded right, and I nodded, and cast my eye down the rest of the sign:

Dedicated in AD 1439 to
SAINT ANNE
and
SAINT MARY THE VIRGIN

The Guild meets here
at 12 noon
on the first Sunday of every month.

The Annual Tithe for
the relief of indigent brethren
is collected on the
26th of July,
which day was kept in ancient times
as the Feast Day of
Saint Anne.

I remembered that Anne was the mother of Mary, and I began to wonder how a virgin could have a baby and be a mother if she hadn't done what Aunt Mary and I had done. I turned to William to ask him what he thought, and I saw Aunt Mary looking out from his face, and the question died on my lips.

He looked at me in a bemused fashion. I took a breath and I said: 'I was thinking of your mother. It must have been the name Mary,' and I pointed to the sign.

He laughed. 'And I was thinking of your mother.'

'My Mother?'

He pointed to the sign. 'Her name is Anne, isn't it?'

I had to stop and think. I called her Mother and so did my Father. In the village they called her Mistress Fenton. If anybody ever came to see her they told me to fetch my Mother, and I could never recall her having a name of her own. I said: 'I'm not sure.'

'Anne,' he said, with a firm nod of his head, 'that's what my Mother calls her – or used to call her.' He bit his lips and looked away, and then he said: 'I'm sorry. I know she's dead, but I still keep thinking of the things I want to tell her, and then I remember that I can't tell her anything. And I see her lying in that grave of hers, and I can feel all that earth weighing her down, and I start to choke, right here,' and he touched the hollow at the base of his throat.

He turned away from me, and blew his nose. Then he turned back. 'Would you mind,' he asked, 'if I walked on my own for a while? It helps sometimes, to be alone.'

I looked at the cobbles and for a moment or two my eyes followed the tracks that the cart wheels had worn in them, and then I said: 'If that's what you want.'

He nodded, and I said we could meet by the pillars at old St Paul's, before the dark blacked out our faces.

He nodded again and gave me a weak smile and his shoulders slumped.

Then he walked away – with a slight limp – and I wondered if I would be like him when my Mother died. I hoped I would be stronger, but I remembered how I had felt in those few seconds when I thought she had died, and I began to think that I would be just like him.

Then I thought of Aunt Mary. She was strong. As strong as those pillars. And I remembered how she had healed me, and I looked at the scar on my arm. It was now no more than a faint line. And I remembered the nights in her bed, and the nights in front of the fire with Simon, and the night Mister Woodgate came. It was the night I read to him. And I heard her words again, I heard her say: 'I'm sorry but he can't read.'

The 'he' was Simon. Was William. And 'he' could read. 'He' could read as well as I could.

This was what I had known deep in my mind. It had been niggling away at me all day, and now, like a ripe boil it burst and filled my mind with puss. I could smell the stench. The sweet sick-making stench that is the stench of rotting flesh. And I knew that she who is now corrupt in her grave, had been corrupt in her words.

She had lied to Mister Woodgate. And she had lied to me who heard her words. But why did she lie? And why did she want to protect him?

I felt betrayed – for I had paid the price of that lie – and I knew that William's mouth would have to become her mouth, and it would have to speak the truth for her.

It would be the price of our friendship. The price of ice that can be walked upon in a time of thaw.

29

I walked to the Tower of London, and along the quays and around the moat and up to Tower Hill. My feet ached and my belly ached. The day had tired me out and I was sick of the sights. I wanted to eat and curl up and go to sleep. I thought about our money, and I knew we had spent enough for one day, but then I smelt the smell of hot bread. It came drifting towards me in waves. I breathed it in but it did not stop the ache, and somehow I found myself standing in front of the bakehouse looking at the pies. They were big, bigger than both my hands put together and the pastry was thick and crusted, and the baker said I could have one for a farthing. I shook my head and he shrugged and I walked away. But the ache would not go away, and I thought of William and that lie that his silence had confirmed; and I bought a pork pie.

It was hot and the steam burnt my nose. It made me think of my Mother and the number of times she had told me not to stick my nose in where it didn't belong. I smiled to myself, and I licked my finger and tried to wet away the pain.

I sat for an hour or more and watched the gleam of the sun die on the banks of mud that line both sides of the Thames. Then I saw the tide rise and drown the banks, as it drowns the paths in The Fens in winter, and when it was dusk and the brown water lay before me like a wet sheet on the grass, I began to make my way to old Saint Paul's. The dusk surprised me. It settled into darkness much faster than it does in the countryside where the hills bump along the horizon, and it brought a sameness, a confusing sameness to every street.

I looked for the pillars of old Saint Paul's. They tower above the roofs to a height of a hundred feet or more, and I couldn't see a sign of them. I kept wondering if the men had pulled them down. But that didn't seem possible, and I began to think I might have taken a wrong turn, and I might be walking away from them instead of towards them.

Then I walked into the hands of a man who was standing right in front of me.

'I'm sorry,' I mumbled, 'I didn't see you.'

He gripped me with both his hands, and he lifted me up in the air and he set my heart pounding. I opened my mouth to scream, and the scream died on my lips.

It was John.

I breathed a loud sigh of relief. 'God,' I said. 'I'm glad it's you. I was dead scared. I thought I was going to be robbed.'

He lowered me to the ground and held out his hand.

I stretched out my hands and turned them over to show that they were empty.

He took his stick, and in the slick of mud that had settled and dried on the cobblestones, he wrote 'MONEY'.

I felt sick, as if I had vomited deep in my stomach. I trembled and my hands shook. They betrayed the fear that was rising within me. 'John,' I said, 'it's me. It's Martyn. Look at me. I'm your friend.' But my words were useless, as useless as the meowing of an unwanted kitten that is about to be drowned.

I looked into his eyes. They were dark grey and overcast, like a sky before a storm. Then I smelt the beer on his breath, and I tried to pull away.

He held me tight, and forced his hand into my pockets. Then he pushed me to the ground and pulled off my shoes, and he took all my pennies and all my halfpennies.

I felt as if I had been raped by a friend. A false friend.

He ran his club through his fingers, and he spun it in the air and he caught it, as jugglers do at the fair. Then he lunged and wacked me on the back of the head.

I sat rocking from side to side, and the lane filled up with mist. It was bright yellow as if it had been dyed with the saffron from Walden.

Then I was sick.

Bits of chewed pork and pie-crust stuck to my breeches and

my shirt and my coat. The smell of it was in my nose, and I could see John and his stick. His lips were moving and I heard him say: 'He won't hit me on the head again, will he?'

He giggled to himself and then he staggered down the lane, and just beyond the black gap, where it looked as if two or three houses had been burnt down, he held out his arm and he stopped a man. He bent over and wrote in the mud with the thin end of his stick. The man shook his fist at him, and John felled him with one blow. I saw him sit beside the man, and then the mists grew thicker and I toppled over. I do not know what happened next.

Sometime on the following day, when the sun was high in the sky and the thunder in my head eased for a moment or two, I tried to stand up. My hands swam in the air and my legs bowed, and I sank back to the ground and drowned in the darkness.

On the morning of the next day I crawled out of the cellar that had wrapped itself around me like a coffin, and I shuffled through the ashes and the burnt beams, and I breathed hard and stopped myself being sick again, and I sat on the cobbles.

William found me about an hour later.

We held each other, and swayed and cried, and he said my pride was hurt. I said it was my head that was hurt, and he smiled and took my arm, and we began to walk. Then he pointed to the sign that read Seething Lane, and he laughed and said it matched my mood.

In the night we stood on the steps of an empty house and peered through the window and tapped on the glass. A man's voice came from behind us and it said: 'I wouldn't break in there if I were you. They hang them for that, they do. And your neck is much too young to stretch,' and he ran his fingers up my neck, and my flesh crept after them. When I turned round he was a shape in the dark, and then he was gone.

I looked at William, and I took his hand and I held it tight.

We slept in an old cellar. It was cold and damp and I woke with a chill in my bones. I stood up and rubbed my hands and tried to warm myself. The noise disturbed William. He rolled over and yawned, and then he took off his shoes and he counted his money. He had two pennies, one halfpenny and one farthing.

He looked at them for a long time and then he handed me a penny and a halfpenny, and said: 'I think we should find Mister Edwards and John. And we should tell him what John did. And we should ask for our money back.'

'He won't give it back. You can never make him do anything he doesn't want to do.'

'I don't mean John. I mean Mister Edwards. He'll make John give the money back.'

'And what if he's spent it?'

'We can ask Mister Edwards for some more.'

'He won't give us any more. He'll say we had our money, and we had to look after it. And this is nothing to do with him.'

'Well, I think he has a moral obligation.'

'A what?'

'A moral obligation. It's a sort of command, from up there,' and he pointed to the sky, 'to do what is right and just. And it means he should repay the money John stole from you.'

'I think you're dreaming.'

'You can think what you bloody like,' and he glared at me. 'Do you have a better idea?'

I shook my head.

'Then we're going to Leadenhall. And we're going now. And if I've worked it out right, this should be his last day.'

The market was crowded.

We found Mister Edwards standing on a barrel shouting: 'Get your goose here! You won't be getting any more. Not this year you won't.'

An old lady waved at him and he eased himself off the barrel and opened up one of the cages and pulled out a goose. He broke its neck with a casual flick of his hand and handed the goose to her. She laid it in her basket and tucked it under her arm. As she walked away the neck slipped out of the basket and it swung from side to side. 'It's having one last look,' William said, and I tried to laugh but it hurt the back of my head.

We edged around the crowd looking for John but there was no sign of him. And I felt a little better.

We pushed through the crowd and William tapped Mister Edwards on the leg.

He looked down from his barrel. 'Do you want a goose?' he asked. Then he recognised William. 'Oh, it's you,' he said, and he leant his hand on William's shoulder and slid off the barrel. 'I thought I had another customer.'

William laughed and shook his head, and Mister Edwards lifted his hat and wiped his brow. 'Christ,' he said, 'this is hot work when you're on your own,' and he took a deep breath. 'I shouldn't be doing this, not at my age I shouldn't.'

He wiped his brow again. 'I wish you'd come along yesterday. You could have helped me. And I could have given you tuppence or maybe threepence. It would have been worth it.' Then he took another breath, and I could hear the sigh in it, and he said: 'You haven't seen John, have you? I don't know where he is. He didn't come back in time to go to Billingsgate and I've looked all over the place and no one's seen him.' Then he noticed me, and without waiting for William to reply, he said: 'Christ Almighty! What the hell happened to you?'

'John attacked him,' William said, 'and he stole all his money.'

'John?' His voice rose like a trumpet and it shrieked disbelief. 'John wouldn't do that. Not to you he wouldn't,' and he shook his head.

'It was him,' I said. 'It was almost dark, but I know it was him. I recognised him.'

He looked away from me. 'John would get drunk. And John would clip you round the ear if you tried to steal a goose. But he wouldn't take your money. I've never told you this before, but I keep my money in a bag and I tie it round his waist and I cover it with his shirt. And he never touches it. Some days he's got more money on him than you could ever dream of. So don't you go telling me he took your money.'

'But I can prove it,' I said. 'He wrote the word "Money" in the dust.'

'Wrote the word "money"? You must be mad! John can't write. He's never written a word in his life,' and he glared at me. 'I don't know what your game is,' and the words died on his lips. A second or two passed, then he said: 'Yes, I do. You want some more money. That's what you want. That's why you're here.

And you're not going to get any. Not from me you're not,' and he shook his fist at me.

I gulped, and William said: 'He did take it.'

Mister Edwards rounded on him. 'Were you there?'

William shook his head.

'So how do you know?'

'He told me.'

He shook his head. 'The boy's a liar. I just proved it. John can't write. God Almighty! He doesn't even understand such things. So how could it be him?'

William's face reddened, and Mister Edwards said: 'I'm disappointed in you. I thought you had more sense. But now I can understand why they used to call you Simple Simon. It bloody suits you. That's what I say,' and he grabbed William's shoulder and pushed himself up and onto the barrel.

'Go on,' he said, 'get out of here. And don't come back.'

I looked at William and said: 'I told you so.'

He pushed me away and shoved through the crowd. As I went to follow him Mister Edwards yelled: 'Simon! William! Whatever your name is, wait for me,' and he elbowed his way past me and he grabbed William. 'I'm sorry,' he said, 'I'm sorry. I'm worried. Worried sick. He's never done this before. Never. And I don't know what to do. I've looked everywhere,' and he wiped his brow and shook his head. 'It's hard at my age. Hard on my feet. And hard on my heart,' and he put his hand on my shoulder and turned me round. 'You should wash that. You should get all the blood out of your hair. It'll help it heal up,' and then he shoved his hand in his pocket and pulled out some coins. 'Here's tuppence for you,' and then he turned to William, 'and tuppence for you. And I want you to look for John. And if you find him I want you come back and tell me. And I'll give you another tuppence. Another tuppence each.'

'And where do we find you?'

'Find me? I'm still at the same place – The Old Cider Master, off White Chapel Street. I've told them I'll stay another week and if I haven't found him by then I don't know what I'll do. He's never done anything like this before. Never.'

Then he seemed to lose sight of us, and he turned and pushed his way back through the crowd.

As we left the market I said to William: 'I'm not going to look for him.'

He gave me a slight shrug.

'And anyway we'd never find him. He could be anywhere. Anywhere at all.'

'I found you.'

I stopped and turned to stare at him. It had never occurred to me that he had looked for me. To me it was an accident. I was there and he came across me. In my pain it had seemed as simple as that. 'Were you looking for me?'

'For two nights, and one day, and all this morning, I walked and walked and walked, though I could hardly stand up straight. I thought you were dead and I didn't know what to do. And I saw myself having to go home and tell your mother. And that was the third time I came to Seething Lane.'

'God,' I said, 'I'm sorry. I had no idea,' and I leant on his shoulder and wrapped my arm around him and gave him a hug. The tears came into my eyes, and I remembered Aunt Mary's lie. The lie that his silence had confirmed. And I knew that I would have to wait to learn the truth.

30

We passed through Ludgate and into Fleet Street and The Strand, and just before Charing Cross a young man was stirring a bucket of whitewash. He stirred my memory and I thought of all the times I had scrubbed and washed our cottage, and I looked at the house that lay before him. It was three storeys high with twenty panels of plaster, and I did not envy him.

He wet the plaster, but he did not scrub it as he should have done, and he took his brush and washed the first panel.

A young lady leant out the first-floor window and called down to him. He smiled and waved his brush at her.

He washed another panel and looked up at her, and said something, but I could not catch his words. Then he wrote the letter I on the next panel and he began to laugh. On the next panel he wrote LO, and on the one after that VE. Then he beckoned to her and in a minute or two she came out the front door, and on the next panel he wrote YOU.

She put her hands to her mouth and smothered her giggling.

William began to laugh and so did I, and a crowd began to gather. The crowd confused her, and she flushed a bright red.

Then an older woman leant out the first-floor window and shouted at her, and she fled inside.

The young man shrugged and turned to the crowd and smiled, and then he changed the I into an arrow that pointed up. It was not a sharp arrow, it was fat and rounded, like a knob, and it made the crowd titter.

Then the young man realised what he'd done, and he whited it out, and his face was as red as hers had been.

We left him to his washing, to his dreams of love and lust and knobs that rise; and we walked past Whitehall Palace and the Banqueting House and into Holbein Gate. The gate was old, with stones and flints arranged in squares, and it looked as though a chequer board had been laid upon it. It was ugly, and I turned and looked again at the Banqueting House. There was something about it that was familiar, but I couldn't think what it was. I began to walk back towards it. The front was made of stone, smooth grey stone. It was ornamented with two rows of columns and topped with a balustrade of carved stone.

About twelve feet from the front, near the palace gate, I stopped and looked down, and set in the cobbles was a square of blood-red marble. It was engraved with a cross and the letters CR.

The blood in my soul froze, and in my fingers I felt the chill of winter, the chill of that January afternoon of so long ago, and I knew that I was standing on the spot where he had died.

This was where they had struck off his head.

For a moment or two the horror of it filled my mind, and I could not think and I could not move. In my mind I saw again that dreadful day. I heard the axe thump on the block. And I heard the crowd groan. And Charles Rex, Charles the King, died again in my mind.

Then I heard the echo of those sermons that marked the day of King Charles the Martyr, and into my mind wriggled the eels, the black eels I called King Charles. I saw their heads come off, and I saw their mouths opening and shutting in wordless agony, as his must have opened and shut.

I was sorry for what they did to him. And I was sorry for what I did to them. I closed my eyes and said a silent prayer.

I know they say we cannot pray for the dead, and I know my Father would not understand a prayer for eels – unless it was to put more of them on his plate – but this was a prayer of the heart. It was not a prayer of reason. And it stayed in my heart, and it lay quiet like a wreath on a tomb.

I blinked my eyes and wiped away the tears, and I said: 'This is where they killed the King.'

William gave me a slow nod, and we turned and walked back to Holbein Gate. We walked in silence, like mourners with a corpse, and it was not till we were standing by the Great Hall in Westminster that I could trust myself to make light of it and say: 'It's much smaller than I thought. The drawings always show such crowds, and they make the Banqueting House look so much bigger.'

He nodded. 'My Father, my Father who is not my Father, he used to say he got what he deserved.'

'My Father used to say much the same thing. And she used to say he was a fool, and he should keep his mouth shut.'

He laughed. 'In our house he used to say she was the fool. And she was the one who was supposed to keep her mouth shut.'

I smiled. 'I suppose neither of them kept their mouth shut, if the truth was known.'

He looked at me and laughed again; and we wandered down to Westminster Steps.

A man was walking up down yelling: 'Oars! Oars! Oars!' His chest had swollen and so had his arms, but his legs were thin and balled at the knees, like the legs of a spinning wheel. He reminded me of someone in my past. Someone I didn't like, didn't trust.

I looked into the waters of the Thames.

It was about an hour or two after midday and the tide had reached its lowest point and turned, and now the waters were running brown and rising fast. A bird with long legs was feeding in the mud. It reminded me of the man with the heron legs – the man I did not trust. Then I remembered the face. It was the face of the ferryman at Vermuyden's Drain.

William walked down the steps and spoke to the man. His face was not the face of the ferryman. The body was, but not the face. In some queer way the oars had shaped his body, as they had shaped the body of the ferryman, and I wondered if they would shape my body if I became a waterman.

It would be the work of a lifetime. A lifetime of crossing and recrossing. And at the end of that lifetime the water would still lie in front of me: rising or falling or resting. It could never be trusted, or taken for granted, and it was the same in The Fens. The water was the water, and the land was the land, and the bridge between them was the boat and the oars, and the man who rowed.

In the waterlands of my mind, in those strange and eerie places where the swamps lie in perpetual darkness, I knew that I did not want to return to the water that gave me birth. I did not want to be a waterman. I did not want to row on the Thames or punt on The Fens, and I wondered why they had not done the sensible thing, the obvious thing, and built a bridge.

In my mind I named it Westminster Bridge, and it crossed the water on heron legs, and it made the waterboatmen row away.

Then William came and sat beside me, and my bridge spread its wings and flew away.

'He says hundreds want to row, but most of the boats have to support a family, and if you don't belong to the family you don't row. It's as simple as that.'

'Is he telling the truth?'

He shrugged, and I said: 'Maybe we should ask a few more.'

'How's your head?'

'Still sore.'

He touched me on the shoulder. 'You stay here. I won't be very long.'

I watched him work his way along the steps and I watched the boats making for the steps at Lambeth Palace. They were rowing into the middle of the river and catching the rip and letting it carry them up stream.

Then a man came rushing up to me. He breathed in my face and said: 'Whores, sir? Whores?'

I felt my jaw drop, and I shook my head, and he rushed away without saying another word. A few minutes later I saw him with a young woman, who was not as pretty as the young woman near Charing Cross, but pretty enough to dry my throat and stir my cock.

I watched her wait, and I watched him ask around, and then he helped her into a boat. He rowed down the river, hugging the shore where the rip was spent, and after fifteen minutes he rounded the bend and I lost sight of him.

I thought of Southwark, and the whores, and those secret things they do in the night, and I fingered my penny and my halfpenny, and I wished that I could finger her.

Then William came back.

I told him about the whores and he laughed in my face. 'It's the way they talk,' he said. 'It sounds like whores, but they mean oars,' and he laughed some more.

I felt a fool. I felt deflated, like a shrivelled cock, and I stood up and kicked a stone into the water.

He shook his head. 'You didn't really think he was saying whores, did you?'

I looked at him and I didn't say a thing, and his face swelled, and he laughed some more.

I walked back to Westminster Hall, and he caught up with me in a couple of minutes. 'They don't want us,' he said in a quiet voice. 'There's more than enough of them, that's what one man said to me. And another said we should hump and lump, and that's all we're fit for.'

'Hump and lump?'

'Bricks. Stone. Wood. Things like that.'

I'd seen the long lines of men and boys at the building plots. Their backs were bent and their eyes were hungry, and the years had leathered their faces.

I could see myself becoming like them. I could see myself waiting, waiting to hump and lump. Always waiting. Always at the beck and call of the man with money.

It was a prospect that filled me with gloom.

In the late afternoon as the shadows began to gather, we joined the smallest line we could find. It was off Fleet Street, in Water Lane, and it stretched across the raw earth and onto the cobbled path. I counted twenty heads in twenty feet; and within an hour eight more boys had locked us into the line.

The dark brought the cold, and we huddled closer together and I felt the warmth of the boy next to me. He was glum and wordless, and lost in his own thoughts, and I did not want to be like him.

I began to think about The Fens: about the sun and the wind and the water and the way they leathered a man's face. It was different from the leathering of London. It was cleaner. It was free from grime. And it was softer, and creased with a smile. I did not want to be leathered by London or The Fens, and I felt caught. I felt that sense of panic, sense of hopelessness that a wild fowl must feel when it beats against the net that has trapped it; and I pulled out my scissors, my useless scissors, and stabbed the air.

William laughed at me, and said: 'They didn't do you much good, did they?'

I looked at him and them, and shook my head. And I thought about John: the man we had not seen, the man I did not want to see again. And I thought about the money he had taken, and the money Mister Edwards had given to us, and I said: 'We have enough money for a week, if we're careful. And then we'll have to go home.'

'I don't have a home any more. He told me to go. And he told me not to come back.' He paused and pulled the collar of his coat up around his ears. 'I thought you'd remember that.'

I nodded; and after a while he said: 'I think we should see Mister Woodgate. I know you don't want to. And I know you think we can get by without him. But, I think you're wrong. I think we need him. And I think we need that work he talked about. And then we can earn some more money.'

'I thought sitting here was going to do that.'

'I don't mean a penny or tuppence or whatever they're going to pay us. I mean a shilling, or two shillings. Enough to eat every day, and buy a hat and some shoes that don't leak.'

'You know what Mister Woodgate would expect you to do?'

'Yes.'

'And you're prepared to do it?'

'Yes.'

'And you think I should do it?'

'Yes.'

In my head I cried. It was wrong. It was a sin and it would condemn him – and me – to the fires of hell. And we would burn for ever, and we would suffer as we had never suffered before.

I took his arm and turned him towards me, and looked into his eyes. They were red and watery, and I could see he was hurting deep inside, and I said, in a whisper: 'It's sin. And we can't do it.'

His eyes slipped away from mine, and after a long silence, he said: 'If you go home, and I am left on my own, it might be the only thing that I can do. And if that is what I have to do, that is what I will do.'

31

When the carts arrived with the dawn, we stood up and a man walked along the line and called out: 'Men are a penny. Boys are a halfpenny. Are you a man or a boy? Boys is what I want. What are you?'

I said: 'A boy.' And so did William, and so did a couple of other men further down the line.

We took the bricks from the carts and stacked them on the plot at the foot of the scaffolding.

In three hours we emptied ten carts.

When I stood back and looked at the piles, and thought that our money was earned, he yelled at us to form a line.

We climbed the ladders – still keeping our place in the line – and passed the bricks from hand to hand and stacked them on the planks.

When we came down the bricklayers were mixing their mortar, and six of the boys who were not boys were told they could run the bricks up the ladders for the rest of the day.

I took my halfpenny – it felt too light for the weight of bricks that I had moved – and I shoved it in my pocket.

We walked back to London Bridge and sat on the steps, the same steps we had sat upon on our first morning in London. The peace of that morning was long gone. The tide was on the way out, but the gaps between the piers of the bridge were too small, and they had banked up the water. It was spurting through the gaps – roaring like a waterfall – and to my mind it made the bridge look like a flood bank that was breached in a dozen places and about to burst.

I leant towards William and yelled and pointed to the

waterwheel – it was in the middle of the bridge, turning and throwing froth into the air – and he cupped his hand to his ear, and mouthed something and then he stood up. I followed him past the stall of the paperman, and I said: 'Shall we see if he's got another paper from Ely?'

He laughed and shook his head. 'Let's get something to eat.'

We drifted up Fish Hill Street. The pies were selling for a penny-halfpenny, and they were smaller than the ones from the baker by Tower Hill. The apples were selling for a halfpenny each and the pears for four-a-penny. We left them where they were, and I ate them in my mind, and we wandered along Gracechurch Street.

About twenty minutes later we found ourselves standing outside Mister Woodgate's shop.

I looked at William and he looked at me, and I shook my head, and he said: 'It took us four hours to earn that halfpenny. I used to do better than that in the kitchens. And the work wasn't as heavy. It was hotter, I'll grant you that. But it wasn't as heavy. And I was thinking maybe . . .'

I shook my head.

He paced up and down, and then he stopped by the step and he peered into the shop, and he turned to me. 'I'll see if he's in. There's no harm in that.'

I grabbed him by the arm. 'If he's out it doesn't matter. But if he's in, he'll want to talk to you, and me. And you know what that'll lead to.'

He shook off my hand. 'I'll just ask.' And he stepped inside the shop.

I grabbed his arm again and pulled. He turned and tried to shake me off. I jerked him hard and we fell against the door. It thumped into the wall and rattled.

His eyes blazed, and he punched me on the shoulder. It sent me staggering into the shop. The old man came running from the back of the shop. 'Get out of here!' he yelled, and he shooed me with his hands.

Then the younger man came running, and he pushed us out the door. 'You go and fight somewhere else!' he yelled. 'And don't you dare come back here again,' and he booted William in the arse. William jumped and swore at him. And the man snarled and shook his fist.

We walked down Bishopsgate in sullen silence. He was in front and I was behind, and every so often he looked over his shoulder, and his eye met my eye.

I let him stare me down, down to the cobbles, and I pretended to be sad and stricken with remorse. But deep inside I was singing for joy. I had wrestled him out of the shop, and away from the evil that lurked there. And it was worth a sore shoulder, and him sulking. And it was worth saying sorry, if that was what I had to say.

He sat down again on the steps at London Bridge, and I sat beside him. We didn't say a word for thirty or forty minutes. Then he said: 'I'm still hungry.'

'We could walk to Billingsgate, and buy some smoked eel. They say it's cheaper down there, in the afternoon, when they have to sell off the fish that won't keep till tomorrow.'

'I don't like eels,' he said. 'The baby eels – the elvers – they're all right, if they're really small. But I don't like the big ones.'

We walked a bit and he said: 'My Mother had an iron plate. It was round and flat with a long wooden handle. I used to hold it in the fire and heat it up, and she'd mix a batter of flour and eggs and stir in the elver. Then she'd grease the hotplate, and spoon on the batter, and when one side was cooked she'd turn them over, and that side would be done in a couple of minutes. And we used to hold them in a crust of bread and eat them hot.'

In my head I could taste those fritters. My Mother used to make them in the bottom of her iron pot, the one with the flat bottom, and we used to eat them with plum pickle and a rasher of fried bacon; and afterwards I'd wipe out the pot with my bread and it would soak up the hot slick of pig fat.

I began to think how easy it had been to work for an hour or two for her, and an hour or two for him, and come home and find food on the table. And I began to think if this morning was a taste of London, a taste of what was to come, I might have been better off taking Aunt Mary's advice and going home and putting up with him, and what he would do to me. And if she was right, I could have protected my Mother in the years to come, when I would grow strong and he would grow weak.

These were dark thoughts, thoughts of sadness and sorrow. They clouded my mind, and they clouded the joy that had been singing deep inside me, and I began to think the unthinkable: could it be that I was wrong and William was right?

It would make right into wrong and good into evil, and it would turn the world on its arse and expose its privy parts. It was an evil thought. A temptation of the devil, and it shocked me to the quick. Then I remembered the quick and the dead, and how long we would be dead, and I tried to put this temptation out of my mind. But I stumbled on a loose cobble, and the temptation would not go, and then I remembered the words of my Mother, the words of my childhood: the devil will go to any lengths to make us stumble and fall from grace. I said a prayer, a silent prayer, and it calmed my mind.

A few minutes later Billingsgate surprised me. It was empty, dark, and cavernous, and it smelt of fish and cold water. We walked right through in a stunned silence, and then we walked to the left. A boat was being unloaded at the quay, and men were rolling barrels into a brick warehouse. The lid of each barrel bore a name stencilled in black letters. The letters were close together and the rolling was blurring them, and I could not read the name.

We sat for a while and I nursed my hunger, and as we stood and half turned and went to leave, a voice said: 'I was wondering when I was going to see you two again.'

He was framed by the door of the warehouse, and on the beam above the door, in letters no more than three or four inches high, ran the words: A. & J. WOODGATE & SONS: MERCHANTS AND CONTRACTORS.

I shrugged, and he said: 'Did you forget the address?'

I looked down at the quay, it was planked with wood and seamed with tar, and I shook my head.

'We went there an hour ago,' William said, 'and you weren't there and I tripped over the steps, and your son thought we were fighting and he threw us out.'

'My son?'

'The young man.'

He shook his head. 'My sons are dead. They died of the plague, and there was nothing I could do.'

'I'm sorry,' I said, 'we thought . . .'

He smiled. 'You're not the first ones to make that mistake. It's the name, I know. I've often thought of changing it. But they were buried in a common grave, and they don't have a stone or a cross to remember them by. And that word, that word "SONS" on my window, and up there,' and he pointed to the beam above the door, 'that's all that's left.' He smiled a sad smile, a smile of loss, and it weighed on me, and I bowed my head.

We sat inside thc warehouse, on the barrels, and I read his name on the lids. He asked about the geese and how much they fetched, and then he said: 'I invited you to dinner, didn't I?'

I thought about the mutton pie he'd talked about. And I remembered the wine he called sack, and I saw my resolve to resist temptation slide away like the grease on Aunt Mary's hotplate, and I said: 'Yes.'

'We finish at six,' he said, 'and then we eat upstairs in The Three Crowns. And I think,' and he paused, 'I think it might be a good idea if we cleaned you up.'

I looked at William. A look of horror was crawling over his face, and I remembered that he didn't like water and lye and washing. And nor did I, if the truth is to be told.

'There's a bathhouse just up from here. The fishermen use it. And they have their clothes washed at the same time. And when they go chasing whores they don't have to pay so much because they smell nice and clean,' and he laughed. 'I'm not suggesting you're going to chase whores. But I am suggesting you do smell a bit ripe, and I prefer my cheeses and not my company to smell like that. And I think our landlord will be of the same mind,' and he laughed again. 'And I must confess that if one of you thought about coming to read to me tonight, I would prefer you to smell nice and clean. So . . .' and he pulled his face into a hard smile.

The woman at the bathhouse was a mountain of pink flesh. She put her hands on her hips, and ran her eye over us. She shook her head and said to Mister Woodgate: 'They'll clean up all right, and I can do their nails and cut their hair. But there won't be time to dry their clothes. They're going to need a good soak, they are. And a good beating.'

'Hmm,' he said. 'A lot of the smell is in the clothes, and it's no use having a bath and putting them back on.'

She nodded. 'I'll tell you what,' she said. 'I've a few clothes here. They've been left behind by those who thought they could have a bath and run away without paying,' and she smiled to herself. 'And I think I could fit them for you. And I could make them look respectable. Fit for company, if that's what you'd like.'

He looked at me, and then at William. 'And what would that cost?'

'Two shillings, including the bath.'

'Two shillings!'

'Hmm,' she said with a smile, 'two shillings each.'

'Each?'

'I'd give them a scrub all over. And for that price I could fit them with under-breeches, and that would keep them smelling nice and clean for a lot longer.'

He gave her a slow nod and put his hand in his pocket and all I could think was: two shillings were twenty-four pence, were forty-eight halfpennies, and each halfpenny took four hours of humping and lumping of bricks, and it would cost forty-eight times four hours to pay for this – and that was just for me – and I couldn't think how many hours that would make. I couldn't do it in my head.

Then she said: 'Take off all your clothes. Everything. And put them in there,' and she pointed to a wicker basket.

We stripped to our breeches and looked at each other.

'You ain't got nothing I ain't seen before,' she said. 'So you get them off, and get into that tub.'

We sank into the warm water. It was brown and scummed and it lapped around the top of the wooden tub. After a few minutes she came and poured in a bucket of hot water. The heat warmed me right through, and my face began to sweat and I closed my eyes. I felt the weight of the bricks slip away from my back, my neck, and my arms.

She stood William in the middle of the floor and she scrubbed and soaped him with lye, and she spread his legs and lifted his cock and peeled back his foreskin and washed his knob. She washed inside his ears and between his toes, and then she poured a bucket of cold water over him. He shrieked and shrivelled and I laughed at him, and she poured another bucket of water over him. She handed him a large square of coarse cloth, and she called it a towel.

Then she beckoned to me, and William grinned, and as I climbed out of the round tub, my arse went up in the air and my balls hung loose – like a dog's – and there was no dignity in it, no sense of propriety. No sense of modesty.

I looked at the ceiling and counted the beams, and emptied my mind when I felt her hands spread my legs.

She daubed lavender water under our arms and between our legs, and she grinned to herself and said: 'He'll like that,' and then she beckoned us to follow her. We walked behind her, stark naked. We walked through the bathhouse and some of the men in the tubs eyed us up and down and one of them yelled: 'They're a bit young for you, aren't they?' She laughed and rounded her mouth and made a sucking sound, and some of them laughed and one of them whistled.

It was the sort of whistle men make to a dog. It was a whistle of command. A whistle to come. A whistle to lie at his feet. It raised the hairs on the back of my neck, and if I had stayed there any longer it would have raised my cock.

We followed her, and I could feel his eyes on my arse, my dog-balled arse, and we walked up the stairs to the first floor, and then up again to a room with an attic roof.

It was packed with clothes.

I laid down my scissors and my pennies and my halfpennies, and she showed me how to button on the under-breeches. They were grey, and they pressed against my skin and they felt soft. And when I moved to take the white shirt she was handing to me, they felt like a hand, a gentle stroking hand. It was strange and sensuous. Never had clothes felt like this before, and she smiled and said: 'Clothes maketh the man. That's what they say. But in your case I think the opposite is true. I think the man maketh the clothes,' and she roared with laughter.

William stared at her, and I felt my face flush.

I tried on three pairs of breeches and two woollen vests, and I padded the toes in my new shoes. An hour later when the heat of the tub was still lingering deep inside my body, she eased us out the door and onto the street.

William was a changed man, not the man I knew. He stood

in a new way. He walked in a new way. And there was no hint of the old simpleton. His hair was close-cropped. It fringed his eyes and sat just above his ears and it touched the collar on his cloak. And when he put on his hat, and the sides fell to form earmuffs, he looked like a man of means, a man of money. He turned to me and said: 'This is what I want to be like.'

By five in the afternoon the dark and the cold had filled the streets, and a light drizzle was turning to rain. We stood outside Mister Woodgate's shop and looked into the warmth and the light. He had called it an office, and he had talked about working office hours, whatever they might be. We watched a man come and go, and we saw a boy deliver some letters, and William said: 'We could wait inside, on that bench.'

We waited for the son who was not the son to go out the back, and we slipped inside and sat on the bench. I felt uneasy about this slow seduction, this slow bending of my will to do what I did not want to do; and I whispered: 'I'm only going to stay here on one condition.'

'Hmm,' he whispered back, 'what's that?'

'When we finish dinner and come out of the tavern, and he walks round here to unlock the door, I'm going to run away. I'm not coming back in here. And I'm not going through that door,' and I nodded to the door behind the counter, 'and out the back to his rooms.'

'Is that fair?'

'Fair?'

'Honourable then.'

'How can you talk about fair and honourable when you know what he's got in mind?'

He shrugged and fingered my cloak. 'You took his money, and soon he'll want what he wants. I think that's fair. And honourable. And you can't say you don't know what he wants. You do. He made it clear. Quite clear. In his own way.'

I fell silent, and the rain began to beat against the window, and I wondered if it would be possible to sleep inside tonight, to stay warm and dry, and not have to do any reading.

Then the older man came bustling into the office. He stopped when he saw us and his mouth sagged. 'I'm sorry, sir,' he said to William, 'and you too, sir,' he said to me. 'I didn't hear you come in. It must be the rain,' and he waved towards the dark and the rain. 'We have a bell,' and he lifted it and rang it, and the son who was not the son came running into the office. 'I'm sorry,' he said to him. 'I was showing these young gentlemen the bell,' and he smiled, and the son who was not the son smiled and bowed to us.

A moment or two passed, and then the older man said: 'How can I help you, sir?'

William stood up and took off his hat and said: 'We have come to see Mister Woodgate.'

'Is he expecting you?'

'He said to come at six o'clock but it started to rain and we didn't want to get wet, and we thought we might wait in here. If that's all right with you.'

He looked at William and he looked at me. 'May I ask the nature of your business with Mister Woodgate.'

'He said to come to dinner, to supper. And I think he would like me to read to him.'

The older man shook his head, and the son who was not the son said to him in a loud whisper: 'And that means I'll have to go home tonight. And look at that bloody rain.'

They sat behind the counter and whispered, but their words did not reach me.

When the hands on the clock touched six o'clock the older man put on a hat and cloak and mumbled: 'Good night,' and he slipped away into the darkness.

At six fifteen, I said to the man who was not the son: 'He's late.'

He smiled and shook his head. 'To Mister Woodgate six o'clock is the time we shut the office. It has nothing to do with the clock. It's the time we finish. Some nights it's six o'clock, and some night it's six thirty, and some nights it's seven o'clock. But to Mister Woodgate it's always six o'clock. We always close at six, that's what he says, and we're never late. He doesn't believe in being late.'

In my head I pulled a face, and for a minute or two my mind walked around this maze of words; and then he said: 'Where did you meet him?'

'Ely.'

'Good God!' and he laughed. 'I suppose that makes a change. Usually he picks them up at Billingsgate and puts them through the bathhouse.' Then the expression on his face changed, and he looked hard at me and said: 'You were here this afternoon,' and he pointed his finger at William, 'and I kicked your arse.'

William nodded, and the man laughed. 'And you've been through the bathhouse. And that bloody old lump of lard has washed inside your foreskin, and patted your balls and dried them off with lavender water.' He shook his head. 'It happened to me ten, twelve years ago. And I thought I was made, in both senses of the word. But it hasn't worked out. Not for me it hasn't, and then he seemed to retreat into himself, and we watched the hands on the clock crawl towards seven.

Mister Woodgate came rushing into the office. He flung his hat on the counter, whipped off his cloak and shook off the water. Then he gestured to us to stand up and turn round. He gave us both a nod and said: 'You scrub up well. And you look good. You look like a pair of clerks. And I think there could be a future for a pair like you. That's what I think,' and he turned to the man who was not his son. 'What do you think, Rutherford?'

'I think they might be promising, sir.'

'Promising?'

'Yes, sir. Promising.'

He turned back to us. The slightest of smiles was flicking on his lips. It was like the flickering of a candle that has just been lit. It might go out, and it might flare and burn. 'Are you promising?' he said to William.

William nodded, and he turned to me and raised his eyebrows.

'I would like to be a clerk,' I said.

'That is ambition,' he said, and the flicker of the candle went out. 'You are confusing ambition with promising. They are two different things.' Then he leant towards Rutherford and said something, and he walked through the office and into the back rooms.

'I knew it,' Rutherford said, 'I bloody knew it!'

I looked at him and waited. 'I have to go home,' he said, 'as soon as we've eaten. And I'm allowed to take his cloak and his hat,' and he turned towards the half-closed door and bowed. 'Such generosity. It's bloody overwhelming!'

Mister Woodgate rushed back into the office adjusting the front of his breeches. 'That's better,' he said. 'Much better. Now come on, come on. It's just on six o'clock and I'm hungry,' and he pushed us out of the office and locked the door.

32 

The landlord leaned over the table and set a pewter goblet, a wooden plate, and a knife and fork in front of each of us. The fork was much smaller than the ones we used at home to fish the meat out of the bottom of the cooking pot, and I was wondering how we would manage, when he placed an oval dish in the middle of the table.

The dish was about six inches high and I could feel the heat pouring off it. When he lifted the lid with his apron and slipped in a large wooden serving spoon, the steam began to escape and it filled the air with herbs and spices and a rich meaty smell that made the juices run inside my mouth.

He brought two flasks of wine to the table and placed them in front of Mister Woodgate. One was small and squat with a thin neck and the other was tall and rounded with a fat neck. At the base of the fat neck, the face of a man swelled up and out, like a large goitre. He wore a beard and bushy eyebrows, and he was old and ugly, and the reds and the browns of the salt glaze gave him a livery look. To me he was a caricature, and I wondered why he was the butt of such cruel humour.

A girl brought us a dish of white beans and a bowl of pickled walnuts, and then she pushed the four candles into the middle of the table and made room for a carving board, a cob of bread and a bowl of butter. She looked at Mister Woodgate and half smiled, half raised her eyebrows, and he nodded to her. She sliced the bread, and then she smiled at him again and asked if that would be all. He said we would like some mugs and some strong beer, and a platter of cheese and maybe some apples after that. And did they have any boiled turnips? And horseradish sauce?

He poured some wine into the goblets and said to William: 'This is sack. It comes from France and there is nothing sweeter. You take a sip and you roll it around your mouth to savour the full flavour. Then you swallow it, very slowly, and it dribbles all the way down your gullet and you can feel the warmth as it spreads through your body. I'll show you.' He took a sip and closed his eyes, and his face became mellow, became holy, like the face of a man who has just received the wine of Holy Communion; and then he looked at us and said: 'Just a sip.'

It was like honey with fire. I could smell it in my nose and my head, and it seemed to reach out and touch my soul. When I opened my eyes he was smiling. He picked up the small flask and held the open neck to his nose, and he closed his eyes and breathed in. 'It's brandy-wine, he said. 'It's for later on. It's very strong. Much stronger than sack, and it does all sorts of things to you,' and he smiled, and I remembered that smile: he was wearing it on the night I went up to his room at Aunt Mary's.

The landlord laid the bread upon our plates, and he covered it with meat, carrots, parsnips, onions and all the other mushy vegetables that floated in his gravy sauce.

I took a mouthful. It was hot. Burning hot. I opened my mouth and puffed out the heat, and Mister Woodgate filled a mug with beer and handed it to me. I took a sip and my eyes watered, and he said to me: 'What do you think?'

'It's hot,' I said, wiping at my eyes, 'and soft and tender. It tastes like fowl, but it's too dark for fowl. And it isn't mutton. Could it be pheasant?'

Rutherford smiled to himself, and Mister Woodgate leant towards William and said: 'Do you know what it is?'

He shook his head.

'It's rabbit,' he said. 'They breed them in Surrey and Essex, in warrens – they're long mounds of earth with a few scrubby trees on top so the roots will hold the earth together – and they keep them fenced off so they can't escape. And as soon as they're full-grown they put them in cages and cart them to London. They're not like your geese. They can't be trusted to walk, or hop along on their own,' and he laughed, and we laughed with him. 'So they cost more than they should, and we don't see as many of them as we used to.'

He poured a little more wine into the goblets, and then he said: 'What did you do today?'

For a moment my mind was a blank, as if it too had been washed and scrubbed in the bathhouse, and then I remembered that William and I had talked about warrens, and I said: 'We saw an old chapel. Just over from here. And it had a sign about the Warrenmasters meeting there once a month.'

'I know the place,' he said. 'I think they're going to close it down. There are no warrens around here any more, so they're running out of brethren. Pity really. They've been here since the time of the Normans,' and he paused and picked at his teeth. 'Did you know they brought the rabbits over with them?'

I shook my head, and he lifted the lid and spooned out another piece of meat. The bone slid away from it, and he smiled to himself and said: 'That's how I like it.'

We ate in silence for several minutes, and my mind drifted back to the day we arrived in London, and I told him about old Saint Paul's and the church in Foster Lane, and how it was full of light. William gave me a sour look, and said he was sick of talking about churches, and Mister Woodgate laughed and asked him if he'd ever tried plum porridge.

I closed my ears to them, and I put my hand on the window panes. They were cold and I could feel the soft beat of the rain, and in the alley I could see the top of the sign for The Three Crowns.

I drank some more and the warmth filled my insides, and I began to see things in a haze. A gentle, seductive haze that was building in my mind like the haze that builds on the horizon in The Fens. Some mornings the haze is nothing but a haze and it's gone by midday. And some mornings it's like John the Baptist: it foreshadows the advent of a storm that will drench the day and change everything that lies before it.

I blinked and wondered if the haze was playing with me, as it so often plays with us in The Fens, and then Mister Woodgate stood up and said: 'I'm going for a piss. The pots are along the corridor, under the table, if you want to use them. The landlord keeps a candle burning there. And he doesn't like you pissing on the floor.'

I turned towards Rutherford who was layering butter and

cheese and walnuts onto his bread, and I said: 'You've been very quiet.'

He took a bite and through a muffling of bread, he said: 'He pisses me off. You think he's very nice. But you don't have to work for him day after day. And you don't have to put up with his moods. And he keeps reminding me that he said yes, and I said yes, and she said no.'

'She?'

He shook his head. 'It doesn't matter. And in a week or two it won't matter for you,' and he turned to William, 'or you. You'll be gone and he'll have forgotten all about you. And if he hasn't found somebody else he'll be running his hand up my arse, and telling me he might be able to make her change her mind.' He poured some of the brandy-wine into his goblet – we had not been offered any of it – and he drank it down in one gulp. 'I'd like to be a soldier-of-foot. That's what I'd like to be.'

'We saw some the other day,' William said. 'They were carrying pikes.'

'I don't want to be a pikeman. In a battle all they do is fend-off troopers and protect musketeers. I want to be a musketeer. I could drill and fire and aim. And I've got a good eye, and I'm strong enough to carry a musket, and it would be a bloody sight better than this.'

He lapsed into silence, and I said: 'How do you become a musketeer?'

'I saw some posters. Down at Deptford by the naval dockyard. We go there once or twice a week. And they had them by the slipway, and on the old Guildhall. It's for a new regiment,' and again he lapsed into silence. Then he came back in a softer voice: 'I might have to be a pikeman to begin with. For a short time. But then I'd be a musketeer and I could come back one night and shoot the bastard. I'd shoot him right here,' and he stood up and grabbed at his crutch with both hands and yelled: 'Bang!' Then he flung his hands away, as though his cock and his balls had been blown to bits, and he doubled over and pretended to be in pain, and jerked himself around the room.

I was bemused – speechless – and I wasn't quite sure what to make of it all.

I filled my mug with the last of the beer. William poured

himself some more wine and then he looked at me and started to giggle, and he covered his mouth with his hands.

Mister Woodgate came rushing into the room. He stopped in mid-step. 'What the hell's the matter with you?'

Rutherford straightened up. 'Colic,' he said. 'A bad attack of colic,' and he turned away from him and looked at us. 'It feels bad. It feels like someone's rammed a bloody great pike up my arse,' and he smiled at us, and I bit my lips, 'and I think maybe I should be going home.'

'No. No,' Mister Woodgate said. 'It's too early. Sit down and we can talk some more. And maybe the rain'll ease off, and you can walk home in the dry.'

Rutherford shrugged, and slipped back onto his stool.

We sat for several seconds, and the pin-prick eyes on the wine flask began to stare at me. I turned the face towards Mister Woodgate and said: 'What's he doing there?'

He blinked, and lifted the flask and peered at the face. 'That's Bellarmine,' he said. 'He was a Roman priest. A cardinal, and now they call those things bellarmines. They're made of stone and clay and some of the bigger ones are very heavy, and we still use a few of them down at the warehouse.'

Then he started to laugh. 'I've just remembered what we used to do when I was young, and a bellarmine was brought to the table,' and he laughed again. 'Here, I'll show you,' and he went to fill our goblets. A drop or two came out. He shrugged. 'Never mind, we can get some more in a moment. You do have some wine in there, don't you?' and he half stood and peered into each goblet, and then he flopped back on his seat. 'Now, you take hold of the goblet with your right hand. Round the stem, like this,' and he held it up in the air. 'Now stick out your finger. The one by your thumb. And twist your hand a bit so that your finger is sticking straight up.' He looked at each finger and nodded. 'And now we stand up and propose a toast to Bellarmine.'

I pushed away my stool, and we all stood with our goblets over the table. 'And I'll show you what you have to do,' he said, and he moved his goblet up and down, and it looked as though his finger was being thrust in and out of some invisible thing.

He smiled at us and said: 'To Bellarmine,' and our fingers thrust into the air and we sipped the wine. 'Now you put the goblet on the table, and you hold your hand up in the air, still keeping your finger stiff, and then very slowly you let it flop, and when it's all weak and limp, you sit down again. And that's how you toast Bellarmine.'

'What he hasn't told you,' Rutherford said, 'is that the papists don't allow their priests to marry. They make them keep their cocks in their breeches. They don't, of course, but that would spoil the toast, so we must pretend they do,' and he laughed and said: 'To Bellarmine,' and we stood and fucked the air, and laughed when our fingers flopped.

Then we did it again, and laughed some more.

Mister Woodgate poured a little bandy-wine into our wine and I breathed in the fumes. The haze in my head became thicker, became like the black dust that the wind lifts from The Fens when the summer has dried the earth that should not be drained and dried and allowed to blow away.

Mister Woodgate said something, but it was caught in the fenblow, and the black dust in my mind smothered his words and his breath, and I heard William say: 'And then we walked through Bishopsgate and up to Holborn and looked at Ely Place.'

'Ely Place. That used to be the palace of the Bishops of Ely. But I suppose you know that?'

I nodded.

'They pulled a lot of it down when I was a boy. It was famous for its gardens. I can remember seeing the roses and the fruit trees. They're all gone now. There's nothing left, not a thing. And you'd never know it ever existed. Funny how things can vanish without a trace,' and then he paused and frowned. 'No, that's not right. There is a trace. There is. And I know where to find it,' and he stood up, and took a candle, and walked out of the room.

I looked at Rutherford. 'Where's he going?'

He shrugged. 'I don't know. And I don't care.'

William yawned. 'I don't know why he's so interested in Ely Place.'

Rutherford blinked and looked up. 'Ely? He went to Ely for the eels. He thinks if he buys things where they are caught or made, he can buy them cheaper. And if he can ship them into

London at a cheap rate, he can make a lot of money. And if he can supply them to the navy, he can make even more money.'

I had thought we were talking about Ely Place, and I let all this slide away from me, and I laid my hands on the table and rested my head on them. And he said: 'There is another reason.'

William mumbled something, and Rutherford said: 'He wants to find new ways of making food keep longer. The trouble is the navy only puts to sea in the summertime, when the seas are calm and the weather is at its hottest. And then the fresh food goes off in about a week, and the sailors are back to salt-beef and a hard biscuit that can break their teeth if it isn't soaked in beer for an hour or two. And he thinks if he could supply better food, fewer sailors would desert their ships. And that would mean the press gangs wouldn't be out looking for new men every time a ship dropped anchor.'

I lifted my head from the table. 'What's this got to do with Ely?'

'He says the people in Ely are just like all the other people in The Fens: sour, morose, and tight-lipped, and they don't like strangers. And he says there's a simple reason for it. They live close to the water and close to the earth, and they know the secrets of both. And some of these are to do with the preservation of food. That's what he calls it. The preservation of food,' and he yawned. 'Trouble is, he's only found one way so far, and it didn't come from The Fens.'

'Hmm,' I said, 'and what was that?'

'He dug a deep pit and lined it with wood and covered it with thatch, and he called it an icehouse. And in the middle of winter he cut the ice off the ponds and lowered it into the house. Then he had a couple of cows killed and cleaned, and he hung them in the middle of the ice. And they froze solid.'

'And he didn't salt them?'

'No.'

'And then what happened?'

'In the early summer, when the ice began to melt, they thawed out and we ate them.'

'Ate them?'

'Yes. There was nothing wrong with them. And they tasted better than salt-beef.'

'And they hadn't gone rotten?'

'No.'

William stood up and stretched. 'So if you could build an icehouse on a ship and fill it with ice, you could have fresh meat for a couple of months.'

'Hmm,' he said. 'But the trouble is when the ships are ready to sail, it's summertime, and there's no ice. And if there was it would soon melt in the heat.'

'So it was a waste of time?'

'To me, yes. But he says it's a start. And don't be surprised if he sits you down, and produces a jug of beer, and wants to talk about food, and how your mothers used to keep it tasting fresh in the middle of winter.'

There weren't any secrets that I knew of, and I shrugged, and William said: 'I know a lady who had a well, and she used to hang her meat in it at the end of a forty-foot rope. And when she pulled it up, it was always cold and she could keep it fresh a lot longer than we could.'

Rutherford nodded, and a slow silence settled on us. I looked into my mug, and ran a drop of beer around the rim; and wished that I was in bed, sound asleep.

Mister Woodgate came back into the room. He had tucked a large book under one arm and draped his hat and cloak over the other.

He placed his candle on the table and handed the hat and cloak to Rutherford and said: 'It's stopped raining,' and then he pushed away the dishes and made room for the book. 'I knew it was here somewhere. I didn't think it would take me as long to find it as it did. But never mind. I've found it now,' and he opened the book, 'and here it is.'

He reached for William and moved him into his own seat, and rested his hands on his shoulders. 'It's from a play by William Shakespeare. He called it *Richard the Third*. They don't perform it any more, it's a political play, and it's gone out of fashion. Some say it's full of lies, and others say it makes a mockery of the monarchy, and others—'

'Excuse me, sir, may I say good night?'

We turned to Rutherford. The hat was masking his face and the cloak was masking his body. He looked like a black windmill, without the white sails that cross the sky and keep the symbol of redemption before our eyes. He looked evil, devilish, like something that should be pushed out into the night.

Mister Woodgate gave him a curt nod, and we said: 'Good night,' and he was gone without a sound.

Mister Woodgate said: 'This is King Richard speaking. At this stage he was still the Duke of Gloucester,' and he pointed to a line on the page, and William read:

'My Lord of Ely, when I was last in Holborn
I saw good strawberries in your garden there.
I do beseech you send for some of them.'

Mister Woodgate sat on William's stool and said: 'You must be careful about Ely Place. It's a strange place, and it still excites the crowds and sometimes, at night, it can become dangerous. And there have been some riots there.

'Riots?'

'Hmm. They don't get reported,' and he smiled to himself. 'It's a way of pretending they don't happen. But they do. I've seen them with my own eyes. And when I've looked for them in the *London Gazette*, there's never anything. Never a word. And that's how they make London look a better place, a safer place than it really is.'

He poured a little brandy-wine into our goblets and stood up, and once again we toasted Bellarmine. And I giggled, and I knew I was losing the thread of his words, and William said: 'What causes the riots?'

He put his hands together and touched his lips as some men do when they pray, and he said: 'Sometimes it's hard to know. They're like a fever, a sort of summer madness. They bloom in the heat and die in the cold, and when they're all over and the streets are quiet, you wonder what they were all about. But it's different in Ely Place. There they always seem to revolve around one thing,' and he turned the wine flask around and tapped Bellarmine on the head. 'It's popery, and it enrages the crowd every time.'

'But why there?'

'It goes back fifty years or more. I was a boy at the time,

a young boy, and I haven't forgotten, and nor have a lot of other people who live around here. The King did a foolish thing. He allowed Ely Place to become the residence of the Spanish Ambassador. And he brought his priests with him, all the way from Spain.' He shook his head. 'Who would have thought we would ever see such creatures here again? We believed we'd seen the end of them when Bloody Mary died. But we were wrong. And here they were again. And they made Saint Etheldreda's – that's the Bishop of Ely's old chapel – into a popish church. It was a bitter blow to those who thought they had rid England of popery for all time. It mocked the Reformation, and the men who fought and died to stop the Spaniards landing here in the time of the great Armada.'

He paused and turned his goblet round and round, and he looked at me, and then he looked at William, and he dropped his voice to a hush. 'And it was made worse by those Englishmen who sneaked into the masses and indulged themselves in an orgy of superstition and idolatry. It was unforgivable.'

He shook his head. 'People haven't forgotten. And they won't. You mark my words. If they think it's coming back again they'll fight on the streets. And calling it a riot or a civil disorder, or some name like that, won't make the slightest bit of difference.'

He opened his book and flicked through the pages, and then he thumped the cover shut. 'There are a lot of plays in here about kings and queens and what brought about their downfall. And I think our own King would do well to remember that his mother is a papist, and so is his wife, and they say his brother is sniffing around the priests. I fear that they may be the cause of his downfall. And when a man comes to write a play about our King, he'll say the Restoration was a mistake because it ended with the King attempting to restore the power of Rome.'

He sat for a while, and my head drifted through the haze of his words, and then he said: 'We are being very serious, and it is too late for this sort of thing. I think we should be making for bed,' and he stood up. 'If you'd like to take a candle, take one each, and follow me; I'll show you the way down the back stairs.'

'Stairs?' I said. 'Are we not going outside?'

He shook his head. 'I have a bedroom and a parlour over the office.'

I stood up and swayed a little. 'But why did we go outside and come in that door down there?' and I pointed to the alley. He laughed. 'It's to confuse the thieves. I put a lock on the outside and old Ramsdale opens it up in the morning.'

I nodded in a vague way. I couldn't think who old Ramsdale might be, but it didn't seem to matter.

We followed him along the corridor, and stopped for a piss in the pots. He leant over my shoulder and had a look, but for some reason or other that didn't worry me. Then we followed him through a room and down some stairs and into another room and into the shop that was an office. It was not as it was in the late afternoon. It was more like the inside of a ship: swaying and rolling in a beery swell.

'I'll get you a couple of quilts,' he said, 'and a couple of pillows,' and then one of you can come up and read to me. And I'll see what you can make of Shakespeare.'

I sat on the floor with my back to the bench and William slid down beside me. He raised his finger in the air and said: 'Bellarmine,' and we fucked the air, and laughed and fell on each other. Then I heard footsteps echoing on the stairs, and I raised my finger and said: 'Woodgate,' and we fucked the air again, and William made a crude sucking sound. Then our fingers drooped, and we toppled over. William lay on the boards and shut his eyes, and I lay upon him.

In my mind I began to read to Mister Woodgate. But my hands shook and my eyes skated around the words and there was no sense in them, and I closed the book. Then I walked in the gardens in Holborn, and I smelt the roses and picked the strawberries, and somebody called me 'My Lord of Ely', and I remembered that I hadn't told Mister Woodgate about my uncle who lived in Ely, and I sighed to myself; and then the eels swam into my mind. I saw them opening and shutting their mouths, and I felt them slithering up my legs. I grabbed my cock and I held it safe, and my mind sank into the black earth of Ely; and like the dead, I lay still, and waited for the day that would bring my body back to life again.

33

I heard a noise and the darkness seeped out of my mind, and I sat up. I opened my eyes, and the door opened, and it let in the light, the hard light of day. It hurt behind my eyes, and in my ears, and all the way round the inside of my head. I rested my head in my hands and I groaned and whispered: 'Dear God. What have you done to me?'

The man at the door chuckled to himself, and he lifted up the flap on the counter and dropped it down; and my head exploded.

I felt hot and cold, and dry in my mouth, and I wanted to piss. I wanted to walk up his secret stairs, and find those pots and piss. But the thought of it. The thought of my head jerking all the way up those stairs, and all the way down again was too much for me, and I crossed my legs and squashed the pain in my bladder, and groaned again.

The man leant over the counter, and his voice shrieked in my ear: 'Drink too much, did we?'

I shook my head and it shook my belly, and I could feel the rabbit hopping around in my belly. It was lively, too lively, and it sickened my belly, and I thought: if I move, I will be sick all over the floor. I pulled the quilt over my head and I sat rock-still in my warren of darkness.

I felt William sit up, and he said: 'Are you alive under there?'

'No.'

The man on the counter laughed. His laugh rolled over me like a thunderclap, and the feathers in the quilt did not deaden it, and in my mind I saw bright flashes of lightning.

I let the quilt slide away and I looked at William. The drink had paled his skin and bloodied his eyes and brought a tremble to his hands.

I tried to laugh but it hurt to laugh, and I sank into a pool of misery.

Rutherford ran into the office. He pulled off his hat and cloak and hissed: 'Morning, Ramsdale,' and he opened and shut the flap on the counter without making a sound. He leant against the door to the back room – it was still shut tight – and caught his breath, and pulled a square of white linen out of his pocket and wiped his brow. 'Christ,' he said, in a voice that was still running fast, 'that was bloody close.'

The clock on the wall put the time at one minute to seven.

In less than thirty seconds the door opened and they both turned and said: 'Good morning, Mister Woodgate.' Their words fell upon each other and chimed, as the voices of children chime when they greet their teacher in the classroom.

He nodded to both of them but he did not speak. Then he looked at us and he looked at them, and he said something under his breath, and they walked into the back room and shut the door.

He lifted the flap and dropped it down, and once again my head exploded, and he came and sat on the bench beside us. 'I thought you might have run away by now,' and he looked at me. 'You wanted to run, didn't you?' I nodded, and he smiled. 'Hmm,' he said, 'I thought you did,' and for a moment he was silent.

Then he looked at William, and shook his head. 'I thought you were the smart one. I thought you knew what you wanted. And I thought you knew how to get it,' and he stared at William for several seconds. 'I'm looking for a man. A man who knows what I want. If you're that man, you can get what you want,' and he let his eyes walk right round the office and they enclosed every corner of it.

William bit his lip and looked at the floor.

'I have to say that I'm disappointed in both of you. I had thought we understood each other. But maybe it was my fault. Maybe I shouldn't have given you so much to drink. And maybe I was expecting too much. So . . .' and he opened his hands and spread his fingers as if to let yesterday run through them. 'I'm not a vindictive man, and if you change your mind and come again,' and he smiled at me, 'and that includes you, I would be pleased to see you. And we would drink less and talk more, and I would listen to you read.'

He stood and paced up and down, and then he stopped with his feet pointing towards us. 'As I said, I'm not a vindictive man and I did promise you some work. Rutherford is taking a lighter to Deptford on Thursday. Full tide is at ten and they'll catch the turn at eleven. So if you're at the warehouse at seven in the morning, you can help with the loading and the unloading, and Rutherford will pay you.'

I nodded, and it pained my head, and I groaned and stood up. I handed him the quilt and the cushion, and I slunk out of the office.

They talk about dogs slinking away with their tails between their legs, and that was how I felt and maybe that was how I looked. But there was one difference. One importance difference: my tail was between my front legs, and the sight of Mister Woodgate, the sight of a master-in-waiting, had not excited me, and I had not wagged my tail at him.

I held onto this thought for the next two or three hours.

It helped the pain to die and it gave me a quiet sense of satisfaction, and I could understand what my Mother used to mean when she talked about her victories. I thought of her, locked in the grip of winter. I thought of her battling the cold; and battling the damp that rises from our earth floor and makes the bones in her feet ache. And I thought of her battling him. It brought a chill to my soul, and I began to think: what have I done for her, for her who has done so much for me?

I tried to think of something, something I had done. But I could think of nothing, nothing at all. And I knew that I wanted my nothing to be something, and I thought about Mister Salthouse, and I wondered if he had done something. And then I had to know. I had to know what he had done, and I turned to William and said: 'I want to go to Ely Place.'

He looked at me and sighed. The colour had not come back into his face and his eyes were still bloodshot. He turned around and mumbled something to himself, and we began to walk towards Holborn.

At Newgate we sat and rested. It used to be the main gate to the west. Now it was a prison, grim and grey, and heavy with menace. High on the walls, grilles of iron covered the windows and locked away the faces that were peering down at us.

My eyes wandered along the battlements; and I was wondering if anyone had ever escaped over the wall, when William tapped me on the arm. 'You see down there,' he said, 'in the shadows by that tavern?'

'Hmm,' I said.

'There's a man. He's walking very slowly, and he's coming towards us. He keeps stopping and looking over his shoulder. And I think it's John.'

I sat up with a jolt. 'John!'

The man had stopped by the door to a shop. I watched him tuck his basket under his arm, and then he turned and searched the crowd with his eyes. 'That's not John,' I said. 'It's like him, but it's not him.'

He came towards us, crab-like, with his face turned to the wall. He pulled the iron ring by the prison door and a bell jangled, and within a minute he was gone.

'He must be visiting someone,' I said, 'and he doesn't want anyone to see him going into the prison.'

William nodded. 'Strange we haven't seen John. I thought we might have.'

'Maybe they caught him. And he's in there,' and I pointed towards the prison.

He laughed. 'Well, I'm not going to pull on that ring and ask.'

'And nor am I,' and I stood up, and looked at the faces pressed to the grille high above me.

John was not among them.

We walked through the gate, and within a second or two the pedlar was saying: 'Good morning, sir. And you, sir, good morning to you too, sir.'

There was something about her, something appealing, and I smiled at her; and she said: 'Is this your first visit to London?'

I nodded. 'And I've come prepared,' and I whipped my scissors out of my pocket and pretended to stab her throat.

She threw her hands in the air and touched her face, and shrieked; and I laughed at her.

'Oh, you did give me a fright,' she said, 'and I didn't recognise you. You look so smart. And you, sir, you look very smart too.'

William nodded to her, and she nodded back and said: 'Maybe I could interest you in a handkerchief,' and she pulled a square of white linen from under her tray. 'A gentleman always carries a handkerchief, a gentleman does.'

He shook his head, and she showed it to me and I shook my head, and we laughed and she smiled at us, and we walked on.

Ely Place stood silent and empty.

We walked along the cobbles and I could hear the water sucking at my shoes. I looked at the plaque on the door and I read the words again and I knew it was after ten o'clock. And it was not later than twelve noon. It was the time for petitions. I raised my hand to knock, but my courage wavered and I walked a little. I walked towards the chapel, and I looked at the great window and the stone that read: 'SANCTA ETHELDREDA'.

I turned to William and said: 'She was the one who founded the abbey in Ely.'

'Hmm,' he said. 'I never thought much of her.'

'Why not?'

'She married the King, and he had to promise not to fuck her.'

'And why would he do that?'

He shrugged. 'They say she wanted to remain a virgin. That's what they say. And when he died she married again. And she wouldn't let the new one fuck her either. And when he got all randy,' and he thrust his arm into the air and jerked it up and down, 'she was scared stiff, and she ran away to a nunnery.'

I had heard the story before but never in words as crude as this, and I laughed, and said: 'It wasn't much of a marriage, was it?'

He shook his head. 'No wife of mine would get away with that.'

I looked at him and smiled. I had never thought of him being married. And I had never thought of myself being married. And I wondered what it would be like to be able to do it whenever I wanted to do it. Then he dug me in the ribs, and said: 'Are you going to knock on that door, or are you going to wander around and think about it for the rest of the morning?'

I bit my lip and walked straight to the door and knocked hard.

A woman opened the door. Her long black dress and her black cap had drained her face and her hands of colour. She leant forward and looked us up and down, and the cross that hung from the chain around her neck swung free. 'Yes,' she said, straightening up and bringing the cross back into the folds of her bosom, 'what do you want?'

'We have a petition,' I said, 'for the Bishop.'

She held out her hand. 'You can give it to me.'

'It's not written down. It's in my head.'

'Then you will have to go away and write it down.'

'I had thought I could talk to Mister Salthouse about it first. I would like his advice.'

She screwed up her face and peered at me. 'Do you know the Reverend Mister Salthouse?'

I nodded. 'I come from Elme. And I was hoping he would see me.'

'Elme? He comes from Elme. Is that the same Elme?'

I nodded again.

'You wait here,' and she shut the door in my face.

I turned to William, and the door opened again. 'What name shall I say?'

'Fenton. William and Martyn Fenton.'

She nodded and shut the door again.

We stood and waited for five or ten minutes, and then the door opened and she said: 'You can come in,' and she pointed to the mat, 'and make sure you wipe your feet.'

34

Mister Salthouse laid his hands on the edge of the table and looked at us, sitting on the other side, and said: 'I thought I'd seen the last of you two. I thought you'd come to your senses. And I assumed your madness would be like a summer sickness: it would come and go, and that would be the end of it. But I see that I was wrong,' and he lifted his hands and looked at his fingernails.

He placed his hands back on the edge of the table and turned to me. 'I did go to see your father. He made me sit down in a chair by the fire, and he told your mother to go outside, and he said he would call her if he needed her.'

I nodded to myself. It was what he always did if a man came to see him.

'I looked at your father and I knew that I could not say what you wanted me to say. He is a big man. A strong man. And he would not have taken kindly to what I had to say. You can call me a coward if you like, and maybe I am, but I am also wise in the ways of the world, and I know that a man should not pry into another man's marriage,' and he paused and fingered the polished wood of the table. 'In the marriage service your mother promised to obey your father. If he is beating her, he is doing it because she is not obeying him. To you this may sound hard and cruel, but that is what she promised to do. She made a solemn vow, in church, in front of witnesses, and she made it of her own free will. And I cannot interfere.'

In his words I heard the echo of Aunt Mary's words, and there was no comfort in them; and as I looked into the polished wood, my tears wet my eyes and they blurred my reflection.

I sniffed and wiped my eyes and I said, in a whisper: 'What did you say to him?'

'What did I say? I told him you were living with your Aunt Mary. I said you had been sick, and she nursed you back to health. And now you were fit and well. And I said you often spoke of your mother, and I thought you were missing both of them.'

'And what did he say to that?'

'He grunted and asked me if there was anything else. I said there wasn't, and he told me I could go. And he didn't thank me for coming, and he didn't stand up, and I had to let myself out.'

I turned to William. The blood had drained out of his face and he looked as though he were going to be sick at any moment. He looked worse, much worse than when we woke, and he made me feel that I had missed something, something I should not have missed.

I turned to Mister Salthouse and said: 'She will suffer till the day she dies because you did not have the courage to do what you said you would do,' and I shook my head. 'You deceived us, and you betrayed her.' I swallowed hard, and the word 'betrayed' stuck in my throat and my mind. And then I knew what William knew – and I felt sick.

I stood up and pushed away my chair, and walked out of the room.

Mister Salthouse ran after me and put his hand on my shoulder. I shook it off; and he said: 'Sometimes it helps to pray. It gives you time to think. Time to put things in perspective,' and he took my elbow.

He guided me down the corridor and into a tiny chapel. I sat down and he sat beside me, and I heard William sit behind us. It was not the Chapel of Saint Etheldreda. It was far too small for that.

For a long time I just sat. My mind was dead. And I could not pray.

The chapel was soaked in gloom. It seeped into me, like the wet fog of evening, and somehow the face on the picture, the face that loomed above the altar, became my Mother's face. It was puffy and purple with pain. It was old and tired. And the eyes were full of tears.

When the gloom began to clear a little, the face became the face of the Virgin Mary, and the years dropped away from her, and so did the pain. She looked young and innocent. But her eyes were empty – as if they had never been lived in.

She was not my Mother and she never would be. My Mother lived inside her eyes, and she was not an innocent virgin. She knew how to spread her legs for a man. She knew the pain of it, and she knew the price of his seed. And one night, long after he had pressed his flesh into hers, and the pain was gone and the price was paid, her voice came to me. It came over the black mountains of sleep that were my Father, and it hung in the quilted valleys that lay between us, and it made this prayer: 'Dear God, this is my cross, and I will bear it in silence. I will bear it for him, and I will bear it for You. And I will bear it till the day I die, if that is what You ask of me.'

I looked at the cross – the cross that nailed her to our bed of pain – standing on the altar between two candles.

A man was hanging on the cross. He was dead. And there was no hope for him, and I let my eye drift down to the front of the altar. It was covered in a cloth of gold that had been embroidered with white lilies, blue crosses and the words: AVE MARIA GRATIA PLENA. For a long time the secret of what I was looking at did not make a mark on my mind.

Then I began to see what I was seeing, and my soul recoiled in horror and a shiver of fear ran down my spine.

I stood up – I could feel myself trembling – and I turned to William and said: 'We have to go.'

Mister Salthouse rang a small bell – it sat on a table to the right of the altar – and within a second or two the lady in black was at the door, saying: 'If you will come this way, I will show you out.'

Outside I turned to William and said: 'I'm sorry, we should never have gone in there.'

'He betrayed her. You know that, don't you?'

I nodded. 'He didn't know what he was doing.'

My mind ran back to the day my Father came to see Aunt Mary. It was the day William came home early, and the cut on my arm was healing. I could get out of bed and walk around, and the haze in my head was beginning to lift. My Father stood at the bottom of the stairs, and I heard him say: 'Do you know where the boy is?' And she said: 'No. I've not seen him, not since he was last here with you, when the corn was cut.'

Her lie was betrayed by Mister Salthouse. And on the day she came to see my Mother, he had known about the lie. He would not forgive her. It was not in his nature to forgive. He would have known she was coming, and he would have waited for her. And he would have made my Mother wait outside.

I could see him and her. And I could hear him. Accusing. Threatening. Condemning. Banning. And I thought about the hurt that tore her soul apart the first time she was banned from our house. And this time, this time was the day she died, and I could feel it tearing her heart apart.

William looked at me. 'Our Father killed her.'

'Yes. I think he did.'

We walked in silence for about half a mile, then William said: 'I cannot take revenge on him, but I can take revenge on the man who betrayed her,' and he stopped and turned towards me.

I looked into his eyes, they were like ponds overflowing with misery, and I said: 'She was betrayed by Mister Salthouse. I think it was an accident, and I think our Father killed her. Not with his hands but with his words. And I think she paid a terrible price for that plan of ours. But,' and I hesitated, 'despite the pain and the anger that is in you – and me – and hard as this is to say, I think the time has come to forgive and forget. And I think we should listen to the words of the Gospel, and turn the other cheek.'

His jaw fell, and he shook his head. 'Forgive! Forget! And turn the other cheek? Christ Almighty, Martyn! Have you gone soft in the head? The only cheeks that man would be interested in you turning are the cheeks of your arse! And if you think anything else you're a bloody fool.'

The colour came back into his face. It was plum-red and it was blazing with anger.

I looked at the ground, and I feared if I said anything it would inflame him some more, and I bit my lip and wished I'd never heard of Mister Salthouse and that bloody plan of ours.

'As far as I'm concerned,' he said, 'Mister Salthouse betrayed her – or exposed her lie if you want to use blunt words – and he killed her. That's what he did. And the fact that he didn't do it with his own hands is irrelevant. And you think about this: if he'd done what he said he was going to do, none of this would have happened. So there won't be any forgiving, or forgetting, or turning of cheeks. What there will be is vengeance. And don't you go trying to tell me it's wrong. I remember that bit in the Old Testament where the Lord God says: Vengeance is mine. Well, if he can have it up there,' and he pointed to the sky, 'I can have it down here,' and he pointed to the ground. 'I'll think of something that will mean the end of that bastard, and if you won't help me, I'll do it on my own.'

We walked on in silence. I kept hoping that the anger would drain out of him, but every time I stole a look at his face it was still plum-red, and his mouth was clenched tight.

About twenty minutes later he said to me: 'Do you remember the young man in Charing Cross, the one who was in love?'

'Hmm,' I said.

Then he told me what he was going to do.

It brought me out in a cold sweat. I shook my head and said: 'You can't do that.'

'Yes I can,' and he dug in his pocket and brought out one penny and two farthings. 'How much have you got?'

I brought out one halfpenny and one farthing, and I said: 'And there's a halfpenny in each shoe.'

'It's not enough.'

'No,' I said, 'it's not,' and I felt relieved, and I turned away so that he couldn't see my face.

'What do you think it would cost?'

I thought a shilling, but I said: 'One and sixpence, or maybe two shillings,' and I knew his plan was dead. Stone-dead. 'Maybe you'll think of something else. Something that isn't so expensive.'

'No. This is what I want to do.'

'They would put you in prison if they caught you. Have you thought of that?'

He shook his head. 'It would be worth it.'

We walked some more, and I was just beginning to think we had walked the madness out of him when he said: 'I know how to get the money. Come on.'

As we came close to Bishopsgate, I began to suspect the

worst. 'Mister Woodgate's not going to give you any money.'

'Who said anything about giving?'

I shook my head, and about fifty yards from the office he said: 'You wait here. I might be a while, so don't get impatient and wander off. And don't come down to the office looking for me.'

I sat by the public conduit and drank some water, and I let it pour over my hands, and an hour flowed away, and then another.

When he came back, he cupped his hands and filled them with water, and rinsed out his mouth three times. He spat the last mouthful onto the cobbles – near my feet – and then he looked at me and grinned, and dug in his pocket.

And when his hand unfolded, I was looking at two shillings.

35

A few seconds later as we began to walk, William said: 'I'm sure it's around here somewhere.'

I shrugged. I hadn't seen the stall he was looking for, and in my heart I was hoping we wouldn't find it. And I was thinking if I dawdled along, it might be shut by the time we did find it, and I was casting around in my mind for something that might distract him, when I realised what he had just done to Mister Woodgate. The shock of it brought me to an abrupt halt.

He turned and stopped, and an angry look crossed his face, and he said: 'What the hell's the matter with you now?'

I looked at him. I did not know how he could have done what he had done, and I said: 'Do you remember that time we talked about whores?'

'You're always talking about whores. What am I supposed to remember?'

'It was the time we talked about men being whores. And I said there's no such thing because we don't have a name for them.'

'Hmm. I remember that.'

'Well, I was wrong.'

He laughed. 'It's not like you to admit you're wrong.'

I shrugged. 'I was wrong. There is a name.'

He stood still, and looked me straight in the eye. 'And what is it?'

I took a step back. 'The two-shilling man.'

He jumped straight at me, grabbed me by the scruff of the neck and hoisted me in the air, and I saw the stall in the distance. Then he rammed his fist in my face. 'You are my brother, and my cousin, and my best friend. But if you ever say that again I'll smash your bloody head in,' and he shook me hard. 'Do you understand?'

I nodded, and he put me down, and I sucked in a breath and straightened my shirt. Inside I was trembling and wanting to run away, but I knew I had to stay. I had to do something to keep him away from that stall. I turned and began to walk away, and over my shoulder I said: 'How did Mister Woodgate know you could read?'

'I told him when you went out for a piss.'

'And did he ask you why she lied to him?'

'She?'

'Your mother. Aunt Mary.'

He came after me, and we walked in silence for about twenty or thirty feet, and he said: 'I never thought of it as a lie. It was what we did. It was our secret.'

'Your secret?'

'Hmm. My Father used to say I was simple. And he used to say I was like him-in-Elme: too stupid to know any better, and too thick to learn. She taught me at night, when he wasn't there. It was our secret, our way of getting even. And it was our way of laughing at him.'

'But why did she lie to Mister Woodgate? Why didn't she tell him the truth?'

He shrugged. 'Habit, I suppose.'

'I think she knew what was going to happen. And she didn't want it to happen to you.'

He shook his head. 'I don't know what she thought. But I do know the walls in our house are thin. And I do know she went to your bed in the night. And maybe she thought you would look after him better than I would. And he would come again. And then she could pay the rent on quarter-days, and we could live in that house a little longer.'

I stopped and looked at him, and I felt sick, and he said: 'There is more. Do you want to know what it is? Are you strong enough to know the truth? Or are you just a smart-arse, clever with words, and clever with all these thoughts of yours?' And he gave me a shove.

I stumbled backwards, and bit my lip, and looked at the cobbles.

'Late at night, when her guests were in bed, she'd go up to their room, and she'd let them fuck her. And that was why they came again. That was why they paid her more than the price of the room. So, don't you go talking to me about whores, or what has to be done. I know what has to be done. She did it. And I did it. And one day you might have to do it.'

The thought dropped into my mind like a stone into a pond. On the surface it vanished without a trace, but it was there in the mud at the bottom. It was watching and waiting, and stirring the waters, and I knew it would not go away. And it made me feel queasy.

We walked in silence for several minutes, then he said: 'I'm doing this for her. It will be the last thing that I can do for her. And I want your help. I know I said I didn't need your help, but that's not true. I do need you. And I want you to remember all the things she did for you, and I want you to do this for her. I think it's the least you can do,' and he paused, and added in a voice that was close to a whisper: 'I don't want to get down on my knees, and beg for help. But if that is what I have to do, that is what I will do.'

I stopped and looked at my shoes. They were damp and splashed with mud, and I knew that I was defeated. I turned around and said: 'The stall is back this way.'

We bought two buckets, two brushes and a bag of lime. The man on the stall said we had enough to wash two houses, and William said we'd give ours two coats. The man pulled a face and took down his sign, and said: 'You don't look like a couple of whitewashers. Not to me you don't. But if you're going to do it,' and he tapped the words on his sign that said 'HOUSES CLEANED AND WASHED', 'I'll give you one piece of advice, and I won't charge you for it. It's this: don't mix your wash too thin because then you'll have to put on two coats and that takes twice as long. And that's not the way to make money,' and he began to cough and go red in the face.

William thumped him on the back and it seemed to ease his coughing. He nodded his thanks and said: 'It comes from breathing in too much lime, when you mix in the water. Do it slowly and you won't end up being whitewashed inside here,' and he tapped his chest, and laughed a gurgling laugh.

As we walked away, I said to William: 'You don't look like a whitewasher to me.'

He smiled to himself. 'No, I would say I'm a signwriter.'

'And what would I be?'

'Ohh,' he said, with a long drawl, 'I think you'd be an archer.'

'An archer?'

'Hmm,' and he began to giggle, 'an archer.'

I stopped and blinked. 'I don't understand.'

He watched me struggling with it for a moment or two, then he said: 'They draw arrows, don't they?'

His words of this morning shot into my head: 'You can paint the arrows if you won't write the words.' And I slapped my head – as if to slap away my own stupidity – and I laughed and said: 'And you talk about me being clever with words.'

He smiled and we became companions in crime. Conspirators, the law would have called us, and it made me think of Guy Fawkes and his papist friends. They conspired to kill King James by blowing up the Houses of Parliament. But their plot was discovered, and they were caught and put to death.

I did not want to be caught, and I began to think about William's plan – it was too simple to be called a plot – and I feared that it would not work, and I said: 'Buggery is not a crime. I think it's a sin, and if it were proved in a church court it would defrock Mister Salthouse, but I don't think it would make a crowd riot. And I don't think it would put him in Newgate. There's no evidence against him. Not here there's not. And I'm not going to stand in front of a court because they wouldn't believe me. They'd believe him. That's what your mother said, and I think she was right.'

'I think he'll confess. I think we'll shame him into it.'

I shrugged. 'Maybe yes, and maybe no.' And it worried me, and I began to think about his chapel and the picture of the Virgin whom he worshipped like a goddess, and I said: 'Do you remember that chapel?'

'What chapel?'

'The one in Ely Place. The one we sat in with Mister Salthouse.'

'No, not really. I just followed you in and sat down. I was thinking about her. And how he betrayed her.'

'It was his chapel, his private chapel, and he prays to the Virgin Mary in there. And that is popery. The evidence is there. It's there for all to see. And if they see it, it will destroy him.'

He looked at me and nodded in a solemn way, and said: 'And I remember what Mister Woodgate said about Ely Place and popery – and I think we should use both ideas.'

Towards midnight, when the lights in the windows had died, and Holborn no longer echoed with the rumble of carts and the tread of feet, we made our way to Ely Place.

On Mister Salthouse's door William painted a large white cross and to the right of it, on the bricks, he wrote 'PAPIST' and to the left he wrote 'PERVERT'.

We stood back and surveyed his work. 'It's too small,' I said, 'and it's too low down. It should be bigger, and it should be above head height. And then if a crowd gathers, as it did for that young man with his "I LOVE YOU", everyone will still be able to read it.'

He nodded and painted a long line of arrows. 'They look all right,' I said. 'We just need them to guide people here. And once they're here it doesn't matter if they can see them or not.'

He came and stood by me. 'You do the left-hand side, and I'll do the right, and if anyone comes for Christ's sake hide and don't make a noise.'

I painted some arrows, and learnt how to stop the whitewash dribbling, and then, in foot-high letters, across the bricks and the stone and the glass of the windows, I wrote: 'THE REVEREND SALTHOUSE BUGGERS LITTLE BOYS.'

I painted some more arrows and some more words and about an hour later when I was nearing the end of the houses, and could see the fields stretching into the distance, a voice – a man's voice – said: 'Papist is spelt with an i. Back there a bit.'

My heart thumped and I turned round and he was pointing back along the trail of arrows, and I said: 'Thank you,' and he said: 'That's quite all right. I have always taken a pride in my spelling,' and he doffed his hat to me and walked on.

I put down the bucket, and my hand shook a spray of whitewash all over the ground, and I had to sit down on the step for a couple of minutes.

The arrows guided me back to Ely Place. It was dead quiet, and there was no sign of William. I painted some more arrows and worked my way down another street, and towards the end I wrote: 'POPERY THIS WAY.'

My feet were aching and my eyes were sore and my hands were white, like the arrows. I made my way back to Ely Place again. There was still no sign of William, so I followed his arrows all the way to Newgate. He was about a quarter of the way up the prison wall – walking along the point where the slope changes to the vertical – and he had just finished writing: 'THE PAPISTS ARE BACK IN ELY PLACE.'

The arrows ran from the words, they ran as far as my eye could see, and they filled me with horror. I could not believe what he had done. What we had done.

I whistled to him, and he turned and waved and slid down the stone slope.

'What do you think?'

I shook my head. 'I'm scared,' I said. 'I didn't think it would look like this. You can't miss it. It's almost too big. Too strong. And when I think of all the hundreds who come out of those gates every day . . .'

'And will follow the arrows . . .' he grinned. 'And that's just what we want, isn't it? Now we can throw these away,' and he went to toss his bucket and brush into a garden.

I grabbed his arm. 'If these were found, and someone started to ask questions, that man on the stall would remember us.'

'Hmm,' he said, 'he would,' and he dropped his brush into the bucket.

We walked back to Ely Place and out to the fields, and we sank our buckets and brushes in a deep ditch. We washed our hands and tried to wash the white spots off our clothes and our shoes, and then we crawled into a hedgerow and cuddled into each other.

As the sky began to lighten, began to outline the leaves and colour them green and brown, I closed my eyes and fell asleep.

36

The chirping of the hedge sparrows woke me. They were hopping from branch to branch about a foot or two above my head, and peeping at the dawn. They seemed close, like a family that had fledged together; and I stayed still and they didn't notice me.

My painting arm ached and my fingers hurt. I clenched and unclenched my hand and wriggled my fingers, and pulled my cloak a little closer. One of the sparrows stopped and put his head on the side and watched my fingers, and I wondered if he saw them as fat worms.

I closed my eyes and listened to the chirping, and I drifted back to sleep. When I woke again the sparrows were gone – like a gentle dream – and the leaves of autumn were bright with sunshine.

I yawned and rolled over and shook William, and we crawled out of the hedgerow and stood up and stretched. We were standing on the edge of a meadow, near a deep ditch. In the water, about twenty feet away, a slick of white had risen from the bottom of the ditch. It was like a long white curl on a head of black hair, and as we watched, the water twirled the ends round and round and it grew a little longer. I picked up a clod of earth and heaved it into the ditch. It parted the curl and covered the surface of the water with strands of white hair. I heaved another clod and then another, and so did William, and they stirred up the water and stirred in the whitewash.

I laughed and turned to William, and the laughter gurgled away. He was splattered with white. It was on his shoes and his breeches and his cloak and his hat, and the spots that he washed in the dark had become splotches of pale white with ragged ink-blot edges. I looked at my shoes and breeches and I took off my cloak: they too were covered in spots and blotches. I had less than him, but I knew at once that I had enough to identify me as a whitewasher, and a signwriter, and if a man was possessed of William's sense of humour, an archer.

I looked at him and said: 'We're going to have to take them off and wash them.'

He stretched out his arms and looked at his sleeves, and then he lifted his leg and looked at his breeches and his shoes. 'That'll take bloody hours.'

'Hmm, it will. But you don't want anyone to know it was you, do you?'

He gave me a slow nod, and we sat inside the ditch, on the slope near the edge of the water, and sponged our clothes and wrung out the water and hung them on the hedge to dry. The sun was almost warm, but the breeze was cold and it cut through my white shirt and my grey under-breeches and I shivered and jumped up and down and tried to keep warm.

I kept feeling my breeches. They felt as though they would never dry, and I scrambled into the hedgerow and sheltered behind the trunk of a tree.

After three or four hours, when the sun was still climbing into the sky, and our clothes were damp-dry, we dressed and walked towards Ely Place.

We rounded a corner and met a crowd of about twenty people. They were muttering and pointing and someone was scrubbing off my words. The words were loath to come off, and somehow, bathed in sunlight, they looked stronger, harder, and they seemed to have taken on a life of their own. They did not belong to me any more. And I heard a woman say: 'If I ever get my hands on the little bastard who did this I'll bloody murder him. God help me, I will!'

I stole a glance at her, and the window, and the whitewash that wouldn't come off, and I hung my head and walked on.

The arrows possessed some strange power. They sped me along the road, and walking became jogging became running, and it wasn't just me that was being affected. It was William, and the two men in front of me, and the boy behind me, and the woman who'd just come out of one of the houses. We seemed to be knotted together and one of the men yelled: 'Do you think it's true?'

And I yelled back: 'Yes I do!'

We began to run faster and I felt a sense of panic; and I could hear loud noises, and shouting, and chanting.

Then we rounded the corner and ran straight into Ely Place. I skidded to a halt and my jaw sagged. We were standing on the edge of two or three hundred people and to my left, just above head height, I read: 'THE REVEREND SALTHOUSE BUGGERS LITTLE BOYS.' I swallowed hard and looked at the faces around me. They were hard, grim, and unforgiving.

Someone shouted: 'Out! Out! Get him out!' It was repeated by a man near me, and then another and another and it ran through the crowd, and it circled all the way around the edge of Ely Place and by the time it came back to us it had become: 'Out! Out! Papist out!'

I looked at William. He was giggling and laughing and jumping up and down and trying to see above the heads of the crowd. A woman shoved me and I shoved her back, and she said: 'I thought you had better manners than that,' and I looked at her. It was the pedlar with her tray folded up and her hat pulled off. I laughed and yelled, 'What do you think?'

'I can't make up my mind. They're such a silly lot round here. They get worked up over nothing.'

'Nothing!' The word stung my pride and killed off my common sense, and I yelled in her face: 'I'll tell you what nothing is. It's doing this to little boys,' and I pretended to shove my fist up William's arse. 'And I've been in his chapel. I've seen the crucifix and the candles. And I've seen him worshipping the Virgin Mary. And I've heard him ring the bells. And I know what he does. I know! Because I've seen it with my own eyes.'

Her face became flushed and her mouth opened and shut several times. 'You said you came from Ely, didn't you? And this is Ely Place,' and she paused and looked me in the eye, 'and you know. Don't you?'

I nodded to her, and our noses almost touched.

She threw her hands in the air, and began to push through the crowd. William grabbed me. 'What the hell did you have to say that to her for?'

I shrugged. I was bubbling with excitement, with madness, and I didn't care. And I didn't want to care. And I yelled: 'Salthouse! Salthouse! We want Salthouse!' Within a second or two my words were running away from me. They were running from lip to lip, and they stirred the crowd and in their wake came a buzz, an angry buzz, like that of bees swarming to attack.

I laughed and jumped up and down; and from behind me a voice cried: 'Make way! Make way!'

I turned and looked up at a pikeman. Behind him were five more. And behind them came the Bishop's coach. I moved away but the others didn't. They stayed firm, and the pikemen halted and the horses shied. The coachman yelled to the pikemen: 'I can't stay, I'll have to turn around. They'll bolt if I stay.'

Two pikemen grabbed the horses by the bridles and calmed them down. Then they walked them round and the coach drove away; and the pikemen began to force their through the crowd.

A boy picked up a stone and hurled it. And so did another one. Then a window broke and the crowd cheered. The boy next to William picked up a couple of stones, and William said to him: 'If you can break two windows I'll give you a farthing.' For a moment the boy stared at him wide-eyed, then he laughed and ducked down and forced himself into the crowd.

Then I began to hear a voice, a woman's voice. It sounded loud and shrill, but I couldn't see the speaker till a couple of men hoisted her up in the air and onto their shoulders.

It was the pedlar.

Bits of her voice came to me: 'Candles . . . and crucifix . . . seen them with his own eyes . . . and the whitewash signs . . . you've read the signs . . . the signs about this,' and she thrust her fist up and down in the air as I had done. And a laugh, a bawdy laugh rippled around the crowd, and she said: 'It's true! It's all true. You ask him,' and she pointed to me.

I shrank into my cloak and pulled my hat over my head and grabbed William, and we slunk along the edge of the crowd.

I heard a window break and then another, and the crowd cheered and laughed. Then the window above the door with the white cross opened, and Mister Salthouse stuck his head out and yelled: 'The pikemen are here,' and he pointed to the men who were still trying to force their way to the door. 'And the troops on horseback will soon be here. And God help you then!'

His threat silenced the crowd, and I yelled: 'That's Salthouse! That's the papist!'

The crowd moaned. It was a eerie sound. Half-strangled, like the wind that moans in the trees when a storm is approaching.

Then another window broke and the pedlar yelled: 'The proof is in the chapel. Look in the chapel,' and another window broke.

From a garret window, high above the white cross, the lady in black looked down upon us. Her hands were touching her face, and she looked bewildered, like a queen besieged in her tower. I thought of Mary, Bloody Mary, and I tapped William on the shoulder and pointed to the window. 'She looks just like Bloody Mary.' He nodded, and so did the man next to him. And then the man whispered to the woman beside him and she pointed to the window and I heard her say: 'Bloody Mary. Remember Bloody Mary?' And her words rippled into the crowd and they fed the fever.

Then someone near the front yelled: 'Heave on the door!' The crowd began to swell and heave and push, and then it calmed for a moment, and then it began to swell and heave and push again.

William grabbed me and we moved along a few yards, but we still couldn't get a clear view, and then two boys were pulling at his sleeve and one was saying: 'Can I have me farthing now, mister? Please. And he wants one,' and he pointed to the other boy, "cause he did a couple for you too.'

William laughed and gave him a halfpenny and said: 'If you do four more you can have another halfpenny.'

The boy grinned and grabbed his friend, and they doubled over and slipped away.

We edged further along the crowd and I stood on a step and grabbed hold of a rail. Then the crowd roared and I jumped up and down and tried to see what was happening. I turned to the lady next to me and said: 'Can you see?'

'I think they've broken down the door.'

I looked at William and grinned, and a window on the first floor was flung open, and a man pushed his head out and waved a crucifix in the air. The crowd fell silent, and a groan, a disbelieving groan ran from mouth to mouth. Then the man waved a candlestick in the air and he tossed it into the crowd, and the mood changed. They laughed and cheered, and then he threw the next candlestick and they clapped and whistled; and the lady next to me said: 'I would have liked one of those.'

I heard a window break and then another and another, and the pikes clustered close to the door. They looked like a crown of thorns and they reminded me of the crown that was forced onto the head of Our Lord. I thought of his trial and how Pontius Pilate washed his hands of him. And I thought of Mister Salthouse and how he washed his hands of my Mother, and I wanted him brought to trial. I wanted him punished. I wanted him to suffer, as I had suffered, as she had suffered. And in my mind I saw him condemned. I saw the crown of thorns forced onto his head. I saw the blood dribble down his face, and I saw the pain in his eyes. I saw the cross that lay before him, and I thought of all the times he said that we must take on the sufferings of Christ and be like him. And I knew that this was his time, his time to stumble and fall, and walk the road to Gethsemane.

I laughed with the crowd and I hooted and jeered like the Pharisees of so long ago; and then the boy was back saying to William: 'We done four for you, and now we wants our money.'

William put his hand in his pocket, and then he said to me: 'Have you got any money?'

I pulled out a coin and slipped it into the boy's hand, and I said: 'Now piss off! And don't come back again.'

He grinned and turned away, and as he bent to run into the crowd, a hand grabbed me by the neck, and jerked me round. I was looking into the face of Mister Woodgate and he was saying: 'What the hell do you think you're doing?' But before I could answer, or even think of an answer, he said: 'And look at your clothes. Just look at them!'

I looked at my cloak and my breeches. They had dried and the spots had reappeared. There weren't as bad as when I woke, but they were still there, like white speckles on a brown egg.

He grabbed William by the neck and pushed our heads together, and hissed into our ears: 'You did this! Didn't you?' And he turned to William. 'And you spent the money on whitewash. Didn't you?'

William nodded, and he jerked us apart and banged our heads together.

My mind exploded into a thousand little bits and they glittered with light; and I sagged at the knees. His hand pulled me back up, and through a haze of dying glitter and little bits that were beginning to clump together again, I looked into his face. It was white and his eyes were blazing like fires set in the snow. I could not feel the heat of his eyes, but I could feel the wet chill of the snow, and it put out the madness that burnt within me. And I felt sick, and I began to tremble.

'And well you might tremble,' he said to me, and he took my arm and he guided us out of the crowd. 'If they catch you,' he whispered, 'they will charge you with inciting a riot. And they will hang you.'

I looked at the ground and scuffled my feet. The word 'hang' was ringing in my mind, and through the ringing came the sounds of laughing, yelling, jeering and clapping. I felt scared. Dead scared. I looked at William. His face was white, whiter than whitewash, whiter than snow. It was dead white. We looked at each other and swallowed hard. Mister Woodgate pulled us close to his chest and wrapped his arms around us and said: 'Listen to me. And listen very carefully. They will not forgive you for this. They will call it a riot, and if this crowd turns nasty that's what it will be. And they will say you started it, and they will hang you at Tyburn. And don't go thinking they won't find any witnesses because they will. There's always someone. Someone ready to take a secret shilling and say what they saw, or what they think they saw. And if they see those,' and he fingered some of the spots on my cloak, 'they won't need any witnesses, will they?'

I shook my head, and he said: 'You have to get out of here and you have to wash those clothes. And the best place would be out in the fields somewhere, and don't come back into the city. Not today and not tonight. And tomorrow, you should go to Aldgate, at dawn, and come in when they open the gate and go straight to the warehouse at Billingsgate. Don't go to any markets or any other places where you might be seen or recognised. Just go straight to the warehouse and you can hide in there till it's time to go to Deptford.'

Then we heard a sudden cheer and a thunderous roar, and he said: 'Forget about them and go,' and he pointed down the road. 'And walk. Don't run. People remember those who run. It looks as though you've just stolen a purse, or someone's after you. So amble along nice and slowly, and keep your hats pulled down over your faces.'

We returned to the meadow with the ditch and we heaved some more clods of earth at the white curl that had grown again on the surface of the water, and we washed our clothes and hung them out to dry. The sparrows were back in the hedgerow, chirping away, and flitting in and out of the leaves. They were possessed of a joy, a liveliness that we did not have, and we sank into a morose silence and dozed in the sunshine.

When the sun was low in the sky and the breeze had dropped and our clothes would not dry any more, we dressed and walked towards the west, towards the spot where the sun would soon drop below the horizon. I could feel the damp in my breeches and I could feel the hunger in my belly, and I was wondering what we could buy for a halfpenny, when we seemed to be caught up in a crowd. Not a big crowd bubbling with excitement like this morning, but a small crowd, sombre and serious. They were grouped around a cart, and they were following the road to Newgate.

A few minutes later, on the corner of a large heath, we could see another small crowd and a cart. A strange structure towered above them. It appeared to be made from three tree trunks, tall and straight and all the same size, and it looked as though they were joined together at the top by three beams. As we came closer the beams opened out and they formed a triangle high in the sky. As the triangle began to fill with the red of the sunset, the cart moved into the tree trunks and then I could see a black shape hanging close to one of the trunks. Men climbed into the cart and up a ladder, and they lifted down the black shape. It sagged and its legs splayed, and I turned to William and said: 'I think this is Tyburn.'

He bit his lips and looked at me, but he did not say a word.

Then the cart and the people began to come towards us, and we stood to the side and waited for them to pass.

We walked to the gallows and stood under Tyburn Tree. The sky was now blood red, and it looked as though the blood from those who died here had washed the sky and coloured the clouds. For a long time I stood in frozen horror, and then my stomach retched and I was sick beside one of the tree trunks, and I looked down at the earth. It was scuffed clean. There was not a single blade of grass to be seen. It was as if every living thing abhorred this place of death and destruction.

Then the blood oozed out of the sky, and the grey of the clouds locked away the sun for another day. And the black of the night filled in the triangle and made it into one of those flat black hats that a judge wears when he pronounces the sentence of death; and I said to William: 'I don't feel like anything to eat.'

He nodded, and as we turned to walk back to the meadow with the ditch, I began to think about Mister Salthouse and to wonder what they had done to him.

37

We huddled into the arches of Mister Woodgate's warehouse and waited.

Twice in the night and again in the morning I had tried to talk to William about Mister Salthouse and what we had done. But he pushed me away, not with his hands but with his manner, and he made me feel alone, alone on the ice that is our friendship.

In my mind I walked the ice – it was firm and it had not begun to crack or thaw – and I crossed the frozen wastelands of the past and they brought me back to him. And he was still my friend.

I put my arm around his shoulder and he half turned and looked at me. His eyes had shrivelled and died, like walnuts that have been kept in the shell too long. I drew him to me, and he buried his head in my cloak, and he began to shiver.

Then he slept for a while, and I watched the mist rise from the waters of the Thames. The mist was grey and silent, like the dawn of an hour ago. It chilled my hands and wet my nose, and at the water's edge it wet the boards of the quay.

To our right Billingsgate was sucking boats out of the mist at the rate of one or two a minute. Its quays were full, and the boats were tying up to each other and forming long chains that looked like floating bridges. The men on the boats were heaving baskets of fish, live crabs and oysters along the bridge till they reached the quayside. Then the porters were grabbing the baskets and hoisting them onto their heads and making the hats that had caught my eye when we first sat on the steps by London Bridge.

That was a week ago today. A week ago, in an hour or two, to be exact. And I thought about the things we should have done, the things we could have done, the things that were lost and gone for ever; and they filled my mind with gloom.

I closed my eyes and drifted in the gloom. I drifted without thinking, or trying to think, and then William stirred, and I opened my eyes. They led me across the quay – it was stumped with piles and swept of life – and then I floated down the river, down the water that would carry us away before the morning was done.

I looked at the seagulls hovering in the mist. They too had been here on our first morning, and they would be here tomorrow; and if we were caught or betrayed by our own stupidity, they would be here on our last morning.

I thought of that last morning. It made me cough and choke and gasp for breath, and it brought me out in a sweat. The sweat was cold and it chilled my body, and I saw the rope at Tyburn. It would chill my body for ever, and there would be no more restless nights like last night. I would rest in peace and the worms would have me. And when I was dug up and someone else was buried in my place, my sightless eyes would not see the spade cut into my bones. And my deaf ears, my dead ears, they would not hear the prayers for him who was to rest in my place.

I let these thoughts of gloom, of death, seep away and I began to think about the lighter. I was not sure what it would look like, apart from being empty and riding high, and I peered into the mist, but there was no sign of such a craft and I began to think it might not arrive. I began to think a promise might not be a promise, but then I looked at my shoes: they were pointing down the river.

It was a sign. A sign to walk the waters as we would say in Elme. And I leant against the bricks and shut my eyes for a moment or two.

Then a long flat boat with four men at the oars came towards us. It came out of the mist with a slow sculling, like something that was drifting or dreaming along. As it touched the quay, one of the men stood up, and when he saw us he shouted: 'Is this Woodgate's?'

I shouted: 'Yes!' and he waved and heaved a rope around the bollard.

Three of the men walked over to Billingsgate and the fourth one sat on the edge of the quay and watched the boat.

About twenty minutes later William woke and yawned, and his eyes had lost their shrivelled look. He stood up, stretched, and wandered down to the boat. When he came back, he said: 'They've gone to buy some bread and cheese and a basket of hot cockles. And he says if we want to do the same we can have some of his vinegar.'

I fished in my pocket and pulled out a halfpenny. 'That's my last one.'

He slid down the wall and pulled off his shoes and held them up and turned them over, and nothing dropped out, and he said: 'They're all gone,' and he slumped in a heap.

A minute or two later Rutherford ambled around the corner and onto the quay. His head was hunched into his coat and his hat was covering most of his face. He stopped and looked at us and said: 'I thought you two mightn't turn up again,' and a slight smirk came to his lips. 'Most don't, you know. Most take what they can get and go, and we don't see them again,' and he pulled a long key out of his pocket and unlocked the door.

Then he reached up and yanked on an iron ring, and in the distance a bell rang, and he said: 'I'm glad you came. It means I won't have to do any humping and lumping today and I can sit by the fire and keep warm for a bit longer.' He stamped his feet up and down, and walked backwards and forwards for a couple of minutes, and then the door opened.

An old man with a yawning face and a white beard, looked at him and grunted what sounded like: 'You're late.'

Rutherford shrugged and turned to us: 'Put your hats and cloaks over there on the hooks,' and he pointed to a row of hooks under the stairs on the ground floor, 'and then you can carry those barrels,' and he nodded to the small barrels that were stacked three high, 'down to the lighter. And I mean carry. I don't mean roll. Rolling froths up the olive oil and bruises the green beans and then the rot sets in, and Mister Woodgate will scream at you if he sees you doing it,' and he paused, 'and so will I,' and he pulled his mouth into a tight-lipped smile.

'Then you stack them by the lighter. Don't put any on board. The oarsmen have to do that and they have to keep the boat balanced while they do it. And if they lose any they have to pay for them,' and he yawned. 'God,' he said, 'I'm tired. And that's in spite of having my own bed back,' and then he smiled, and this time it was a wide open-mouthed smile. 'And I noticed that my bed hadn't been slept in the other night,' and the smile became a grin, a dirty grin that linked him and me and William into a secret that was like a common currency: we could pass it among ourselves and in time it would be devalued.

I smiled and looked away, and then I picked up the first barrel. It was heavier than it looked, and he knew it, and he laughed, and said: 'When you've finished you can come upstairs. Old Harris owns a flat pan and he fries eggs and sausages and bread, and sometimes he has a couple of rashers of bacon. And the sooner you come the more you'll get.'

The barrels became heavier and heavier. I placed one on the warehouse floor and rolled it with my foot, and I was tempted. But I thought of the money we were promised, and I sighed to myself and picked up the barrel and lumped it down to the lighter.

An hour later, I ran the crust of bread around my plate with the point of my knife and soaked up the last of the warm fat and the egg yolk, and I sucked at it, like a boiled sweet, and then I leant back and sighed.

It was warm in Old Harris's room, warm and dark. The three of us settled on his bed, close to the fire, and if I had closed my eyes I could have gone to sleep. I watched the flames break the coal apart, and I was thinking how much nicer it was to build up the turves and watch them smoulder and spark and touch each other with tiny fingers of flame, when I remembered the smell they made. It was rich and deep, like the smell of a sweet tobacco, and it did not claw at my throat like coal smoke. Then I remembered the white shells that come out of the turf. They look like snail shells, bleached of the browns that make them hard to see against the earth. And I remembered the ones that I had collected – I had them crawling along the beams above our bed – and I was wondering what had happened to them, when Rutherford came back into the room and said: 'He wants to see you two. You go up the next flight of stairs and he's in the room at the front. The one that looks onto the quay.'

Mister Woodgate was standing behind a table. His back was to the windows and the shadows were darkening his face. For a long time he stared at us, and then he shook his head and said: 'Your Mister Salter or Saltcellar, or whatever his name is, has been arrested. And I hear they have him in the Tower.'

I shuddered and remembered the stories of Traitors' Gate, and the axe and the block, and the two princes who were never seen again, and I whispered: 'The Tower. Why the Tower?'

'They say it's for his own protection.'

'But they don't come out of there alive.'

He smiled. 'That used to be true. But now we have the law, and it will protect him. And if he's innocent he'll be released.'

'But what if they find him guilty?'

'They will defrock him, and then I think they will keep him locked up in the Tower till the day he dies.'

'Dies?'

'Of old age or the infirmities. It's more likely to be the infirmities: swollen legs or the rheumatics or phlegm on the chest. They've killed more men in there than the axe has ever done,' and he gave us a grim smile.

William looked up and said: 'But won't they ever let him out?'

'I wouldn't think so,' and he brushed both his hands over his head as if to brush the hair that was not there, and he said: 'But I do remember them letting one man out, and strangely enough,' and he paused as if to think about it a little more, 'he was from Ely. And he was the Bishop. Has anyone ever told you about him?'

William and I shook our heads.

'His name was Wren – if I remember it right – and he was imprisoned by Cromwell, and it wasn't till the King was restored about ten years later that they let him out.'

'And what happened to him?'

'As far as I know he went back to Ely and became the Bishop again,' and he paused and looked at me. 'Do you remember him now?'

I shook my head. 'No. We never studied bishops at school, and I don't know anything about them,' and then he asked the question I had been dreading: 'Why did you do it?'

I shrugged and looked at my feet, and he turned to William: 'Will you tell me why you did it?'

William looked at the floor and kept his mouth shut tight.

I could feel Mister Woodgate looking at me, but I did not raise my eyes.

After a while he turned to look out the window. 'Christ Almighty!' he yelled.

He rushed to the door and bellowed down the stairs: 'Rutherford. Come up here!'

Rutherford ran up the stairs and into the room.

'Look at that,' Mister Woodgate said, jabbing the window with his finger.

I moved closer to the window. An oarsman had gripped a barrel at both ends and he was shaking it up and down, in the same way my old Granny Wilkes used to shake her butter churn.

'You get down there,' Mister Woodgate said, 'and you stop that, and you make sure they treat them properly.'

Rutherford nodded and rushed to the door, and Mister Woodgate called after him: 'Did you count the barrels?'

'I did it last night.'

'And how many are there?'

'Sixty-six.'

'I can only count sixty-two from here. You get on that boat and count them again, and then come back to me. And I want to see your delivery document. I want to see that you've written it out for sixty-six barrels. And next time you stay down there and watch them load that lighter. That's what I pay you for, in case you've forgotten.'

Rutherford flushed and bit his lip and rushed out the door, and the three of us stood and listened to his feet thumping down the stairs. When the thumping ceased Mister Woodgate turned to the window and for a minute or two he stared out of it and then he turned back to us and said to me: 'Was it your idea?'

'My idea?'

'The whitewash.'

I shook my head.

He turned to William. 'So it was your idea.'

William hung his head and bit his lips and Mister Woodgate

began to laugh. 'I don't know what possessed you, but I have to tell you I thought it most entertaining – after you were safely away that is. And I hear that last night people were still going out to Ely Place to have a look,' and he came from behind the table and looked at my shoes and my breeches, and then he turned me round. Then he did the same to William. 'Most of the spots are gone, and the few that are left could be stains, so they don't matter,' and he picked up a chair and carried it over to me and said: 'Sit down,' and he fetched another one for William and said: 'And you too,' and then he seated himself on the other side of the table, and smiled. 'I don't think anything like that has ever happened before in Ely Place. And I hope it never will again,' and he smiled and shook his head.

'I was worried about the *London Gazette,*' he said. 'I thought if they reported it there would be a chance of someone identifying both of you. And I was worried that someone might have seen you come into the office, or maybe someone in The Three Crowns would recognise you, and I didn't like the thought of that. So . . .' and he paused and stared hard at us, 'I had a word with the proprietor. At first,' and he spread his hands in a dismissive way, 'he wouldn't listen. But then, I told him that putting it in the paper would spread the idea, and soon we might have a pack of idiots painting signs on houses every night. And I told him I would be unable to renew the public notice, the advertisement, I have been placing in his paper, if his paper was seen – even by implication – to be promoting such despicable conduct.'

He smiled, a soft gentle smile. 'So you see, I have been helping you, in my own way, and there may be some other way I can help you.' Again he smiled. 'That's what friends are for. So tell me,' and his voice dropped to a whisper, and he looked at William, 'why did you do it?'

William twiddled his fingers for a moment or two, and then he told him about his mother, and how he had revenged her death. And he told him about my Mother and how we had tried to help her, and how we had failed.

I told him I felt sorry for Mister Salthouse, and he wanted to know what he'd done to me. I shook my head, and said: 'It's in the past,' and I looked at the table and I could not trust myself to say a single word.

For a long time he didn't say anything, then he locked his hands together and rested them on the edge of the table, and said: 'Rutherford knows nothing about this. He's been to Ely Place and seen what you did, but he doesn't know that you did it. And it would be best if you didn't say a word to him about it. Don't even mention the subject to him, or to anyone else. And if you have to talk about it, come back to me and talk about it, but don't talk to anyone else. No one. Do you understand?'

I nodded and so did William.

Then he said: 'I think you should stay down in Deptford – at the naval dockyard – for three or four weeks. I'll talk to Rutherford. He can have a word with our man at the slipway, and he should be able to get you some work for a couple of weeks, maybe longer. And then,' he shrugged, 'if you want to come back, you can come back. And maybe I can listen to some more of your reading,' and he smiled at William.

He stood up and we stood up, and he said: 'One last thing. What you did was quite remarkable. It shows a lot of foresight. The law would not agree with me, but then the law is not in the business of buying and selling, and finding new ways of doing things, and making a profit. I am. And I suspect that if some of this foresight could be channelled into thinking about food and its preservation,' and he waved his hand at the crocks and the jars and the bottles that lined the shelves on both sides of the room, 'you might do very well,' and then he smiled. 'And I might even get you to write one or two of my advertisements in the *London Gazette*, but there would be one proviso.'

'Proviso?'

'Hmm. I wouldn't let you put any arrows around it. I would insist on a plain border,' and he laughed.

38

The four oarsmen sculled the lighter into the middle of the Thames and picked up the rip of the ebb tide. Then they lifted the blades of their oars out of the water, and like a big black beetle with four legs stiffened by death, we drifted down the river.

The sun had burnt away the mist of the early morning and I hung my hand over the side and let the water flow through my fingers. The water was cold and brown, and the smell of fish, the smell of Billingsgate drifted with us.

In my mind I said goodbye to Mister Woodgate, and I thought about our last few minutes together. He talked about Lambeth and the kilns and the blue and white plates he called Delft, and he said: 'I used to import them from the Low Countries till we fought the Dutch and the trade was stopped. And then the King licensed the new kilns in Lambeth and I knew the trade would never come back. So I had to think of something else, and that was when I became interested in the preservation of food.' Then he paused and frowned: 'And it's just occurred to me that if you can't find any work in Deptford you might be able to find some in Lambeth at the Delftware Kilns.'

He took a card from out of his drawer and wrote on it, and said: 'You give this to Mister Muckleberry. He borrowed some of my Delft tiles once and copied the designs. He liked the windmills, the boats with the sails set, and the canals with the locks. I told him he should send an artist up to The Fens to draw some English scenes. But he wouldn't do it. He said people liked the foreign ones,' and he shrugged and laughed. 'He said they looked smarter and more expensive, and they were what he called the fashion. And he said people wouldn't want The Fens because they're cold and wet and miserable, and who wants to be reminded of a place like that?'

I fingered the card in my pocket – he called it an insurance – and I let these memories slip away, and I watched the Tower grow bigger and bigger. The stones were almost white like meat that has been sucked of blood in an eel trap; and I thought of Mister Salthouse trapped in there. And I remembered thinking about the eels and the way they wanted to escape, wanted to find their freedom when they were in my trap. I remembered letting some of them go, and I wished I could let him go.

Then I remembered Bishop Wren, who was given his freedom at the time of the Restoration, at the time of my birth, and in my mind the sky darkened, and the fireworks exploded, as they had exploded so many times before, and they filled my head with showers of red and yellow and green. But this time there was no joy in them, no sense of celebration, and under my breath I said: 'I'm sorry. I didn't think it would end like this. And if I could take back the past and start again, I would do it. I would do it for you.'

Then Rutherford turned towards me and said: 'I've had enough of Mister Woodgate. And I've had enough of every bloody thing I have to do for him,' and he smacked his fist into the palm of his hand. 'It doesn't matter what I do, or how long it takes, or how hard it is to do, he still finds something wrong with it. And he tells me. He tells me every bloody time. And I'm sick of it. I'm sick of it right up to here,' and he drew an imaginary line across his forehead. 'You saw him today. That was nothing. That was restrained. That was him putting on an act for . . .' and he stopped and stared at me.

'He's offered you my job, hasn't he?'

I shook my head, and he turned to William. 'So it's you. You're the one he wants.'

William blanched and shook his head.

'Yes,' he said, 'you're the one,' and he grabbed him by the arm and squeezed hard. 'You're the one. Young and strong,' and he squeezed harder. 'And she'd like you,' and he let go of his arm and pulled off his hat. 'And she'd like your pretty face and your green eyes and your black hair,' and he nodded to himself. 'Yes, she would. And then he'd have to give you up,' and he giggled to himself.

Then he turned to me. 'But then there's always you, isn't there? Coming along behind, so to speak,' and he shook his head and sank into silence.

I looked down at the water that was sloshing around in the bottom of the boat, and I tried not to think about his words and what they could mean for me, and I said: 'Who is she?'

Rutherford lifted his head and watched the oarsmen on the right dip their oars and steer the lighter back into the current, and then he turned to me and said: 'She? She is his niece. His brother's daughter. She lives with him in Plymouth. She's an only child and when he dies she'll inherit his share of the business. And when Woodgate dies she'll inherit his share. And the man who marries her will marry the business, and he'll run it, and that's what they want.'

'Then why haven't they found a man they can trust, a man who knows the business and can make it prosper, and made her marry him?'

He shrugged and watched the water for a moment, and then he said: 'They both wanted me to marry her. And I wanted to marry her. But she . . . she didn't want to marry me. And her father would not insist upon it.'

The three of us sat with our thoughts for a minute or more, and then he said: 'She's a bit dumpy, and bit older than me, and she's not that good-looking, but what does it matter? He knows my cock works. And he knows I could have given her a son. That's what they want: a son and heir. And he could have been five by now,' and his head slumped forward, like that of a man weighed down by mourning. 'And what are they going to do if she dies?' he asked in a voice so quiet he might have been talking to himself. 'There's no one else. No one. And now they're getting bloody desperate,' and he sat up and grabbed William in the crutch – by the balls – and he jerked him off the seat. 'This is what they want from you. And this is what they're going to get.'

William slapped his face.

Rutherford sprung to his feet and punched William on the nose.

The lighter lurched and rocked, and the barrels rattled.

An oarsman swung round and grabbed at Rutherford, and yelled: 'If you want to fight, you fight over there!' and he pointed to a quay about twenty yards away. 'And I won't be coming back for you.'

Rutherford sat down and shook his head, and William rubbed at his nose and looked at his feet.

For a long time we sat in silence, and then Rutherford turned his back on William and leant towards me and said: 'I could have run the business. And I could have made it prosper, like you said. And I've got a lot of good ideas.'

'Hmm,' I said, trying to pretend that nothing had happened, 'and what would you have done?'

'Done? I would have opened a warehouse on the Medway and another down in Portsmouth.'

'But they're a long way away.'

'To you and me, yes, but not to a ship,' and he leant back a little. 'The navy's been building and repairing ships at Deptford for more than a hundred years. But I can see them opening more yards on the Medway. It would bring the ships closer to the coast and make the channel easier to defend. And we're going to have to go where the fleet goes. It's as simple as that.'

'So you'd close down the office in Bishopsgate?'

'Heavens no. We couldn't do that. The shipowners all come to London. This is where we sign the contracts. And besides, the Navy Office is still in Seething Lane. You probably don't know where that is.'

'Oh yes I do,' I said, and I touched the bump on the back of my head, and it still hurt. 'That was where I was knocked on the head and robbed of all my money.'

He laughed. 'That would make a change. It's usually Mister Woodgate who gets robbed down there.'

I looked at him, and he half smiled. 'Before we can sign a contract to supply the navy that bloody old rogue Peps – or whatever his name is – has to have a little inducement. He means a bribe, but that's the way he puts it, and it never shows on the contract. And that's the price of doing business with the navy.'

We drifted along and I watched the shoreline for a while, and he said: 'There's one other thing I'd do. I'd forget all about this preserving of food and give 'em what they want. I'd give 'em the three Bs.'

I blinked and looked at him. 'The three Bs?'

'Bread, beer and beef. That's what they want, and that's what I'd give 'em.'

I nodded and said: 'Mister Woodgate was telling me he can make more money from what he calls fancy goods. He says the officers can afford to pay for them, and he was showing me a biscuit he's made from pork and turnip soup. And he says you can break it up and simmer it in water, and the soup comes back again.'

'He's being making them down at the bakery, after they've finished baking the bread and the ovens are still warm. But he can't make them keep.'

'That's what he told me. And I told him about my Father keeping wheat in a crock, and sealing the top with beeswax. And I suggested he packed them into a crock and filled up all the gaps with dried peas and that would get rid of all the air. Then he could seal the top with wax, and when they made the soup they could stir in the dried peas.'

He stared at me for a couple of seconds and his face became hard. 'Jesus! Another bloody little dreamer. He'd like you, he would,' and he nodded to himself. 'Maybe I've got it wrong. Maybe you're the one he wants, and maybe all this business with him,' and he nodded towards William, 'is just a way of testing you,' and his head slumped and he kicked his foot against the barrel that lay between us.

Then he straightened up. 'He's very cunning. More cunning than you'd believe. And I know there's nothing left for me. Not now there's not.'

'But when he's dead, and this niece of his is the new owner she might want you to look after the office in Bishopsgate. And maybe she'd listen to some of your ideas.'

He laughed. 'She might. But every time her husband looked at me he'd see the man who thought he could run the business. And he'd know that I used to think about fucking his wife. And he wouldn't want me. And I'd be out the bloody door,' and he paused. 'And I think it would be better, much better, if I went now, while I'm still young enough to do something else.'

I felt sorry for him, and I said: 'But what would you do?'

'Do? I'd do what I've always wanted to do. I'd join a regiment and be a soldier, a musketeer,' and he paused. 'Do you remember me telling you about the posters?' I didn't, but I nodded, and he said: 'I saw them down here at Deptford. And they were wanting men to sign up. I don't remember where the regiment was going to be stationed, but that doesn't matter, does it?' and he sat back and shut his eyes.

As we closed on the quay at Deptford, we could see into a courtyard. Hundreds of men were milling about, and one of them had climbed up a ladder and he was trying to say something, but the hooting and the jeering were drowning his words, and Rutherford said: 'That reminds me. Did you see the crowd in Ely Place the other day?'

I shook my head, and he said: 'It was bigger than this one. A lot bigger. And it turned into a riot. And they had to call out a troop-of-horse,' and his eyes became soft and dreamy for a moment, and then he went on: 'I'd like to be a trooper. But each man has to supply his own horse, and I don't have any money, and I couldn't afford all those oats they eat,' and he looked at me and sighed.

William turned to him. 'What happened in Ely Place?'

Rutherford stared at him, as if shocked to discover that he still had a voice after such a long silence, and then he said: 'The troopers drew their swords and lined up to charge, and the crowd went quiet. Deadly quiet they tell me. Then people started to scream and run, and all the troopers had to do was sit and wait,' and he laughed. 'And I hear they've been questioning some old woman who sells trinkets at Newgate. And now they're looking for a couple of men who bought a lot of whitewash and painted arrows everywhere,' and he reached out and steadied the boat as the oarsmen brought it into the quay. 'They say they're both young and well dressed, and they might catch them. You never know,' and he stepped out of the lighter onto the steps.

I followed him up the steps and he said: 'I've been thinking a lot about that regiment. And I think I might sign up. I think I might do it today, before I change my mind,' and he looked at me and his face broke into a smile.

It sounded like madness to me, but I gave him a nod that said yes, because that was what he wanted; and I pointed towards the crowd and said: 'What are they here for?'

'They come looking for work every morning, and when there's nothing to do they sit around and drink till the money runs out. And then they cause trouble,' and he paused, and smiled. 'It could be the regiment is going to be stationed here, to protect the slipways and keep that lot in order.'

Then he spoke to the oarsmen for a moment or two, and he turned to us and said: 'You two stay here while they unload those,' and he nodded at the barrels. 'I'm just going to have a look at the posters over there,' and he turned towards the wooden fence that was about forty yards away, and his face fell. 'They've gone! They were over there. On that fence. And they've gone.'

For a moment or two he didn't seem to know what to do, and then he said: 'There were some more in the High Street, by the church or the old Guildhall, if I remember right. You stay here and I'll be back in a couple of minutes.'

He came back about thirty minutes later and sat down on the barrels. His head drooped, and his shoulders slouched, and he looked at me and said: 'They've gone. I can't find one. Not a single solitary bloody one,' and he kicked at the barrels with his foot. 'I suppose some of that bloody lot over there,' and he kicked his foot towards the crowd, 'signed up. And now they don't want any more,' and he slumped into silence.

The lighter pulled away from the quay, and I said to him: 'Aren't they going to take you back to Billingsgate?'

He shook his head. 'It's cheaper for me to walk back and pay the toll on the bridge. So that's what I have to do,' and he stood up and told us to grab a barrel.

About two hours latter when the barrels were stacked in an ice-cold room at the back of a stone storehouse, and the delivery document was signed and sealed, we followed Rutherford down to the slipyard.

Just above the tideline, a ship was lying on her side. Her hull was black with tar and hairy with seaweed. The sun had opened her barnacles and filled the air with the stench of rotting fish.

I walked around to her other side. The masts were lashed to a row of iron rings, and they looked like trees that had been blown down in a storm and stripped of all their leaves.

The outer planking around her bow, from the line of the deck to the line of the keel, had been pulled away. The ribs were still attached to the inner-planking, and they looked dark and gaunt, like ribs of old beef, half-butchered but still with all the innards, all the secrets intact.

I began to think about those secrets, those sailor-secrets, those bowels that open in the bowels of the ship. I began to feel cold, like a man with the flux, and I saw it as an omen, an omen of what could be but must not be. And I began to sweat, to tremble; and I knew that I had to avoid the ships and the sailors and the things they say they do in the night.

Then the sun came out from behind a cloud and it made the ribs look bright and fresh and full of life, and there was no hint of evil hiding within them, and I said to myself: 'You're dreaming. You're imagining things that are not there,' and I walked over to the next slipway and sat beside William.

I could see Rutherford inside a shed talking to a man, and in front of him, four more men were lifting old planks and tracing the outline onto new lengths of wood. One of them picked up an adze, and with his legs wide apart he began to swing it backwards and forwards – like a pendulum on a clock – and chips of wood flew into the air. After a while the smell of raw wood began to drift over us. It was heady, almost like pine, and it made me remember my Father and the day he repaired our punt.

For a few minutes my mind drifted with the punt on the flat waters of The Fens, and I breathed the clean air, and it calmed my mind; and then Rutherford came back and said: 'You're to be here at seven in the morning. Come to that shed,' and he pointed to a small one with a tile roof and black weatherboards, 'and ask for Mister Shepherd. He says you can start by cleaning the bottom of that ship over there,' and he nodded at the one with the hairy hull. 'And he says to warn you about the press gangs. He says they sent a couple of ships down the slips yesterday and they're short of men. And he thinks they'll be out tonight looking for some of that crowd who were hanging around this morning. So he says to stay out of town tonight. And tomorrow night – if he likes the way you work – you can sleep in that shed of his.'

He pulled out his purse and gave us threepence each. I said it was more than I expected, and he shrugged and said: 'It's what he told me to give you.'

I slipped my threepence into my shoe, and then I wondered about the soldiers – and how much they were paid – and I said: 'Did Mister Shepherd know anything about the regiment?'

He shook his head. 'He hasn't seen them for a week or more, and last time he saw their house it was all locked up. He thinks they're just as bad as the bloody press gang. He says there've been a lot of rumours about them, and some of his men didn't arrive for work one morning. And he thinks they were hit on the head and forced to enlist when they sobered up. And as far as he's concerned there's only one difference between a regiment and a ship,' and he paused to add weight to his words, 'you don't get seasick on the land.'

We laughed and William said: 'Is the regiment to be stationed here?'

'No. It's for some place he's never heard of. And like me, he couldn't remember the name,' and he shrugged.

I wasn't sure what to say next. William was pretending to look at the ship – the four men had brought over the first of the new planks and now they were fitting it to the bow – and a heavy silence settled upon us. Then he said: 'I don't know if I'll ever see you again, but if I do, I'll know what it means,' and he scuffed his feet. 'And I'll do what you want me to do,' and he paused and took a deep breath. 'If I can't get into a regiment I won't have any choice, will I?' and he turned and walked away.

I looked at William and he looked at me, and we both shrugged, and then we followed him – at a distance of twenty or thirty yards – through the docks and past the guard house with its flag and Royal coat of arms, and up the road to the marker stone where he turned to the right and we turned to the left.

In the Market Place we bought four slices of cold beef, four pickled onions, two bread buns and two mugs of black beer; and then we walked down to the marshes and sat in the rushes.

The tide had rippled the sand and uncovered the mudflats, and it had left a brown scum on the seagrass. I watched a spider paddle through the scum and I watched the godwits feeding at the water's edge, and then I began to feel sleepy and I lay back and looked up at the sky and William said: 'I feel sorry for Mister Salthouse. I didn't think I would but I do.'

'So do I,' I said. 'I never thought I would, but I do. And I can't explain it,' and I watched the clouds drifting into each other, and then I said: 'I feel sorry for that silly old woman who sold me the scissors.'

'He said they were questioning her, didn't he?'

'Hmm.'

'Well, she did stir up the crowd. And in her own way she did just as much as we did.'

'For Christ's sake! We did it! You and me,' and I sat up. 'She got a bit excited, and she told them what we said. And that's all she did.'

He pushed at the mud with his foot for a moment or two, then he said: 'Do you think they'll arrest her?'

I shook my head. 'They'll want her as a witness against us.'

'But what if they do arrest her? What would we do then?'

'We couldn't do anything. Even if we went to Newgate and confessed it wouldn't do her any good. If they think she's guilty they'll lock her up. And they'll lock us up with her. And that would be that.'

He bit his lips, and I lay back and looked at the clouds again. The thought of her, and what they could do to her if they did arrest her, emptied my soul of life, and I felt sad and miserable; and then I flicked the spider off the seagrass and watched it drown in the mud.

When it was almost dark, we walked back to the town – there was nowhere else to buy anything to eat – and we bought a plate of whelks and a couple of loaves of bread from the lady at the shellfish stall. Her bread tasted soft and fresh but her whelks were overcooked, and chewy, like gristle. We threw most of them away and she shook her head at us, and I could almost hear her saying tut tut, and I yelled out: 'They were bloody awful.'

She gave me a toothless smile. 'The sailors like them,' she yelled back. 'They like to chew on them. And they say mine are good for chewing,' and she let out an evil laugh.

I knew she wasn't talking about whelks, and she annoyed me,

and so did the thought that we had wasted a halfpenny on them. I screamed at her: 'You're a bloody old whore. And I'm not a sailor. And I want my money back.'

She laughed again, and pressed her hand into her skirts, and pointed to the private place at the top of her legs. 'That's where it is. You can come and get it if you want to.'

I shook my head, and William yelled out: 'I bet it smells like your whelks after a day in the sun.'

'You rude little bastard!' she yelled back. 'I hope the press gang gets you.'

'And you should watch out too,' she yelled at me. 'They were in Dartford the other night. And they say they're coming here. And you wouldn't want to be a sailor. Not with your looks you wouldn't,' and she laughed some more. Then she turned her back on us and packed up her stall, and walked away with the rolling gait of a sailor.

William laughed at her, and he leant towards me. 'You know why a sailor walks like that?' I shook my head. 'Because he's had too many cocks up his arse,' and he laughed some more.

I glanced at the ground that was black and oily like the sins of the flesh, and I bit my lips.

William looked at me. 'Are you all right?'

I had not told him about the things my Father had done to me, and I shrugged off his words and said: 'I think we should get out of here, right away. Just in case.'

He shook his head, and held out his hand. 'It's starting to rain. I can feel it. And I don't like getting wet. And anyway they say the press gangs wait outside the taverns. So all we have to do is stay away from them, and hide somewhere warm and dry, and they'll never find us.'

We walked around Deptford, and in a quiet alleyway, well away from the High Street and the lights of the taverns, we found a large house. It was shuttered and there was no sign of light. We climbed over the gate and into the brick porch, and we curled up in the shadows, on either side of the door, like a pair of guard dogs.

I listened to the steady drip of the rain, and I thought about the day. I thought about Mister Woodgate's niece, and I said:

'She's a bit dumpy, and a lot older than you, and she's not that good-looking, but I can see you and her—'

He gave me a shove and laughed. 'And I can see you scratching your head, and trying to think of a new way to preserve bloody old eels.'

I laughed, and closed my eyes and sank into a blackness that felt soft and warm.

39

'What have we here?'

The voice bored into my sleeping mind, and I could feel my leg being prodded.

'Get up!' said the voice. 'Both of you. Come on.'

White stockings and blue garters swam into my vision. They were about a foot away from my face. I remembered what they'd said about the press gang, and it dried my mouth.

I moved my hands away from his shoes and I pushed myself up. I brushed against his breeches and his grey coat, with its blue cuffs and pewter buttons. The buttons bore the image of a lamb with a halo. It was holding a flag with a cross, and like the saints of old with their bland faces and their dead eyes, it was a picture of innocence; but that was not what my senses were telling me about this man.

He was fingering one of the buttons, and uncovering the circle of dark grey cloth that lay behind it. It gave the lamb a second halo, and it gave his coat a faded look, and it made him look as though he'd been out in the hot sun for too long.

He placed his right hand on my shoulder and his left hand on William's shoulder, and he pushed us against the door. 'Come to volunteer, have we?'

'Volunteer?' It was a word I had not heard before, and there was something about it, something that didn't sound right. It made me feel nervous. 'I don't know what that means.'

'Well now,' and he slid a key into the lock and propelled us both inside before we had a chance to break away, 'it means you're here of your own free will. And you want to join the regiment, without any force or coercion, as it says in the regulations.'

He closed the door and opened the wooden shutters.

A long table with a chair tucked under it stood in the middle of the room.

I looked at William. His back had slumped, and his legs had bowed, and his arms were flopping about in a peculiar way. He was starting to hum a tune, a tune I knew but could not name.

I hissed at him, and the man glared at me.

He didn't look like a sailor, and he didn't look like a soldier. I'd seen them in London, by the Palace of Whitehall. Those on foot were wearing red coats, and those on horse were wearing blue coats with breastplates. So who was this man, and why did he think we wanted to join a regiment?

'I don't know anything about a regiment,' I said.

He pointed to a poster. It was pinned to the wall, in the shadows to the right of the fireplace.

I knew without thinking, without forming any words in my mind: it was Rutherford's poster. It was the one he had been looking for.

I read the words and they froze my soul and chilled my body, and I turned and stared at the man.

'I'll read it for you,' he said. 'None of you can ever read, so I wan't waste my time asking you to try.' He took off his hat, it had been shading his face, and now I could see his skin: it was brown and leathery. 'This is what it says:

'By command of His Majesty
KING CHARLES II,
His Excellency, The Earl of Middleton,
is authorised to raise a further fifty men,
to serve in his Regiment.

'Such men are to be unmarried.' He looked at us. 'You're not married are you?'

I laughed, and William made a silly sniggering sound that grew into a loud neighing, like a horse makes when it's frightened.

The man looked at him, and frowned, and then he turned back to the poster. 'And it goes on to say: "And fit in mind and body and of a good moral disposition."' He turned to us. 'We won't worry about that. They think we should set a good example to the heathen, but it's nonsense, as you'll soon find out,' and he grinned to himself.

'The next few lines say we'll pay you, and feed you, and look after you, and you'll serve in the Regiment for the rest of your life. When you're dead, and it doesn't say this on the poster but I can tell you: the whole Regiment will parade for your funeral. We make a grand sight with our flags and drums and pikes and muskets; and it's quite an occasion, as long as you're not the man in the box,' and he laughed. 'And then of course there's this little bit at the bottom that says: "The Tangiers' (Lord Middleton's) Regiment-of-Foot and Horse is entrusted with the defence of His Majesty's Royal City and Port of Tangiers."'

William looked at me and shook his head.

I turned and looked at the door.

I felt trapped. I glanced at the floor, and I remembered my Father cursing the heathen and saying they came from Tipperary, and no man in his right mind would ever want to go there.

'I don't want to go to Ireland,' I said.

'Ireland? You're not going to Ireland. You're going south, to Tangiers,' and he smiled. 'You could say you're going to go as far as an Englishman can go.'

I tried to think of the south. We had learnt about it, one afternoon when it was hot and the classroom windows were wide open. A fly came buzzing around and I can remember thinking if the lizard would eat the fly that would be the end of the buzzing. And there was something else about an end, an end of land, but I couldn't think what it was. Then I remembered the name of the place and I said: 'Cornwall?'

He opened his mouth to reply, but before he could say a word, a door to the left of the fireplace swung open. It made a grating sound. It spun him around, and he stamped to attention. 'Good morning, sir!'

A man strode into the room. He looked like a soldier. His coat was red and his cuffs were green, and the curls of his wig brushed his shoulders. He sat on the chair and looked up at me. 'That one doesn't look old enough, Sergeant.'

'Begging your pardon, sir. I'd reckon him to be about thirteen.'

'Thirteen? He looks about ten to me.'

'Shall we have a look at him, sir?'

The man at the table nodded.

'Pull your breeches down,' the sergeant said to me.

'Pardon,' I said, not wanting to believe what I had just heard.

He didn't reply. He grabbed my breeches and pulled them down. They flopped around my ankles like brown cowpats. He walked to my side and pulled up the front of my shirt and snorted. Then he pulled down my under-breeches. 'He's thirteen,' he said. 'He's got to be with that wad of hair.'

The man at the table ran his fingers up and down the lace that hung from his neck. It was a simple act of straightening but somehow it was more like stroking, or feeling, and it made me feel nervous and ashamed. And it made my cock swell and rise.

'Why do you think,' said the man at the table, 'that some are big and some are small?'

The sergeant grinned. 'I wouldn't know, sir. They say the Lord has His reasons, and we should be grateful for what we are about to receive.'

The man at the table smiled and covered his mouth with his hand. Then he nodded to the sergeant. It was an intimate nod. The sort of nod that people make to each other when they want to keep something secret, and I knew at once that I was to be their secret, their dirty secret. And I knew that they would make me do what I did not want to do.

And I wanted to get out of there.

I stole a sideways glance at William. He was holding the top of his breeches with both hands. His knuckles were white and veined with red and yellow, like the legs of a rooster.

The sergeant leant towards my ear. 'I was wondering,' he said, 'if you've kept yourself clean,' and he raised the front of my shirt a little higher and bent forward to take a closer look.

I nodded and tried to cover my cock with my hands.

He laughed and let go of my shirt.

The man at the table took his hands away from the lace at his throat, and he placed them flat on the table. 'Pull up your breeches,' he said.

I pulled them up and tucked in my shirt and retied the cord.

'After a display like that, you may like to know that the men have a name for it; they call it standing to attention,' and he chuckled. 'I have to accept that you are old enough to join the regiment.'

'Noooo!' William screamed. 'No! No! No!' And he danced around the room on the tips of his toes. The sergeant grabbed at him, but he slipped out of his hands. He ducked under the table and around the man's legs, and he leapt in the air. Then he ran at me, and spun me round, and hissed: 'We've got to get out of here!'

I was still ashamed and half confused. I turned round and looked at the door and the window and the open shutters, and I couldn't think what to do.

The man at the table grabbed at William. He missed and he yelled: 'What's your name?'

William laughed. It was the mad drooling laugh that he used to make when he was in Ely, pretending to be an idiot. He was reverting, in front of my eyes, he was becoming a fool again. He mouthed his name, without making a sound, and the man shouted at me: 'What's his name?'

'William,' I said, 'William Fenton.'

'No it's not! That's not my name! That's his name. He thinks he's William the Conqueror,' and he shrieked with laughter.

The sergeant and the man at the table looked at each, and William began to pace up and down. 'My name is Simon,' he said. 'Simple Simon,' and he bowed to the man at the table. Then he began to hum the tune that I hadn't been able to recognise earlier on, and he burst into song. "Simple Simon met a pieman, going to the fair,"' and he threw his arms in the air as if he were meeting this imaginary person. '"Said Simple Simon to the pieman . . ."'

The man at the table jumped to his feet. 'He's a bloody idiot! And I don't want him! You should never have let him in. And you can get him out of here. Right now!'

The sergeant rushed to the door and pushed up the bar. His face was flushed and his mouth was open and two of his teeth were sticking out, like fangs. He snarled at Simon, and pulled at the door.

Simon grabbed at me and we ran.

The sergeant flung his arm in the air and hooked me under the chin. I jerked to a halt, and he punched at Simon.

Simon staggered and the sergeant shoved him out the door and slammed it shut.

Then he kneed me in the back.

I gasped and sagged, and he pushed me back to the table.

He was panting, and filling my face with the stink of pickled onions. I tried to pull away, but he held me tight. 'This young man has come to volunteer, sir.'

'Have you come to volunteer?'

I shook my head and whipped the scissors out of my pocket, and thrust them at his throat.

He laughed and a look of glee came into his eyes. He hit my hand away and kneed me in the back again. I gasped, and my eyes filled with tears.

'Have you come to volunteer?'

'No.'

The sergeant kicked my ankle. The pain made me dance up and down, and it made my feet slide apart. His hand streaked between my legs and grabbed me by the balls.

He squeezed them hard, and then he pulled. He pulled so hard I thought he was going to pull them off. And I felt the taste of sick rise in my throat, and I tried to breathe and I could not breathe and I doubled over.

He grabbed me by the neck and lifted me onto my toes. Then he kneed me in the arse. It made the man at the table go in and out of focus, and it made me flay the air with my hands and my feet.

'Have you come to volunteer?'

'Volunteer?'

'Hmm,' he said in a soft voice, 'to sign up, of your own free will.'

I shook my head, and he lifted me up again, I flinched – I was expecting his knee – but he grabbed me by the balls again and squeezed them hard. Spots appeared before my eyes and I felt my insides go soft, like the jelly that comes from the hoof of a cow. I tried to swallow, I tried to say no, but nothing came out of my mouth.

He dropped me on my feet. The jolt was hard and sudden, and it slammed into the top of my skull, and it jerked my head backwards and forwards.

It was an act of surrender. It was my body's way of saying, yes.

The man at the table smiled. 'I knew you'd see sense.' He opened a drawer at the back of the table and brought out a book, a quill, and a small pot of ink. He opened the book, and dipped the quill in the black ink and wrote two or three words.

Then he looked up. 'What year were you born?'

'In 1660,' I gasped. 'It was the year of the Restoration.'

'So it was.' He fussed with the end of the quill for a moment and then he wrote the date. 'And where were you born?'

'In Elme.'

'Where's that?'

'Near Ely.'

'Ely?' He made it sound like a question. He looked up at the sergeant. 'Didn't that fellow come from Ely? The one they hanged yesterday. At Tyburn.'

The sergeant nodded.

'I thought so.' He looked up at me. 'You might know him. A big brute of man. With a thick neck. He didn't have anything to say for himself and it took six of them to get the rope around his neck. And after half an hour he was still kicking away. They called for a friend to pull on his legs and help him die, but no one came to help.'

In my mind I walked again on Tyburn heath and I saw Tyburn Tree. I saw the triangle of death, and the sunset and the blood red sky. I saw the red become black, become clouds that were black and blue and heavy with snow.

I saw the snow begin to fall. For a few moments it was soft and gentle. But then it began to change. It picked up the wind, the wind that is the air we breathe, and like a man who wants to live but knows he has to die, it began to rant and rage and storm against what is. What has to be. And it clothed the heath and the tree and the black shape that hung upon it; it clothed them all in white, in the white that is the shroud of death.

I knew that shape was him. It had to be him. But I had to ask, I had to hear it from someone else. 'Do you know his name?'

He looked up to the sergeant. 'Can you remember his name?'
He shook his head.

'It was a common name. Jack or John. Something like that. I remember thinking it was a common name for a common thief.'

I shook my head, and he shrugged. The clouds grew darker and the storm raged again in my mind. I could feel the drifts of snow building against the insides of my eyes and I couldn't see what lay beyond them. I began to slide away into a drifting dreaming state. My head was frozen, and my balls were on fire, and my heart was thumping so hard I thought it was going to burst out of my chest. Then I heard him say, in a muffled voice: 'Catch him. Before he falls.'

When I opened my eyes, I was still standing and he was still sitting at the table in front of me. I pushed away the sergeant's hands, and I swayed a little. Then I found my feet.

'Are you sure you don't know him?' he asked.

I shook my head, and he shrugged. 'Where did you say you came from?'

'Elme.'

He paused. 'My name is Captain Lacey. I am an officer. And when you address me, or any other officer, you will call him "sir". Do you understand me?'

'Yes, sir.'

'And where were you born?'

'In Elme, sir.'

He dipped the quill, wrote in the book, and sanded the ink. He turned the book towards me, and he held out the quill. 'Put your mark there,' and he pointed with his finger. 'Make an X.'

I made an X, and I read the entry. 'My name is not William Fenton,' I said, 'it's Martyn Fenton. Simon was making a joke. It's what he does. It's why they call him simple.'

'You call me sir! What do you call me?'

'Sir.'

'And you want me to cross out William, and write in Martyn?'

'Yes, sir. That's my name, sir.'

'Look!' He ran his finger down the page, and then he turned back to the previous page and ran his finger down that. 'Not one mistake. Not one single mistake. I don't make mistakes, and I'm not crossing out William. That's the name I was given, and as long as you're in this regiment, that will be your name.' He stared into my eyes, then he shut the book with a bang, as if to tell me the matter was closed. I looked away from him, for a second or two, then he said: 'Can you read and write?'

I nodded. Then I realised I hadn't said sir. 'Yes, sir. We had a classroom in our village.'

'Hmm,' and he put the tips of his fingers together. 'In that case, I think it would be best if you wrote your name in beside the cross. Then you'll never be able to say it was a mistake. Will you?' He opened the book and turned it towards me. 'And write William. William Fenton. You do know how to spell William?'

'Yes, sir.'

He waited for the ink to dry, then he shut the book, and looked at the sergeant. 'Is there anything else?'

'He could be lying, sir.'

'Lying?'

'About the reading, sir. Some of them can read their name and that's about all.'

'Hmm,' he said, 'you could be right.' He reached into the drawer and pulled out a news-sheet – it looked old and crumpled – and he slid it across the table. 'Down the bottom there, on the front page, where it says: "TANGIERS: The finest Jewel in the King's Crown", you can read me some of that.'

I picked up the news-sheet. It was the *London Reporter*, and I could remember seeing some of them on the stall.

I found the place and began to read. 'Since work was begun on the building of a stone breakwater (which in common parlance is called The Mole) Tangiers has been able to provide a safe anchorage for His Majesty's ships. From this anchorage, more than one thousand miles south of these shores, His Majesty's ships have been able to pursue the infamous Barbary pirates to the innermost reaches of the Mediterranean Sea, and as a consequence the seas around the Straits of Gibraltar have been made safe for the passage of ships engaged in lawful trade.'

I paused and looked at him. I felt sick in my heart and sick in my belly. I tried to think what a thousand miles would look like, but the snow was still drifting about in my mind, and it was covering everything and I was losing my sense of distance.

The Captain reached for the news-sheet and slipped it into the drawer. 'You'll find that Tangiers is surrounded by walls and forts and deep trenches, and it's always coming under attack from the heathen Moors.'

He placed the book, the ink, and the quill in the drawer, and slid it shut. 'They come out of the hills in their thousands, like sand on the wind. They think that Tangiers belongs to them but we know that it belongs to His Majesty. And you and I, and Sergeant Brandon here, and all the men who wear this uniform, are going to defend Tangiers. We are going to fight. And we are going to die, if that is what we have to do. And we are going to make sure that it continues to belong to His Majesty.'

He stood up and placed his hands on the back of the chair and pushed it under the table and he said: 'I think a young man like you could do well,' and he smiled, 'could do very well,' and I heard the stress on the word 'do', and I felt his eyes crawl up my legs and over the front of my breeches.

Then he turned to the sergeant. 'That idiot out there has been jumping up and down and looking in the windows. Would you close the shutters and leave us? I think this young man could be one of our new clerks, and I would like to hear him read a little more.'

40

Dear Mother,

I am writing this letter in my mind because I know that if I wrote it on paper you would have to ask someone to read it to you, and I do not want anyone else to read what is meant for you and you alone.

Earlier today, when we were marching in the rain, we saw four men carrying a body to the graveyard. I thought of the service for the dead, and I thought of that dreadful Day of Judgement when the dead shall come forth again and all hearts shall be opened and all secrets shall be known. And I thought if I wrote this letter in my mind, you would be able to read it on that dreadful day.

Then I remembered that some people say the dead are still with us and they can see into the hearts and the minds of the living. And I thought if this is true, and you die before me, then you will be able to read this letter before the Day of Judgement, and you will know what is in my heart.

I would like to think that this letter will soothe away some of the pain that I have caused you, but I fear that this will not be so, because I have to tell you that on the very day you gave me back my innocence, I lost it again. I lost it to Mister Salthouse. He was not the man you thought he was and I cannot tell you all he did, but I can tell you he did not deserve to be called Reverend. And now for his sins he is imprisoned, and I think he does not deserve that either. I know there is a confusion in this, and I do not understand it, but it is how I feel, and I cannot explain it any clearer.

And I have to tell you that I have lost the name you gave

to me, and now they call me William Fenton. But in my mind I will always be Martyn. I will always be your son. And when I think of you and hear your voice, I will hear my name, my name that was; and it will bind me to you and you to me.

And I have lost the boy who lived within me, and now they say I am a man, and they have dressed me in a long grey coat, an iron breastplate and a backplate. On my head they have placed an iron helmet, and in my hand I carry a pike. I have lost whatever it was that made me into me, and now I look like all the others, and they look like me. And to those who see us marching by, we look like what we are: pikemen, soldiers-of-foot.

I know that Mister Salthouse came to see Father, and I know that he did not say the words I asked him to say. His courage failed him. And because he failed, I failed.

I wish there was something I could do, something I could do to help you. But I know in my heart there is nothing I can do, and I know what Father will do. And I am afraid for you. And it makes me cry in the night. And I am sorry, sorry that I cannot help you any more.

I know you always said I should be stronger, and I wish I could be more like you and Aunt Mary. But I am not like you, or her, or the men I am marching with. Their eyes are set on the future and mine are set on the past; and when I think of the past I think of the love you gave to me, and I go soft and quiet inside. And then I want to be back home. I want to be in Elme, with you, and I want to watch the waters rise and I want to smell the smells that are the smells of home.

And I have to tell you that I bought you a gift in London. It was not large or expensive, but it was what you wanted: a pair of scissors with a sharp point. I know that I will never be able to give you this gift, and I want you to know that in the years to come, when they cut something, they will cut me to the quick, and I will remember you – you who will never be blunted in my memory.

And I have to confess that I don't understand why I wanted to come to London. Now that I have seen it, it seems such a silly thing to want to do, and I have no desire to go back. The pavements were hard on my feet and the noise was hard on my ears, and the smoke caught in my throat. And the crowds

– you would have hated the crowds. They push and shove and they have no manners. And they sneer at us and the way we dress, and the way we talk, and they know nothing of The Fens, of the waterlands that are the land of my birth.

When I think of all that I have lost a black mood settles upon me; and dry feet, and hills on the horizon, and the look of London, will never make up for what was mine and will never be mine again.

A week ago they forced me to take an oath to serve the King, and now I am a soldier in a Regiment of Foot. There are forty-seven of us, or forty-eight if I count the sergeant, and we are marching towards Devon and the ship that will take us to Tangiers.

They say Tangiers is as close to hell as a man will ever get in this life. They say the heat sets your lungs on fire, and when the winds come, they do not blow out the fire. Instead, they fill your head with noise, and the noise can drive you mad; and there is no escape.

The pike is making my shoulder ache, and I do not like all this marching, and I do not like having to obey orders. And I do not like the thought of having to fight, of having to kill a man with whom I have no quarrel. I remember the eels. I remember letting them go. And I remember what you called my soft heart. And I think you were right then, and you would be right now, and it is making me feel sick in my head and sick in my belly.

They have told us we will not be coming back to England, and I'm looking at the fields and the trees and the last of the wild flowers, and I'm thinking I'll never see them again. And they are beautiful, more beautiful than I have ever seen them before. And there's a lump in my throat, and I'm trying to tell myself not to be so stupid.

I keep thinking of Simon. The Simon we used to say was stupid and simple, and I can remember Father saying: 'I don't want that idiot in my house.'

He's not an idiot or a fool, and he's not stupid. I think he's very clever. He escaped from the regiment, and I didn't. And I fear that if anyone is a fool or an idiot, it is me.

And one day I can see him married, married to an older

woman. And I can see him clothed in money, and wise beyond his years. And I think you would like to know – will be proud one day to know – that he is now one of us. He is a Fenton.

And I keep thinking of Father, and our bed, and the things he did, the things he taught me to do. And hard as it is to say or think, I know now that he has prepared me for the days and the nights that lie ahead; and there is in me a bitterness for I have found again the things I sought to flee. And this time I cannot flee from them.

I know that I will never be able to sit beside you and talk as we used to talk. And I know that your hands will never be able to hold me as they used to hold me. And when I think of the winter, and the cold, and what it does to those hands, it brings a sour taste to my mouth and it wraps my soul in sadness.

My sadness is white, like a snow-washed shroud. It is strewn with red poppies, and they are dying. They are dying for you, and they are dying for me, and I am starting to cry, and the road ahead is beginning to blur. I am having trouble thinking, and I keep telling myself I am sorry . . . and I can write no more.